PAINT

THE

WIND

Other Books by Linda Cardillo

Dancing on Sunday Afternoons
True Harvest
Two Mothers: A Saigon Pilgrimage
Across the Table
Love That Moves the Sun
Italian Tales
A Thing Miraculous
The Smallest Christmas Tree
Come Sit at My Table

First Light Series
The Boat House Café
The Uneven Road
Island Legacy
A Place of Refuge
Catríona's Vow

PAINT
THE
WIND

LINDA
CARDILLO

Bellastoria
Press

ISBN: 978-1-959102-15-1

Paint the Wind

Bellastoria Press

P.O. Box 60341

Longmeadow, MA 01106

Cover art

"On the North Sea"

By Olga Wisinger-Florian (1844–1926)

This painting is in the public domain.

In memory of Maja Hollstein,
Tante Maja

Gemalt hätt ich dich: nicht an die Wand,
an den Himmel selber ...:
als Berg, als Brand,
als Samum, wachsend aus Wüstensand –

I would have painted you: not on the wall,
on the sky itself.....:
as a mountain, as fire,
as a rising desert wind.

Rainer Maria Rilke, from the poem
"Wenn ich gewachsen wäre irgendwo"

Author's Note

ALTHOUGH ROOTED IN THE history of Vienna at the beginning of the twentieth century, *Paint the Wind* is a work of fiction. While most of the characters are products of my imagination, the artists of the Secession—Gustav Klimt, Egon Schiele, and others—as well as the salonnière and art critic Berta Zuckerkandl, were historical figures. The words and actions I ascribe to them are imagined, but they are grounded in my research and consistent with what I understood about these individuals from historical records and journals.

The art exhibitions depicted at the Secession, the School of Applied Arts, Salon Pisko, and the Isabella Stewart Gardner Museum are fictional, but are based on the vibrant exhibition culture at the time the story is set. Women artists flourished in Vienna in the early twentieth century, but two world wars and the Nazi destruction of what was considered "decadent" art caused their work to be forgotten. It is only recently that the art world is rediscovering these artists.

PART ONE

VIENNA

1902-1906

Chapter One

THE FIRST TIME ANDREAS Brenner painted me, I was fifteen.

I sat in stillness, speaking not a word and keeping my hands folded carefully like the schoolgirl I still was, and I watched him. His brushstrokes on the canvas were like a caress; his eyes, studying my own, seemed to be searching for something more than shape or color or the length of my very dark lashes. Later, much later, he told me that it was my soul he was seeking. The genius in capturing a likeness that causes onlookers to say, "But that is *exactly* how she looks!" is not in the angle of the cheekbone or the curve of the lower lip. The true great portraitist knows that he must plunge below the surface of the flesh and paint from within.

But I knew none of that then. As I said, I was a schoolgirl, my parents' only child, and subject to their wishes. My father, the Greek merchant Kostas Sircos, was intent on making his mark on the Viennese society into which he had married. On the walls of the elegant homes he had supplied with priceless antiquities, Persian carpets and Indian chests carved with peacocks and amaranth, my father noted the portraits: thin-lipped ancestors in powdered wigs; innocent children in impossible outfits frolicking with small dogs; plump, satisfied wives displaying a ruby brooch or sapphire earrings.

A portrait, my father decided, was one of those possessions that signaled status. He commissioned Andreas Brenner on the advice of the opera singer Magdalena Viktor, a recent client. She had been ecstatic with the results of young Brenner's work. Although still in his twenties, Brenner had the sight and the hand of a much more experienced artist, she told my father.

Had my father listened carefully to the nuances of Madame Viktor's praise, he might have recognized the danger of inviting the young artist to paint me. Until the moment Andreas Brenner walked into our home carrying his easel, a stretched and gessoed canvas, and a battered wooden box of oils, I had been a naïf, unaware and untouched. I had not known hunger of any kind. I did not know what it meant to be consumed by need.

Perhaps my father thought, as many fathers do, that I was still a child. He was a shrewd businessman, and it may have suited him to hire Brenner because, despite his talent, his price was well below that of the older, more established portraitists in Vienna. Whatever my father's reasons, accidental or intended, his choice of Brenner to paint my portrait changed my life.

In the weeks leading up to his arrival, my mother sorted and fussed through her wardrobe and mine. (Brenner had been commissioned to paint us both, on separate canvases.) I have inherited my father's black hair and olive-tinged complexion and my mother's blue eyes. "Aegean blue" is how my father described them the first time he met my mother, Marie-Therese Cronberg, at sunset on the steps of the temple at Sounion, where she had sprained her ankle in a fall and he, a young Greek in a linen suit, had carried her to safety.

"You must wear a dress the color of the Aegean," my mother had decided as she riffled through my armoire, fingering the fine cloth that had adorned me on special occasions—Christmas Eve at my grandparents' house in Hietzing, my confirmation, various excursions to matinee performances of the ballet and the opera. But none was Aegean blue. So, with my father's blessing, we made an appointment with my grandmother's dressmaker and set about the city on a hunt for silk the color of my eyes. When we found it, my mother was ecstatic, and I felt quite grown-up to have so much attention paid to how I would appear in the portrait. In retrospect, my parents could have spared the cost of the new dress and simply instructed Brenner to give whatever I was wearing in life the color blue in the painting.

My father, certainly, was no stranger to masking whatever was plain or ugly or unsatisfactory in reality and creating the illusion of beauty. But it seemed important to my parents that the dress indeed be blue, and blue it was.

Overcome with self-importance, I was disappointed that the style of the dress did not match my vision of what a young girl would wear for her first portrait. I was thinking

John Singer Sargent's *Madame X*, and my parents were holding in their mind's eye Mary Cassatt's *Elsie in a Blue Chair.*

The dress was demure, with long sleeves and a neckline that revealed only my collarbone. I pouted and begged my mother for a more sophisticated dress; I even whispered to the dressmaker to cut the neckline lower. Neither of them would bend.

I didn't want to be immortalized as a child, but had only a vague idea of how to portray myself as a woman. As a result, I was uncomfortable and sullen when Brenner entered our home and set up his easel in our music room, where the northern light filtered through two tall windows.

He spoke only briefly to me, directing me to a chair he had positioned at an angle to the windows. Once I was seated, he studied me for a few moments and then approached me.

"Tilt your head slightly to the left, like this." He reached for my chin with his hand. His fingertips were rough with callouses and smelled of turpentine. One of his nails was chipped, and the skin on the hand that held his brushes was crazed with lines of color—magenta, burnt umber, cerulean.

My nose grew accustomed to the odors that permeated even the fibers of his shirt and the strands of his hair that fell across his forehead when he leaned toward me to adjust the collar of my dress or straighten my shoulders.

I was used to the robust affection of my father's embrace—strong enough to carry my mother down the cliff of Sounion or lift me in one swoop onto a carousel horse at the Prater. Brenner's touch was at once both professional and intimate. He did nothing that even raised an eyebrow from my mother, sitting with her embroidery in a corner of the room. But each time he touched me, it was as if he were a blind man confronted by the unfamiliar and tracing it with his fingertips to identify it.

I found myself leaning into his touch, longing to be identified. To be seen and interpreted by an artist is not the same as standing in front of a mirror and receiving its unfiltered reflection. I was curious to learn who he was seeing.

"Smile just a little, Maya," my mother prompted me from the corner. "This isn't the dentist."

But I was still resentful about the dress and, besides, thought smiling was for children, enticed by the promise of an ice cream if they behaved. I wasn't eager to smile for my mother.

If Andreas Brenner had asked me to smile, however, I would have complied in an instant. He did not. In fact, at my mother's remark, he caught my eye with his and shook his head in a gesture so subtle it was clearly meant only for me—a secret passed between us in plain sight. From that point on, I trusted him to see me not as a child to be coaxed but as a young woman meeting his gaze as an equal.

That first morning was exhausting. Sitting still for any length of time has never been my habit. When I had visited my father's parents on the island of Skiathos, I would run barefoot on the beach, stopping only to pick up a wave-polished stone or a shard of amber-hued conch shell. I climbed pine-covered hills with my father, thrusting my walking stick into the dusty earth. Even in Vienna, I preferred to walk to school rather than take the trolley.

I was far from the beach in our music room, stiff in my chair. But then Brenner asked, "Where would you most like to be right now? Don't answer me out loud; just go there in your head."

I nodded in understanding and chose my summers in Greece. Other Viennese daughters might have images of the botanical garden or the Danube to entertain them while they sat staring at a spot on the wallpaper. But only I had the stone houses of Skiathos with their whitewashed stoops and bougainvillea climbing over blue doorways; the olive trees in my grandfather's orchard, bent from centuries of clinging to the hillsides; the harbor teeming with vessels; the dockside raucous with tavernas spilling onto the sidewalks and serving ouzo and crisply fried anchovies.

Brenner seemed to approve of my choice of reverie, because he nodded and threw himself once again into transferring what *he* saw onto his waiting canvas.

When the session was over, he covered the canvas with a cloth. I wanted a glimpse, but he refused. An unfinished work should not be viewed prematurely, he told my mother and me, as it tended to lead to disappointment or false expectations. He assured us that later, we would have time to absorb what he had created. He asked my mother if there was a cupboard where the canvas could be stored under lock and key, and she led him to one in the hallway.

I was disappointed, my vanity unsatisfied, my curiosity thwarted. I was impatient for Brenner to return.

Each morning, I devoured my *Brötchen* and coffee in the kitchen, not waiting to breakfast with my parents, and then spent an hour dressing for Brenner. That is how I came to think of it. Not dressing for my portrait, but for *him*. Something happened to me when I entered the music room and he was waiting at the easel. At times, he was industrious, blending colors from the white metal tubes in his box. But just as often, I would find him perched on the red wooden stool my mother had had brought up from the basement, his arms folded across his chest, his eyes staring at—no, studying—the face on the canvas that he would not let me see.

At those moments, I waited quietly in the doorway, a part of me respecting the artist at work and not wishing to disturb him but another part studying his face as intently as he did mine. I was looking for something—a glimmer of admiration for my unusual beauty; a sign that he was waiting for *me* with as much anticipation as I felt as I counted the hours until he reappeared.

When he looked up and saw me, he held my gaze, swallowing me whole, measuring the flesh-and-blood face standing before him against the one on the canvas. He nodded—whether in greeting or in agreement that the two images coincided wasn't always clear. Was he pleased to see *me*, or pleased that his work was achieving its end?

I took my accustomed place and basked for the next two hours in his attention. He seemed to be attuned to my thoughts. When my energy flagged, he sensed it in my posture or my wandering eye and called me back to the present with a joke or the suggestion of a sip of tea. If a hair was astray and distracting, he approached and smoothed it away. His touch, at first soothing, interesting, now made me flinch—not from pain or displeasure, but from an excitement that I'd never before experienced. His finger grazed my ear as he tucked a curl behind it, and I felt the touch reverberate throughout my body.

I wondered when he looked at me if he could see what was unfolding within me, the discovery I was making of how it felt to be seen—truly seen—by a man. It wasn't uncomfortable, but it was something I wished to keep hidden—from my mother definitely, but also from him.

I didn't think of it as forbidden, but it was not something I wished to share. It was too new, too fragile, too precious.

But it suffused me, warmed me in ways Brenner must have seen. When he suggested once again that I go in my mind to where I truly wanted to be, I did not go to Skiathos. I went, instead, into his arms.

I sat for Brenner every morning of my entire fall school holiday. In the afternoons, when I normally would have been sipping hot chocolate and gossiping with my girl-friends at Café Sacher, reveling in our freedom from algebra and Latin and the rigid expectations of the Sisters of Notre Dame de Sion, I sat instead in the music room and watched Brenner as he painted my mother.

"You don't have to stay," my mother assured me.

"It's fine," I told her. "Sister Marie assigned us a book to read over *Ferien*. It's a quiet time to get it finished."

So I paged through the tome but did very little reading. Instead, I studied Brenner when he wasn't focused on me. The second afternoon, I tucked a few sheets of sketching paper into my book and, while my mother assumed I was conscientiously taking notes, I roughed out in soft charcoal the lines and planes of what had become for me such a compelling face.

Later that night, I tacked the drawing to the side of my night table so that with my head on my pillow and my face turned toward it, it was exactly in my line of sight and the last thing I saw before I drifted off to sleep.

Chapter Two

WHEN THE WEEK WAS over, Brenner took both canvases back to his studio to finish them. With pain, I watched from our front parlor windows as he left. The end of this interlude in my otherwise ordinary life seized me more emphatically than I expected. Suddenly, the sketch that inspired my nightly dreams seemed a poor substitute for the face itself. I left the parlor, grabbed my hat and coat, and told my mother I was going for a walk. A week of being cooped up in the house had been enough, I told her.

She waved me off, more familiar with this version of Maya than the bookworm who had sat every afternoon in the shadows.

Brenner wasn't difficult to follow, even in the bustle of a late Friday afternoon in Vienna. The canvases and his easel, now collapsed to a manageable size, were stowed in a large knapsack carried on his back. In his left hand was the wooden case. He was tall and easy to spot, even though he had a few minutes' lead. I walked briskly at first to catch up to him, politely but firmly offering my excuses as I passed those taking a more leisurely pace.

When I was within a few meters of him, I slowed down and caught my breath. I hadn't expected to be so breathless—as I've said, I'm an energetic girl, used to moving quickly through the world. My heart was pounding. I'd been much closer to him during the sitting, but that had been a controlled and well-defined setting, under the observation of my mother's watchful eyes. Out here on the street, I was aware of just how reckless my decision to follow him had been. I had no idea what I was going to do next. Part of me wanted simply to keep him in sight, for that alone was enough to send a wave of pleasure washing over me. His stride down the street was as purposeful as his brushstrokes had been; he didn't appear to be burdened by the weight of his knapsack but rather carried it with pride, like the shield and colors of a knight identifying his allegiance.

Everything about Brenner proclaimed him an artist, and I found that thrilling. It was enough to be in his presence.

I was so focused on Brenner that I didn't notice the crowd was thinning as he turned off the Ringstrasse and headed toward a more remote neighborhood, less prosperous than the one my family inhabited. He stopped at the doorway of a tavern, but instead of going in, he held open the door and then turned directly toward me.

"We seem to be headed in the same direction. Would you like to stop for a beer on the way?"

An amused smile played around his lips, and I felt my face redden. How long had he known I was following him?

"Don't worry. I'm not going to send you home to your mother, at least not right away. I'm sure you're thirsty. Come and sit."

I followed him into the noisy and dim bar. He was greeted by several patrons, some of whom raised their eyebrows as I trailed behind him. I was glad I wasn't wearing my school uniform or a ribbon in my hair.

He found us a small, round table near the back and ordered us each a Pilsner from the barmaid as we took our seats.

"So, you wanted to see your portrait so badly that you were going to follow me to my studio and sneak a glimpse?"

Perhaps it was better if he thought that was my motivation. I would rather he assume I was a vain and spoiled princess than an infatuated schoolgirl. But what I really wanted was for him to see me as a woman. An object of desire, not a child to patronize.

I managed to find some sensible words to explain my unexpected presence. "I'm a student of art. I'm interested in your process—how you complete a painting. I didn't mean to follow you, but I was out for a walk after you left and noticed you. I thought I could catch up with you and ask you about what you'll do next."

He took the beers from the waitress and handed me one. At least he hadn't ordered me a lemonade.

"To your portrait," he said, lifting his glass toward mine.

"I noticed you sketching the other afternoon when your mother was sitting. What was your subject?"

"I take private art lessons. My teacher requires daily sketches, like a writer would keep a journal. They don't have to be elaborate or complicated. In fact, she prefers that I draw everyday things, like teapots and candlesticks, from life."

"And you were drawing candlesticks?"

"There are no candlesticks in the music room."

I didn't want to tell him that I had drawn his face, but I didn't want to lie either. I tried, instead, to draw the conversation away from my art and toward his.

"What will you do now with the portraits? How will you finish them?"

"The final touches are refinements only. A smoothing out of the surface. I won't alter what I saw in your face. I try to capture that immediately and don't rethink or rework what I first discovered."

"Will you show me?"

The knapsack leaned against the bench, tempting me to discover its contents. Even in the midst of the tavern, permeated with the aroma of fermented grain, I could smell the oils.

"Not here. Too dark. Too much risk of a spilled beer ruining the work. But if you want, you can see them at the studio."

That was indeed what I wanted. I glanced hesitantly at him, then out the window at the darkening sky. It was October, and although the winter solstice was still two months away, the days were already increasingly shorter.

I had left the house without a thought about my intentions. I'd been reckless and impulsive, driven only by the desire to still see and be seen by Brenner. I hadn't imagined anything beyond that. Faced now with his invitation—casually offered but laden with potential far beyond the opportunity to see the portrait—my emotions careened from one end of a swinging pendulum to the other. To go with him was the fulfillment of what had propelled me in the first place. But something held me back—more than the gathering dark and the alarm my lengthening absence would cause at home. As young and foolish as I was, I sensed my own vulnerability and the danger Andreas Brenner represented. To accept his offer now was to reveal the secret I had protected since he first began to paint me. If the invitation truly was as careless as it sounded, it meant far less to him than to me. Andreas Brenner was a man who could hurt me.

And so I withdrew.

"Another time, perhaps. I should go. Thank you for the beer."

I pulled on my coat and hat and extended my hand in farewell. He took it and held it.

"You were a delightful subject, far more interesting than the debutantes I'm often commissioned to paint. I hope you like the final portrait."

And then he bent and kissed the hand he held.

It was a gesture I'd seen repeated countless times in the society in which my family moved. But until that moment, I hadn't realized what an intimate act it could be. This was no mere social convention, a quarter-inch of air between lips and skin. Brenner's lips were close enough for me to feel their warmth, their softness, their openness.

I pulled my hand away, stunned by the depth of my response, and wove my way to the front of the crowded tavern. When I looked back, Brenner was already in conversation with the men who had greeted him when we arrived. He didn't look up as I slipped out the door and hurried home.

I was already back at school when Brenner delivered the finished paintings to my parents. I arrived home late in the afternoon to find the portraits side by side on the mantel. My father sat in his favorite chair, holding a glass of wine; my mother stood behind him, her hand lightly on his shoulder. The two of them were silent, studying the paintings as if they hung in a gallery at the Kunsthistorisches Museum.

"Maya, come see what our young artist has accomplished!" It was my father, clearly pleased, who invited me in.

The images staring back at us captured the striking resemblance between my mother and me that many fail to see because of the difference in our coloring. In her portrait, she appeared bathed in golden light that reflected off her pale blonde hair and roses-and-cream skin. But the delicacy of her coloring was in contrast to the strength of her features—her cheekbones, her nose, her chin could have been those of one of the Caryatids that support the Erechtheion on the Acropolis. My father has always called her "my goddess." It is that facial structure, in addition to the blue eyes, that she and I share. But in my mother, I saw those features as those of a classic beauty, and in myself I saw only angularity and awkwardness.

I approached my own portrait to get a closer look at how Brenner had interpreted my unusual face. It was not that of a child, I was relieved to see. But I was startled by how accurately he had captured what had been going through my head. I saw heat and sensuality in the directness and fire of my eyes, in the fullness of the mouth that I had refused to shape into a smile. It was the face of a woman forming, flowering. It was frank, not demure. It was hungry, not satisfied. It was me.

The smile that had been missing when I sat for Brenner now teased its way onto my lips. I had my back to my parents, and I wondered if they, too, saw this transformation. Their daughter no longer a child. I struggled to conceal in that moment what the portrait so clearly revealed, at least to me.

"Come here, Maya, and see the paintings from a proper distance. Up close as you are, you are only seeing brushstrokes and patches of color."

I turned, wary and cautious.

"Don't you like what he's done?" My mother, ever sensitive, had seen my face.

My father interpreted my reaction a different way. "She's just realized what a great beauty she is," he said. "You are both my beauties, and I'll spend many happy hours with these two images looking down at me every day."

While my parents discussed the permanent location of the paintings—remain above the mantel, flank it on either side, or hang on the opposite wall above the sofa—I slipped down to the kitchen for a cup of hot chocolate and a quiet moment by myself to savor the Maya that Brenner had discovered and re-created.

Chapter Three

THE PORTRAIT BECAME A guidepost for me over the next few years, like an ensemble that I grew into. It wasn't that Andreas Brenner had painted me to look older than my years, but that he had anticipated the woman I was becoming. The painting instilled a kind of pride in me—not because it made me see myself as beautiful and therefore superior in some way, but because it gave me a glimpse of the power in my striking and unusual face, and an understanding of how much of one's beauty comes from what is within.

By the time I was nineteen, I was no longer the awkward adolescent arguing with my mother about the cut of my dress. Despite my father's initial misgivings, which were overcome by my mother's adamant campaign, I earned a place at the University of Vienna—one of only a few women admitted. The university was a compromise on my part. I would have rather studied studio art at the Academy of Fine Arts, but the Vienna art establishment refused to allow women. I elected to pursue art history, learning what I could from the masters.

I began my studies with a sense of myself that had come, in many ways, from Andreas Brenner's portrait. I carried myself boldly; when I entered a room, I intended to command it.

In fact, I *had* to project an attitude of confidence, because most of my male classmates and many of my professors considered it either ridiculous or an outrage that a woman thought she was capable of higher intellectual study.

My first days at university were a heady taste of freedom after the rigorous structure of the nuns. Choices abounded in the courses I would study, the friends I would make, even in whether to sit in a vast amphitheater to listen to a droning lecture on Aristotle or to slip across campus to the student canteen for a cup of coffee and a lively discussion of politics or aesthetics.

I was studying art history and spent many hours in the galleries of the Kunsthistorisches Museum, my notebook in hand to record the curve of a limb or the effect of light and shadow on a scene. I was interested not only in the classical works covered in the university's curriculum but also in the art that was being created now—in the lofts of Vienna and Paris; in the sunlight of Spain and the Riviera. I began to frequent the pubs and coffeehouses in the neighborhoods where artists congregated, eager to engage in conversation with Gustav Klimt or Koloman Moser. One afternoon, I stumbled into a heated discussion taking place at a coffeehouse among an animated group populated by a few people who were known to me.

"Maya, come pull up a chair and join the fray." Max Huber, one of the lecturers in my art history courses, moved his chair over to make room for me, clearly relishing the debate. "We're arguing about art and commerce—private vision and public taste. Sander here thinks Andreas is prostituting himself because he's making a living selling his art."

I noticed this wasn't a group of students alone. Older men were also at the table—a professor, a couple of artists, and, directly opposite me, the Andreas to whom Max had referred—Andreas Brenner.

I hadn't seen him since he had bought me the glass of beer and I had refused his invitation to see the unfinished portraits. His face did not register recognition, and I chose not to remind him who I was. His reputation had been growing, according to conversations I overheard between my parents—a development that was particularly important to my father, who saw his choice of Brenner as prescient as the value of our portraits increased along with Brenner's fame.

I watched and listened as I sipped my coffee. Brenner seemed amused by the discussion, even though it was his life and his art that was being questioned. Perhaps he had made peace with the fact that he was a commercial artist; perhaps he used his career as a portraitist to support a more avant-garde body of work that he painted for himself and not for the drawing rooms of Vienna's elite. He revealed nothing; he did not defend himself. Instead, he let Sander rage about pandering to conventional norms and declare that portraits were not art. I nearly choked on my coffee.

"I've just come from two hours in the portrait gallery of the museum," I felt compelled to interject. I was the only woman at the table, and suddenly all eyes were upon me. "Have you forgotten that some of the greatest paintings are portraits created for exactly the same reasons Andreas paints? To satisfy the desires of a patron. Or is the measure of true art in your eyes inversely proportional to its value in the marketplace?"

"But Andreas is catering to the small minds who wish to be immortalized in oil. He glosses over imperfections, limns the harsh line or unfortunate shape of chin or nose to create the illusion of a far more attractive subject."

"Have you seen any of his portraits? In my opinion, he is not concealing or obscuring anything, but rather peeling away layers of camouflage to reveal the essence of an individual."

I realized I was treading dangerously close to revelations I didn't want to expose at this table—not to the intellectuals batting around an idea and not to Andreas Brenner.

"You appear to have a champion here, Andreas, who claims to know your work. Perhaps you should hire her to promote you."

"I'd rather paint her," he said, and looked directly into my eyes, just as I remembered him doing when I sat for him.

I stared back, challenging him. But I didn't speak out loud what I was thinking: *You have.*

The conversation moved on to other topics at that point. When I finished my coffee, I gathered my things and rose to leave. Max invited me to return another afternoon.

"We can always use some of your fiery comments to liven the discussion. You're a match for any of us."

I promised to come again and turned away from the table. I had gone only a few steps when I felt a hand on my elbow.

"I meant what I said back there. I'd like to paint you."

"I have only a student's allowance at my disposal. I couldn't afford you."

"I didn't mean as a commission."

"What do you mean then?" He still had his hand on my arm, and I was reluctant for him to let me go. But I believed he still didn't recognize me. How many faces had he painted since mine? Had they all blended into one?

"Be my model. I'll pay *you*."

"Why me? Aren't there dozens of women in Vienna from whom you can choose?"

"I've painted most of them. They were schoolboy exercises compared to you. If it's not of interest to you, I'll not pursue the idea. But your beauty is both unusual and familiar."

I allowed a brief smile to flit across my face. He meant familiar in its broadest sense—my Viennese features—not the particular familiarity of our past encounters. But I was flattered, enjoying the attention of someone captivated by my looks. Despite my intellectual pursuits, I was still a woman who liked to be told she was beautiful.

"Very well. I accept. Where? When?"

He released my arm to retrieve a card from his pocket.

"Here's the address of my studio. Does tomorrow at eleven suit you?"

It did. We parted at the door of the coffeehouse. I looked at my watch and saw that I had a class to attend in ten minutes. I raced to campus, doing my best to cast aside the excitement I felt about the next portrait Brenner would paint of me.

I didn't tell my parents. Although I still lived under their roof, my daily comings and goings as a university student were my own business. But I also knew they would be horrified to find out I was posing as a model for an artist—even Andreas Brenner.

I arrived at his studio shortly before eleven. I have my mother's sense of time—not my father's. The early fall air had been brisk, and I had relished the walk, my curiosity mounting the closer I got to Brenner's neighborhood. I was enjoying the idea of myself as the object once again of his acute observation, his intense scrutiny. No longer the tentative adolescent struggling to define herself as a woman, I was looking forward to meeting Brenner on more equal footing.

The building was relatively new, and suffused with in-direct Northern light from tall, floor-to-ceiling windows. I rode the lift to the top floor and stepped into a sky-lit room. A tile stove in the center emanated a welcome heat. Three or four easels supported canvases in various stages of completion—all formal, conventional portraits for which he'd become known. The warmth of the air in the room heightened the odors of linseed oil and turpentine, mingled with coffee and tobacco.

Brenner was arranging pillows on a divan that had been draped with a shawl enhanced by embroidered flowers in deep colors of magenta and yellow.

I waited in the doorway, absorbing what I had only imagined years before. When he turned from his task, I greeted him.

"Good morning." I extended my hand.

He strode across the room, appraising me as he walked.

"Welcome. I see that this time, you weren't afraid to accept my invitation to my studio."

So he *had* recognized me. I wrestled with whether I should take this newfound knowledge as a warning. I'll admit, I had been flattered back at the café that he'd found me interesting enough to paint. But now I suspected another motive behind the invitation, and it made me uneasy.

I'd been an art student long enough to understand that the relationship between artist and model is fraught with layers of complexity. Who, after all, is really in control? The model is naked; she turns herself over to the artist's vision of her; he tells her how to arrange herself—in the languorous pose of a lover promising pleasure or the haughty position of a patroness holding the viewer at a distance. I've often wondered what was going through the minds of the women painted by the masters, and whether they were a source of something more than simply the flesh-and-blood figure onto which the artist placed his own interpretation. Did the model's gaze outward at the artist, her sense of her body and its power and its mystery, in any way infuse the artist's depiction of that body?

I wanted to find out for myself—but not if I couldn't trust the artist's reason for painting me.

"Why did you ask me to model for you?" In addition to my looks being at odds with the Viennese ideal of beauty, I'd never quite mastered the art of subtlety my mother had attempted to instill in me growing up.

"You won't get what you want if you demand it, Maya," she had warned me.

Brenner didn't appear fazed by my directness. "I asked because I found your transformation from the girl on Elisabethstrasse stunning, although not surprising. You possessed an intangible boldness even then. I wanted to explore what it would be like to paint you again—without your mother sitting in the corner. Or will she still be there, in your head? Because if she is, I'm not interested."

He turned with a shrug, as if to dismiss me.

"I can assure you that my mother will not be joining us." I surprised myself by how quickly I jumped to answer him, to direct him back to me.

"Fine. You can undress over there." He pointed to a corner where a flimsy Japanese screen scattered with cherry blossoms stood. "Put on the red gown that's draped over the chair. Only the red gown; nothing else. And pile your hair on top of your head."

I moved across the room, conscious that his eyes followed me and aware, in following his instructions, that I had just ceded control to him. I stripped off the layers of my clothing fiercely, as if to prevent myself from reconsidering. The red dress was silk. It slid over my bare skin like the water of baptism.

"Are you ready?" The impatience in his voice was palpable. I heard the scratch of charcoal on the canvas on the other side of the screen. Was he already sketching?

I emerged from the meager nod to modesty that the screen had provided. The gown floated around me, affording me a freedom of movement that my own garments lacked.

"That's exactly what I'm looking for," he said, looking up from the sketchpad. "Keep moving around the room. Inhabit the dress. I want it to possess you before you pose."

I drifted, through the blue smoke of his cigarette, across the floor in my bare feet and around the studio as if it were a ballroom. A cello played in my head, and I began to dance—a melancholy waltz. I lifted my hands above my head and swayed, my partner the heated air in the room.

"Stop there."

My arms were outstretched, beckoning. My eyes were wide open. Strands of my hair had slipped from the chignon I had fashioned. Parts of the silk clung to my body where I had begun to sweat. Brenner began sketching furiously, his hand moving quickly and decisively across the canvas.

In the four years since I had watched him work, his methods had become more frenetic, more intense and inward. He rarely met my gaze, but instead cast his eyes over me in a sweeping glance, all the while keeping his sketching hand in motion. I felt as if I, Maya, had disappeared, replaced by the abstract concept "woman in a red dress."

It was not what I expected. I wanted to be seen. I wanted the painting to be what it was because of *me*.

"I need to put my arms down. Have you anything to drink?"

"Fine, take a break. There's coffee on the burner. Brandy in the cupboard."

I poured myself a cup of the bitter brew that had been sitting too long in the pot and wandered over to the canvas. I remembered how adamant Brenner had been about not showing me my portrait before it was completed, but I was intent on reminding him that I was no longer the child of his client.

"Does it bother you if I watch? I'm a student, after all. I'm eager to learn."

"You're not like other models I've hired. But that's no surprise, given what I saw yesterday at the café. Most of the women who pose for me are happy enough to display their bodies, take their breaks out on the balcony, and ignore what's happening on the canvas."

"Is that what you prefer? A model who stays out of the way, both physically and intellectually? If that's what you're looking for, don't expect me to continue to model for you."

He began to fill in with color the outline he had created with his rapid strokes. His eyes were on my image, not on me.

"What is it that *you* are looking for? Why did you agree to model for me? You surely don't need the money."

"I meant what I said yesterday about your talent. You get under the skin of your subjects. You've gotten under my skin."

As soon as I said it, I wished I could call it back. I felt like the adolescent daydreamer who'd been obsessed with her first taste of passion. But I couldn't deny that Andreas Brenner had awakened something when he first painted me. And I knew that he was about to do it again.

We worked until dusk began to muffle the city. As the street lamps shed their haloed light on the pavement below the studio, I shook out my arms to release the rigidity of my pose.

"I'll be leaving now," I told him as I moved across the room to the screen and my own clothes.

"Expected for dinner on Elisabethstrasse?" He said the words in a sneer, taunting me as the good Viennese daughter who went home to bone china and crystal, her afternoon of slumming it in the artists' quarter coming to an end.

"As a matter of fact, no, I have another engagement." I didn't, but I was damned if I was going to give him the satisfaction of defining me as the bourgeois dilettante, defying her background for a few hours before scurrying back to the safety of home.

In truth, I *was* defying my parents. Had they known what I had been doing that afternoon, my father would probably have threatened to make me quit university. I knew I was taking a risk in accepting Brenner's dare. Because that was what it was—a challenge, not an idle offer that he extended to every woman he might want to paint.

The afternoon had been a wild ride of emotions—exhilaration coupled with fear. The freedom of the red dress had been a revelation. Unhampered by the trappings of Viennese fashion and enhanced by the absence of undergarments, my body had reacted with relief and then joy.

I dressed hurriedly, putting on not only my clothes but also the façade that would protect me once I left the studio. I would need it when I returned to my parents' home and when I moved about the world I inhabited at university. I was wary of being labeled Brenner's model, further diminishing whatever intellectual weight I carried.

Nevertheless, I had felt a striking sense of my own power as I watched Brenner fill the page with my image. Was this how a muse experienced her influence? I wondered. Did I want to be Brenner's muse? And at what cost?

Chapter Four

I DIDN'T SEE ANDREAS again for several days, and my reaction to his absence careened from irritation to longing and then to fear. Was I becoming obsessed with him? If so, I wanted to wrench that yearning out of my heart. I had fought a lengthy battle with my parents to obtain their permission to attend university after an equally exhausting experience convincing the Faculty of Liberal Arts that I was a qualified candidate. I was one of a ridiculously small cohort of women accepted. Even though women had been allowed to study there for twenty years, we were still rare birds in the lecture halls. By accepting Andreas's dare to model for him, I was risking my credibility as a serious student.

Andreas had claimed to find my outspoken comments at the café intriguing. I had always been confident I would hold my own in a challenging conversation about art and its meaning, but in taking off my clothes in Andreas's studio, had I also stripped myself of my intellectual life? I was furious with myself for falling under his arrogant spell, furious with him for treating me like a plaything. He had dangled the modeling request as a challenge, a slightly dangerous adventure, and I had found it as enticing as a shiny object.

Alone in my room on Elisabethstrasse, I threw things as I undressed—a jeweled comb pulled forcefully from my hair and cast on the dresser, my stockings tossed carelessly over a chair, my chemise left in a puddle of silk on the floor. I stood in front of the mirror, looking at my body as Andreas must have. I am tall. I am dark, with my father's black hair and tawny skin. I am strong. As a child, I scrambled over the rocky cliffs of my grandparents' island of Skiathos. As an adolescent, I hiked the Dolomites and the Alps with my parents. My father taught me to sail on the Wolfgangsee and later on the Aegean. I was, after all, the son he never had. And so he passed on to me the skills that might have gone to a brother.

I learned to read the wind. I learned to love the wind.

Had I betrayed this body, which I had commanded until I posed for Andreas? As soon as I began to yearn for him to call me back, I was reminded I had already ceded power to him. At university, I forced myself to avoid the café where we had encountered each other. I refused to seek him out, although I had to resist the urge more than once to follow the street that led to his studio. I went to lectures. I retreated to the library in the afternoons. I went back to Elisabethstrasse for dinner.

My mother, ever watchful, commented on my moodiness and distraction.

"This is exactly what I was afraid of when we acquiesced to your desire to attend university."

"What do you mean, Mama?" I kept my tone calm, but I knew exactly what she meant. Was I so transparent that she suspected I had done something risky? Surely she couldn't have guessed I had modeled for Andreas, but she knew something had changed within me.

"Your excitement in starting your classes has dissipated. You seem to be only going through the motions of attending your lectures physically, but I doubt you're mentally engaged. You used to arrive at the dinner table bursting with ideas, arguing with Papa about some obscure theory. Now you barely open your mouth except to eat, and even that has diminished. What has happened to you, *Schatzi*? Has the glow of intellectual life lost its appeal?"

I believe that is what she hoped—that I had experimented with the challenge of university study but now found it either too hard or too boring, and was ready to abandon it for a more traditional path.

"Not at all, Mama. Forgive me if I seem less talkative at dinner. I'm simply lost in thought."

She studied my face in silence. I'm sure she wanted to ask me, "About what?" but perhaps reconsidered whether she truly wanted to know.

"Sometimes I'm truly lost in trying to understand you, Maya. I am merely concerned that you seem unhappy. If you are not, I will let it rest."

"I am not unhappy, Mama. But I have a lengthy reading assignment. If you'll excuse me, I'm going up to my room."

I left my half-eaten dinner on my plate and retreated to my books. I hadn't lied to her. I wasn't unhappy. I was angry. I was tortured by wild swings in my emotions—the incredible euphoria of being seen by Andreas and the fear that I was losing myself to him. My books offered little relief. I couldn't concentrate. Had it not already been dark, I would have grabbed my coat and taken a brisk walk in the park across the street from our house. Instead, knowing I had to do something to dissipate the energy surging and seething within me, I opened a tin of colored pencils and decided to transfer to paper what was roiling inside me.

I still had the sketch I had made of Andreas four years ago; it was hidden under a loose floorboard in my room, as though it was a forbidden love letter. I retrieved the sketch and stared at it awhile, recalling the emotions of the adolescent girl who had created it, exploring her first experience of passion, so unformed, so hungry. Did I understand any more deeply now what was drawing me to Andreas? I certainly knew what was holding me back—Mama, who was probably still sitting at the dining table, baffled by a daughter who did not conform in so many ways. I knew I was on the precipice of something, hesitating to leap into the unknown. I did not want to be afraid.

I began to sketch Andreas's face again, using my first drawing as if it were an underdrawing. But this time I used color and poured into the image all my ambivalence, the push and pull of desire and fear. When I finished, I was exhausted. My hand cramped from gripping the pencil and sweat trickled between my breasts, as if I had raced around the park in a most unladylike fashion.

I held the paper away from me and studied it. Although the face was Andreas's, the emotions emanating from it were my own. I had used the colors in layers, building up the image to convey the ambiguity and complexity of my feelings.

The drawing was raw, searing, honest in ways I was not able to express in words. It occurred to me that rather than choosing to draw a self-portrait, I had instead superimposed my own internal life onto Andreas's visage. That intrigued me rather than disturbed me. I acknowledged that my entanglement and fascination with Andreas Brenner had begun long before I had posed for him the second time. Something was compelling me. And that night, I made the decision to surrender to it.

Circumstances at home unexpectedly opened an opportunity for me to act on my decision. My parents had received an invitation from relatives in Salzburg to spend a few weeks attending opera performances and concerts. My mother was an enthusiastic music lover and my father was happy to indulge her whenever the occasion arose. I convinced them my studies were too important for me to join them and wished them an enjoyable trip.

The day after their departure, I sought out Andreas. I preferred not to confront him in the café, where our encounter would be sure to arouse attention. We had left each other in an unsettled state, and our meeting would inevitably be intense. Instead, I went to his studio. I knew he painted in the late morning when the light was at its peak.

I took the lift, the clanging metal grid work reminding me that I was about to enclose myself, define myself, in relation to Andreas. Rather than knock, I opened the door and walked into the room. The familiar aromas of tobacco, coffee, and turpentine enveloped me. Even after only one modeling session, I felt at home in this space.

Andreas had his back to me. He was not alone. An older woman, draped only in a flowered gauze shawl, was posing for him. She lost her focus when I entered the room, her gaze taking me in with a mixture of disdain and curiosity. She turned her world-weary expression away from me and addressed Andreas.

"Who's this, your latest conquest?" She flicked her head in my direction, and Andreas turned.

I stood my ground. I knew I belonged there and wasn't going to be dismissed.

Andreas said nothing to me but spoke to the model. "Get dressed. I have enough here. There's cash on the table."

He wiped his brush as she stomped off the platform. While she dressed, I poured myself a cup of coffee and lit a cigarette. Andreas continued to clean up. Each of us was waiting out the other, a child's game of who would blink first. But I had come with intention, and I was not going to be thwarted. I moved toward the windows, my coffee cup in hand, and waited. When the model finally left, slamming the door behind her, I heard the slap of the wooden-handled brush on the table, and braced myself for either a verbal outburst or the clattering of paint tubes and bottles of spirits onto the floor, swept there by Andreas's hand. But instead, his voice was gentle, almost pleading.

"I didn't expect you to come back." I could tell by his tone he wasn't mocking me as the bourgeois princess willing to dare and defy only so much.

"I didn't expect to come back, at least not as I left."

"Why did you?"

"Because I want to be fearless. And when I am with you, you ignite that part of me that is ready to explore my deepest secrets."

We still stood several feet apart. His eyes revealed a hunger I had not seen before. A hunger for me.

"Paint me," I whispered, and began to unbutton my blouse, not behind the screen but standing in front of him. Locked in place, he watched me as I watched him. My eyes never left his as layer after layer of my clothing dropped to the floor. With each article, I removed yet another layer of my mask, another level of my being. I wanted him to see all of me, from the tiny mole under my left breast to the scar on my thigh I had gotten scrambling over rocks on Skiathos when I was ten.

By the time I had finished, we were both breathless. I thought then that he would cross the distance between us, lift me in his arms, and carry me to the bed near the stove. He did not. I saw the tension in his muscles, the restraint with which he held himself back, and then realized that he was about to take that energy and desire to the canvas.

"Stay exactly as you are." He could barely speak the words.

I watched silently as he wrestled a large canvas onto an easel and began with rapid, bold strokes to transform my naked body into a portrait of longing and defiance. How do I explain what happened during those hours as I stood, my body pulsing with aching need while he worked, throwing his own hunger onto that barren surface? The air between us crackled with intensity, an electric storm building over the mountains. Neither of us spoke. When he finally put down his brush, we were both near collapse. I don't remember which one of us moved first. But when he reached me, I clawed at his shirt, desperate for the sensation of his skin against mine. By the time he, too, was naked, we were on the floor, the burgundy of the carpet an echo of the blood thrumming throughout my body, our coupling magnified by the last few hours—no, years—of my longing.

I welcomed the pain when he first entered me, embracing it as a confirmation of what I had anticipated when I stepped off the lift and into his studio. I was plunging into danger, exhilaration, and an unknown fraught with both intense pleasure and terrifying loss.

I touched the blood on my thigh, understanding how fitting it was as a symbol of this passage, and with my finger smeared the dark red fluid across his cheek and mine.

The shadows from the windowpanes were stretching across the floor, casting half of Andreas's face in darkness. He was asleep, turned toward me, one arm flung across my belly, his fingertips stained with pigment. Despite the encroaching dusk, I didn't stir. Rather than scrambling to hurry home as I had the last time I modeled for Andreas, I found in myself a stillness that was new to me.

I ached in a curious melding of pain and remembered pleasure. After our first mindless, ravenous coupling, we had moved to the bed, where we had made love two more times before both of us had succumbed to sleep. I woke first. With the weight of Andreas's arm preventing me from moving without disturbing him, I remained still and savored the peace of this singular moment of my life.

My eyes roamed the studio, familiar to me in its surface chaos, an amalgam of Andreas's divided attention. To one side, the society portraits, the paintings that paid the rent and made him the darling of every mother hoping to enhance her daughter's beauty and attract the "right" suitor.

But arrayed against another wall, a growing number of canvases that spoke of Andreas's grasp of the pain and raw emotion of human existence. The portrait he had painted of me today would take its place among those.

I could see it easily from where I lay, propped against its heavy easel. Observing it now, sated as I was with our lovemaking, I could still feel the coiled tension in my limbs, the longing in my heart, the trembling in my lips. The woman on the canvas was tortured with waiting, held back by her own will, and overwhelmed with anticipation for an imagined yet unknown joy.

Her expression was defiant and so clearly focused on the lover across the room that anyone viewing this painting would be confronted with their own desire.

How had Andreas done that? Or had he only been able to paint such palpable yearning because I had presented him with it—transparent, unabashed, and, in that moment, without guilt. A smile emerged on my face, unlike the visage of the woman in the painting, which conveyed both an invitation and a challenge. That face said, "Come to me, but only if you dare."

"Why are you smiling?" Andreas had woken and propped himself on his elbow. His paint-spattered fingertips traced my lips.

"I am remembering how I felt earlier."

The peacock spread his feathers in an extravagant display. He thought I was referring to our lovemaking. I didn't dissuade him. Power isn't easily shared, and I thought it best to hold in secret the potent role I had played in the creation that I knew in my heart would become known as Andreas Brenner's masterpiece.

The languor of the afternoon was seeping away in inverse proportion to the lengthening shadows and the increasing chill of a room where neither of us had fed the stove, so heated were we by our own passion.

I stretched my arms over my head.

"My next portrait of you will be this pose," he murmured, stroking my thigh. I stopped his hand from roving further.

A fleeting expression of thwarted desire passed across his face, but I kissed it away.

"Have you forgotten so quickly that I was a virgin a few hours ago? I am both sated and extremely sore."

"Are you about to run away again?" He sat up, the supple limbs that had enfolded me now shifted away just enough to cause me to shiver as the cold air skittered across the floor.

"Not at all," I answered, still lying in the pose he envisioned for my next portrait.

"Do you want to paint me now?" I said it softly, but it was still a dare.

He shook his head and flexed the fingers on his dominant hand. "Like the virginal model, the artist is also sore."

I sat up and, despite the cold, took his cramped hand and began to massage it.

It was past twilight when we finally rose—Andreas to relight the stove and I to quickly wash, gather my discarded clothing, and dress. I was struck by how confined and uncomfortable I felt with each additional layer I put on. Wearing the red silk dress the first time I had modeled for him had given me a sense of freedom in my body. But this time, without even the semblance of a covering, my nakedness had given me knowledge—an awareness not only of sinew and bone, muscle and blood, but of the mystery between piercing emotion and its manifestation and transformation in art.

I experienced my body as energy, chafing to escape from the finely embroidered undergarments, starched linen blouse, and heavy woolen suit that now encumbered me.

"I'm ravenous. Is there anywhere we can go to get a decent meal?" I thought some food and a glass of wine might quell my prickling unquiet. Something hearty, like goulash and spaetzle.

"Are you not expected at home for dinner?"

"Are you trying to send me away?" I smiled, confident he was not.

"Not at all. I'm only surprised. But I suppose after today, nothing you do should surprise me."

"If you must know, my parents have left Vienna for a few weeks to visit relatives in Salzburg."

"Why didn't you travel with them?"

"I chose not to miss my lectures. I have no intention of losing my place at university."

"And yet you chose to miss them today."

"Yes, I did." I placed my hat on my head. "Are you going to take me to dinner, or am I to forage in my family's kitchen for a hunk of cheese and a crust of bread?"

He threw on his coat with a flamboyant gesture and swept open the door to the studio.

"I know just the place."

The bistro where he took me, not far from the Opera House, was raucous and patronized by a mixture of artists, musicians, and actors. Andreas was apparently well known there, and I was definitely scrutinized as we made our way through the crowd to a table near the rear of the dining room.

I truly was hungry, having eaten only a Brötchen with butter and ham before I had embarked on my mission that morning.

Andreas laughed as I reveled in the goulash, the tender chunks of pork coated in a wine-rich sauce with bits of onions and peppers adding to its savor.

"I've never seen you eat before. It's a revelation."

"What, that I enjoy food?"

"You devour it—as you embrace all of life, Maya. You are a miracle."

I mopped up the last of the gravy with a piece of bread torn from the loaf. And then I licked my fingers.

Chapter Five

ANDREAS PUT ME IN a cab after dinner. When I arrived home, I was relieved to find the house quiet. With my parents in Salzburg, Gertraud had left me a covered dish of noodles and meatballs in the kitchen, with a note that said she was retiring to her room but was available if I needed her to run a bath or prepare clothes for tomorrow.

I required neither the food nor the assistance. The last thing I wanted was the judgmental eyes of Gertraud observing my body. I didn't know if there were outward signs when a woman had made love for hours, but I certainly felt different, emotionally as well as physically. In addition to the soreness, there was a sense of both having been known as well as knowing.

I had read accounts of intimacy, but they were romantic fantasies that only hinted at the power of what I had experienced in Andreas's bed.

I put the untouched meal away in the icebox and climbed the stairs to my room. The heightened energy that had sustained me all day was waning, and I was suddenly exhausted. I could barely undress myself before I collapsed on my bed.

I thought I would sleep deeply. But flashes of sense memory coursed through my body, reigniting an intense longing. I touched myself where Andreas's lips and hands had explored my body. Despite the constant drumbeat of sin imparted by the nuns at Notre Dame de Sion, I found myself curiously free of guilt.

At some point during the night, I finally succumbed to sleep. I am usually an early riser, but my body ignored the dawn as I burrowed under the duvet. It was Gertraud, alarmed that I had not appeared for breakfast, who came to my door and called my name.

When I didn't respond, she opened the door and raised her voice.

As I stirred and lifted my head, I heard her catch her breath.

"*Gott sei Dank*," she whispered, and crossed herself. "I was afraid you were ill, especially when I found the food in the icebox and realized you hadn't eaten one of your favorite meals."

I mumbled my apology for causing her concern. "What time is it?"

"Past eleven. Are you expected anywhere today? Shall I draw a bath for you?"

I rubbed my face and pushed strands of hair out of my eyes. I hadn't bothered to braid my hair before I got into bed. Hairpins were strewn across the pillow, and my usually contained tresses were a mass of tangles. What other signs of disarray might be apparent on my body? I had washed quickly at the studio, but I couldn't peek under the sheets to check if traces of blood remained on my thighs. The last thing I wanted was for Gertraud to be helping me in the bath. I leaned back against the pillows and attempted to look wan and drained, which probably wasn't far from my actual condition.

"You were right. I am feeling somewhat off. I think it's best if I rest for a few more hours."

"You don't look like your usual energetic self, I agree. Did you eat some of that unfortunate food at the university canteen? Who knows how long they keep it warmed over? Did you vomit?" She looked under the bed for the chamber pot. "You smell very sour. I'll go make you some *Kamillentee*. That will settle your stomach."

As soon as she left, I pushed back the covers and crossed the room to the mirror. I lifted my nightgown, looking for any outward signs that my body was decidedly no longer in its virginal, untouched state. What had I expected? A glow? A secret knowledge that anyone with a shred of experience would recognize? What I saw instead was what I realized Andreas had seen the night before as he painted me. Ripeness. Willingness. Hunger.

I dropped the nightgown and grabbed my hairbrush from the dresser. I was detangling my hair when Gertraud returned with the tea.

"I can do that for you, Maya. Sip your tea while I braid."

I let her care for me, welcoming even that chaste touch as she wove the plait.

"You're still wearing your earrings! You must have truly felt awful last night—to forget your jewelry and leave your hair still pinned."

I bent my head, trying to mask the smile. Of all the words I might have used to describe my feelings when I had climbed into bed the night before, "awful" was not one of them. Distracted, perhaps, by memories; pleasured, certainly, in ways I had never imagined; but most of all, I had felt powerful.

After she finished braiding my hair, Gertraud left me to rest.

"I'll make some soup for when you feel up to eating. Something light."

I waited until I heard her descending the stairs. I had no need for more sleep, but it would have been impossible for me to leave the house without arousing suspicion. I pulled on a dressing gown and paced, overcome with a nervous energy that might have gnawed at me had I not redirected my agitation, my sheer need to be with Andreas again, into a plan that could place me back in the studio without alarming Gertraud or my parents. Mama and Papa were not due home for weeks. I knew I could convince Gertraud I had recovered within a few hours and claim I had an appointment with a professor, which wasn't so far from the truth. Andreas was indeed a kind of tutor to me, although not in the creative arts.

Longer term, I would need a more elaborate scheme to keep my parents unaware. But I would deal with them later. It didn't occur to me at all that Andreas might not want me back. I believed I had conquered him. Hadn't I set out the previous morning with only one intention, and hadn't I achieved that?

There was water, albeit cold, in the pitcher on the washstand, and I filled the basin and bathed myself. Like Gertraud's braiding, even the friction of the wet cloth on my skin sent heightened sensations through my body. Every nerve ending was singing an unfamiliar tune, at times melodious and at other moments jangling and off-key. I also detected the smell Gertraud had labeled "sour." As unfamiliar to me as the explosion of pleasure the lovemaking had incited, it was both earthy and metallic, sweat and blood, mingled with Andreas's own distinctive scent of coffee, tobacco, and linseed oil. Rather than repel me, it conveyed me back to the studio. The scent was so different from the powdered and perfumed bodies that swirled around the drawing rooms and ballrooms of my parents' circle.

As I turned to dress, I found my clothing from the night before in a pile on the chair next to my bed. As I lifted my chemise from the top, I saw with horror that there were traces of blood on my drawers. By some grace, Gertraud had been too concerned with my sickly appearance to turn her attention to my carelessly discarded garments. I grabbed the drawers and riffled through the rest of my clothing to check for stains. Everything else was without a trace, but I stared with indecision at the fragment of silk in my hand. Hide it? Wash it? Burn it? Whatever I did, Gertraud would find it. I acted quickly before she returned with the soup, and stuffed the lace-trimmed evidence of my lost maidenhood into the satchel I used to carry my notebooks back and forth to university. When I left the house later, Gertraud wouldn't question why I had it. I pulled fresh undergarments from my lingerie drawer and donned a wool dress and jacket. My suit from the previous day reeked of smoke and onions from the bistro, and I hung it to air out.

I gathered up the stockings, chemise, and blouse from the day before and placed them in the hamper. I was rushing around like a child who has broken her Oma's cherished figurine and is trying to hide the fragments, all the while knowing that eventually, Oma will discover the figurine is missing. Would my efforts to conceal the evidence of my transformative encounter with Andreas be as futile? How long could I sustain the charade?

Another knock on the door startled me out of my reverie.

"Maya, I have some soup for you, and the mail."

I opened the door.

"You're up and dressed! I'm so relieved. Come sit and have some broth."

"Thank you, Gertraud. I'm feeling much better."

I dutifully accepted the soup and flipped through the stack of envelopes she had brought up. My breath caught when I saw the handwriting on a small, gray envelope.

"Is everything all right, Maya?"

I slipped the gray square under the other mail and dutifully lifted my spoon and blew on the liquid.

"It's a little hot. That's all. I'm truly fine, Gertraud. I'll come down in a while. I have an appointment with my tutor at three o'clock."

"Are you sure you're up to it? I can deliver a message if you want to postpone the meeting."

"That is kind of you, but I should go."

"Very well, but you work too hard, Maya. All this studying and reading and writing, I see the toll it's taking on you."

She surveyed my room as she made up the bed, hung the duvet out the window to air it, and tidied my bedside table. She crossed to the commode and slipped the washcloth and damp towel off the rack. I'm sure if my clothes had still been on the chair, she would have scooped them up and off to the laundry. I held my breath, willing her not to check the hamper.

"Thank you, Gertraud. I'll be down shortly." I nodded toward the door.

With the damp towel draped over her arm, she finally left. I waited until I heard her footsteps become quieter and quieter as she retreated down the stairs, and then I slipped the letter out from its hiding place. I slit it open and read it, skimming the words to reassure myself it was not a message of dismissal but instead one of longing. While waiting for Gertraud to leave, I had felt physical pain, fearing that Andreas regretted the encounter I'd forced upon him and that he was pushing me away.

"Oh!" A brief, hopefully barely audible exclamation escaped my lips when I read his words. The note was no declaration of love or even passion. It was simply a request scrawled in urgency to meet him again at the studio that afternoon. There was no stamp on the letter, so he must have brought it himself, slipping it through the slot in the door or, more likely, paid a boy to race across town to deliver it.

I tucked the note into my pocket, smoothed my hair, and picked up my satchel. I left the house without Gertraud noticing.

Andreas was waiting for me in the studio. We crossed the floor to each other without words, and with eager fingers pulled at sleeves and buttons, lifted shirt and dress over our heads, slipped out of undergarments, and fell into bed. Nothing and everything had changed from the previous day. We were no longer strangers to each other's bodies, and our familiarity with the geography gave us confidence to explore further.

"You are a quick study," he murmured to me. I thought again of how appropriate it was that I had described him to Gertraud as my tutor. Any concerns I might have had that he would quickly tire of me and my naïveté seemed misplaced. I knew he had experience with women far more knowledgeable than I in the ways of love, but I also knew that it was not my untouched state that had first appealed to him. It was my curiosity, my longing, my hunger, that he found so compelling and that he met with hunger of his own. We were each other's obsession.

While my parents remained in Salzburg, we repeated our afternoon assignations without interruption. I was careful to return home for dinner after that first night, so as not to arouse Gertraud's suspicions. As long as I ate well and retired quietly to my room, she was content in her role as my chaperone. I was not about to abandon or jeopardize the place I had fought so hard to secure at university. I knew I needed to study away from the distractions of Andreas's hands, whether they were stroking my limbs or painting them on a canvas.

One afternoon, when I rose from my languid pose on the bed after only an hour and began to dress, Andreas was simply amused.

"Going so soon? No voracious appetite this evening, either for goulash or me?"

I swung around from the mirror over the washbasin as I pinned my hair. I suspected that telling him either reason for my departure—appeasing the housekeeper acting *in loco parentis* or reviewing my lecture notes on the art of the Italian Baroque period—would only have elicited his ridicule. His teasing, despite his own voracious appetite for me and my rapid assimilation of the role of lover, reminded me I was not very far removed from the schoolgirl whose daydreams he had once inhabited. I responded in a light tone, displaying the same playfulness.

"I find that a small taste of something delicious is often more exciting than a full meal. It leaves the palate hungry for more. The anticipation of the next bite can be exhilarating, don't you think? Tomorrow, then, for a sampling of more items on the menu?"

As he helped me with my coat, he leaned in to kiss my neck and then nipped at the tender flesh just above my collarbone. I laughed to cover up my surprised exclamation and fought the urge to rub the spot. But I took care to wrap my scarf snuggly around my neck. No need to display the evidence of our lovemaking as I made my way home on the trolley.

As brief as our afternoon encounters were, they filled us in expected ways. Andreas was both a passionate and patient lover, and my discovery of the pleasure my body could bring me was a revelation. The aftermath was equally stunning. Rather than drift off into a dreamy haze of exhaustion, Andreas would pull himself away from my finally spent body and *paint*.

He didn't bother to dress, but confronted the canvas nude with legs astride and energy rippling through his arms as I watched. He moved as a man inspired and invigorated, and I came to understand with a sense of wonder that I was the reason. I did not speak a word as he added layer upon layer of vibrant color to a series of portraits—all of me. After that first nude painting, created out of desperate longing and unfilled need, he began a new one each afternoon. Over the weeks we spent together, one could see the evolution from hunger and unknowing to satisfaction and awareness. The paintings were raw emotion, incredibly physical, and breathtaking in their honest portrayal of sexual awakening.

My own wonder at what Andreas was creating was matched by the exuberance with which he approached not only the canvas but me as the object of both his art and his ardor. It was exhilarating. It was addictive. It was dangerous. I reflected on the ambivalence I'd originally felt after modeling for him in the red dress and the deliberate choice I'd made to abandon any semblance of preserving my reputation as a serious student. I had no doubt that my liaison with Andreas would soon seep into chatter at the coffeehouses and eventually make its way into the corridors at university. Surely someone had seen us at the bistro that first night. Anyone with eyes would have recognized the intimacy, despite the formality of our clothing and demeanor.

I told myself I didn't care. That what I had gained in these few weeks had been worth the price, not only in my discovery of sexual pleasure but also in the sense of power I wielded as the origin of the explosion of Andreas's creative output. I believed without reservation that the series of paintings accumulating in the studio would be as transformative to his career as my metamorphosis from virginal girl to emerging woman, and that his rise would not have happened without me.

I was a fool.

Chapter Six

A FEW DAYS BEFORE my parents were to return from Salzburg, I prepared Andreas for what I knew would be a major restriction in my freedom. I was hoping to set his expectations—to limit his expectations, actually.

"I won't be able to come as frequently as I have," I began, trying to set a casual tone as I dressed to leave. "Exams begin next week." I didn't want to begin my excuses by mentioning my parents.

"But we still have the weekend, or are you going to secrete yourself in the library and bury your nose in your notebooks? I thought you'd abandoned your scholarly, diligent pursuit of book learning for the wider university of life, where real art is created—not in some dusty lecture hall where the professors are only looking back. The Secession is defining the future of art, saving it from the constrictions of the classical realist tradition espoused by old men."

"I agree I'm learning more from you than from my professors—in more ways than one." I looked back at him over my shoulder with a wide smile. "But I'm not about to give up my seat in that lecture hall just yet. I've had to fight to get it, and I'm not going to jeopardize it by failing my exams." I thrust a hairpin into my chignon as if it were a sword aimed at a challenger.

Andreas held up his hands, acknowledging my raised ire.

"I enjoy your anger, Maya. Your face is as flushed right now as when we are in the midst of lovemaking."

He moved across the room toward me and wrapped his arms around me from behind, bending his head toward my ear to whisper.

"What's to keep you from studying here? Stay the weekend. Don't go back to Elisabethstrasse, to your narrow maiden's bed. Tell your Gertraud you are sojourning with friends and send her off to visit relatives for a few days."

It was tempting. But Gertraud would be sure to report my absence to my parents as soon as they returned, and I could imagine the inquisition that would inevitably follow. It would be polite, but as soon as I gave them the name of a friend who might have extended the invitation, the next time they encountered her family, they'd offer thanks for the hospitality to their lonely daughter and be faced with blank stares. No, I couldn't risk it.

I turned into Andreas's embrace and kissed him. "It's a lovely idea, and one I'll hold in reserve for another time, when I can plan ahead and enlist a friend willing to lie for me. For now, I must go. I'll find a way to let you know when I can return."

I gestured toward the canvases lined up against the wall. "Use the time to put the finishing touches on those. They are astonishing."

"They are my love poem to you."

I was taken aback by his words. Andreas had been a passionate lover, but tenderness and romantic utterings were not his wont.

I placed my hand on my heart and bowed my head in thanks, trying to hold back the tears. For all my claims of independence and determination to be a strong, modern woman, the word "love" was enough to undo me. Before I succumbed to that word and threw away my resolve to leave, I choked out a barely coherent farewell and walked out of the studio.

When I reached the street, I looked up at the windows. I could see Andreas, lit cigarette in his mouth, standing before the paintings, arms crossed and very still.

It was just as well I hadn't stayed the weekend. A letter awaiting me at home announced that my parents planned to return a day early. The next afternoon, they arrived in a flurry of luggage and tales of parties, concerts, and family gossip. I had spent the early part of the day ensconced in the university library turning the pages of art history tomes and furiously making notes, knowing that my parents would be expecting my full attention at dinner. My mother's excitement in recounting their visit postponed any inquiries she might have made of me and how I had spent their time away. I listened intently to her stories, exclaimed at the appropriate moments, and expressed exactly the right amount of regret that I'd not been able to share the delights of the trip. Fortunately, they had not invited guests for dinner and I wasn't expected to entertain anyone beyond them. I refrained from excusing myself early to study, staying with them for the entire evening, and promised I'd be ready to attend Mass with them in the morning.

I collapsed into bed and thought I'd fall asleep immediately. But the reality of my parents' presence and the return to the structured days of our household hit me with unexpected despair. I had ignored the glimmers of warning that had surfaced on that first morning after Andreas and I had made love, when the ease of fooling Gertraud had lulled me into complacency and procrastination. I had promised myself then I'd find a way to sustain the compelling need that drove me into Andreas's arms every day while maintaining the façade of dutiful daughter and diligent student. But now that my parents had returned, reconciling the daughter they had left nearly a month ago with the woman I had become so fully in Andreas's arms was an overwhelming challenge that I was not sure I could meet. How long could I keep up the façade before they—especially my mother—detected the urgency and passion with which I had suddenly embraced a life that would appall them?

I was dressed and waiting for them in the hall the next morning when it was time to leave for church. My mother tucked a loose curl behind my ear as she studied my face in the morning light. Was she already seeing something I had taken such pains to hide?

"I hope your anxiety about your exams has not robbed you of sleep or caused you to bite your lips as you did as a child whenever you were faced with a quiz at school. You look tired, and your lips seem swollen." She pressed a hand to my forehead.

"I'm fine, Mama. It's true, I've been studying in preparation for exams, but I'm confident. I ate some goulash with hot peppers yesterday, and you know how my lips swell up from them."

"You should know better than to indulge in spicy food. We'll go to breakfast at Sacher after Mass and have some egg dumplings." She tucked her arm into mine, and we headed out the door to where Papa was waiting with the carriage.

Mass was its usual mix of soaring music, mumbled Latin, and social gossip. I had a challenging but brief moment of hesitation at the Agnus Dei when I realized I couldn't avoid taking Holy Communion without inviting my mother's probing quest as to the reason behind such a radical departure from my usual behavior. While I have never been especially devout, despite my convent education, I had learned years before to go through the motions so I could be left in peace to wander through my imagination while the priest intoned the prayers or exhorted the congregation about good and evil.

In becoming Andreas's lover, I had already defied the moral rules of both the Church and the society that my family orbited. To defy the stricture that one shouldn't receive the Eucharist in a state of sin was simply one more step in my departure from the life my parents had expected me to live. I resolved to act as I had every Sunday since I'd received my first Holy Communion, dressed like a little bride and celebrated with a family party in the garden and the gift of a gold medal of the Virgin Mary.

I stood, smoothed my skirt, and joined the line of the faithful to the altar rail. I knelt and received the host the priest placed in my mouth. No lightning broke through the stained-glass windows of the cathedral striking me dead, so I returned to my pew and knelt with my head buried in my hands to hide the secret smile spreading across my face.

As promised, we broke our fast at the Café Sacher, where my parents were happy to be welcomed back by both the staff and friends who had followed us from the Stephansdom. I ordered whipped cream for my coffee and devoured my egg dumplings. I ate with perhaps more relish than my mother remembered, as indicated by the slightly astonished glance she cast at my empty plate, the last bits of butter and egg wiped clean with a corner of a roll. How could I explain to her that *every* sensory act, not just sex, had been heightened for me? The ravenous appetite I'd had the first evening, when Andreas took me to the bistro, had become a natural accompaniment to our lovemaking.

My father was merely amused. "I never expected studying to stimulate one's appetite. Is it the paintings of all those Dutch still lifes, filled with fruit and slaughtered game, that make you hungry?"

I had to hold myself back from licking the plum jam off my fingers. *Remember not only where you are, Maya*, I warned myself, *but who you still must be to your parents.*

This was going to be harder than I anticipated.

We returned home, and I retreated to my room to study until dinner. I truly wasn't anxious about my exams. Although the attitude of my professors toward the women in the lecture hall was often dismissive, and some refused to even acknowledge our presence, I had resolved to absorb as much as I could from their classes and then supplement my learning with reading well beyond the course curriculum. I'd spent hours in the Kunsthistorisches Museum and the Belvedere Palace, sketching masterpieces until I understood how the artists had created such magic. I was ready.

On Monday morning, I kissed my parents goodbye, picked up my satchel, and set off for the university. The atmosphere within the building was stifling—a combination perhaps of overheated pipes, sweating students, and silence punctuated only by the whisper of pages being turned in exam books and pens scratching out theorems and essays. I had only one exam that day and retreated to the canteen for a coffee and a bowl of soup when I finished.

It was quieter than usual. No raucous arguments bounced across scratched tables, not even from the group that had originally pulled me into the conversation about Andreas. How long ago that seemed! They were the last people I wanted to see, given their connection to him and the possibility that they might know of our liaison. I didn't think Andreas would have talked about me with them, but I wondered if they remembered how he had left the group to follow me the day he invited me to model for him. I didn't trust myself to dissemble and act indifferent to the mention of his name. For the first time, away from the isolation of the studio and the intensity of our passion for each other, I felt vulnerable. Was I simply yet another of Andreas Brenner's conquests?

I slipped into a seat at a corner table and propped open a book, not only to occupy me as I sipped my soup but also to discourage interruption. It was exam week, after all; people would respect someone clearly studying.

Or perhaps not.

"Maya, may I join you?"

It was Liesl Baumann, one of the three other women in my class. She unwrapped her scarf as she sat down.

"What a relief to have that over!"

She peeked at the title of the book I was reading. "Are you already preparing for the literature exam on Wednesday?"

"Refreshing my memory." I lifted my spoon to my mouth to keep the conversation at a minimum.

"I haven't seen you around lately, not even at the last few sessions of class. Were you ill?"

"No."

I could see her struggling to determine whether to push on with her questioning. The words "Then why . . . ?"

were on the tip of her tongue. We weren't close, but we four women had developed a bond born of solidarity. We were perceived by both the class and our professors as "the women," if they even thought of us at all.

"I was concerned that you had resigned your place. Of all of us, I considered you the strongest, the most confident of your right to be here. And it dismayed me to think you had left."

I was stunned. What I had initially expected when she started asking questions was unwelcome curiosity or an attempt to form a connection that I truly didn't feel with her. But now, I was more uncomfortable. Would the strength she saw in me be obliterated if she had any idea where I actually had been in the time I had been absent from university?

I recovered enough to answer her with something anodyne.

"I'm very much still here. I preferred to prepare for exams away from the distractions this place can sometimes throw in one's path." I waved my hand around to encompass not only the canteen but the wider campus.

Liesl nodded. "I know what you mean. I'm relieved to hear it."

I had finished my soup and was equally relieved to have a reason to depart. I placed my book in my satchel and picked up my tray.

"Good luck with your remaining exams."

After I left the canteen, I made a brief stop at the student mailroom to check my box. A familiar gray envelope was tucked within, the scrawling penmanship declaring my name. I opened it immediately.

The note was brief: "3:00 p.m.—the studio." A statement, not a question.

I wasn't expected at Elisabethstrasse until dinnertime. I had told Mama that I'd study in the library after my morning exam. Nothing stood in the way of my making good on Andreas's veiled presumption that I would come to him. Nothing except my own discomfort after my conversation with Liesl. I've never been one to care that much about how others perceive me, despite the modesty drilled into me by the nuns and the example set by my mother, for whom acceptance by society meant everything. Marrying my father placed her as an outlier, but his wealth, his business acumen, and his exotic good looks won them favor in their ever-revolving circle.

Perhaps it was the uniqueness of my parents' marriage—the romance of their meeting at the Temple of Poseidon at Sounion and their defiance of traditions on both sides about whom one should marry—that ignited in me the longing to define myself apart from Vienna's interpretation of womanhood. Whatever formed the basis of my rebellion, I had no doubt that each encounter I'd had with Andreas Brenner had shaped me. My infatuation with him when I was a girl of fifteen; the revelations of both freedom and power when I modeled for him; the all-engulfing passion when we made love.

I weighed the uneasiness triggered by Liesl's assessment of my self-confidence against the obsession represented by the note in my hand. Then I crumpled the paper, its ink already smudged, shoved it into my pocket, and strode toward the trolley. Perhaps if I had been forced to wait, I might have reconsidered, reversed my steps, and climbed the stairs to the library. But I could feel the track humming with the approach of the car before I saw it, and allowed the mesmerizing clacking rhythm to align with my heartbeat. Andreas himself might have been there in the trolley car, hand outstretched to help me climb aboard, so strong was the pull of his message.

Given the timely arrival of the trolley, it was well before three when I let myself into the studio. Andreas had given me a key after I had suggested the eminent practicality of my possessing one. I had enumerated on my fingers how useful I could be—shopping for art supplies, stopping at the market for coffee and bread, or picking up his newspaper and cigarettes when I got off the trolley. I had clearly caught him in an amenable mood. He had laughed, threaded the key on a silk ribbon, and slipped it over my head like a necklace.

I heard the voices as I closed the door behind me and set my satchel on the table. Men's voices, praising, negotiating, strategizing. I held back, not wishing to interrupt but also eager to listen. It took me only a few moments to recognize the topic—the canvases Andreas had painted of me. The men were discussing exhibiting them at the Secession Building.

I hadn't thought they were ready. Andreas had spent hours working on them, moving from one to the next, but always turning away in frustration. Perhaps in the few days I'd been gone, he had finally realized their completion. Why else would he have called in the men now standing in judgment?

With no intention of remaining in plain sight when they turned away from the portraits, I quietly slipped out of the studio. The lift was no longer up, so I descended the stairs as quickly as I could. I left the building and took refuge in the coffeehouse across the street, sitting back from the windows but still able to see when the men finally departed. I sipped my coffee with unsettled emotions. An exhibition at the Secession was the prize Andreas had burned for, and I had known with certainty when he painted that first nude—stripping away my mask of bravado and revealing such palpable longing—that it was the defining work of his career, the painting that would launch him into the circle of luminaries to which he craved to belong. It was my daring, not my beauty, which had provoked him. I had been consumed with igniting his talent as well as his passion for me. Now that I had succeeded, I pondered what that success meant not only for Andreas but for me. The paintings would no longer reside propped against the wall in the studio. Vienna was about to see them.

I felt as naïve as the fifteen-year-old girl who had once followed Andreas across Vienna, playing with the illusion that my modeling would remain as private an encounter as our lovemaking.

I saw a flurry of movement across the street as the Secession men emerged from the building, buttoning coats and wrapping scarves around their necks. As they moved off, I rose from my table, paid for my coffee, and stiffened my spine. If I thought the loss of my precious virginity had been a milestone in my life, I wondered what the loss of my reputation, my very identity, would mean for me.

It's a little late for that, isn't it? I asked myself. As the lift rose, I knew that I was stepping off into an entirely new life.

Andreas was pacing by the canvases as I entered the studio. The expression on his face as he turned toward me was at once victorious and childlike—wonder and disbelief that a dream had come true, mingled with absolute conviction that he deserved the accolades he had just received.

We celebrated at the bistro, where he could share the news with his colleagues, the same artists who had mocked him for his society portraits. I sat back, nursing my glass of Sekt and saying nothing. None of them had seen the paintings yet, so my role in their creation was still unknown. I knew that wouldn't last, but I wanted to savor my anonymity for as long as I could. The exhibition wouldn't be mounted until the end of December. By then, I would be well done with my exams and far from any lecture hall where a professor might connect the face in the portraits with the nearly invisible woman sitting attentively in his class.

For the remainder of my exam schedule, I did not return to the studio. It hadn't taken much to assuage Andreas's demands for my presence when I phrased my intention to stay away as serving *his* need to focus on preparing the paintings without distraction.

My parents appreciated my daily company at dinner, fussed over how diligently I was studying, and even found the words to commend me for not giving up, despite their bewilderment at my commitment to obtaining a university degree. It was the calm before the storm.

Chapter Seven

ON THE NIGHT OF my last exam, my parents surprised
me with the gift of two weeks in Bad Ischl. I accepted it as
a reprieve and an opportunity to armor myself before the
Secession exhibition opened.

I wrote to Andreas and told him I would be traveling
with my mother and would see him on my return. He did
not reply.

I spent my time in Bad Ischl soaking away the stiffness
in my body and calming the agitation in my mind. The
hours spent posing for Andreas, combined with an almost
equal number of hours spent over my sketchbook at the
Kunsthistorisches Museum or studying the monographs
of my professors at the university library, had taken their
toll on my muscles. At the same time, the recent developments involving Andreas's portraits had caused me much
consternation. The warmth of the baths and the sulfurous
air wafting over the water helped to dispel my sense memories of the studio. Allowing my thoughts to drift as I
floated was a necessary emptying of the turmoil that had
confronted me since I had overheard the Secession artists
discussing the images of me.

I believed fiercely that I needed to free myself of any anxiety I had about the revelation of those images in order to prepare myself for what I expected would be an avalanche of notoriety.

I leaned back against the stone rim of the bath. Had I ever felt shame? The nuns at Notre Dame de Sion had certainly tried their best to instill in us a deep sense of mortification as daughters of Eve. As strong as I had been intellectually as a student, I had not met Reverend Mother's expectation for my behavior. My rebellion had been subtle, more a refusal within my own mind to embrace the ideal of womanhood presented to us in the classroom and the chapel. I had learned early in my education that by going through the outward motions of piety and obedience, I could slip unobserved into my own reverie about what I wanted in my life. I became quite adept at fingering my rosary beads and moving my lips while imagining a world beyond the walls of Notre Dame, in which I was free to be the Maya of my own definition. So no, shame was a foreign emotion to me.

Nevertheless, I had no illusions that the spectators at the Secession exhibition would be marveling only at Andreas's groundbreaking interpretation of human longing. The murmurs would start, of course, with those who recognized me—the artists and intellectuals who were willing to spar with me in an argument about art but who would jump at the opportunity to disparage me as "only a model" after all. Their dismissive comments would soon seep into the widening circles of those who considered themselves arbiters and connoisseurs of art. It would not take long for my name to surface in an offhand remark at a salon or the opera, or in a review of the exhibit in the latest issue of the *Neues Wiener Tagblatt*.

I needed to prepare myself, not only for the Vienna art scene to identify and vilify me but for word of my role to reach my parents. It chafed me enormously that Andreas would not have reached the pinnacle of the Secession without me; I had presented him with the body, rising like Botticelli's *Venus*, as well as the spirit that informed my interactions with him. I believed intensely and whole-heartedly in Andreas's genius, and that belief would have to sustain me as I faced the repercussions of my sacrifice to his art. I had stripped myself bare, not in removing my clothes but in revealing the raw vulnerability of a woman on the verge of discovery—the embodiment of Fear and Desire.

I slipped under the water, a baptism of sorts, sealing my conviction that I had done the right thing. My sureness in Andreas's brilliance would be the armor I was seeking. Or, if not armor, at least a weapon with which I could defend myself. Merely taking refuge behind walls was not an option. I had been the instrument of Andreas's achievement, and I would continue to be.

My mother remarked on my demeanor as we traveled back to Vienna after our fortnight of respite.

"It relieves me to see you so rested. Ever since we returned from Cousin Margarete's, I was worried that you were exhausted, overwhelmed by your studies and your relentless drive to excel. Papa and I are proud of you, Schatz, but the cost seemed high in comparison to your health."

"I'm well, Mama, and I'm grateful to you and Papa for both supporting me in my quest and offering me this opportunity to rejuvenate my body and my spirit." *I feel quite strong and ready to face whatever comes*, I added silently.

I considered going back to the studio after our return; Andreas had not written while I was away. No gray envelopes awaited me in a neat pile in my room. Although he had been on my mind at Bad Ischl, it had only been in the context of how I would face the inevitable repercussions of the exhibition. I hadn't longed for him as I had during the days when he had been painting me as well as making love to me. The obsession that had consumed us both seemed to have waned in the weeks I had been away.

The next few weeks at home were busy with preparations for Advent and Christmas. My new classes would not start until after the new year. I wandered through my days at home, occasionally meeting friends from Notre Dame for coffee, but I found those conversations unfulfilling. In the few months I'd spent studying and then caught up in my relationship with Andreas, Martina and Sigrid had fully entered society. Their lives focused on balls, gowns, and gossip. I listened to their chatter over slices of *apfelstrudel* and bit my tongue to keep from challenging them over the emptiness of their pursuits. They had been just as studious as I at Notre Dame. Our friendship had blossomed over philosophical discussions and deep critiques of the books we were reading. How had our lives diverged so radically? Perhaps because I was already an outlier, the dark-haired girl who spent her summers with her Greek grandparents, the daughter of a couple who had defied both cultures in choosing to marry. Both Martina and Sigrid were bright enough to continue studying, but neither had pushed her parents as I had. Neither had felt the urgency I had experienced, the hunger to learn. Neither had ached with the discontent that had spurred me. I always seemed to need more—more challenge, more inspiration, more danger. There appeared to be little of my life I could share with Martina and Sigrid that I thought they could understand. They seemed to still be children caught up in the whirlwind of Vienna society like Clara on Christmas Eve in *The Nutcracker*. They were filled with innocent dreams represented by a kiss on a hand, gloved in silk, while I had peeled away more than a glove. I could only imagine their reaction to the Secession exhibition, except they probably would never see it, held back by propriety from exposing their eyes to the scandalous work of an Expressionist artist probing the hidden emotions beneath the layers we present to the world. They would, however, hear about it.

I left the café feeling vastly more worldly and completely alone.

The next day, I went to the studio, lying to Mama that I was joining Martina for an excursion to Schoenbrun.

I used my key when I arrived, not even knocking. But the studio was deserted, the stove unlit. The paintings were gone, no doubt crated and transported already to the Secession Building.

Despite the emptiness, I felt none of the loneliness I'd experienced at the café the previous day. I felt, instead, at home. The slant of the light through the windows, the mingled odors of Andreas's art and Andreas's body, the casual disarray of the bed.

I sat on the mattress, pulled the down comforter to my nose, and inhaled its familiar scent. Without thinking, I slipped off my shoes, wrapped myself in the voluminous warmth, and laid back.

It was nearing dusk when I heard the key in the door and then the snap of a match being struck. I hadn't left anything by the door, as I often did. I had no satchel that day. He wasn't aware I was there. A small shiver of relief escaped my thoughts. He was alone. No Secession members this time, but also no woman. It occurred to me only then that while I'd been away, he might not have been alone.

I stirred and stretched in the bed rather than calling out his name. He caught the movement out of the corner of his eye and turned abruptly, grabbing his umbrella—to be used as a weapon, I supposed, against an intruder. But the umbrella clattered to the floor as soon as I spoke his name. With a few strides, he was at the bed, and then I was in his arms. The lull to my senses that my immersion in the waters at Bad Ischl had induced was disrupted as soon as I felt his breath on my neck, his voice uttering my name, his hand on my breast.

We did not take the time to undress completely, only enough for me to open to him and pull him in. In those few minutes, all my concerns were obliterated.

"I missed you," he whispered when we collapsed side by side. "I missed this," he added, stroking the bare skin of my thigh above my stockings, "and I missed recreating your image again and again."

"Does the Secession want more paintings?"

"No, they are quite satisfied. It is I who am not satisfied. I could paint you for the rest of my life. Every time I look at you, you reveal something new—the vulnerability of your gaze; the defiance of your mouth as you turn your head over your shoulder; the pale, smooth skin of your inner arm as you reach your hands above you in a gesture of utter submission. How do you do it? I swear you have bewitched me."

"You cede me too much power. It is *your* eye that sees these things, *your* hand that brings them to life on the canvas." Although I believed that I did indeed have a certain power in the emotions I presented in my poses, I also believed that it served neither of us to reveal how pivotal I was to his creativity. He needed to trust his own genius. I was merely an instrument, like his brushes.

We lay sated for a brief time in silence, until I rose and began to smooth my rumpled skirt and find my underwear buried among the twisted sheets.

"You're leaving, when you've only just arrived?"

"*You've* only just arrived. *I've* been here for hours. I am still expected at Elisabethstrasse. You've chosen a woman who is not free to come and go as she pleases. I still live under my father's roof, subject to my father's will."

"Then come and live under my roof."

His words stilled my hands, which until that moment had been lacing up my boots.

"Or are you only playing at a game, Maya? You light a match and then run away to safety when the conflagration you ignited throws off too much heat. How long before the expectation that you appear for dinner becomes the assumption you will entertain the attention of some rich, young son in your parents' social circle, and then the demand that you give up the foolishness of your studies and marry within society?"

"That's not fair. I have no intention of abandoning my studies and certainly not of renouncing you. How little do you know me to think that this is some daring adventure for me before I settle into a life that I consider stifling and empty?"

"How long do you think you can keep our liaison a secret from your family? How long do you intend to lead two lives? What do you think is going to happen when the exhibit opens at the Secession?"

"It will only be a matter of time before my parents learn of the paintings. I'm prepared. I'm not ashamed, Andreas, and I did not enter into our liaison, as you call it, unaware of the consequences."

"Then why do you still take refuge behind the façade of dutiful daughter?"

"Because I have no financial independence, Andreas. I'm not an heiress, and this"—I waved my hands around the studio—"is still very new to me. The effect you have had on my life from the first moment you entered it has been extraordinary. But I'm still trying to reconcile the woman I have become within these walls with the daughter my parents love. I know I cannot continue to lie to them. I've been trying to determine how to tell them before my world collapses."

"Then preempt the fallout from the exhibition and tell them now. I meant what I said: Live with me."

The solitude and peace of Bad Ischl seemed to have lulled me into the illusion that I could master the looming crisis of the exhibition simply by believing in Andreas's brilliance, that somehow all would be forgiven by my parents because of their belief in me.

"I am a fool, aren't I?" For the first time, I also admitted to myself I was afraid, perhaps because I was finally confronting the reality of what I had so passionately and recklessly done. Was I not the strong, brave, defiant, nonconformist I believed myself to be? I recognized that Andreas was daring me to commit to that vision I had of myself.

"A brave fool. Believe in yourself the way you believe in me, Maya." He kissed the top of my head as I pulled on my coat.

"I'll be back. Not tonight, but soon. Before the opening."

I left, still frightened of what the future would bring. As I rode the trolley back to Elisabethstrasse, I leaned my head against the cold window, trying to imagine the conversation with my parents and being unable to find the words.

I arrived home to find that dinner was delayed. Thank God, Papa had had a late meeting with a customer for some Persian rugs. I retreated to my room, distracted and unready to sit in the parlor with Mama, who undoubtedly was waiting for a recounting of the excursion she believed I had been on all afternoon. I glanced around at my surroundings, filled with the treasures my father had gathered from around the world, as well as my cherished books and the sketchbooks I'd filled since childhood. I ran my fingers over the spines and realized I was choosing what to take with me and what to bid farewell.

How was I going to accomplish this?

I imagined both the pain and the outrage my announcement would precipitate. My mother collapsing in tears, questioning, "Maya, how could you?" and my father physically stopping me from leaving, both responses equally effective in paralyzing me. If I were to do this—no, when—it would have to be in a public place with Andreas nearby, perhaps with a cab at the ready to take me out of reach, both physically and emotionally.

It would take a few days of quietly moving some clothing and those precious books to the studio. I sat at my desk and hugged myself, suddenly chilled despite the fire in the stove. I was stripping my life down to essentials, staring into a future where the stove would not be lit by a solicitous Gertraud, where dinner would not be served on a damask cloth set with porcelain and silver, where the comforts I'd been surrounded with my whole life would be replaced by independence and the opportunity to define a life free from the deadening constraints I had watched Martina and Sigrid succumb to.

I got up and began to sort through my dresser, determined not to paralyze myself with agonizing decisions. I took what I could fit into my satchel unobtrusively, buckled it closed, and walked down to the dining room when I was called to dinner.

Over the next few days, I repeated the process, occasionally layering my skirts or blouses as I dressed and covering the bulk with my coat before my mother saw me leave the house. Hiding my clothing was easier than disguising my mood, however. I was filled with a combination of excitement and dread. I could not allow my parents to discover my plans before I announced my departure, because I knew I would succumb to their intentions to keep me at home, whether it was my mother's entreaties or my father's demands.

Andreas was at first amused by the lengths to which I was going to quietly move my life to the studio, but eventually he questioned whether I was simply postponing the inevitable confrontation.

"I'm nearly ready. It's been a challenge making my room look undisturbed despite how much I've removed."

I looked around the studio, now beginning to show signs of my presence.

"You're sure this is what you want?" he challenged me.

I stopped folding the blouse in my hand. Was Andreas having second thoughts and using his own doubts to question my intentions? Rather than wonder, I confronted him.

"Are you sure this is what *you* want? My constant presence, whether it's me in the flesh, or the scent of my fragrance in the air, or my books piled on the floor by the bed, or my stockings hanging on a rod by the stove. It's all of me, Andreas. I won't be hurrying home to Elisabethstrasse in the evening, leaving you to whatever diversions fill your nights."

"Yes, this is exactly what I want—you filling both my days and my nights. Do you not understand the effect you've had on my art? Your presence nourishes me, inspires me, transforms me. I have never painted with such intensity and abandon. You have freed me, Maya."

I did understand that. I had seen his talent expand with every pose, every glance, every word I had directed toward him. In some ways, he was *my* work of art, as much as the images he created of me were his.

It was so easy to feel possessive of those nudes now being uncrated and hung at the Secession. They were more than my body. They were my whole being elicited from Andreas's hand and brush, but provoked by my body as the instrument of *my* vision. I had had as much responsibility for their power as Andreas had.

"I believe you," I said. "I believe in us."

I tossed the blouse toward a chair and led him to the bed.

Chapter Eight

THE SECESSION EXHIBITION WAS scheduled to open on New Year's Eve, with a lavish reception. I planned to spend Christmas with my parents as we always had, entertaining my mother's family—my grandmother, aunts and uncles, and cousins. The following day, I would break the news to my parents and turn their world upside-down. No need to compound the pain by announcing my decision before Christmas Eve and thereby inviting the entire family into the scandal. Enough dissection would occur in the aftermath, but at least they'd all be back in their own houses and not sitting around the Christmas tree at ours when it happened. I could at least spare my mother the humiliation of her sisters shaking their heads and repeating the warnings that had greeted her decision to marry my father.

It was my cousin Paula who had once told me about the family's opinion of my mother's marriage and its impact on me. Paula had overheard the aunts one day chattering over *Kaffee und Kuchen*.

"You mark my words, his flamboyance and foreign ways will one day influence Maya. Look how he spoils her, and those summers on that godforsaken island with his parents. The grandfather raises goats! Maya runs barefoot with the village children. She comes back to Vienna brown as a nut, and Marie-Therese always has her hands full in September getting Maya to adapt to civilization again."

So, no, I did not want to give my aunts the opportunity to criticize my mother at a family holiday. There would be time enough for that after the exhibit opened, not that any of my aunts would debase themselves enough to attend the Secession show. They already had voiced their disapproval of Klimt's eroticism. They would much rather admire the monumental paintings at the Kunsthistorisches Museum. No, they would not experience their niece's body on display themselves, but they would undoubtedly hear about it from their extensive network of gossips.

So we all spent Christmas Eve feasting on roast goose, spaetzle, and red cabbage, with apfelstrudel for dessert. Bottles from my father's extensive wine cellar graced the table and helped considerably to smooth the rough edges of the family gathering. My parents reported dutifully on their visit to Salzburg, and I lavishly described the pleasures of Bad Ischl, hoping to circumvent any pointed questions about my decision to attend university. Suffice it to say, no one in my mother's extended clan thought well of my choosing to study. Some remarks did make their way into the conversation, but I was able to deflect the criticism by recounting the hours I had spent in the museum in front of their beloved paintings, sketching and absorbing the gorgeous techniques of their eighteenth- and nineteenth-century artists.

"At least you're studying the classics," Tante Letty sniffed, "and not the atrocious distortions and garish colors of those Secessionists."

I smiled benignly, which took great effort. My usual reaction would have been to climb on a metaphorical soapbox and berate the closed minds and bourgeois tastes of my aunts. But I held back, not only because my words wouldn't have penetrated their rigid opinions, but also because I might have easily slipped into a passionate and vociferous defense of the art of one particular Secessionist.

My parents had no idea that Andreas Brenner had reentered my life, and I could not risk even a hint of his presence on the eve of my departure. In a quiet moment, I glanced around the table. Silver candelabra filled with towering candles cast a honeyed glow over the assembled guests. Crystal goblets filled with burgundy and Sekt clinked in response to the myriad toasts and blessings that were offered at various moments. If I blocked out the shrill voices, it was a scene of both beauty and comfort, a scene and a life I was about to forsake. Was I ready?

"Maya, where are you? You seem to have drifted into another world." Tante Clara called me back to the present. She continued when she had my attention.

"I told your mother earlier this evening, Uncle Werner has hired a new young law clerk, a nephew of the Bauers'. Very serious; a book lover, I'm told; and also not unpleasant to look at."

She gave me a wink. "You studious young women claim to want a learned man, but in my experience, you still gravitate to the handsome ones. I've invited you and your parents to dinner on the Wednesday after Sylvester to meet him. Consider it my Christmas gift to you."

I was about to sputter a protest, but stopped myself when I realized the futility of expressing any opposition to my meddling matchmaker aunt. By the time the meeting was to take place, I'd scarcely be marriageable by the standards of Viennese society, and certainly not welcome to attend a dinner at Tante Clara's and Uncle Werner's. So I smiled and thanked her. Out of the corner of my eye, I caught my mother's nod of approval, mingled with relief that I hadn't made a scene.

Shortly before midnight, everyone bundled up for the journey to the Stephansdom for Midnight Mass. I shared a coach with my parents, one more bittersweet last moment. I expected Mama to bring up Tante Clara's invitation, but instead she tucked an errant curl behind my ear with her gloved hand and surprised me by commenting on my appearance.

"Your hair looks lovely this way. After seeing you the whole autumn with such a severe chignon, which I know was to emphasize your seriousness at university, it's lovely to see you pay attention to your looks. You're a beautiful woman, Maya. Don't hide your beauty just to prove how intelligent you are."

Such words coming from Mama were a revelation. Throughout my early adolescence, she had fretted about my unconventional looks, seeing me through the eyes of her family and friends. I wondered what had prompted her remarks. I *had* made an effort with my hair that evening, a compromise between the conservative look that had served me reasonably well in the lecture hall and the wild tresses captured by Andreas's brush on the canvas. In my appearance and demeanor at Christmas Eve dinner, I was performing my role as dutiful daughter for the last time.

I thanked Mama for the compliment, despite the barely veiled criticism contained within it. I bit back the retort aching to be expressed. What was the point? Tomorrow I'd be gone, no longer racing back and forth between two disparate worlds. My defiance needn't be voiced, so I tamped down the smoldering resentment and pressed my forehead against the window, now iced over from the frigid cold. Even though I couldn't make out objects with any clarity and saw only the intermittent glow of streetlights, the cold glass soothed me. I was beginning to develop a headache from all the wine.

We disembarked in front of the cathedral into a swirling crowd of well-wishers and made our way inside. The High Mass was a stifling mélange of aromas—incense, wet wool, expensive perfume. The heads of multiple worshippers drooped in sleep before being nudged by sharp elbows to wake up. As the priest droned on with his prayers, I recognized that each minute that passed was bringing me closer to freedom. By the time the last notes of "*Stille Nacht*" had been sung, I was hardly still. If my body had reflected the effervescence of my mind, I might have danced down the aisle. As it was, I was constrained not only by the slowly moving line of congregants ahead of me but also by my mother's presence.

I was exhausted when we reached home. The strain of the role I'd played all evening, along with the anxiety of anticipating the unfolding of my careful plans the next morning, had taken a toll on me.

I undressed slowly, fingering the burgundy silk of my gown as I hung it in the armoire. Would I ever wear it again? Exasperated with myself, I pushed the voluminous folds of fabric into the depths of the wardrobe. I was being maudlin and ridiculous, as I'd clearly been all evening, clinging to bourgeois regrets. I was not about to abandon my dreams for a frothy dress. If anything, I was renouncing a life that such a ball gown represented.

I unpinned and braided my hair, hoping the repetitive, mindless motion would calm me as I ran through in my head what the morning would bring. I would breakfast with my parents at Café Sacher. Before leaving the house, I would remember something in my room and go back upstairs, but instead of retrieving the forgotten item, I would slip into my parents' room and leave a letter addressed to them. The letter contained the words I feared might get drowned out in the drama sure to unfold after I announced my decision at the café.

I held the letter now in my hands as I sat in bed, unable to sleep. The envelope was cream-colored, thick, with my initials embossed on the flap. Within, on two crisp sheets, were my gratitude and love and my impassioned plea for understanding.

You have raised me to be thoughtful and caring, but also curious and adventurous. You've supported my quest for education and encouraged my independence. Now I ask you for understanding as I take a step that I know on its surface you will find incomprehensible. But it is a step I must take in order to discover who I am as an artist, unfettered by the constraints I've tried to accommodate. Society—and you—have expectations for what young women may and may not do. I've been torn apart in my soul trying to live a double life, that of an artist and that of your dutiful daughter. I have left not because I do not love you, but because I love you so much that I can no longer lie to you about who I am and who I desperately long to be.

I wrote their names on the front of the envelope and tucked it into a book on my bedside table. For much of the night, I tossed restlessly, not from doubt that I was doing the right thing, but from fear that some interference would arise in the meantime—a blizzard that prevented us from leaving the house or one of them becoming ill during the night. I finally slept, only to be awakened by a knock on the door in the morning. It was Mama. Gertraud had gone back to her village in the mountains for the holiday, and had left before dawn.

"*Frohe Weihnachten,* Schatz! Time to dress for our outing."

I threw off the covers and shivered as I placed my feet on the floor. As I dressed, I focused on my actions, pulling on my underthings and fastening my stockings, lifting my dark green wool dress over my head. I did not want to get lost in yet another internal journey, wandering through last moments. Sweeping my hair up in the style Mama had complimented me on the night before, I secured it with my pearl hairpins and slipped matching earrings into my lobes. With a last glance in the mirror, I swept out of the room and descended the stairs. Mama was waiting.

"Papa is outside with the carriage. Are you ready?" I nodded, and we left the house. I was halfway down the walk when I exclaimed, "Oh no! I've forgotten something. I'll be right back."

The question "What?" was still on my mother's lips as I raced back inside and up the stairs. I grabbed the letter, its weight now heavier in my hand, and crossed the corridor to my parents' room. I had deliberately left this step until the last moment. It wasn't that I wanted to give myself the opportunity to back out of the decision, but rather that I wanted to force myself to act quickly—get in and out without raising Mama's suspicions. I propped the letter on the pillows and hurried back down the stairs.

"You're quite flushed, Maya. There was no need to rush. We would have waited. What was it that you needed to retrieve?"

I adjusted my hat, which had become slightly askew in my haste, to give myself a moment to answer. "My gloves." I pulled them out of my reticule and put them on.

The carriage clattered over the pavement as Papa drove. His horses were his pride and joy, their coats gleaming and their bridles decorated for the holiday with ribbons and bells. In addition to the carriage pair, he also kept a thoroughbred that he rode in the park whenever he wasn't traveling on one of his merchant expeditions. He hadn't grown up with horses. The terrain of Skiathos had been more suited to mules. But as soon as he was financially able, he'd purchased his first horse. He taught me to ride when I was ten, and it was one of the activities we had shared. I pulled the carriage blanket tighter around me to ward off a chill that was not caused solely by the weather. I was doing it again—checking off yet another aspect of my life that I was now giving up. I doubted there would be many horses in my future.

Despite the anxiety I felt about my ability to leave and break my parents' hearts, the prospect of no longer lying, no longer hiding, was a freedom that had been out of reach until now. It was the prospect of that freedom, of defining my life on my own terms, that had driven me in the last weeks and would sustain me in the next hour.

Papa brought up the carriage in front of the café and handed the reins to our groom. With a flourish, he opened the door to the carriage and offered his hand to each of us as we descended to the sidewalk. We swept through the etched glass doors, out of the frigid air, and into the over-heated dining room, redolent with the aromas of coffee and buttery pastry and simmering *Weisswurst*.

We sat at our usual table adjacent to the windows. I intentionally took a seat facing the street in order to watch for Andreas's arrival. It was too warm to keep my coat on, and in any case, it would have prompted a comment from Mama, but I was reluctant to hand it over to the maître d'. I needed it close at hand when the final moment came. Instead of relinquishing it, I draped it over my shoulders.

In response to Mama's raised eyebrows, I shrugged. "I'm feeling a slight chill every time the outer door opens."

Papa ordered for us. Our Christmas breakfast never varied, a tradition that had begun when I was old enough to sit with decorum, whatever Christmas doll I had received the night before settled in a place of honor on my lap. Instead of a doll, my gift from my parents this year had been a brooch, an heirloom from my great-grandmother. I had pinned it to the silk scarf draped around my neck, a fluid cascade of pink roses and green leaves on a black background edged with black fringe. The brooch was an emerald that caught the light of the winter sun pouring through the window.

Our coffee arrived, steaming, and I brought my cup to my lips, inhaling the fortifying aroma before I sipped. The liquid was strong and dark and exactly what I needed. The conversation with my parents drifted over reflections on the night before and anticipation of the week ahead, filled with social obligations, concerts, and Tante Clara's dinner. Intermittently, our words were interrupted by greetings as other families made their entrances. It was a familiar dance, stifling in its predictability, each step choreographed eons before and carried out by the participants without a thought that it might have been different. Perhaps they clung to the formality and ritual as a bulwark against the changes that were sweeping through Vienna. The café was a bubble of privilege and insularity—the damask and crystal, the hushed voices, and the string quartet unobtrusively playing the familiar melodies all reinforcing the assurance that here nothing had changed. A few streets away, the city teamed with faces and rituals far different from the genteel pretensions of the nobility and the wealthy. Czechs, Hungarians, Romanians, Jews, had all made a home in Vienna in the last fifty years. Two million of us filled the ever-expanding boundaries of the city. My family might have been outliers in this room, except for my father's prowess in acquiring wealth and a wife who epitomized the Viennese ideal of womanhood. Mama was still beautiful, and despite her misstep in falling literally at the feet of my father on the temple steps on Sounion, she was also still well regarded. Most of society was unaware of her wayward daughter, an intellectual who studied at university. I had made an effort to dress elegantly and act with grace until the last moment, and I realized now that I would not make a scene and destroy my parents' fragile hold on their place in the city.

It was at that moment that Andreas appeared in my line of sight. He had dressed flamboyantly, in contrast to my severe and proper garb. He wore a burgundy velvet jacket, a voluminous scarf of magenta and olive green threads wrapped several times around his neck, and a Tyrolean felt hat complete with feather. He was difficult to miss, which had been his intention. He stood back from the window, but it was clear he had seen me. I brushed a stray curl behind my ear as a signal, and then he turned away. We were in the last stages of the meal, and I placed my knife and fork across my plate. Our waiter hastened to remove the platter, but my father waved him away from his own.

"Another coffee, Bitte."

The waiter looked at Mama, who nodded. I declined. As he moved away from the table, I recognized my moment had arrived, but the words I had rehearsed for days refused to come. So, instead, I improvised.

"I'm sorry I didn't mention it earlier, but I have plans for the rest of the day. My friends are waiting."

"But it's Christmas Day. Aren't they spending it with their families?"

"They celebrated as we did last night. I'll be late."

I rose as decisively as I could without creating a disturbance. To forestall the objection I could see forming on my father's lips, I bent to kiss them both.

"Frohe Weihnachten. *Ich danke euch für alles.*" Merry Christmas. Thank you for everything.

And I was gone, leaving my father stiff and grim and my mother in a state of disbelief. I knew she would rearrange her expression immediately in order to avoid questions or wagging tongues. I saw the waiter return with their coffees, and they resumed their meals, disappointed but not horrified. That would come later, when they returned home and discovered the letter.

I pushed open the doors and motioned to Andreas to move away from the windows.

"That seemed to go more smoothly than you anticipated."

"They think I'm gone only for the afternoon."

"You lost courage. You're not coming home with me."

"I decided not to make a scene. They'll learn the truth in the letter I left for them. Did you hire a cab? They still might follow me."

He led me around the corner to the waiting carriage. Once inside, he took me in his arms.

"I have a surprise for you. I thought we should leave the city for a few days, given that your parents will surely search for you. A friend has a lodge in Tyrol. We can stay there. I already packed your bag. The cab is taking us to the train station."

My heart was racing, and I began to shake.

"Are you chilled? You're shivering." Andreas drew me closer to him and took my hands between his, rubbing them. I was about to make some excuse about going from the overheated café to the frigid street, but I knew it wasn't the change in temperature that had precipitated my trembling. Tears began to prick my eyes, and I withdrew my hand from Andreas's grasp to wipe them away.

"Are you regretting your decision so soon? If so, I can direct the carriage back to your parents." His voice was tight, a tone of dismissal that I knew was masking hurt.

"Not at all. These tears have not sprung from dismay but from exhilaration and, I have to admit, disbelief that I am actually here. I know my departure will be more challenging in the days to come, but for today, I'm going to savor my freedom."

He took my hands back and kissed them.

We slipped out of the carriage and into the train station quickly. I did not look back to see if we'd been followed, but I saw Andreas scan the cabs behind ours as he paid the driver and grabbed our bags.

"I've already purchased the tickets. We should go directly to the train. We travel first to Bolzano and change there for Meran."

The main concourse was sparsely populated. I realized that, because of the holiday, a limited number of trains must be running. Ours was most likely the only one today leading to our destination. We walked briskly to the platform, found our car, and climbed aboard. Our compartment was empty, and I sank into my seat as Andreas stowed the luggage in the rack above. The exhilaration I'd felt in the cab had dissipated. Leaving the café without being stopped by my parents had been only the first step, albeit a successful one. I knew there were many more challenges facing us. I chewed my lip and tapped my foot, waiting for the final whistle and the movement of the train. My trembling had subsided, only to be replaced by a nervous energy, as if my own movements could fuel the train. Finally, the screech of metal upon metal and a lurch of the car signaled that we were on our way at last. The compartment remained ours alone, and I looked out the window, watching the snowbound city recede from view. Andreas retrieved a flask from his pocket and offered me a sip of brandy. The fiery liquid slid down my throat and warmed my belly. I leaned back against the velvet seat and closed my eyes. My sleepless night, combined with the anxiety of anticipation, had left me exhausted. Perhaps now, hurtling away from my parents and my past, I could sleep.

Chapter Nine

IT WAS NEARLY MIDNIGHT when we arrived in Meran. I had slept fitfully during the long journey, at times curled up against Andreas and at other times shifting restlessly to find a comfortable position. Unlike on my trip to Bad Ischl, we had no sleeping accommodations.

We were two of only a handful of passengers who had changed trains at Bolzano for the spur to Meran. I pulled my collar close around my neck against the frigid mountain air as we descended to the platform. Andreas retrieved the address of the hunting lodge from his pocket and strode toward the one waiting carriage outside the station, an open sled that fortunately was piled with blankets. We climbed in and huddled together as the driver negotiated the road along the river and then out of town into the forest. Night sounds greeted us along the way. An owl took flight above us, either disturbed by the bells on the horses' bridles or intent on the hunt. Its wingspan only inches above us, it sent a current of air that lifted the curls that had slipped out of my coiffure. In the distance, a wolf howled.

At last, the sleigh came to a halt at a gate, and the driver motioned that we had reached our destination. Andreas retrieved our bags, paid the driver, and helped me down onto the snow-covered path. Ahead, beyond the gate, we could see the outline of a building and began to make our way through several inches of snow to get to it.

I was dressed for a day in the city and hadn't thought to change on the train into more sensible clothing. After trudging several meters, we reached the lodge. Andreas found the key above a window ledge and, after a few unsuccessful attempts, managed to open the door. He struck a match and searched for a lamp while I stood just inside. It felt colder inside the lodge than it had in the sleigh, and I hoped we'd find a supply of wood as well as a lamp.

After a few curses, Andreas located a lantern, and the shape of our surroundings became clearer. The lodge was rough, clearly a hunting cabin with practical, hand-hewn furniture. The most welcome sight was a tiled stove in the far corner. I was pleased to see Andreas kneeling at the open grate where kindling and small logs had already been set inside. I moved quickly to his side, hands outstretched to the flames Andreas had coaxed into existence. Once the fire was established, we explored the lodge further. A bunk room adjacent to the main room offered some thin ticking mattresses on rope-strung beds and a trunk filled with coarse blankets. I retreated back to the stove and tested the cushions on a built-in daybed.

"I don't think the heat will penetrate to the bunk room. I'd rather sleep here closer to the fire."

A drawer under the bed yielded some pillows and a down comforter. I wrapped the latter around me and invited Andreas to join me.

"We can keep each other warm under this."

He added a few more logs to the stove, slipped out of his boots, and climbed into the bed with me. At first, our objective was simple—get warm. Except for our shoes, we were still fully clothed, including coats, hats, and gloves. I could barely sleep, not only because of the cold but also because it was dawning on me that my escape had been successful. Despite the frigid air and primitive accommodations, I felt an exhilaration that bubbled up out of my lungs as uncontrollable laughter.

Our only light was the glow of the fire, but I could detect an expression of consternation on Andreas's face.

He sat up abruptly and asked, "Are you unwell? You appear to be in the midst of hysteria."

I managed with a few hiccups to calm my unrestrained laughter in order to answer him.

"Hysterical joy."

I hugged him through the layers of wool to convey how very well I felt at that moment.

Somehow ignoring air so cold we could both see our breath, we managed to remove our many layers of clothing, burrow under the feather blanket, and make love, punctuated by my irrepressible laughter.

Then we slept, waking several hours later to sunlight casting a glittering display on the frosted windows and a fire nothing more than cold ash.

We pulled our clothes on under the covers, then ventured out of bed to restart the fire. We had depleted the logs that had been stacked inside, forcing us to don coats and boots to retrieve more from the covered porch. When I opened the door, I gasped at what had been invisible in the darkness the night before—a vista of the mountains across the valley, the river frozen between the lodge and the village. In direct contrast to the frigid air, the sunlight cast a magical spell that created the illusion of warmth. Branches laden with ice glittered in the light and rustled with winter music.

"Andreas, come and see the light!" I was mesmerized by the variegated shadows on the snow, from a deep indigo to a smoky periwinkle. I spun around, absorbing every aspect of our hidden nest. When the cold finally defeated my explorations, I loaded my arms with logs and made the first of several trips back inside. Andreas restarted the fire while I hunted in the kitchen for a kettle. Andreas had wisely packed some provisions for the trip—a round loaf of bread, cheese, and salami. In the kitchen cupboard, I found a tin of ground coffee, some jars of pickled beets, and marmalade. We made a breakfast feast and ate on the floor by the stove.

"How long will we stay here?"

"Only a few days. We need to return by Sylvester for the Secession opening."

"My parents will still be looking for me when we get back."

Andreas nodded. "We can't hide here forever. At some point, you'll have to confront them."

"I know, but for now, I want only to live in the present. Let's take a walk in the woods and then spend some time in the village. We should get some provisions; what we have here won't last very long. As lovely as our breakfast was, I know I'll be starving by noon."

We bundled in our warmest clothing, banked the fire in the stove, and headed out along the path the sled had taken as it carried us the night before.

We walked briskly, stopping now and then to take in breathtaking views over the valley. Retrieving a pencil stub and a small notepad that I had tucked in my pocket, I sketched a few images that struck me as we ventured farther into the forest—stark tree branches with a few berries not yet plucked by hungry birds; a tall fir tree so laden with snow that its branches draped to the ground.

We reached the village red-cheeked and famished.

"First, *Mahlzeit!*" I tugged on Andreas's sleeve when I saw the warm glow of windows from a *Gasthof*. Aromas of bacon, roasting potatoes, and barley soup greeted us when we entered.

A warm, hearty meal was exactly what I needed. We attracted curious stares as we settled at a table near the stove, but the proprietor, an energetic woman with both mirth and girth, greeted us warmly. We ate with gusto and, once sufficiently warmed by both the food and the fire, ventured back out to a market recommended by our hostess. While I shopped, Andreas went to the railroad station to get the timetable for our return to Vienna and to find a driver to pick us up later in the week.

By the time we had accomplished our errands, the sun was much lower in the sky and well on its way to being hidden by the mountain. With the incentive of returning to the lodge before darkness, we urged each other to quicken the pace. We were trudging uphill laden with sagging bags of groceries, including a few bottles of wine, but we made it back just as the last sliver of sunlight slipped from sight and the brilliance of the morning disappeared into a monochromatic landscape.

I deposited our supplies in the kitchen while Andreas restarted the fire. I found a corkscrew and some tin cups—no crystal goblets—and poured each of us a well-deserved measure of wine. By true darkness, we were settled once again before the stove, enjoying *Abendbrot* and the silence of the woods.

We spent the next three days in a bubble of domestic bliss—daytime walks, venturing farther afield each day, away from the village and toward higher ground; meals of roasted chicken and Wiener schnitzel served with red cabbage, and *Kaiserschmarrn* for dessert. In the evenings, by the light of the oil lamp, we sketched or read, our feet intertwined as we stretched out on the rug. At night we made love. It was much easier than I had anticipated to ignore thoughts of what awaited me in Vienna, so immersed was I in the natural beauty of the Ötztal Alps and the intimacy of time spent only with each other. No distractions or obligations pecked at our attention.

It was what I imagined a honeymoon would be, although I didn't say that word to Andreas. The idea of marriage to him was the encapsulation of the hidebound bourgeois life he believed he had rescued me from.

Our idyll came to an end too quickly. By the last day, I could see Andreas was impatient to return to Vienna. The exhibition had been hung before Christmas, with him overseeing every placement and lighting, but he wanted to have time to review the space again and address anything he deemed amiss.

With reluctance, I packed up my belongings and wrapped food for the journey. The sled arrived; we locked up and headed down to the valley. I turned to cast one last look on the sturdy dwelling that had given us so much happiness. Then, taking a deep breath of cold, clean Alpine air, I turned back to face the unknown—my parents, the art world, and a new home.

Chapter Ten

We arrived back in Vienna the evening before Sylvester. After depositing our bags in the studio, we reclaimed our urban lives as if we had never been away. Andreas was eager to catch up with his colleagues, so we headed for our neighborhood *Kneipe*, hazy with cigarette smoke and buzzing with the usual debates about the state of the arts in Vienna. We had only been away for a few days, but Andreas was anxious to plunge back into this world, as if we'd been away for months. I was hungry enough to join him, but wasn't looking forward to a long night of drinking and dissecting whatever scandal we'd missed. I didn't expect the news of my abandoning my parents' home would have reached these quarters, rendering me safe from discovery for at least another day, but I knew all that would change as soon as my face and body were unveiled at the exhibition. Someone who knew my parents would undoubtedly attend the opening.

Places were immediately made for us at our usual table, as chairs scraped back and hearty welcomes were extended to us.

"Where have you been? Hugo from the *Tagblatt* has been sniffing around trying to get a scoop on the exhibition. He said he'd heard it was bound to send shock waves through the city. We could all claim to know nothing, since you've kept those canvases well hidden, Andreas. But what is the harm in telling us now, with so little time left before the opening?"

Andreas smiled and squeezed my hand under the table. The curiosity that had clearly been building while we'd been away was exactly what he was hoping for.

"You'll just have to wait, like the rest of the critics. Part of what I hope to achieve depends on the secrecy. I can tell you, it's like nothing I've ever done before."

"Perhaps Maya will give us a hint. You've seen the canvases, haven't you?"

I could feel my cheeks redden, and quickly took a sip of wine to steady my nerves.

"I *can* tell you it's the best work Andreas has produced so far. He's carved a new direction that I fully expect him to continue. The paintings are positively thrilling."

The inquisition was temporarily quelled when the waiter brought our goulash. Despite the teasing, the group seemed genuinely glad to have us back. Although I had originally intended to limit my drinking, I found myself reaching for the wine several times, caught up in the convivial spirit of the evening. But I also found myself seeking both solace and strength in the wine, fortification for the days ahead. And in some way, I was also avoiding the reality of what our return to Vienna meant. Perhaps I was mimicking the recklessness of soldiers on the eve of battle, knowing that on the morrow they might die.

We fumbled our way back to the studio well past midnight, leaning on each other as Andreas unlocked the door to the courtyard. Just as I had been driven to bury my fear in the wine, I also sought to obliterate any thought at all by taking Andreas to bed as soon as we entered the studio. Our lovemaking that night had nothing of the tenderness and joy of our sojourn in the Alps, nor the insatiable passion that had inspired the canvases destined to transform Andreas's career and shatter my parents' perception of their daughter. Instead, the sex was impelled by the need to forget.

I woke the next morning to the aroma of coffee and the sound of Andreas splashing in the washbasin as he shaved.

"What time is it?"

"Nine. I'm leaving for the Secession hall shortly to oversee the final details. With three artists' work on display tonight, I want to make sure nothing got rearranged while we were away."

His tone was brusque. I knew he was anxious, but I sensed that he was also regretting that he had left the city, and that he placed the responsibility for doing so solely on me, even though it had been his idea.

"I'll be back this afternoon to change." He wiped his face, pulled on his jacket, and left.

I took my time getting out of bed.

I desperately needed a bath after a week in a hunting lodge with no tub. If I had been back on Elisabethstrasse, Gertraud would have run the water for me, filled the ample tub with bath salts, and warmed the towels. Because there was no Gertraud anymore, I finally threw back the covers, put wood into the stove, and began heating water. I dragged our tub out from behind the screen and placed it close to the fire, gathered soap and towels, and started to fill the tub with the heated water.

The first time I'd seen the tub, it had surprised me. I had expected Andreas to have a utilitarian, galvanized vessel in keeping with the relatively spartan elements of his household. But instead, it was a magnificent copper soaking tub. It was my first insight into Andreas's indulgence of his sensual pleasures.

When the water was deep enough, I slipped in and leaned my head back, drenching and then shampooing my hair. The quickly cooling temperature of the water didn't allow me a luxurious soak, but it sufficed to slough off both the grime and stiffness of nights spent on a daybed and hours in a cold train compartment. I dried off in front of the stove and combed out the tangles in my hair before opening the wardrobe to decide what to wear. I flipped through the dresses until my hand stopped.

The red dress. I knew that one of the paintings on display would be the one Andreas had painted of me that first day I had modeled for him on a dare. I had put on the red dress then at his request, so wearing it again tonight would send an absolutely undeniable message. The woman in the red dress in the painting was the same woman in the nudes that formed the majority of the exhibition. And there I would be in the exhibition hall, the unmistakable muse, available for every male eye to undress me and envy Andreas.

Did I dare wear it? Perhaps that dress would always represent a dare to me, but it could also signify my defiance and make a profound statement. Yes, I am the woman in the red dress, the source of everything you see here on these walls. I pulled the dress out. It needed ironing.

By the time Andreas returned, the tub was empty and back in its place, and I was ensconced in red silk, my hair loose and adorned with only a simple feather. Over long black gloves, I wore some Persian bangles my father had brought back from one of his excursions.

Andreas reacted with a mixture of disbelief and praise when he saw what I was wearing.

"That's brave of you, but I love it. It's a performance as shocking as the paintings."

"A reinforcement, perhaps, of how groundbreaking your work is. I want tonight to be a success for you, Andreas. You've earned it."

His lips formed a thin smile, superstitious of exalting too soon but convinced of his triumph nonetheless.

As we prepared to leave, I straightened his tie. "You cut quite a dashing figure when you clean up."

"It's more like girding myself with armor. I have a bit of armor for you as well."

He stretched out his hand and slid off the onyx ring he had worn since I had first met him—a ring that anyone who knew him would recognize as his.

"I've never removed this ring before. It's a part of me that I now want you to wear. You have possessed my soul. Let this ring be a symbol of our possession of each other."

I let him slip the ring on my right hand. As distinctive as the red dress, the ring would mark me tonight as his.

"Shall we go and face the hordes at the gates of artistic judgment?" He handed me his arm, and we left in a burst of nervous energy, running down the stairs and out into the bustle of the city on New Year's Eve.

We arrived early at the Secession hall as planned, but instead of leaving my cape in the cloakroom, I kept my gown covered. To reveal it too soon would only be a distraction. The other artists arrived soon after, and we all clustered around the wine and punch. One of the men was exhibiting for the first time, like Andreas, and shifted from foot to foot, his eyes darting around the room as guests began to trickle in.

Gustav Klimt arrived with an elegant woman at his side dressed in an unmistakably Parisian gown and extravagant hat. They both had attracted whispered attention as they moved across the room. He extended his hand to all three artists one at a time.

"Welcome, gentlemen, and congratulations. I'm eager to immerse myself in your work. I've heard a great deal about all of you from my colleagues." He rubbed his hands together, and then turned to the stunning woman whose presence had caused such a buzz. "May I introduce Hofratin Berta Zuckerkandl."

Berta Zuckerkandl! Her salon and her art criticism in the *Wiener Allgemeine Zeitung* were the most influential in Vienna. Her opinion tonight would either raise Andreas to great heights or destroy his career.

She smiled warmly. "I'm quite excited to see your work. Gustav insisted that I come, and here I am." She turned, took Klimt's arm, and began her tour of the gallery.

Andreas squeezed my hand and took a deep breath. Throughout the conversation with Klimt and Hofratin Zuckerkandl, I had remained in the background, not willing to draw attention to myself yet. Once attendees had begun to observe the paintings, I would make myself more visible, the living embodiment of what they were experiencing on the walls.

I sipped my wine and urged Andreas to begin circulating among the guests. He kissed my hand and moved out to the growing crowd. The Secessionists had apparently done a good job of publicizing the exhibition.

I watched as people we knew approached first the paintings and then Andreas. Their faces revealed their visceral reactions to the images—discomfort, wonder, hunger. I knew the power of those paintings to elicit longing. They made the viewer want what Andreas's strokes of paint conveyed in translating my own hunger. I smiled, slipped off my cape, and then ventured into the throng, gliding through the rooms.

Chapter Eleven

THE SPACE WAS CROWDED, and the viewers jostled for position in front of the paintings. The vast exhibition hall was divided into smaller galleries with temporary white walls. Each of the artists whose work was on display had his own dedicated area.

Murmurs rising to an animated chorus from Andreas's corner signaled the response we both hoped would greet his work. I deliberately avoided the buzzing commentary and instead withdrew to the other galleries, where only small knots of viewers quietly observed the paintings.

The artists stood awkwardly, occasionally casting a glance in the direction of the commotion and trying to carry on a conversation with individuals who seemed to be known to them—family or patrons, perhaps. I assumed Andreas was similarly chatting with exhibition attendees, the only difference being that he was basking in the attention rather than anxiously comparing the size of his audience as the other artists were.

I was surprised not to see any supportive women at their sides. Did they not have models, if not muses? Of course, others may have wondered the same thing about

Andreas, as I was nowhere near him at that moment. Part of my motivation for keeping my distance was to give him the spotlight. I expected that my appearance next to the paintings would distract from his role as creator. Vienna was always eager for a scandal, and the initial reactions of the public were best left untainted by my presence. But I also held back to prepare myself before I entered the fray. The magnitude of my decision to become the object of Andreas's notable debut confronted me in that moment of solitude. The roar from the gallery was beyond what either of us had anticipated. My anxious nights contemplating the consequences of my modeling had not been unwarranted.

As I had imagined, Andreas's portraits of me were not to be ignored, slipping into the shadows of anonymity. I braced myself against a wall near the entrance of his gallery and listened. The cacophony I had heard from a distance evolved into distinct comments as viewers emerged from the din. I kept my face turned away when anyone passed me to hide both my identity and my rising ire.

"Outrageous! Brenner has gone beyond the pale."

"These young men want only to defy and destroy. One expects as much from the Secession, but not *this* far."

I recognized the voice of my art history professor, hardly someone I would expect to attend a Secession exhibition. I knew I would need an especially strong spine the next time I entered the lecture hall. He rushed past without recognizing me as either a student in his class or the subject of the paintings.

But interspersed with the outrage, other observations emerged.

"He has captured the unseen desires of humanity. Uncomfortable, true, but what is art's purpose, if not to bare the soul?"

"Who is the model? I've never seen her image before, but perhaps because he was capturing her as truly virginal—not only her sexual awakening but her initiation into the artist's milieu."

"Strikingly beautiful. The embodiment of passion."

"Extraordinary."

Fortified by the positive comments, I ventured into the gallery. Andreas was still surrounded by a gaggle, although the animated conversation appeared to be a scene of philosophical discussion, not outrage. I took my time circling the room, stopping at each painting when I could get close enough.

I was deeply engrossed in experiencing them in the context of the exhibition, as opposed to the cluttered and all-too-familiar studio in which they had been created. The austere setting of the hall and its stark white walls, with little of the embellishment of the city's established museums and galleries, emphasized the visceral human nature of the art. It took my breath away, despite my familiarity with the canvases in their original state.

But all were not exactly as I remembered them. Andreas had added new details since I had last seen them, elements that intensified the raw emotion and the sheer physicality of my longing—the streak of blood on my thigh, the bloom of heat rising up my outstretched neck as I turned to face the viewer.

"It's breathtaking, is it not? This is my second tour around the room, and I see something new each time. I suspect that no matter how often I come to the paintings, they will reveal yet another truth."

Berta Zuckerkandl was at my side. "You have had a role in this, my dear. I've seen other work by Brenner, and nothing he's done before compares to this. You may not have wielded the brush, but your hand has its imprint here." She glanced around the room, where others were now whispering, heads together, and nodding toward us. "They already know who I am. It's you they have recognized. It was quite smart of you to wear the red dress, but I hope you realize the price you are about to pay for your part in Brenner's success tonight. Don't let the notoriety prevent you from bringing your sensibilities and understanding to whatever it is *you* wish to do."

She squeezed my hand and floated away. I took a deep breath, raised my head, and turned to face the crowd, a knowing smile on my face. Andreas broke away from the circle of avid philosophers to reach for my black-gloved hand. The group separated enough for me to join them. Familiar faces from the pub were momentarily speechless. A few of them swept my body, eyes darting from the painting behind me, *Woman in a Red Dress*, to the flesh and blood that had inspired it.

As the group plunged once again into their spirited arguments, I kept my own comments to myself, sometimes biting my lips to restrain myself. This was Andreas's night, not mine. It was also clear to me that no one other than Hofratin Zuckerkandl was interested in what I had to say. I was the object that had inspired the art, not the creator. And so I remained as mute as the paintings. But they, without language, conveyed more than any of the words being formed around the circle.

We ended the evening at a party hosted by Max. We drank excessively, danced to exhaustion, and sampled some hashish smuggled in from the Ottoman Empire by Max's brother. We crowded onto the terrace at midnight to watch fireworks and resumed our frenetic celebration after the sky was clouded with the smoky remnants of the pyrotechnics. At some point, we collapsed on couches and slept.

We missed the dawn of the new year, not waking till early afternoon, and then Andreas and I returned to the studio. We'd had little time to discuss the success of the exhibition, but in the quiet and privacy of our home, Andreas took me in his arms.

"My muse."

Then he knelt before me, buried his head against my belly, and wept.

Chapter Twelve

WE HAD TO WAIT until the second of January for the reviews. I raced down the steps and across the street to the newsagent, gathering every periodical that had an art critic. Thus laden, I returned to the studio and spread the papers on the bed, where Andreas and I began thumbing through them. The reviews were a reflection of the verbal comments I'd heard from my hiding place at the exhibition. The conservative arbiters of traditional taste screamed "Outrage!" and "Pornography!" But the columnists in the vanguard of the new art making its way across the continent were excited, praising Andreas for his use of color and his ability to peel away the layers of armor with which we shroud our secrets.

The review I was most eager to read was Berta Zuckerkandl's. She wrote as she had spoken to me, praising Andreas but also mentioning the inspiration that had driven his remarkable exploration of the human spirit. She likened his images to the music of Gustav Mahler.

All was well as we combed through the pages, sipping our coffee. But my hand was stilled and I nearly spilled my drink when I came across an illustration from the exhibition of a woman standing before *Woman in a Red Dress.* The caption identified me as the woman.

"How did the newspaper know my name?"

I threw the paper at Andreas. He caught it, saw what had upset me, and shrugged.

"Many people attended the exhibition, Maya. It was inevitable that someone would recognize you."

I started pacing. "My father reads the *Tagblatt.* It's only a matter of time before he sees it and makes the connection to you. It won't take him long to find us."

"We knew that, Maya. Did you truly expect to remain hidden forever? What can he do now that you are here? You don't need his money. Come here, my muse. I won't let you go."

He stilled my agitation and held me, and for a while, I absorbed his strength and calmness. We dressed and left the studio for dinner at the Kneipe. The usual crowd was there, except for Wolfgang. Somebody commented that he was nursing a virulent case of jealousy after reading the reviews. The rest of them, in various stages of their own careers, seemed more in awe of Andreas's success than envious of it.

It was late when we returned to the studio, and we weren't particularly observant. As we entered the courtyard and Andreas reached for the keys, a hand grabbed his arm and twisted it behind him.

I screamed, thinking it was a thief, but a pair of arms wrapped around me and a familiar voice whispered in my ear.

"We won't hurt him, but you are coming home with me, Maya. Enough of your search for artistic expression. I went to the Secession exhibition today after seeing your name and your image in the *Tagblatt*. I saw much more than a woman in a red dress. How could you betray us? What possessed you to bare your body to the world? I won't let your mother see it. It will kill her. If you don't come, Antonio will break his hand."

Andreas struggled under the grip of the other man, whom I recognized as one of my father's seamen, another Greek named Antonio. He was much stronger than Andreas.

"It's useless to put up a fight, Andreas. He'll maim you, break your hand, if I don't go with my father."

I turned to my father. "I'll go. Let him be."

"Before we leave we are going upstairs to get your belongings. I want every trace of you removed from his sight." He led me to the lift and we entered the studio while Antonio kept Andreas below in the courtyard. Papa watched as I pulled my clothing from the armoire and my books and sketchbooks that were scattered around the room. When he was satisfied that I had collected everything, he took me back to the courtyard and marched me to the gate and a waiting carriage—not his, or I would have recognized it. Antonio released Andreas only after I was in the carriage. Weeping, I leaned out the window and shouted to Andreas.

"I'll find a way back!"

PART TWO

SKIATHOS

1907

Chapter Thirteen

Mama was waiting at home. I had never seen her in such a state of disarray. Her hair was down, the blonde that had gleamed in the Greek sunshine when she had first entranced Papa was now streaked with gray, and dark smudges beneath her eyes attested to the insomnia that must have plagued her since my departure. She wasn't dressed, but stood in the hall wrapped in a carelessly tied dressing gown.

Papa held my arm with an unfamiliar pressure as we entered the house.

"Apologize to your mother."

"I am sorry, Mama, if I caused you worry."

It was Papa who replied. "What did you expect, Maya, when you callously lie to us and disappear for days, leading us to imagine the worst—that you'd been kidnapped or even killed?" His voice was barely restrained. The fury I had avoided on Christmas Day at Café Sacher had merely been postponed. "And then to discover your naked body adorning the walls of that damn Secession exhibition. What were you thinking? Thank God Mama has not seen those paintings."

Throughout Papa's tirade, Mama remained speechless. It was only then that I realized how vacant her eyes were, how sallow her skin, and how listless and defeated her body appeared.

"Oh, Mama, you've taken drugs!"

I tried to reach out to her, but Papa still held me fast.

"Of course! Dr. Schindler prescribed laudanum to calm her nerves. Take a good look at what you've done to your mother, and then go to your room."

I climbed the stairs quickly once Papa released my arm. After I was in my room, I heard the key turn in the door. He had locked me in like a prisoner. I threw myself face down on the bed and sobbed for the loss of my freedom, but also for the loss of my parents' love. Even though I had anticipated their anger, being confronted with the reality of it was devastating. My mother was clearly ill, barely recognizable, and my behavior had driven her to despair. I punched the down pillow. Why was the price so high?

I slept fitfully, not bothering to undress. In the morning, Papa unlocked the door and told me to come to breakfast.

"Tidy yourself. You're no longer living in a slum."

I did the minimum, tucking in my blouse but leaving my hair loose. Before I left my room, I removed Andreas's onyx ring from my finger. I placed it instead on a narrow gold chain that I fastened around my neck and then tucked under my blouse.

Mama was not in the dining room, and Gertraud slipped back to the kitchen as soon as I arrived, avoiding my gaze.

"Sit down and listen. I've decided, and your mother agrees, that you cannot remain in Vienna. The scandal is only simmering right now, because most people we know haven't yet seen the exhibition, but it's only a matter of time before the whole city is aware of your escapade. Once that happens, who knows who will be poking around here trying to identify you and write sordid details about your relationship with that painter? I regret ever inviting him to our home. I've already removed the portraits from the parlor.

"So you can't stay here, and sending you off to one of your aunts' will damage your mother's already fraught connections with her sisters. The only salvageable solution is for you to go to your grandparents' on Skiathos."

I nearly dropped my coffee cup. "Skiathos!" The distance it would put between me and Andreas, between me and my short-lived freedom, enraged me. I started to protest, but Papa slammed his fist on the table, causing the jar of plum preserves to jump.

"You have no say in this, Maya. Your ability to make wise decisions is clearly impaired. You and I will depart for Trieste this afternoon, and from there board a ship to Greece. I hesitated telling you even this much for fear you would try to get word to that predator. You will remain in your room until we leave. Pack your belongings. Gertraud will bring you a tray for lunch. I suggest you have a bath. It will be a long trip, and not a luxurious cruise."

He dismissed me with a wave of his hand and turned to his newspaper. I rose and left the room. As I turned for the stairs, I glanced at the front door. How far would I get if I left at that moment, with no coat, no money, and no doubt a guard at the front steps? Was there any way to reach Andreas? I might be able to post a letter at the train station if we were traveling to Trieste by rail, but Papa hadn't said, and we could just as likely be going by carriage. Nevertheless, I resolved to be ready if an opportunity presented itself once our journey was underway.

Once again, I acted the dutiful daughter and did as Papa said. An empty suitcase was waiting in my bedroom, probably retrieved from storage by Gertraud. Alone, I packed and then took a bath. I was dressed in traveling clothes and sitting on my bed when I heard a hesitant knock on my door.

"Maya, may I come in?"

It was Mama. I answered and heard the key turn, opening the door.

She appeared much the same as she had the night before, although her hair was now neatly braided and she was wearing a fresh nightgown. She was also much more talkative.

"I want to speak to you before you leave with Papa. I need to understand why you found the need to defy everything we thought you held dear—our love for you, the life Papa built for us, even your place at university, which you fought so persistently for. What possessed you to throw away a future we had supported? We accepted that you were not going to be happy following the path of other young Viennese girls. While we—especially, I—hope you will one day marry, we recognized your intelligence and drive and understood we could not hold you back, even knowing what a challenging life you would have trying to satisfy your insatiable desire to be an educated, independent woman. We supported you. It is incomprehensible to me that my brilliant daughter did not foresee the chaos her decision to model would unleash. I am not even speaking of the pain you have inflicted on us and the scandal that will keep the tongues of Viennese society wagging. I'm talking about your life, your ambition, your desire to accomplish something with the many gifts you have. Maya, I know you are furious with us right now, but I beg you to think about what you truly want while you are away. Do you want to be labeled as Brenner's whore for the rest of your life, dismissed as an object of someone else's vision?"

"I'm not his whore. I'm his collaborator, his muse, his inspiration." I sputtered the words, taken aback by my mother's observations. Clearly the laudanum had worn off, and she had come to my room primed for battle.

"Oh, please, Maya. I've seen the paintings."

"But Papa said . . ."

"Papa is not aware that I went to the exhibition. I needed to see for myself with the eyes of a woman, not an enraged father who believes his daughter is still a child."

I was speechless.

"You were no longer a virgin when he painted those nudes. You were his lover."

"His lover, not his whore."

She shrugged. "There is more than one way to define a whore. Are you pregnant?"

"No!"

"Well, at least there is that. I am still devastated for you, but perhaps not for the same reasons as Papa. Nevertheless, I agree with him that the best course of action is for you to leave Vienna right now. Everything needs to cool off—everyone's reaction to the exhibition, your affair with Brenner, your headstrong tendency to act without understanding the consequences."

"You don't understand. Without me, his art will suffer. This decision of yours and Papa's will destroy his life as well as mine."

"No, Maya, it is you who do not understand. I do not care what happens to Andreas Brenner. He exploited you for his own gain. I know you think I am old-fashioned and hidebound in my adherence to society's dictates. But would someone with such conventional views have not only allowed you to attend university but also encouraged you? It is I who convinced your father of the rightness and wisdom of such an unorthodox path for his daughter. I will tell you now why I championed you, and why it is breaking my heart that you have thrown away that opportunity. And for what—lust and a fleeting moment of notoriety?"

She took a breath, giving me a moment to reflect on what she was saying, a perspective that was very much in line with my own fears about what would ensue after the unveiling of the portraits.

"Let me tell you why I fought for you. Before I met your father, I was a student of music. I had private instruction because my parents forbid me to study at the Vienna Conservatory. I played and composed for the piano. I even gave a recital of my original work that was well reviewed. But it was 1875. If you think society's constraints now are unbearable, Vienna at that time was bound tightly by rules defining the proper role for women, especially women of our class. My parents were adamant that my music would never be a profession, but merely an adornment. I was furious. I was fortunate to have a sympathetic aunt, your Grosstante Irmgard. She whisked me away to Greece to calm the waters in my parents' house. I cried, I ranted, and then I fell on the steps of Sounion and fell in love with your father."

"But your dream of composing!"

"I put it aside when you were born. I couldn't reconcile my life as a wife and mother with my ambition to bring my music to the world. Perhaps I didn't try hard enough, but I was bombarded with expectations from my family to live a certain kind of life, and Viennese society left little room for loosening the bonds that restricted women's lives. I also knew I had a role to play in fostering Papa's success in business. I didn't want you to face the same challenges. That is why I persuaded Papa to allow you to attend university, and that is also why I cannot fathom why you squandered that precious seat in the lecture hall and the library."

Any resistance I had to my parents' decision to send me away was seeping out of me like air from a balloon. Listening to my mother had drained me far more than my father's fury. Her disappointment in me for my seeming rejection of the life she thought I wanted and that she had fought for me to have had thrown me into turmoil.

I wanted to protest, "It's not the same! I haven't given up my dreams or discarded my ambition to further Andreas's career!" But I couldn't, in all honesty, say that. All my illusions about the power I held in my relationship with Andreas and his art seemed ridiculous in the light of my mother's observations. I didn't want to believe how blind I had been.

All I could do was apologize to my mother again. I took her hands in mine.

"Thank you, Mama. I am truly sorry for the pain I've caused you."

She kissed me. "I know, Schatz. Use your time away wisely. I won't come down to bid you farewell. I cannot bear to watch you ride away."

And then she left me.

As I hoped, we traveled by train to Trieste, but my plan to mail a letter to Andreas from the station was thwarted by my father's vigilance. He never left my side, except when I insisted on using the ladies' room, and even then he waited immediately outside the door. I had thought I might ask someone to post the letter for me, but the restroom was empty except for an elderly woman who did not understand German and waved me away in apparent fear. Did I seem dangerously unstable in my desperation to get word to Andreas? It had been less than twenty-four hours since my father had come for me at the studio, but I was already on the verge of despair. In another day, I'd be on a ship and completely beyond reach.

I washed my hands and face and rejoined my father. We had barely spoken since leaving the house, and I had no desire to provoke him into another tirade about my behavior by even acknowledging him. Andreas and I had departed from the same station for Meran just over a week ago. I forced myself not to dwell on that memory, if only to spare myself the pain of more loss than I was already experiencing.

Each time I thought I might be able to wrest myself from my father's side, not only to slip the letter into a post box but also to escape into the city, I found the watchful, hulking presence of Antonio, along with others recruited from my father's warehouse. He had left nothing to chance. A chill rose in my spine. I would never again be able to leave unobstructed as I had on Christmas Day when I walked out of the café.

We boarded the train. I knew it was pointless to search the platform for Andreas. He was not coming to rescue me. I was on my own.

My father had reserved a sleeping compartment for our ten-hour journey and arranged for dinner to be brought to us. He was allowing no possibility for me to leave the train along the way. We ate in silence as the train sped south, first toward Graz.

I had put down my napkin when my father spoke as if he were musing to himself and not actually addressing me.

"He's a Jew, you know." He took a sip of cognac and waited for me to react.

I was confused. "Who is?"

"Brenner, of course. I did some investigating before I found him. His birth name is Aaron Bochner. Comes from a village outside Warsaw. Apparently, he saw the wisdom of removing the taint of Judaism from his name if he was going to convince Viennese society to hire him as a portraitist."

Andreas's reluctance to share with me any details of his past or his family now made more sense, although several of his fellow artists were also Jewish and they hadn't changed their names or hidden their backgrounds. Was it to further his career, or was it shame? I might have understood the former, but why had he held his origins secret from me?

"Your silence indicates you didn't know. For all your physical intimacy, it's clear he was a stranger to you. Your recklessness astounds me, Maya. I've always thought you were astute, especially when it came to people, but I can see I was mistaken. What other lies of his did you believe? That he loved you? That he would marry you?"

I remained impassive, listening to my father's cruel words. He had never spoken to me like this, which reinforced how angry he was with me. I saw no point in arguing with him.

"I'm tired, Papa. I'm going to get ready for bed."

Our compartment had a private lavatory, so I couldn't even gain a few minutes' respite to use the toilet at the end of the railway car. When I had finished washing up, I crawled into the narrow berth and turned my back on my father. Sometime later, I heard water splashing into the sink, and then the light dimmed. Before long, I could hear my father's snores. I was exhausted, but even the rhythmic pulse of the train rolling over the tracks was not enough to lull me into sleep.

Early the next morning, a porter rang a bell as he moved up the corridor outside our compartment. The train would arrive in Trieste within a half hour.

"Dress warmly," my father said sharply. "We'll sail shortly after we arrive, and the weather will be frigid on the open sea."

He was right. During the crossing, we encountered not only frigid temperatures but also rough seas and high winds. I spent most of the voyage in my cabin, curled into a ball on my berth with a basin close by.

The trip took more than two weeks. I lost weight, didn't have a bath or wash my hair, and was barely able to hold down a bowl of soup.

By the time we arrived on Skiathos, I was a shadow of my former self.

Chapter Fourteen

AT THE PORT IN Skiathos Town, my father hired a fleet of donkeys to carry the supplies he had brought for my grandparents up into the hills above the harbor to their home.

Our arrival in the neighborhood drew notice immediately. Kerchiefed women retrieving water at the fountain stopped their conversation to watch us. Two old men smoking on a bench outside a taverna nodded as my father acknowledged them, greeting them as *Theío*, or uncle. The neighborhood was smaller than I remembered, but most of the landmarks remained—the cobbled square, the church, the mayor's house. My grandparents' home was on the outskirts of the town, with commanding views of both the harbor and the cove to the south.

Like my father, my *pappou* had gone to sea as a young man and prospered, returning intermittently with money to support his widowed mother and provide dowries for his sisters. One year he had returned with a wife, my *yiayia*. As a child, I had only vaguely been aware that my grandmother was not like her sisters-in-law or the other women on the island. It had not seemed at all unusual, for example, that my grandparents' house was filled with books, just as my home in Vienna had been. My childhood summers on Skiathos had been paradise. I never questioned if my grandmother was homesick for a life very different from the one she had adopted in marrying my grandfather.

After his seafaring days were over, my grandfather built a trading company with a fleet of ships and a large warehouse at the port. He also took over the farm that had been in his family for generations, growing olives that were crushed into oil before being exported and raising goats and sheep whose milk my yiayia transformed into feta and yogurt.

We arrived at the gate to their house, one of the largest on the island, and my father called out "*Mitera! Pateras!*" A window on the upper story was thrown open, and my yiayia's face appeared, accompanied by a shriek of joy. She left the window, and I could hear her calling out to someone in the house as she descended to greet us. Bursting out of the door, she ran to my father, who had dismounted his donkey. It was the first time I had seen him smile in all the days since he had pulled me away from Andreas.

He embraced and kissed her.

She held his face in her hands and studied him with wonder, as if he were a ghost, presumed dead and now returning to her. Although I had not been back in ten years, I had always assumed that my father had visited his parents on some of his voyages, but perhaps not.

It was only after welcoming her son that my grandmother noticed me.

"Is this Maya, my little *engoni*, now a grown woman?"

She held out her arms, and I bent down to receive her hug. She was much shorter than I, sleight of build but strong, I discovered, as she wrapped her sinewy arms around me.

"Come, come inside and tell me everything. I've sent our workman Dimitri down to the warehouse to fetch Pappou."

My father insisted on unpacking the donkeys first, concerned with the threatening skies. Our trek up from Skiathos Town had been dry, but he had warned me that January was notoriously wet and cold in the Sporades. I helped to haul the sacks of food and boxes that I assumed contained objects unavailable on the island. My grandmother directed us where to stack them. By the time everything was inside, my grandfather had arrived and we went through another round of welcomes.

My grandfather was more subdued than my grandmother, expressing a gruff pleasure in seeing us but astute enough to know we hadn't arrived unannounced in the middle of winter for a social visit. When we were settled in front of the fire with hot cups of green mountain tea laced with honey in our hands, my grandfather wasted no time.

"So why are you here? We are grateful for the money and gifts you send to us, of course, but you yourself have been a stranger. I'm old, but I'm not stupid. There's only one reason why you've brought Maya. Is she in trouble?"

My father stiffened. My grandmother sighed and shook her head.

"She's not with child, if that is what you mean."

"Then why have you brought her?"

They were talking about me as if I wasn't in the room. I wanted to speak up and began to open my mouth, but my father put his hand on my arm to stop me.

"She's become involved with people we consider a bad influence, and we think it's best if she's away from Vienna for a while."

I realized my father wasn't planning on revealing everything. His motivation in withholding the details, I concluded, was not to protect me or to prevent the scandal from spreading to Skiathos but rather to protect himself. He didn't want his parents to judge him as unable to control his daughter.

"We'd like her to stay here with you."

My grandfather considered the request. "How long?"

My father shrugged. "Several months, at least until the summer."

I gasped. I knew his reasoning. By summer, the Secession exhibition would be a vague recollection and most of my parents' friends would be away from Vienna.

"And you? How long do you plan to stay?" My grandmother's voice gave evidence of longing.

"A week, maybe two. I'll help with work at the warehouse and make sure Maya is settled."

My grandparents exchanged a look and nodded to each other.

"Very well."

My grandfather went to a cabinet and retrieved a bottle of Metaxa and two glasses.

My grandmother rose. "Come, Maya, I'll show you to your room, and you can help me make the bed. Then we can start preparing dinner."

As my grandmother and I climbed the stairs, I could hear the pouring of liquid, the clink of glasses, and the murmur of voices. I wondered how much information my grandfather would extract from my father, then realized I didn't care. Let them know. Let them be horrified.

The weather was as my father had predicted—rain that varied from heavy downpours to a damp mist that clung to our clothing and blurred the view from the upper windows of the house. On one of the rare clear days, I had been able to see the serpentine path that descended through the undergrowth to a small cove where my Theío Paraskevas and cousin Nikos moored their fishing boat.

My father spent most of the day at the warehouse with my grandfather. In the evenings, they both went to the taverna. My days were spent with my grandmother, who, after assessing the wardrobe I had brought with me, decided I needed clothing more suitable to island life. She opened an armoire in the attic and hauled out a collection of blouses and skirts.

"These belonged to your aunts. Only one of them had a daughter; the rest, only boys or no children at all. So these clothes got put away for another day."

She looked me up and down. "None of them was as tall or slender as you, but I think we can alter them enough to fit you."

So while the men discussed business and the politics of the island, we spent our days taking in seams and lowering hems,; washing and bleaching cotton blouses in *alysiva*, lye water made from ashes and rainwater, until they were as bright as the sunshine reflected off the peak of Mount Olympus; and even darning wool stockings. I'd originally shuddered at wearing the stockings, but came to appreciate the warmth they provided as the damp and cold seeped into every crevice of the house. My sun-kissed memories of August on Skiathos were worlds away from the gray winter landscape that surrounded me.

Within a few days, I could reasonably pass for a Skiathan maiden. My hair was braided and wrapped around my head and I wore a long woolen skirt topped by a crisp white blouse. The clothing was familiar in its style, similar to the confining Viennese uniform of women of my class in Vienna and very different from the more daring clothing I had begun to wear in the art world. Covering my body with high necklines and long sleeves reminded me that attitudes toward women had not progressed here on the island. We were assumed to be temptresses who needed to swathe ourselves in layers of fabric to prevent the men who saw us from having sinful thoughts of lust. It was no wonder my modeling had enraged my father. Despite his sophisticated life in Vienna, his ideas were rooted in the soil of Skiathos.

At night in my room, I poured my anger into stripping off the clothes that symbolized my imprisonment but found no real relief.

Several days after our arrival, I woke one morning to find my grandmother bustling around the kitchen with even more than her usual energy.

"*Kalimera*, YiaYia."

"*Kalimera*, Maya. I'm glad to see you're up at last."

I wanted to point out that it was barely past dawn. I was only standing before her because of the racket she was making and my inability to drown out the sound by putting my pillow over my head.

"Start peeling these potatoes." She directed me toward a bushel on the floor.

"What's all this for?" I gestured toward the phyllo dough she was rolling out, a basket of eggs, and a large bowl of feta draped in cheesecloth.

"Your father, of course. Word has reached the far corners of the island, and everyone wants to see the elusive Kostas Sircos before he disappears again. He and Pappou slaughtered one of the yearling goats last night, and it's roasting in the big oven of Stathis, the baker. You and I will make the *tiropita* and bake the potatoes. Your Aunt Maria is bringing the baklava. Your Aunt Ekaterina made the *fasolada*, and your Aunt Anastasia baked the bread."

After YiaYia and I assembled large baking sheets of tiropita filled with feta and eggs, she sent me out to the field behind the house to pick cabbage to be cooked with onions, leeks, and rice.

My aunts arrived over the course of the morning, exclaiming over my transformation from child to woman.

"Little Maya, not so little anymore."

Then they rolled up their sleeves, tied on their aprons, and proceeded to prepare a feast for their brother.

"The prince, the prodigal son," they joked in pretend annoyance. It's true he was the only son and put on a pedestal because of it.

I saw in their faces hints of my own. I heard in their laughter and blunt language a lack of restraint that I had not experienced among my Viennese aunts. If any of these women had arrived in Austria, they would have been considered peasants. In spite of my resentment at being torn from my life in Vienna, I felt a kinship with my aunts in ways I had forgotten since my childhood summers. It had been more than just the sunshine, the sea, and the freedom to roam the countryside with my cousins that had shaped me then. I was more like these women than I had realized. Not only did I resemble them physically, with my dark hair and olive skin, but I shared what I saw as a comfort with and pride in their bodies. My aunts were strong, feeding heavy logs into the kitchen fire, carrying mounded platters of food to the trestle tables they had set up in the dining room and wielding knives with vigor to attack the sack of onions they had hauled up from my grandmother's root cellar.

They weren't ashamed of the sweat their labors generated, but simply wiped it away with the edge of their aprons. They kneaded each other's backs, made my grandmother sit down with a cup of tea when the last of the tiropita had gone into the oven, and broke out my grandfather's Metaxa for themselves.

"A toast to our brother for giving us the opportunity to celebrate."

My Aunt Maria, the oldest, raised her glass, and we joined her in a joyful "*Yamas!*"

I recognized the pattern etched in the glasses. Czech crystal that my father had brought home one day for Mama and Gertraud to pack carefully before he shipped them to Skiathos.

By the time Dimitri arrived from the baker's with the roasted goat, the rest of the family and other members of the community had gathered in the house—uncles and cousins, the mayor, the priest, and the doctor, plus other men and their wives from the neighborhood who had grown up with my father.

My grandparents sat at the table surrounded by all their children and grandchildren. Amidst the noise of multiple conversations, the ruckus of storytelling and teasing, and demands for my father to fill in ten years of wandering, YiaYia and Pappou observed it all with expressions of bittersweet gratitude. Their son had returned, but he would not stay. I knew I was a poor substitute, a burden with a shameful past that needed to be kept from the rest of the island. If Skiathos was anything like Vienna, the secret in my grandparents' house would not be contained for long.

I barely spoke during the meal. I was seated at the far end of the table, where I could easily move back and forth to the kitchen to carry away empty platters and return with more bounty. It was the best way to remain almost invisible. A few glances from villagers registered my presence, something to be tucked away in the moment and brought out like a sweet morsel the next time they sat with a neighbor over a cup of tea or shared a glass of Retsina with other fishermen in the taverna. The daughter of Kostas Sircos. Why was she here? Not just for a visit with her father, but staying.

On one of my trips to the kitchen, I was intercepted by my cousin Leonidas.

"Maya! Are you hiding here in the kitchen? Every time I tried to catch your eye at the table, you weren't there. I wanted to say welcome back."

He pulled me into a powerful embrace and then gently tipped my chin up.

"What? Not happy to see me?" He spread his arms wide. "Not enthralled to be surrounded by this beauty?"

"Leo, it's so good to see you! Forgive me for not greeting you sooner. I'm just trying to help YiaYia. There are so many people to feed, especially people I don't know."

"So you *are* hiding. I don't remember you being as reticent as a little girl. If I recall, you kept up with all us boy cousins and never wanted to be left behind. Have you turned into a proper Viennese lady after all these years away, or have you become the artist you dreamed of being?"

"Neither." *If you only knew, Leo, would you be shocked?*

"I heard from my mother that you'll be staying a while." He leaned against the china cabinet, arms folded, and waited for me to respond. When I didn't answer, he asked me directly. "What exactly did you do that led to your exile?"

"You don't know?"

"I believe your father made YiaYia and Pappou swear to silence."

"To protect his reputation or mine?" I spat out the words.

"Do you want to tell me? I promise on the graves of our ancestors that it will remain with me."

I wavered. I was desperately lonely, and I had fond memories of Leo from childhood. I looked away from him as I spoke. I wasn't going to tell him everything, and I didn't want him to recognize I was holding something back.

"I was modeling for Andreas Brenner."

"Should I know who he is?"

"A well-regarded artist."

"Why did that upset Theío Kostas?"

"It didn't just upset him. It enraged him."

Leo caught my meaning. "You were modeling without your clothes on?"

I nodded.

"Brave girl. But I thought you were an artist yourself. Why weren't you painting instead of being the object of someone else's art? Why aren't you painting now when you're free of that role?"

I turned and stared at Leo. When had he become so perceptive? Or had he always been and I'd simply forgotten? I pushed back as I always had with him, refusing to allow him the satisfaction of knowing he had spoken the truth I was avoiding.

"I'm not merely modeling. I'm learning from him, gleaning the elements of his craft as he paints me."

"Bullshit."

I turned away again, feeling the heat of my anger and my shame rising, spreading from my breast under my dress up my neck and into my face.

I wanted to throw the tureen in my hands at him.

"If you'll excuse me, I've got to get back to the dining room with this fasolada before it gets cold." I nearly ran out the door.

I'm sure my face was flaming when I slipped back into my seat at the table. I had told myself I didn't care if people knew why I was here, but it had bothered me more than I expected to be confronted by Leo. I had idolized him as a child; he was the older brother I'd never had. He had taught me to swim, shown me how to write my name in Greek when I was only four, and rescued me from a too-high branch in a tree I had climbed to watch my father's ship sail away.

I didn't want to disappoint him, but I knew that would be impossible. He had spent his entire life on Skiathos and had more than likely absorbed the moral code that had existed here for generations. The gangly teenager I had tearfully bid goodbye ten years before had grown into a handsome man. When he had held me in the kitchen, I had felt protected and welcomed in a way that I had rarely experienced before—not since arriving on Skiathos, certainly, but also not in Andreas's arms. Leo's embrace had reminded me of how safe and loved I had once felt when my father had held me.

Up until my conversation with Leo, I had been simmering with resentment but not flailing. I'd been under control, hopeful that my exile would be ended by a daring rescue from Andreas. But Leo had held up a mirror to me, and I pushed away the pathetic image I saw there.

Andreas was not going to save me. Certainly not by coming to Skiathos, but also not in the studio. Leo was right. Why had I, who prided myself on my independence and daring, succumbed to such a traditional role? I had thought I was flouting the Viennese society that was so important to my parents by posing for Andreas. No other daughter in my family's tight social circle would have dared even to enter that studio, let alone take her clothes off there. But was I simply trading one subservient role—the bourgeois debutante on the marriage market—for another? I shook my head to dispel the doubts that Leo's words had triggered. No, I insisted. I had power over Andreas equal to his over me. I had felt it in my body as I presented myself to him, forcing him to explore the secrets I was conveying.

"Maya, where are you?" It was my younger cousin Irini, disturbing my reverie from across the table. "I've been trying to get your attention. Would you like to go for a walk later—after we clean up, I mean? The men are probably going down to the taverna."

I could see she was anxious to get away, and I understood her impatience and boredom. She must be almost sixteen by now, I thought, old enough to want to be away from watchful eyes. Even island girls have secrets.

"Of course I'll go with you. Shall we get started in the kitchen?"

We were joined soon by two of my aunts. YiaYia had been coaxed to rest and had gone upstairs with Anastasia. With so many hands, the washing up was quickly dispatched.

Irini announced to her mother, Theía Ekaterina, that she and I were going for a walk. I caught a glance between Theía Ekaterina and Theía Maria. Was I not to be trusted with the innocent Irini? But Maria, as eldest, seemed to make a decision, shrugged, and waved us off.

"You both earned a break. Irini, stay clear of the cliff walk. Your father reported it's muddy from the rain and slippery in spots."

"We'll be careful. I want to show Maya the old chapel."

We took our coats from the hall and emerged into the fresh air. After hours in the heat of the kitchen and then the press of humanity in the dining room, the coolness to my face was a refreshing change. Irini ran ahead, almost dancing from the relief of being outside. She was still the sprite I remembered, a tiny thing who took after YiaYia rather than our sturdy aunts.

I followed her beyond the paddock where the donkeys grazed and up a slight rise. We passed vineyards, stark in their winter nakedness and olive orchards, their silver green leaves glimmering in the winter light. All showed signs of careful tending. Trees and vines had been pruned and younger trees had been wrapped in canvas.

We eventually came to a clearing with a small, white-washed church in its center. Irini pushed against the scarred oak door, and its ancient, rusted hinges screeched in complaint. I had to stoop to enter through the portal. Inside was musty but new candles sat on the stone altar and a few wooden benches remained. Everything appeared to be in miniature and therefore a perfect size for Irini.

She took me by the hand and led me up the nave. It took only ten steps to reach the altar.

"The chapel was deconsecrated years ago when Pappou paid for the renovations of the Church of Agios Nikolaos. 'A more fitting symbol for the Sircos name' is how my father described Pappou's decision.

"I come here when I want to be alone, away from my brothers. I brought you here to let you know you are welcome to use it as a refuge anytime you need it."

"That is so kind of you, Irini. Do you often need to escape?"

"I have three brothers—Nikos, Theos, and Grigoris. You saw them at dinner—noisy, bossy, and messy."

"I remember them as boys, and I agree completely with your description." I laughed, as I recalled the memory of my rowdy cousins.

"Until you arrived, I was the only girl in the whole family. I'm so glad you're here! May I ask you something?"

Here it was, confirmation that word was getting out among the family about Kostas Sircos's wayward daughter. I began to understand why Irini had brought me away from the house to question me.

"No one will tell me why you are here. I know it's not for a short visit with Theío Kostas because he is leaving and you are staying."

"My father wants me to stay awhile to reclaim my Greek roots. He felt I was losing the language and the culture." My explanation wasn't entirely a lie. Papa definitely believed that my wild ways would be reined in by the strictures of behavior that defined the culture of Skiathos.

"Your Greek isn't bad, although sometimes your vocabulary seems limited."

"That's because the last time I was here, I was ten years old. Perhaps you could help me improve my Greek."

"Oh, yes, I'd love to do that. We could meet here and talk. I've always wanted a sister."

"And now you at least have a female cousin."

We went back to the house arm in arm. Irini seemed satisfied with my reason for staying, and I had no intention of enlightening her further, as I had with Leo. The life I had led in Vienna that had caused my exile would be both shocking and unbelievable to her. I was not about to be the one who revealed to her that women's lives could be as messy as those of her brothers.

My father left a few days after the feast thrown in his honor. As I stood in the doorway, adorned in my Skiathan clothing, he appraised me and saw not the sullen, sinning daughter but a facsimile, a reproduction, of what he wished his daughter to be. We did not embrace. The two weeks with my grandparents as intermediaries had not closed the distance between us.

"Be good for your grandparents" were his parting words to me.

"Give my love to Mama" were mine to him.

I turned back into the house before he was out of sight.

Chapter Fifteen

I SETTLED INTO A routine with my grandmother of housework and meal preparation that kept my hands busy and helped me to survive each day without collapsing into despair. My grandmother would not tolerate any idleness. After all, my presence put a burden on the household; I was another mouth to feed, another body in need of a bed and clean clothes. But she also indicated to me in the early days after my father left that my assistance would not only provide her with some relief but also give me an outlet for the frustration and anger that simmered within me as the days between my life in Vienna and my existence on Skiathos multiplied. I had little time or energy to dwell on my loneliness, or my fear that Andreas had already forgotten me and found a new model.

It was only at night when I retreated to my room that I had time to reflect on my situation. I often fell asleep imagining wildly unrealistic scenarios of escaping Skiathos and making my way back to Vienna. During the day, I moved through my chores in silence. I could not blame my grandparents for my imprisonment and didn't want to inflict my pain on them, so I washed dishes, swept the floor, chopped onions, kneaded bread under my grand-mother's instruction, and learned how to gut a fish. The monotony of my days was endless. Like the mist-shrouded landscape around the house, the colors of my life had seeped away. No more bold strokes of vibrant pigments on Andreas's canvases, no more passionate embrace of bohemian life in the artists' quarter.

My very being felt surrounded by a cloak of sadness and despair. I had lost my identity—the strong-willed, passionately curious, clever woman I had once known myself to be.

My isolation was a devastating contrast not only to the intensity and intimacy of my relationship with Andreas, but also to my intellectual life of challenging and often heated conversations over the bitter coffee and Turkish cigarettes that seemed to be the only sustenance of my friends. My life in Vienna was often frenetic and raucous and infuriating, but the energy fed me, made me feel alive in every sense.

Here, I felt my senses had dimmed. I wandered through the house after my chores were done, restless and unable to settle myself. I thought if I found a purposeful task, I might pull myself out of the morass of emptiness into which I had sunk. I had packed my traveling writing desk, an ingenious contraption that held my monogrammed stationery and the fountain pen my parents had given me when I graduated from secondary school and passed the Abitur exam. I decided to write a letter every day to Andreas, despite my inability to send them. My father had left strict instructions forbidding me any contact with Andreas or anyone else in Vienna. He rightly surmised that I might persuade someone to act as a go-between in my efforts to reach Andreas. I thus had no way for my letters to make their way from Skiathos Town across the Aegean, through the Corinth Canal, the Gulfs of Corinth and Patras, and then up the Adriatic coast to Trieste and on to Vienna. I had traced the route on a maritime map Pappou kept in his office at his warehouse. Perhaps not as fraught and complicated as the journey of Odysseus, but still overwhelming in its complexity.

Nevertheless, I began the daily practice of writing to Andreas. In the beginning, the words came easily, despite the trauma of my departure and the devastating aftermath of my arrival on Skiathos. I was still Maya then. My rage sustained me at first. I was furious with my father, of course, but also with myself for my naïveté in thinking I was truly free. But as the days passed and the weather itself locked me in the house, I gradually came to the understanding that my sojourn would last far longer than I anticipated, and that realization drained my anger and left me in a state of emotional paralysis. I was numb, and the sensation served as a form of protection, like the swaddling of an infant to keep it from flailing. The more I withdrew from the painful realization that my life was now bound to Skiathos, the fewer words emerged from my pen every night. It did not take me long to forgo the letters entirely. I had nothing to say. I had no hope to express of one day finding myself once again in Andreas's studio,

Andreas's arms, Andreas's bed. The memory of that bed also began to fade, leaving me a shell who could not even recall the exquisite touch of my lover—a touch that had revealed a side of me that had delighted and astonished me.

I bound up the letters with a thin strip of fabric left over from the alterations of my aunts' dresses. I attached so little value to the letters that they didn't even deserve a ribbon.

One morning when the foul weather had abated slightly, my grandmother greeted me at breakfast with an announcement.

"Today we go to visit your Aunt Ekaterina. Dress warmly. The wind is strong and may bring more rain."

We left in the late morning and walked down the hill into the town. My grandmother had a large bundle with her, which I offered to carry, and a tin of her sesame seed cookies that we had baked earlier in the week.

When we arrived at her house, Ekaterina greeted us with enveloping hugs. She was expecting us.

We gathered in a central room that served as both a dining room and a parlor. A fire in the hearth cast warmth over the entire space, and we sat on cushioned benches surrounding the fireplace. I was disappointed to learn that Irini was at school and wondered if Theía Ekaterina and YiaYia had planned the timing of my visit to protect Irini from the modern ideas I had brought with me from Vienna.

Over tea, YiaYia guided the conversation away from any deep probing of why I was on Skiathos. It seemed even close family members like Theía Ekaterina were to be kept from the truth of my shameful behavior. YiaYia directed my attention to a corner of the room.

"Theía Ekaterina is a master weaver."

I got up to examine the loom that filled nearly a quarter of the room. Shelves around it were filled with skeins of wool. Some were the natural shades shorn from sheep, but several had been dyed in brilliant shades of burgundy and violet and the deep green of the pine forests climbing the hills beyond the town. I stood at the loom and stared in wonder at the intricate pattern taking shape in the frame.

"What will it be when you finish?"

"A wall hanging to keep out the draft in Irini's bedroom."

"It's beautiful!"

I caught the look that passed between my grandmother and my aunt. Was this visit some kind of plot to lift me out of my despondent mood? I could sense the words my grandmother was holding back. You see, Maya, art exists on Skiathos as well as in Vienna.

I turned to my aunt. "How did you learn?"

She laughed and pointed to my grandmother, who held up her arthritic gnarled fingers.

"We moved the loom to Ekaterina about five years ago, when my hands could no longer manage the shuttle. She weaves practical materials like linens for the house and cotton for clothing, but her skills have advanced far beyond what I taught her."

"Is this a traditional design?" I pointed to the loom.

"It's a variation of an ancient island pattern."

Both women looked at me, satisfied smiles on their faces, as if the plan they had hatched was unfolding as expected. They waited for me to ask Ekaterina if she would teach me. But I didn't. As beautiful as her work was, I saw it as anachronistic, an homage to a past that rigidly defined what was possible. She had called her design a variation, but I imagined if I walked through the town, I'd find several wall hangings with the same colors and shapes as hers. I smiled and offered a concession, disappointing their hopes for an acceptable enterprise for me but acknowledging my admiration for Ekaterina's craft.

"May I watch you weave someday?"

"Of course, Maya. I could show you how I manipulate the loom, if you like."

She wasn't going to give up, but she avoided the word *teach*.

"Come back tomorrow after dinner."

We left soon after my grandmother handed Ekaterina the bundle she had brought, which contained raw wool.

"This is from the summer shearing. Dimitri found it in the barn, forgotten under stacked wood. It's a wonder the mice didn't discover it."

"*Efcharisto*, Mitera. I'll wash and card it. I have some dried berries I can use to dye it. Maya, you can help when you come tomorrow."

Before returning home, YiaYia and I stopped at a small shop that offered dry goods and served as a post office and a café.

"I need salt and flour. Your father usually writes ahead to ask what we need, but apparently he didn't have time for that. Come. Be prepared for the stir it will make. Any stranger's arrival in town is cause for curiosity, but word has certainly reached those who weren't at the house for the feast. The appearance of Kostas Sircos's daughter after ten years will generate enough inquisitiveness to fuel the rumor mill for weeks."

As my grandmother predicted, our entrance into the shop brought conversations to a standstill. No one bothered to disguise their curiosity, but instead stared openly. I understood more clearly why my grandmother's first task had been to outfit me as a Skiathan when I had been deposited in her house by my father. I caused enough of a commotion dressed modestly. I could only imagine what the reaction would have been if I had shown up dressed in my bohemian finery. No doubt I'd have been labeled a loose woman fresh from the city of the devil. I expected that impression might still be forthcoming as my sojourn on Skiathos continued, but at least in these early days, I was a proper young granddaughter accompanying her yiayia to the market. My grandmother spoke only to Nota, the shopkeeper, who wrapped our purchases and asked no questions. Without acknowledging any of the other customers, YiaYia and I left the store and returned home.

The next day, I went to Ekaterina's by myself to help her wash, card, and dye the wool. YiaYia cautioned me to go directly to Ekaterina's house.

"You remember the way. Don't wander and don't stop to speak to anyone you pass. Dimitri will come and get you before nightfall."

"Not even people I met at Papa's feast?"

"No one. They will try to engage you with questions, but only to extract information they will use like currency to curry favor or damage your already tenuous reputation. It's better to just nod a greeting and move on."

Her warning seemed extreme to me, but I understood enough about island culture to heed her advice. Every household had secrets that were best held close, especially households like that of my grandparents, whose lofty status relied on the reputation of my father. By nature of being his daughter, my behavior on the island or my history, if it became known, could ostracize my family. Consequently, I hurried through the village to Ekaterina's house, arriving in a state of breathlessness.

"Maya, are you ill? Did a dog chase you? Were you accosted by old Alexis, drunk again?" She looked up and down the street to find the source of my agitation. But of course, nothing was in sight except for some damp leaves caught in the wind.

I shook my head. "Only my imagination. YiaYia put the fear of God in me to come straight here and not be distracted by talking to anyone."

Ekaterina shook her head in sympathy. "My mother is a suspicious old woman who sees danger around every corner. Don't let her frighten you. The town is more afraid of her than she has reason to fear them."

"Why is that?"

"Your grandmother has healing powers, or didn't you know that? A lot of people here believe she can cast spells or call down curses. However, mostly what she does is prepare remedies for fevers and agues, and serve as the island midwife. She's delivered more than 500 babies over her lifetime. Even at her age, she still answers the call to births. If it's out of town to one of the hamlets in the hills, Leo goes with her, over her objections."

"If she does such good, why is she feared?"

"Some people are jealous. Some people believe she's privy to the secrets in a family when she goes to help a woman through a difficult birth or sits in death watch with a dying fisherman. It's what she knows that frightens them."

"Does it ever worry you? Is she right to be so distrustful? Has anyone ever tried to harm her?"

"Listen to you! So many questions. YiaYia knows how to protect herself and the family. She will protect you here. Now come. We've got wool to clean before I can get to my loom."

We spent a peaceful afternoon washing the raw wool in a galvanized tub and hanging it to dry before Ekaterina sat down at her loom. Once again, I was struck by the difference between my Greek and Viennese aunts. I could not imagine Tante Clara roughening her pampered hands with the kind of physical work that Ekaterina engaged in. But I also knew the hollowness of Clara's life—her preoccupation with fashion, society balls, and maintaining a façade of propriety and wealth. I knew I didn't want the life of a Viennese society matron, but I doubted I could be happy confined to life in an island community still trapped in the eighteenth century.

But I did admire Ekaterina for the skill she had acquired and her ability to produce something of value and beauty for her family. She seemed at peace at the loom, a peace my own life lacked. It wasn't just the disruption of being exiled to Skiathos. I knew that I had also been agitated in Vienna. A growing sense of emptiness had begun to creep into my consciousness. I'd pushed it aside in Vienna, caught up as I was in Andreas's quest for acceptance by the Secession.

But the longer I remained on Skiathos, the more my unease surfaced.

Not long after working with Ekaterina I was surprised to receive a letter from my mother. My father's departure had been so final, that I had feared being cut off from my parents as well as Andreas. Although Mama had agreed with Papa to send me away, she was at least reaching out. Her words were mainly ones of admonition—to learn from my exile, especially in thinking about what I wanted in life apart from Andreas. But she also shared news of Vienna. I saw the gesture as a kindness, and wrote back to her. I was still angry, but she was offering me a tentative link to my former life, and I took it. Over the months, her letters continued.

Chapter Sixteen

THE RAIN AND GRAYNESS that enveloped the island persisted for several days. Except for occasional trips to Nota's market with YiaYia or visits to Ekaterina to help with carding and dyeing the wool, I spent most of my days in the house. When my chores were done, YiaYia would offer me the pick of her library. After Leo had taught me to write my name in Greek, my father had made sure I could read and write as well as speak his native language. YiaYia's books were an eclectic mix of Greek literature, poetry, and religious works. It intrigued me that a woman as learned as my grandmother had agreed to settle on a remote island, and that, once there, had transformed herself into the island healer. One day, as I helped her distill some wild herbs we had picked together, I asked her about her past.

"How did you learn to do this?" I waved my hand at the shelves of salves and tinctures that were her stock in trade. "From the books in your library?"

She laughed. "Hardly. I learned to heal the ills of those who come to me from my mother-in-law, your great-grandmother, Afendra. She could neither read nor write, but she had knowledge in her fingertips and her nose. I began to write down what I observed as I assisted her, but not in the beginning. In the early days of my marriage to Pappou, I was skeptical of her remedies. More than a few times when I was in the town with her, I heard the word 'witch' muttered as we passed. The speaker would touch the blue Mati amulet everyone seemed to wear, as if to ward off the evil eye. I was an educated woman, not superstitious, but those encounters sent chills up my spine."

"Why did you change your opinion of her?"

"One day, one of the fishermen was brought to her. He had slipped on the deck of his boat, slick with fish, and had impaled his leg on a large hook. He'd been out at sea, and it was almost two days before he got to her. The wound was already festering, and he was feverish. She cleansed the wound, dressed it with honey, and made him a tea of willow bark to lower his fever. If we'd been in Athens, I believe a surgeon would have amputated the leg, but my mother-in-law understood what the loss of a limb would have meant to the fisherman and his family. She kept him here and nursed him through the night and the next day, and the wound began to heal. After that, I no longer doubted her, and vowed to learn from her everything I could. I became her apprentice."

"But why did the villagers think she was a witch?"

"They saw her healing as somehow supernatural, miraculous. But when she failed, when someone died, they thought she'd put a curse on him. Primitive beliefs are difficult to uproot here on Skiathos. It still feels very much like the eighteenth century at times. This tincture is ready. Line up those bottles on the table, and we can strain the liquid into them."

Her eyes flashed with pain, and I thought she had a headache coming on. Ekaterina had told me to watch for signs of distress and encourage YiaYia to rest. But it wasn't a physical ache that had stabbed her. Instead, it was a bitter memory. Her gaze shifted from the simmering pot in front of us to a spot across the room. She gestured with her spoon.

"The last time I saw my mother-in-law, she was standing over there by the window watching Pappou, her son, saddling the donkeys. A small bundle of her clothing was at her feet."

"Where was she going?"

"I didn't know. Pappou thought it better, a protection for me, not to know. Only years later did he tell me he'd brought her to the nuns who live as hermits on Mount Stavros."

"But why?"

"A young woman's body had washed up on the shore below the cliffs at Megas Gialos. It was no accident. A fisherman had seen her fling herself into the sea. It was rumored that she was pregnant, her lover an off-islander who had abandoned her. At her mother's urging, she had gone to Afendra weeks before for help in bringing on her monthly blood, but the tea had failed. Distraught, the girl had taken herself to the cliff, believing she was better off dead than a shameful burden to her family.

"The girl's mother, recognizing her own guilt in sending her daughter to Afendra, instead accused Afendra of cursing her daughter. The girl's father, devastated by both the loss of his daughter and the sin she had tried to commit to rid herself of the baby with Afendra's help, rose up against my mother-in-law. Mad with grief and rage, he stirred unrest in the village, reminding others when Afendra had been present at times of unexplained illnesses or bad harvests or a storm at sea that had shattered fishing boats against the rocks. Someone whispered the word 'witch,' and soon it became a chant. Pappou's cousin Vangelis heard the gathering fury in the taverna and came to warn us.

"Pappou made the decision that night to take his mother away and ordered me to take refuge with Vangelis in a neighboring hamlet. Your father was two at the time, and I was pregnant with your Aunt Maria. I hugged my mother-in-law goodbye, and her parting words were to take my notebooks—all that I had learned from her—with me to Vangelis's. 'Don't leave them behind in the house,' she had begged me.

"I watched them go by a little-used path that led away from the town and down to the cove where Pappou had moored his boat. I spent three days with your father at Vangelis's place, while Vangelis and his brothers and more men from the family guarded our house from the mob that was forming in the village. They came with torches screaming for Afendra, and when they were denied her, they ransacked our house, smashing her jars of herbs and remedies, destroying the beehives, and trying to set fire to her workroom. Thank the Lord, they didn't succeed. The mayor, who was roused from his bed, hastened to the house. He exhorted them to go home and pray that no one in their family fell ill or injured themselves, because Afendra Sircos was no longer here to heal them.

"I came back on the fourth morning and had no time for tears as I set about cleaning up the mess. Vangelis's wife helped me. It was a month before Pappou returned."

"When did you take on Afendra's role as healer?"

"I had no intention of calling down on us again the wrath that had been unleashed, and used the skills I'd learned from Afendra only in the family. It was nearly a year later, after Maria's birth, that I was faced with a decision one morning. One of the fishermen from Plakes showed up at our door. I told him Pappou was down at the warehouse, but he said he had come for me. His wife was in labor. The child, her first, was coming too soon, and she had no one. Her mother was dead. His mother was on the mainland visiting relatives. That's how his wife found herself alone. I was about to send him away, telling him to seek help elsewhere. But something touched me. To this day, I believe it was the voice of Afendra telling me not to be afraid, and that I had been given a gift I should not squander.

"I agreed to help. I brought your father and Maria to Vangelis's wife, packed a bag with what I thought I might need, and followed the fisherman to his cottage near the water.

"It was more a shack than a home. One room. It was well kept, but meagerly furnished with only one window and barely enough light, even in midday. The fisherman's wife was moaning on her bed, drenched in sweat, a look of wildness in her face as a contraction surged through her.

"I had only borne two children, but I had accompanied Afendra at several births, and knew how to begin. I directed the fisherman to build up the fire, haul in several buckets of water, light as many candles as he possessed, and find at least one other woman to attend his wife.

'Have you no sisters or cousins or neighbors?' I challenged him. He was distraught—understandably so, given the state of his wife—but I needed him to act, to do those tasks over which he had control.

"While he was gone following my instructions, I examined his wife.

'What is your name?' I asked her as I wiped her brow. She could barely utter an intelligible sound, but managed to eke out in a whisper, 'Angeliki.'

"I needed little time to ascertain that her baby was lying sideways in her womb. I had seen Afendra turn a baby only once, but I knew it was the only chance for this mother and child to survive. I could have berated myself for listening to the voice of my mother-in-law; I could have told the fisherman that there was nothing I could do for Angeliki. I could have advised him that it was in God's hands and, when he finished with his tasks, he should pray. But I didn't. When the fisherman returned with a neighbor, I sent him outside. My experience of men at a birth ranged from uselessness to disgust to horror. He would only have been an impediment and might have interfered if he saw what I was going to do. The neighbor woman was no stranger to me. She knew I was Afendra's daughter-in-law but apparently had not been one who had considered Afendra a witch. When I explained what I intended to do, she understood. She had assisted before at a breech birth. Afendra must have sent her to me, I thought with gratitude.

"Between Angeliki's contractions, I described to her what we were going to do. I didn't know how much she comprehended in her agony and fear, but I could not wait for her to calm herself. And so I began to manipulate the baby, remembering with my hands the movements of Afendra's hands. Angeliki's screams filled my ears and my heart, but I kept going. I knew that I held in my hands not only the lives of Angeliki and this baby, but also my own safety and that of my family. Afendra's disappearance and the destruction of her medicines had satisfied the village, but we, especially I, had remained ostracized. I was, after all, her acolyte. I could have been called a witch in training. That is why I had receded from any engagement as a healer.

"But now I was thrust into the middle of a dangerous situation by my own choice. I pushed aside those thoughts as I struggled to keep up my strength and move that baby. I don't know how long I worked, only that my arms ached, but I succeeded. The baby's head was now positioned at the top of the birth canal. Angeliki's strength was nearly at its limit. I fed her some honeyed tea and, with the help of the neighbor, got her up and ready to deliver.

"Angeliki's son was born shortly after midnight. He was decidedly unhappy to be out in the world, but a few moments at his mother's breast were enough to soothe him and present him to his father. After we bathed Angeliki and the baby, remade the bed with fresh linens, and set the bloodied sheets to soak in a basin, I sat by the fire with a beaker of water. It was too late for me to return home, and I wanted to stay the night anyway to check on Angeliki. I knew enough about the risks of childbirth, especially one as difficult as this one, to make no assumptions that the danger was passed. I dozed in the chair throughout the night, periodically checking Angeliki for fever and the baby for difficulties breathing, but his lusty cries every two hours reassured me that this one had a strong will to live despite the ordeal of his birth.

"In the morning, I was surprised by Pappou, who had come to walk me home. He had gotten word through Vangelis of my whereabouts and was familiar enough with his mother's midwifery to know that babies had no reasonable timetable for being born.

"As we walked the path I had chosen to follow the day before, he asked me if I had decided to take up his mother's calling. I searched his eyes for fear or for a sign that he was about to forbid me from continuing what I had set in motion by going to Angeliki. I searched myself for the misgivings that had plagued me during Angeliki's labor. I knew they had been dispelled not by a successful birth, but by my embrace of the gift Afendra had imparted to me. I was going to continue, and Pappou, God bless him, recognized that he couldn't stop me."

Chapter Seventeen

IT SNOWED AT THE end of February, surprising me. I was used to such weather in Vienna, but because I had only spent summers on Skiathos as a child, I woke with amazement to a landscape transformed overnight.

YiaYia teased me at breakfast.

"Did you think winter never came to Skiathos?"

I shook my head. I suppose I should have learned, after all the rain and damp cold, that my childhood memories of endless sunshine were an illusion, but I truly didn't expect snow. We kept to the house for a few days. The paths, slushy after a few hours, froze at night. YiaYia had already bound the ankle of Theíos Yiannis, Ekaterina's husband, after he slipped on his way to the cove. YiaYia and I made use of the confinement to continue to distill herbs and prepare ointments. After listening to her decision to carry on the work of my great-grandmother, I understood more clearly what compelled her to do her work. And in spite of my unremitting resentment, I had begun to learn something of her healing arts working at her side. Still, I had no intention of accompanying her the next time she was called to a birth.

On Skiathos, I was immersed in a world that was far more physical, visceral, and unfiltered than anything I had experienced in Vienna. Andreas had often expounded on the idea of living life in its most raw state, embracing the wild, unfettered by the trappings of civilization. But he had no idea what that truly meant. From the moment I had set foot on the ship that brought me here, I had confronted the power of nature and its impact. I had glimpsed, as well, the lives of the women in my family, whose toil and strength kept their families fed and clothed and comforted despite the challenges of a harsh environment. I was overwhelmed by what I had encountered and wasn't ready to add child-birth to my new experiences.

For that reason, I stayed behind one night when a neighbor's boy knocked on the door to ask for YiaYia. His mother was in labor. YiaYia packed her bag and left with the boy.

"I'm not sure when I'll return. Pappou should be back around ten from the taverna. If you are still awake, please let him know."

By eleven, there was still no sign of Pappou and the snow had begun to fall again. I banked the fire, left an oil lamp burning by the door, and went to bed. As usual, my sleep was long in coming. After finally drifting off, I was startled awake by a loud crash and a moan. I pulled on a woolen shawl and peered over the railing to the lower hall, where Pappou was sprawled across the floor. The front door was still open, and an icy wind was blowing snow into the house. I raced down the steps, pushed the door closed against the gusting snow, and bent to check if he was breathing. My first impression was that he was drunk. But then his body shook in a spasm of violent coughing and his skin was hot to my touch. Between bouts of hacking, he croaked out YiaYia's name, Kaliope. I tried to explain that she was assisting at a birth, but he was so feverish and wracked with coughing, my words were not reaching him.

I knew I couldn't leave him on the floor, which was already wet with melted snow. I managed to get him into a sitting position and then slipped behind him, grabbed him under his arms, and dragged him to the stove, where I propped him up against the sofa. We were both drenched in sweat by the time I got him there. I peeled off his soaked jacket and covered him with one of Theía Ekaterina's woven blankets.

I had no idea where YiaYia had gone, and even if I did, I realized I'd more than likely get lost in the squalling snow searching for her. I tried not to panic as I listened to Pappou's desperate, constant coughing.

I built up the fire in the stove and tried to soothe Pappou's fevered brow with a damp cloth. In his delirium, he pushed away my hand, as if recognizing it was not the touch of his beloved Kaliope.

I am not a nurturing person. I am impatient with sickness. When I am not well, my reaction is one of anger with myself for succumbing. Illness has always been something I've viewed as an annoyance to overcome. For the first time, faced with my grandfather's suffering, I was frightened. The instincts possessed by my great-grandmother and the training absorbed and perfected by my grand-mother were in neither my fingertips nor my heart.

The only help I could call upon was memory. When I was a child and had contracted an ague, Gertraud had nursed me with broth and honeyed tea and a tent fashioned of muslin filled with vapors from an aromatic tincture that opened my lungs.

Holding on to that image, I slipped away from Pappou and into YiaYia's workroom beyond the kitchen. Thank God earlier in the week, when we'd been distilling, I had paid attention to the purposes of each herbal remedy. But the room was dark, and in my urgency as I fumbled for a lamp, my hand knocked over several bottles lined up on the workbench. I retreated to the kitchen for a candle and started over again, this time more methodically, try-ing to still my worry as the wretched sounds emanating from Pappou echoed through the house. Finally, my eyes alighted on bunches of eucalyptus and sage and strips of willow bark hanging from the rafters. I pulled them down; returned to the kitchen for towels, a kettle of water, a cup, and a bowl; and brought them to Pappou. He was mutter-ing nonsense between bouts of coughing, and continued to swat at my attempts to cool his fever.

I set the kettle to boil on the stove and began to con-struct the tent I remembered from childhood. In frustra-tion, I realized the towels I had grabbed in the kitchen were too small. But the tablecloth on the dining table was not. I pulled it off and managed to drape it over Pappou by propping it up with chairs. When the water had boiled,

I made a tea of the willow bark in the cup, crumbled the eucalyptus and sage leaves into the bowl, and covered them with more of the boiling water. As the bracing aroma released by the herbs reached my nose, I climbed under the tent with Pappou. He barely knew I was there, but I held the steaming bowl under his face as the vapors rose, surrounding us like the mist that creeps inland from the sea.

"Breathe, Pappou," I urged him, hoping he could hear me in his delirium. When the infusion cooled, I slipped out of the tent. I mixed honey and brandy into the tea and fed it to him with a teaspoon, cradling him against me like an infant despite his size. I repeated the steaming bowl of herbs two more times until his coughing subsided. Holding him, I leaned back against the sofa as his breathing became more regular. He slept. I dared not move for fear of disturbing him and starting the cycle of coughing again, so I closed my eyes.

Sometime later—I don't know if it was minutes or hours after I had drifted off to sleep—Pappou stirred and sat up abruptly. Once again, he called out for YiaYia.

"YiaYia is away at a birth, Pappou."

He looked at me and our position in front of the fire in confusion, and then glanced toward the front door, now firmly shut against the storm. A glimmer of memory lit up his face.

"I remember leaving old Panagiotis's place. It had begun to snow again, and the cough that was bothering me in the morning roared back. I lost my breath climbing the hill.

The only thing that kept me going was the fear I'd fall and freeze to death under the snow."

"You made it back to the house and collapsed just inside the door."

"But how did I get here? Why am I no longer coughing?'

"I dragged you close to the stove to warm you. Then I made you an infusion to soothe the cough."

He grunted in acknowledgment.

It struck me that this was the first time since my arrival that my grandfather and I had spoken to each other, just the two of us. Because he spent his days at the warehouse, I typically saw him only at the dinner table, where we were often joined by family members. He was a gruff, intense man who did not suffer fools. More than once, I had overheard his criticism of a worker or a neighbor. To me and of me he had little to say. He tolerated me in the house, but that was all.

He shifted his position, and I saw him wince in pain.

"I'm going to my bed." As he attempted to stand, he stumbled. I rose quickly and grabbed him to steady him.

"Let me help you, Pappou."

He shrugged off my supporting arm, just as he had pushed away the cold cloth I had tried to soothe him with during the night. He wasn't delirious now. He was simply proud. But he took only a few steps before reaching out for one of the chairs I had used to prop up the tent. He looked ahead. There was nothing more for him to hold on to between the chair and the stairs. I was right behind him and ready when he turned and motioned to me to come.

I said nothing, but placed his arm over my shoulder and wrapped my own arm around his waist. I could feel the tension in his body as he struggled to bear most of the weight himself. When we reached the stairs, we both girded ourselves for the coming challenge. I knew I couldn't persuade this stubborn man to go back to the sofa, and so we began the trek to the upper floor. His breathing was labored, and his face was rigid with the effort. In some ways, moving him was more difficult than it had been the night before, because then he hadn't resisted me. This time, he was determined not to show weakness. I worried that the exertion would trigger his coughing again, but knew he wouldn't listen to me if I told him to remain downstairs. When we reached the landing, he stopped to rest. Beads of sweat had formed on his forehead, and he was shaking.

I waited silently for him to catch his breath. Finally, he began to move again. When we reached the bedroom, he collapsed on the bed, his face a rictus of pain. And then, of course, the coughing he had managed to suppress with sheer stubbornness exploded with terrible force.

I was exhausted and angry and frightened. Everything I had done during the night had been for naught.

"I'll be back, Pappou, with something to help you." I spoke with a calm that I did not feel.

I raced down the stairs, threw more wood on the fire, and slammed the kettle onto the stove. While waiting for the water to boil, I paced, wishing like a child for my grandmother to return home and make everything better.

I looked out the window. Dawn was approaching, but the snow had not abated and was piled in drifts blown by the fierce wind. It was unlikely that I'd see YiaYia anytime soon. I feared that the remedies of the night before might not work again. Once again, I explored the workroom. Forcing myself to concentrate, I made a more thorough search and found YiaYia's notebooks. I turned the pages, searching for Pappou's symptoms, my fingers tracing Yia-Yia's precise handwriting. I cried with relief when I found "violent coughing." A tincture of poppy would suppress the cough and provide temporary relief. I kissed the book and turned to the neatly labeled bottles on the shelves. As I knew, everything was in alphabetical order, but I had to remind myself of the Greek word for poppy, *paparouna*. I clutched the precious bottle and returned to Pappou, berating myself for the time it had taken me.

His coughing had not subsided, and there was blood on his shirt. With trembling hands, I wiped his mouth; this time, he didn't push me away. He allowed me to help him sit up and give him a spoonful of the tincture.

"What is this?" He managed to croak a few words after swallowing the liquid with a grimace.

"A tincture of poppy. It should calm your coughing." I waited for a few minutes, not expecting immediate relief but hoping the medication might at least slow his breathing. As always, I was impatient.

"I'll be back with something else to help."

I retreated downstairs and prepared another bowl of eucalyptus. With the tablecloth over my arm, I climbed the steps again, carrying the steaming bowl.

Pappou fussed as I once again constructed the tent.

"What's this?" He swatted at the draped cloth.

"This helped you to breathe last night. The vapors . . ."

He waved his hand in grudging acceptance as I held the steaming bowl close to his face. My whole body ached, and my head was pounding. I wanted nothing more than to crawl into my own bed. With relief, I watched the combination of the poppy tincture and the vapors silence his coughing before the water in the bowl had cooled. He finally slept, probably more from exhaustion than my ministrations.

I stayed at his side. When weariness overcame me, I bent my head down onto the bed and fell asleep.

I woke to a calloused hand covering mine. In his sleep, Pappou must have reached out for me.

I heard sounds downstairs, the clatter of dishes and the screech of the iron door of the stove opening, and I sighed in gratitude. YiaYia was home.

I slid my hand out from under Pappou's grip and crept from the room.

YiaYia was sitting at the kitchen table with a cup of coffee.

"I saw that you were both asleep and didn't want to disturb you. I could surmise from the paraphernalia around the bed what had happened, but tell me everything."

And so I did.

After I finished, YiaYia touched my face. "Despite your father's shame over your behavior, Maya, you have a courageous heart and a sharp intelligence. Your quick thinking saved Pappou's life. God bless you."

I may have saved Pappou's life that night, but healing him was beyond the skills of both me and my grandmother. When Theíos Yiannis arrived later in the morning to clear the paths to the house and the barn, YiaYia sent him to fetch Dr. Bakarezos.

After Yiannis left, she explained to me, "I could have gone myself, but Dr. Bakarezos and I are not on the best of terms. He will be only too pleased to be called in to a case that requires more than my skills. He accepts that women don't want him for birthing their babies, but believes the certificate he displays on the wall of his clinic anoints him as superior to me in all else. He will gloat."

The poppy tincture was beginning to wear off by the time Dr. Bakarezos arrived. Pappou was awake and uncomfortable while submitting to the doctor's examination and pronouncements. I remained in my room until he left and then found YiaYia.

"It's a lung infection, which is no surprise. He's prescribed morphine to calm the cough."

"That's all?"

"Dr. Bakarezos has no imagination and no understanding of herbal remedies. I'll send Dimitri to the pharmacy for the morphine, but you and I will continue the vapor tent and infusions with honey and lemon."

She had included me in carrying on the treatment. I smiled, put on my apron, and returned to the workroom to prepare more eucalyptus and sage.

Pappou recovered slowly. And although I was the one mixing the herbs and brewing infusions, I was no longer directly caring for him. The intimacy and intensity of that night he fell ill receded in his memory. I assured myself it was for the better, that he would heal faster if he could forget the pain and distress. But I regretted that he had also forgotten the small moments of rapprochement and acknowledgment between us. I suspected that he would not take my hand again, seeking reassurance and comfort, and that saddened me.

Chapter Eighteen

By late March, Pappou was well enough to leave his bed and sit on the terrace in the sun. The snow had melted, Clean Monday had marked the beginning of Lent at the end of February, and we were already deep into the observation of the holy season. The slower pace of winter, when weather had kept us confined mainly to the house, had been replaced by a frenetic level of activity. Preparing for Easter involved throwing open doors and windows to allow the early spring winds to dispel the dust and the clouds of sickness that had hovered over the family. Rugs were beaten; walls and windows and curtains washed; tables and chests polished with lemon oil. Outside, once the mud had subsided, my cousin Nikos, Irini's brother, tilled YiaYia's vegetable garden while Pappou oversaw and criticized from his chair on the terrace.

In addition to tending to the preparations at home, we were also expected at church for prayer and penance, as well as to scrub the sanctuary of winter soot and the accumulated odors of sweat and incense and candle tallow. YiaYia, my aunts, and I joined the other women of the neighborhood in this yearly ritual. Once again, I could not imagine my mother or my Viennese aunts tying up their hair and getting down on their knees to wash the marble altar steps of St. Stephan's or heating irons to press the starched altar cloths embroidered by the lined and gnarled hands of the women of Skiathos.

We celebrated Easter on April 9 and over the course of the month the entire island burst into green, from the mountains above the town to the gardens in backyards and clay pots on every doorstep.

But I was indifferent to the beauty.

My grandmother, ever perceptive, recognized my emotional state.

"Maya, this isn't a prison. You are pacing like a convict confined to a dungeon. It's finally spring, when you can recognize, once again, the Skiathos you remember. It's time to gather flowers for the May wreath. Take this basket and go outside. You'll find a meadow of wildflowers beyond the edge of town, toward the cove where Theíos Yiannis keeps his fishing trawler. Now go!"

By the time I reached the path toward the cove, I had shaken off my resentment. Following my grandmother's direction, I headed uphill. As I reached the top of the rise, I gasped with amazement. Spread before me was a swath of color that reminded me of one of Gustav Klimt's landscapes. A wave of poppies tumbled down the hill. I plunged into the meadow, brushing my fingertips along the petals, still moist with dew, imagining how the flowers would look in the May wreath. I began cutting stems and gathering them in my basket.

I was nearly finished when I noticed movement on the opposite hillside. A fair-haired woman was stepping back from a canvas propped on an easel.

It was clear the woman was not Skiathan. Her clothing and her presence alone in an isolated valley were signs of her being a stranger. Also, no Skiathan woman had the time to be painting landscapes in the middle of the day. Ekaterina had her loom, and Theía Anastasia had her embroidery. But they were seen less as artistic pursuits and more as useful, practical talents that were appropriate for a woman.

I was fascinated and intrigued. What had brought her here? Surely, Skiathos wasn't recognized as an artists' haven, like the south of France or the German village of Worpswede. Perhaps she was someone's wife, a visiting functionary with business in Skiathos Town, and painting landscapes was her way of entertaining herself while her husband was occupied. I knew of women in Vienna who dabbled in watercolors, painting still lifes to adorn the walls of their morning rooms.

Her art interested me far less than the near certainty that she was not Greek. Until that moment, I hadn't acknowledged how hungry I was for companionship with someone who might recognize the life in Vienna I'd been torn from.

With resolve and no hesitation in my step, I picked up my basket of flowers and strode through the meadow. My movement caught her attention, and she exclaimed a startled "Oh!"

Although she was wearing a wide-brimmed hat, she still held up her hand to shield her eyes from the sun. As I approached, she greeted me in heavily accented Greek, an accent I recognized immediately.

"*Guten Tag*," I returned her greeting.

"Elise Goldberg," she introduced herself, and extended her hand to me after wiping it on a rag. "You speak German flawlessly."

"Maya Sircos," I reciprocated. "I am Viennese."

"What brings you to Skiathos?"

"A family visit." I was not willing to elaborate. "But why are you here?"

"To paint, of course." She gestured with her brush to the partially completed canvas.

I moved closer to view it. I expected to see an amateur's literal creation of the scene before us—green grass, red poppies, puffs of clouds in a blue sky. In other words, a child's rendering of a commonplace scene.

Instead, the canvas vibrated with the hum of spring life and swaths of vivid color. Her style was bold, confident. It held elements that were familiar to me, part of the movement that was gaining adherents among the artists I knew, but her interpretation of the landscape was unique. And then I realized I'd seen her paintings before.

"I know your work! You were part of the *Acht Kunstlerin-nen* exhibition last fall at Salon Pisko!"

"So you are familiar with the avant-garde! I didn't expect to encounter someone here who understood what I am trying to do. Quite often, casual observers are surprised or even curl their lips in disapproval, but you did not. Are you a painter yourself?"

"I don't paint, at least not since I was a schoolgirl, but I'm a student of art history. I'm aware of the changes that are taking place all across Europe."

I wondered why she hadn't been part of the circle of artists in Vienna who were known to me, despite her work being on exhibit in the city, but then I remembered that most of Andreas's colleagues barely recognized the work of female painters.

"Where are you from? And why Skiathos? It's hardly a crucible of experimentation in art."

"My home is in Linz, but I've traveled widely to study. I have already been to Paris, to the crucible, as you call it. I'm here as a traveling companion to my twin brother, who is a novelist. He recommended Skiathos as a rare opportunity. He knows it as a port from his days as a merchant seaman."

"How long will you stay?"

"Through the summer. I've only been here a few days, but I'm already enthralled. If you'll excuse me, I'd like to take advantage of the light before it moves beyond the mountain."

She turned back to her canvas, dismissing me.

I retrieved my basket and began to retrace my steps across the meadow, but then stopped and turned around.

"May I invite you and your brother to tea?"

She put down her brush and beamed. "That would be delightful!"

We settled on a day later in the week and exchanged addresses. She and her brother were staying at a guesthouse near the harbor run by the widow Asimina.

When I returned home, I was excited to announce to YiaYia my discovery of a countrywoman in the poppy meadow.

"I've invited her and her brother to tea. I hope that's not an imposition."

Her response surprised me.

"They are strangers, Maya."

"My mother was once a stranger here."

"And remained a stranger. She visited rarely, making it clear to the family here that she did not wish to know us or share in our lives. She was civil, but not loving. At least she allowed your father to bring you here. But after her last visit, when you were ten, it was she who put a stop to your coming. So you have not chosen a good example to convince me to open my home, especially to someone who shares your mother's supposed sophistication as a citizen of Vienna. Why should I be judged as primitive or uneducated in my own home?"

Her comments about my mother stung, but it was true that Mama had come with Papa and me to Skiathos only a few times. My mother had never disparaged Papa's family, but her own family had held them in disdain.

"You are neither primitive nor uneducated, YiaYia, but unless Elise meets you, she may never know that and may persist in thinking of Skiathans as beneath her. If we invite her, we can dispel those ideas."

"Why is this so important to you? You seem intent on this in ways I haven't seen you express since you arrived."

It finally occurred to me that YiaYia's reluctance to have the Austrians in her home was less about her concern for their opinion of her and more about the danger they represented as a possible connection to Andreas.

"I am lonely for the world I left behind. She speaks my language—not just German but the language of art. I have no friends here, YiaYia, and perhaps she might become one."

YiaYia did not respond at first, but set her lips in a thin line.

"When you were a child, you would often seize on an idea, something you wanted to do that was beyond the limits of your age or capability—climbing a tree as high as Leo could go or exploring the caves by Lalaria."

"Things my boy cousins did all the time."

She nodded her head. "You often came back with scraped elbows or muddy skirts. You were determined to keep up with the boys. Although I often scolded you for your escapades, I will admit to you now that I thought it was a good thing. It made you strong and fearless, qualities I did not believe the sheltered life you led in Vienna could ever provide you. A woman needs to be strong, Maya."

She threw up her hands. "Oh, alright. They are welcome here. If I said no, you would still find a way to spend time with her. I'd rather meet her on my own turf and learn who this woman is who has so enthralled you."

I hugged her, not only for agreeing to host Elise but also for what she revealed about who I was.

I was not the only member of the family to have encountered an Austrian visitor. Nikos recounted a meeting in a taverna by the docks with an Oscar Goldberg, whom I realized must be Elise's twin

"He must be wealthy if he's staying through the summer and isn't obliged to work," Nikos said, shaking his head. Like the women of Skiathos, whose toil caring for families and homes was without respite, the men of the island could not fathom a life spent without the endless battle of extracting a livelihood from the sea or the land.

No one in my family would perceive as work the painting and writing with which the Goldbergs occupied their days. But I did. Especially Elise's commitment to her craft.

My discovery of Elise interrupted the acquiescence to my exile that I had managed to reconcile myself to. I had learned over the winter that to rage against my father's decision harmed only me. I had come to an accommodation that at least had given me a reprieve from sleepless nights fraught with longing, not only for Andreas but for the freedom I had experienced in the midst of a bright, vibrant, and constantly exciting city. I had resigned myself to the role of dutiful granddaughter, especially after Pappou's illness. The chains that bound me to the island were not physical shackles but emotional ones. I did not believe I could flee my grandparents as I had run from my parents in Vienna. I was unwilling to sever the bonds that had shaped me in childhood and that I knew had had far more impact than anything else on who I was now.

But Elise's presence, her art, awakened in me once again the agitation caused by the knowledge that I had been cut off from becoming my true self. Without Andreas to inspire to new heights, my sense of purpose and power had dissipated into an ephemeral fog without definition. Elise's question, "Are you a painter?" had begun haunting me shortly after she had uttered the words.

Why wasn't I? I challenged myself. I had found pleasure in making art as a child and even in the early days of my relationship with Andreas. The sketch I'd made of his face the day I had confronted him with my passion remained a secret possession. I had chosen to carry it with me to Skiathos, hidden in my prayer book. I had folded and re-folded it countless times, and the colors were beginning to fade.

After my conversation with Elise, I opened the book and studied the drawing, tracing it with my finger. As I felt the nerves in my fingertips move across the now fragile paper, I also felt the numbness that had protected me since my arrival start to recede. In its wake I felt pain—pain at my blindness in subsuming my own gifts in order to foster Andreas's talent.

The next day, I found a pencil by the calendar Yia-Yia used to note the expected dates of the births she would be assisting as midwife. She had shown me the clusters that occurred nine months after particular feast days—Epiphany, Clean Monday, and especially Saint John the Baptist. "I have to plan ahead, because I cannot be in two places at once. I know who has family close by and can assist if I get called away to another birth. I make note if this is a first birth or a more experienced mother," YiaYia had explained.

I considered taking the pencil without saying anything, as if my purpose was something to be hidden. But I shook off that need for secrecy. What possible scandal could be attached to my spending some time sketching?

"YiaYia, I'm borrowing your pencil for an hour. I'll put it back when I'm done."

She stopped stirring the octopus ragout in the pot on the stove and waved her hand to send me on my way to do whatever I intended with the pencil.

Rough paper that had been wrapped around packages from Nota's shop filled a basket near the stove. I plucked a large sheet, smoothed out its folds, and left the house. I deliberately turned away from the house and strode up the path that I had first walked with Irini when she took me to the chapel. It wove in and out of the forest, sometimes in shadow and other times in the brilliant light at the edge of the sea. The way was rough, strewn with rocks and thick with tree roots bordering the path, forcing me to slow my pace and take care with every step, especially at the cliff's edge. I passed the clearing with the chapel and continued to climb, finally reaching a spot where I could go no higher. A glimpse of red clay tiles on the roof of the house below me was visible beneath the canopy of pine trees. I sat on a ledge covered with moss and wiped the sweat from my face with the edge of my skirt. Tilting my head to the sun, I absorbed its warmth. Leo had teased me that I would lose my Viennese complexion before long, and he was right.

I had seen this same landscape for over a hundred days since my arrival. At times, it had been shrouded in mist, with only memory delineating its contours. Today, the angle of the sun sharply defined the rocky ledges, the needles of the Aleppo pines, and the tender leaves of emerging undergrowth. Here and there, spring flowers nestled among the subtle greenery.

At first, I had intended to draw a broad swath of the landscape—the sea on the horizon, the rising cliff on the side of the cove opposite my vantage point, and the densely growing trees that flourished throughout the island and contributed a major source of its economy. But my eye was drawn from the expansive distance to a minute aspect of nature. I rose from the ledge and moved toward an oak tree. Circling its trunk was a cascade of striated fungus with ruffled edges. When I got closer, I examined the delicate pattern and reached out to touch it. It had an earthy odor and a spongy texture. Its flared edges and variegated colors in spirals of brown, orange, and green fascinated me. I wished I had paints or pastels to capture the variations in color, but had to satisfy my desire to reproduce the fungus with only shades of pale gray to black.

I sat on the ground on a patch of soft moss, took up the pencil, and began to sketch the fungus, line by line—some razor thin and others achieved by placing the side of the pencil flat against the paper. At first, my hand was tentative and the image was small and tight. I was trying too hard, approaching the task with rigidity rather than willingness.

I wanted to crumple the paper. My attempted sketch was an embarrassment caused by my own inactivity, my own unwillingness to lift myself out of an emotional paralysis that had become far more confining than my father's decision to banish me from Vienna. But I only had the one sheet with me. I turned it over, flexed my fingers, and began again.

In recent years, practice had made me far more adept at capturing faces, but I dismissed my lack of experience with other forms as a weak excuse for the poor quality of the product. The natural world had presented me with a challenge, and I was going to rise to meet it.

As a schoolgirl, I'd been required to keep a notebook of daily sketches of simple objects that I encountered in the course of the day. The practice was an exercise to train our eyes in observation and our hands in recreating what we saw. I had put away the notebook years before, but the lessons I'd learned in filling it had not abandoned me.

I asked myself what I was trying to accomplish with this sketch. The answer was to bring to the page my awe and fascination with an element of nature that was both beautiful and poisonous. That fungus was sapping the life out of the tree to which it had attached itself. A minute spore caught by the wind had burrowed its way into the bark and bloomed, flourishing while it robbed the tree of its own life force.

The very specific definition of my drawing, so precise and almost architectural, was a far cry from the exuberant vitality of Elise's painting and the work of Andreas and his colleagues in Vienna. But I felt the discipline of the exercise was necessary to my fledgling attempt to recapture the joy of my childhood pastime. I needed to prove to myself that I could first recreate what I saw in the world. The time to develop my vision would only come later.

In the following days, I scavenged for bits of paper while also wearing down YiaYia's pencil, which I had to take a knife to several times to whittle a sharp point. I wandered around the garden or through the house, seeking out objects to draw. YiaYia noticed the growing stack of paper scraps and turned them over one by one. Occasionally, a smile of recognition would light up her face.

"These are quite good, Maya. I remember the drawings your father sent in letters when you were a girl. Even then, you had an eye for transforming the world around you into something magical. It's a gift."

YiaYia's praise pierced my armored heart. I had anesthetized myself against the pain of loss caused by my exile using not the laudanum of anxious Viennese matrons or the opium of intense young men in the artists' quarter but rather the sheer force of my will. When my grandmother's words broke through the protective armor, however, I found myself crying. I had a gift, a gift that I had denied in my pursuit of power as Andreas's muse.

I wiped away the tears, feeling foolish. YiaYia's words were only a grandmother's loving opinion, not a review in the *Neues Wiener Tagblatt*. Nevertheless, they had awakened a long dormant joy. Beyond the pleasure that creating the drawings had given me, my art had brought my grandmother a moment of delight, and I knew I needed that sense of purpose. I wanted something I created to move people. I wanted to make more magic.

Chapter Nineteen

THE GOLDBERGS CAME FOR tea three days later. They attempted, with their rudimentary Greek, to converse with YiaYia. Oscar's Greek was the language of the ancients. YiaYia finally got up and made excuses about a new baby and mother she needed to visit and left us to pick up in German, where we—at least I—desperately needed the conversation to proceed.

I delved in like a starving sailor finally on terra firma stuffing himself with meat and vegetables after enduring hardtack and raw fish for months at sea. We talked of Vienna, the Secession, and another women's exhibition at Salon Pisko. Oscar regaled us with tales of his travels to India and Persia. He revealed he was writing a novel but would not discuss its topic.

Elise teased him. "Artists have no way to hide their works in progress the way writers can tuck their notebooks in a drawer and lock them away from prying eyes."

"You could always cover your canvas with a cloth," he retorted.

"But as soon as I am out on the hillside, it's exposed once again for anyone to see. I can't bear being confined in a studio, so I must work en plein air. I want to paint landscapes to capture nature's beauty and wildness and strangeness. It's simply not possible if I'm surrounded by walls. I need to absorb the atmosphere with every sense, not just my sight."

I was enthralled by her description of her process, and also by the banter between brother and sister. As an only child, even though I had cousins in both Vienna and Skiathos, I'd never experienced the ease and intimacy I saw on display between Oscar and Elise.

I rose to get more sweets from the kitchen. Both of them had devoured the *Hamalia*, cookies made from ground almonds, sugar and orange blossom water, exclaiming over their deliciousness. Elise had licked her fingers clean of the dusted sugar. When I returned with a platter of baklava, I found her standing by a chest near the window. In her hand was a sheaf of papers, my drawings. I knew I hadn't left them out, but then remembered YiaYia stopping by the chest before she left the house. She must have put them there. Elise was shifting through the stack, taking in the images one by one.

"Who made these drawings? I couldn't quell my curiosity after I saw the first one."

I put the tray down and somehow found my voice. "They're mine."

I could have downplayed their importance to me, called them only informal sketches, and feigned indifference. But I didn't. I waited.

Finally, she spoke. "You have both a remarkable eye and an exciting technique. I don't think I've ever seen such depth and variety of strokes. Did you only use a pencil? It's extraordinary what you've managed to achieve with such a simple medium. I thought you told me you hadn't painted since childhood."

"I hadn't, but after meeting you that day in the meadow, I came home and started to draw again. Our conversation prompted me to ask myself why I hadn't continued with my art. There were no paints in the house, so I improvised with a pencil."

"Well, your improvisations are quite remarkable. And you haven't had any instruction since you were a schoolgirl?"

I shook my head.

"Maya, you must continue. You have talent that shouldn't be allowed to atrophy. But you need to develop it, give it a strong foundation."

"That's very kind of you to say, Elise, but I'm not sure that's possible. You haven't been on Skiathos long, so you may not realize that such an opportunity for any kind of training simply doesn't exist here. There are no art teachers, not even an informal group of artists."

"Oh, I've noticed. We've never been anywhere like this before, where we haven't been able to find kindred souls pursuing their vision and sharing their interpretations. It's been quite lonely."

"Now, Elise, I warned you Skiathos was isolated."

"I know, Oscar. I know you wanted to write in peace without being bombarded every evening in a coffeehouse with some nascent poet's excruciating exploration of death and love. But I wasn't expecting to be so lonely and hungry for intelligent conversation. Your company is wonderful, dear brother, but we know each other too well."

"I've been lonely, too." I wanted to call the words back as soon as I said them and almost slapped my hand against my mouth as a rebuke. Instead, I grabbed the tray of baklava and thrust it in front of Elise.

"More sweets?"

Elise looked at me. I'm sure my face was bright red.

"Of course you're lonely. I've only been here two weeks, and I'm falling asleep over my book in the evenings instead of arguing about the role of art in the modern world. I can't imagine what it's been like for you."

Elise plucked a square of baklava from the platter. "It was such serendipity that you were picking flowers in the meadow I was painting the other day, like we were meant to encounter each other. I have an idea. Would you be willing to paint with me this summer? We could share paints. I have more than enough, and we could critique each other. We could form our own women painters group, a *Frauenkunstverein*."

"I would love that. But I'll need more than pigments if I'm to develop my talent."

"Then allow me to be your instructor. I've given art lessons in Vienna and various other places we've traveled to and stayed in for a while."

"That is so generous of you, but I must pay you."

"I would be more than satisfied if you paid me in pastries."

"It would be my pleasure, but I can't meet you every day to paint. I have responsibilities here." I waved my hand around the house.

"Understood. Perhaps we could meet once a week. Would next Thursday suit you? We could meet in the meadow. I'll bring my supplies, and we can get started."

After Elise and Oscar left, as I gathered up the coffee cups, I marveled at how the day had been unlike any other since my arrival. It had lifted my spirits not only to be speaking German but to be discussing art and the life I left behind. I thought the reminder of all I had lost might have provoked me to despondency, but Elise's vivacity and generosity of spirit had instead offered me a bit of home and hope. She had even at one point said we would be creating a Little Vienna, the three of us. She included Oscar in our club, and I realized how much I had missed a masculine perspective. Oh, I was surrounded by men here—my grandfather, my uncles, my cousins—but on Skiathos, men and women led separate lives. Divisions were pronounced. The lines between men's work and women's work were not to be crossed.

Oscar was unlike the Skiathan men I knew, but he was also unlike Andreas and the other artists in that circle. Perhaps it could be chalked up to his being a writer and not a painter. Elise had identified one difference between the two—how closely a writer can hold his work in progress, while most of the artists I knew tended to splash their pigments boldly onto canvases and vociferously proclaim that their art revealed humanity's true face.

When YiaYia returned, she found me in the kitchen washing up.

"Did you have a good visit? The man who could only speak ancient Greek, was he able to converse in modern German?" She smiled. "The sister is the strong one, not only because she spoke better Greek." She put her apron on and began to gather the vegetables to prepare dinner.

"You only spoke to them for a few minutes. How did you make that judgment?"

She touched her finger to her head. "I have to understand a situation quickly as a healer. She is the one making decisions for them. He appears content to let her. So what did she decide? Will you see her again?"

"I should no longer be amazed by you, YiaYia, but I am. Yes, she led the conversation. She invited me to paint with her and offered to share her materials. I won't have to wear your pencil down to a nub."

I joined my grandmother at the table and helped her peel potatoes, carrots, and onions. At one point, she reached over and patted my hand.

"It's good you'll be using these hands to make something beautiful."

The following Thursday at seven in the morning, I headed for the meadow with a jug of tea, an egg sandwich, a full tray of baklava wrapped in paraffin wax paper, a wide-brimmed hat, and one of YiaYia's old aprons.

Elise was already in the meadow, her easel assembled and a wooden box open on the grass beside her, filled with an array of pigments in tubes and small bottles of linseed oil and turpentine.

As I got closer, I was jolted by the smells, which pulled me back to Andreas's studio so suddenly it caused me to gasp.

"Are you unwell?" Elise's face reinforced the concern in her voice.

"I'm quite well. Just remembering how much I missed these familiar aromas."

"Please help yourself. I've prepared a canvas for you. It's propped up against that boulder. We'll have to find a carpenter who perhaps can replicate my easel. So what do you want to paint today?"

"I'm not sure yet. I'll wander for a few minutes. Please don't let me disturb you."

She picked up her brush. "Very well. I have only one piece of advice: Begin boldly. Your drawings are quite precise, almost architectural, which suits the medium of pencil and paper well. But paint is more freeing, at least for me. See color before you examine the details. Observe the light as it becomes obscured by clouds or spills over the hillside unimpeded."

And so I wandered, letting my eyes sweep over the landscape. I remembered Elise speaking the other day about absorbing the outdoors through all one's senses, not just sight. I had moved away from her paint box and lost the studio smells, but what wafted toward me on a gentle wind was the aroma of spring, of green shoots and yellow pollen. I sat down, removed my boots and stockings, and felt the moist earth between my toes. I heard humming and fluttering and chirping. As Elise had suggested, my eyes registered swaths of color.

And then I picked up the canvas, a brush, and a palette, and I began to paint.

Chapter Twenty

Elise and I painted until late afternoon. After cleaning her brushes, she wandered over to my canvas, sat on the grass, and studied it. Her arms were folded, as if to keep her hands still so they did not reach for my brush.

"How do you feel about your first day?"

I shrugged. "I am more adept at recognizing the success or failure of someone else's art."

She raised her eyebrows. She seemed on the verge of asking me, "Whose art?" but then held back. I was relieved. I shouldn't have intimated that I was close enough to any artist who would listen to my opinion.

"Come now, Maya, surely you have some feeling about what you've attempted here, and I am emphasizing the word 'feeling.' I'm not some professor at the University of Vienna full of pompous ideas about what is and isn't art. What do you feel?"

"Honestly, I feel uneasy. I feel stiff, like some rusted piece of machinery that has sat unused for too long. I started the day full of expectation, open to the suggestion you made to pay attention to all my senses, but when I look at this canvas, I see nothing of the energy I wanted to convey. Like my drawings, this feels too precise, too literal."

"Good!"

"How is that good? I've always believed good art to be deeply expressive of human emotion, revealing layers of passion or joy or despair. This"—I gestured with my brush to the canvas—"is an accurate rendition of a meadow that could have been captured with a camera."

Elise stood up and approached the canvas. "A photo cannot recreate the depths that I see here. It cannot layer color over color, revealing the myriad shades in a single bloom stirred by the wind. I see the eye and hand of a singular artist in this painting. This is your interpretation of the meadow, albeit still tentative. My assessment is that you have a great deal you want to say with your art. You are only at the beginning of discovering how to say it."

She smiled. "Now clean your brushes and let's eat some of your grandmother's baklava."

After we'd eaten and packed up, we walked together to the road where our paths diverged, one path leading to the guesthouse of the widow Asimina and the other to my grandparents' home.

"I will see you again on Thursday," she said. "Until then, try transforming one of your sketches into color."

When I returned home, I opened the gate to the garden and deposited my canvas and the box of paints Elise had given me on the bench outside the house. Then I paced back and forth in front of the painting, trying to see what Elise had seen. Was this the work of a nascent talent, as yet untrained but with a developing vision? Or was it simply a schoolgirl's assignment, good enough to meet the standards of Notre Dame de Sion, technically proficient but lacking a soul? Settling on the latter possibility, I decided the painting said nothing. I wanted to slash the lifeless canvas, but the material was too precious.

Instead, I opened a tube of titanium white and painted over the poppy-filled meadow.

When I entered the house, YiaYia was in the kitchen gutting a fish.

"Yiannis brought it from his catch today. Too small for the market, but it's enough to make a fish soup for us."

"Do you need some help?"

"Of course. How did the painting go with Elise?"

"Fine." I didn't want to reveal my disappointment or show her the now blank canvas. I took out my frustrations on the onions and potatoes. After supper, I made excuses about being tired after a full day outside and went up to bed.

YiaYia and Pappou exchanged knowing glances. I had expected Pappou to grumble something about painting not being work, but he was uncharacteristically silent. I lit the oil lamp on my dresser and turned to undress, then stopped short when I noticed a package on my bed. At first, my heart raced with a foolish thought that Andreas had found me and sent me a letter, but the parcel was too bulky. Had my mother sent a gift, books, or clothing?

I tried to still my excitement, but it had been a while since my mother had written. There was no address on the package, neither directing it to me nor indicating who had sent it. With disappointment, I recognized the wrapping paper and string. It was the same paper I used for my drawings, from Nota's shop. Perhaps YiaYia had bought me a pair of boots. She had fussed about how wet the meadows were at this time of year. My hopes dashed of finding anything remotely pleasing, I unwrapped the package, saving the string and carefully flattening the paper to use for my drawings.

But as I turned over the last fold, I looked in amazement at a collection of art supplies—a thick pad of paper, charcoal, graphite pencils, ink, and a pen with several different size nibs. I searched for a card or some indication of who had sent it. When I didn't find one, I assumed it was another gift from Elise.

The fatigue I'd felt earlier left me. I set everything out on the table next to my bed and fingered each implement. A knock on my door interrupted my reverie. It was YiaYia.

"You found the package?"

"Yes. When did it arrive? Did Nota say who purchased it?"

"She didn't need to."

"So it was Elise?"

A look of pain passed over her face. "No, Maya, it wasn't Elise."

I was confused. Had YiaYia herself purchased the materials?

"It was from you, YiaYia? Thank you!"

She shook her head sadly, and I remembered the look that had passed between my grandparents before I came upstairs.

"Pappou bought me these materials?" I was incredulous.

"Pappou is not so blind to who you are and what you desire, Maya. He saw the drawings and how you save every scrap of paper. He blustered about you thinking we were too poor to afford paper and went marching down to Nota's. He would have bought out her entire stock for you, Maya, not out of pride but out of love. He's not forgotten what you did for him. This is how he expresses his thanks."

"I am so sorry for assuming it was Elise. I'll go and thank him right now."

YiaYia put out her hand to stop me. "I have a better idea. Draw him a picture and leave it quietly for him. He's a man who doesn't make or want a big fuss about anything. He didn't even want me to tell you the package was from him. That's why he left it on the bed instead of presenting it to you himself, but I suspected you might think it was from Elise. I only told you otherwise because I didn't want you to hurt him."

I grasped YiaYia's hands. "I don't want to hurt him either."

I kissed her cheeks, and she left me with a blessing, marking a cross on my forehead with one of her thumbs.

Over the next few days, I departed from my usual choice of subjects, the natural world or still lifes of household objects. Instead, I began to sketch my grandfather when he wasn't aware I was watching him. In one drawing, I captured his portrait—the lined face marking years spent at sea and his eyes revealing a world-weary intelligence. In others, I drew full-length images of him leaning on the pasture fence, watching the new goats cavort on the grass.

I finished the drawings in pen and ink with a wash for shadows and background, then hung them to dry in my room. When they were ready, I slipped them onto his plate at the dinner table.

That night when he sat down, he picked them up, one in each hand, his eyes moving from one to another. Then he glanced across the table at me.

"A good likeness."

"Efcharisto, Pappou."

After completing the drawings of Pappou, I realized that my next painting with Elise should not be another landscape. When we met at our usual spot, I brought the painted-over canvas and one of the sketches I'd made of Pappou. Using the drawing as a starting point, I transferred an outline of his image to the canvas with a thin brush dipped in a thinned-out burnt sienna. Then, with color, I created an entirely different version of Pappou than the pen and ink drawings. The rustiness of my skills that had been apparent in the brushstrokes of my first painting was scrubbed away. My arms felt looser, and my hand no longer cramped as it held the brush. I felt a fluidity to both the shape and the coloring of my grandfather's image. I painted him, not as a literal version of my memory of him but as my sense of him. I was beginning to grasp what Elise had meant about not only seeing my subject but also feeling it deep in my core.

I was surprised by the tenderness that surfaced in the portrait. His face still contained the gruffness and cynicism that eighty years on this earth had shaped, but it held much more than just that. I had learned that my grandfather was more complex than the image he portrayed of an astute businessman and powerful head of a prosperous family. His quiet generosity and devoted love of his wife also made up who he was.

Elise examined the portrait with concentration and then looked at me.

"Although I haven't met him, I know who this man is, purely on the basis of your painting. Brava, my friend."

My days took on a rhythm after completing the portrait of Pappou. Although Elise and I met only once a week, on the other days I rose before dawn, and after my coffee, painted for a few hours until YiaYia needed me. She gave me an old cotton coat to wear while I painted when it became clear that an apron was barely sufficient to protect my dress. My strokes, which had been so tentative and unsure that first day I had painted with Elise, became energetic and muscular. I felt as if I were dancing as I approached and receded from the canvas. The physicality of my process often meant that not all the paint ended up on the canvas. I sometimes finished with not only a colorful coat but also a green cheek or a turquoise eyebrow.

The seeds planted by the challenging questioning of both Elise and Leo had taken root. I was no longer haunted by the words that had provoked me to take up YiaYia's pencil. Why aren't you painting? Aren't you a painter?

My painting became both a release of my emotions and a balm smoothing the jagged edges that my exile had inflicted on my soul. But it also opened me up to the longing for Andreas that I had suppressed—a searing need for the intensity, for the challenges, and, yes, for the touch. I poured my yearning onto the canvas, but it was a poor substitute for the double-sided sword of our love. I was still cut off from what had fed my spirit, and I still hungered for it.

Had I been in Vienna, would I have plucked a few of my best paintings and dared to present them to Andreas for critique? A part of me admitted to my reluctance to open myself to his appraisal. Our relationship was deeply entangled with our roles as artist and muse. How would he react if I stepped into his milieu? But I realized with a wry acknowledgment that if I were in Vienna, I would not have produced any art at all. There would have been nothing to reveal to Andreas.

Chapter Twenty-One

MY COUSIN LEO HAD been trying to coax me to join him for an evening with young people. I had resisted until one evening when YiaYia spoke bluntly to me.

"Maya, when your father brought you here, it was not to punish you but to protect you. You're not a prisoner here. I'm an old woman, but I still remember what it felt like to dance. Go with your cousin. Let go of the shadows you've brought into this house. Even if it's just for an hour."

After Leo arrived, we walked down the hill in companionable silence. He seemed to recognize that gloating about my acquiescence would probably provoke me, and wisely kept his mouth shut. I considered him like a brother, with all the aggravation that entails, but I never doubted that he cared about me. We could hear the music before we reached the square.

"What's the occasion?"

"Have you been away so long that you've forgotten the feast of Klidonas? It's Saint John's Eve."

As we drew closer, I could see the bonfires and hear the shouts and cheers as young men and boys leapt over glowing coals. Piles of freshly harvested oregano filled baskets on the steps of the church. The air was thick with smoke from the fires and the pungent aroma of oregano. I was a child of ten the last time I'd been on Skiathos during Klidonas. I remembered hovering on the periphery as the older girls in the village had carried out the ritual that would reveal their future husbands. I had chafed at being too young to participate, and my mother had dismissed the practice as primitive, pulling me out of the house where the young women had gathered.

"Do the girls in the village still perform the divination ceremony?"

Leo raised his eyebrows. "Are you hoping to dream of your lover tonight?"

"I detect some mockery, dear cousin. I'm simply curious."

"If you want to join in, I'm sure Irini would take you along. You surprise me, Maya. Perhaps you are rediscovering your Greek roots."

I shrugged. I didn't know what I wanted. We set out to find Irini.

We found Irini in the midst of a group of young women bubbling with excitement. All of them were dressed in elaborately embroidered jackets with fringed scarves wrapped around their heads. I wished I had carried a sketchbook with me so I could capture both the vivid plumage on display and the effervescence radiating from the group. Leo gestured to Irini, and she left the circle to join us. Her face was flushed, and she danced across the cobblestones. Her necklace of bronze discs and beads tinkled as she approached, matching her joyful mood.

"Maya, you came! Leo was determined to help you escape, but I didn't believe he would succeed."

She grabbed my hand. "You should come with me to the ceremony. Do you remember it?"

I looked at Leo. Was this his plan from the beginning, to pull me into the life of the island?

Leo kissed us both on the cheek. "I'm off to jump over some coals and find a large bottle of ouzo. Come to Manolis's when you're finished."

Irini brought me to the others and introduced me. Despite my Greek features, which had been so unusual in Vienna, I was acutely conscious of how different I was from these young women. But Irini's enthusiasm pulled me in, and I linked arms with her as we started to walk.

"We're gathering at Olympia's house. Did Leo tell you I was chosen to draw the water from the well? It's such an honor and a responsibility."

Irini babbled the entire way, and I smiled to myself as I imagined the effort it would take for her to carry the water later without speaking. The water used in the ceremony was called *omilito neró,* silent water, because the woman carrying it must do so without saying a word.

"Will you come with me to the well?" Irini was sixteen, and I remembered myself at that age. Innocent and protected, but longing for experience of the world, a world that was both exciting and terrifying. What would Irini dream tonight? What lover would reveal himself to her?

When everyone had arrived at Olympia's house, her yi-ayia welcomed the girls and reminded them of the sacred nature of the ritual. The water Irini carried would be poured into a clay pot, and each young woman would drop a belonging into the vessel. The pot would be bound in red fabric and prayers offered before being brought outside for the night—an offering to call forth dreams of the man each was meant to marry.

Some of the younger girls, Irini's age, giggled and whispered. I could understand how the romance of the tradition would appeal to them. For the women closer to my age, I could see the longing in their faces, in the way they held their bodies. Whether the man of their dreams lived down the road or only in their imaginations, they were pulled toward the vessel of water with both hope and desire.

Irini was bouncing on her feet, anxious to begin. When the grandmother gave her blessing, Irini and I made our way swiftly toward the well. For all her chattering earlier, Irini was now quiet, carrying the pitcher she would use to transport the water. At the well, she filled the pitcher to the brim and then turned back to the house. Her silence and her slow steps were a sharp contrast to her exuberance earlier. She had fully embraced her role, and I could see that the ritual was truly sacred to her.

I wondered what my Viennese friends would think of this feast, what they would think of me for taking part in it. Even though I considered myself an outsider, only an observer, I could understand why the women did it.

The door was flung open as we arrived, and Irini held the pitcher high as she approached the clay pot on a table in the middle of the room. With a flourish, she poured the water. One by one, the women drew near and removed an earring or a bracelet or a medal, murmuring a few words and dropping the objects into the pot. Irini was the last to approach, but before she let go of the necklace that had made music, she turned to me and whispered, "What will you offer Maya? Do you not have a dream to be fulfilled?"

I was about to shake my head in denial. I didn't need ancient magic. But Irini's question stopped me. The longing I had sensed in the other women was as palpable as the hidden desires the artists in Vienna were attempting to reveal in their raw and passionate paintings. I felt something stir in me and reached around my neck to unclasp the chain that held the ring Andreas had given me. I had been wearing it ever since I had left Vienna with my father. It was warm to the touch, retaining the heat of my body. I dropped the ring, chain included, into the vessel and stepped back. My heart was pounding and I felt lightheaded, relinquishing control as I let go of the ring. Olympia led the prayers around the pot as two of the young women covered the top with a red silk shawl.

I bowed my head as I listened to the chanting. Although I understood the words, I did not join in the prayers. When the prayers were finished, the women gathered at the door, led by Olympia carrying the bowl.

"What now?" I whispered to Irini.

"We'll follow Olympia to the garden, and she'll place the vessel outside under the stars. Our prayers and wishes will rise to the heavens during the night and return to us in our dreams."

She squeezed my hand as we left the house. Once the pot swathed in red had been left on a stone in the garden, the women dispersed. Most, like Irini and I, were headed toward the beach, where bonfires had been lit and where the chances of discovering the object of one's dreams were far greater than in a secluded garden. At the beach, we found Leo.

"Ready to leap into a new life, Maya?" He pointed to the line of people that had formed, all of whom were waiting to jump over the coals.

"Oh come, Maya!" Irini was pulling me toward the glowing embers. "You've done only part of the feast day rituals."

She tucked her skirt up around her belt and moved toward the bonfire. I did the same and took off my shoes to make it easier to run. Shouts and cheers accompanied every attempt to leap. Some of the young men ahead of us were quite drunk, and I suspected many of them would be nursing burned feet the next morning. When it was our turn, Irini went first, running furiously toward the fire and lifting her skirts as she sailed over the coals. She was laughing as she landed on the other side. I took measure of the distance and focused on the far side of the bonfire. At first I was hesitant, but then I remembered the girl I had once been on this island and took off as fast as I could. After a few seconds of disbelief, I managed to get to the far side of the bonfire. It had felt astonishing to be up and over the coals with the heat reaching its tentacles for my feet.

After we retrieved our shoes, Leo guided us to a table outside a taverna in the square. While we waited for our vanilla sodas, I removed a few hairpins and knotted my chignon at the nape of my neck.

"Let your hair down, Maya. It will only come undone again when we are dancing."

I was about to protest about the dancing but stopped myself. I had already embraced every other tradition of Saint John's Eve. Why stop now? I shook out my hair.

"Take me dancing." I grabbed Irini's and Leo's hands and pulled them away from the table. Leo led us toward the group of dancers and my dress floated around me in ripples as we raised our hands and moved into the circle of the *Kamara*, the traditional dance of Skiathos. The music of the square had a rhythm and an energy to it that seemed to enter the bloodstream of each dancer, consume their thoughts, and take over their bodies. We all became one organism, moving in unison, and danced until we were exhausted, exhilarated, euphoric. I collapsed against Leo's chest, laughing.

"Thank you," I said, and kissed him on the cheek.

Leo linked arms with each of us. "Let's get you two home to your dreams."

YiaYia was waiting up for me, reading in the parlor. She closed her book when she saw me standing in the doorway and appraised my appearance.

"You're no longer wearing the chain around your neck."

My observant grandmother missed nothing. I felt the blood rising to my cheeks.

"Did you place it in the Klidonas bowl?"

I nodded, hoping not to be the recipient of a lecture on the inappropriate choice I had made in matters of love. But instead, YiaYia approached me and kissed my cheeks.

"I remember the night of Klidonas when I dreamt of your grandfather. I'm not a superstitious woman, Maya." She waved her hand toward the bookcases lining the walls. "I read too much, or so the town harpies tell me. But Klidonas is more than superstition. The ancient mysteries are powerful, and our dreams reveal more to us than the romantic wishes of girls full of longing for love. I've read Freud. Don't look surprised."

"I'm not surprised, YiaYia, only awed."

"Pay attention to what you dream tonight, Maya. It may be a visitation from your lover, but be open to other loves that may make themselves known to you. Now, I'm weary from reading by this lamp. I'm off to my own dreams."

I followed YiaYia up the stairs and retired to my room. She hadn't needed to be explicit about other loves. I knew she was planting a seed that might or might not take root in my unconscious. I had learned over the years that my grandmother had an infinite supply of patience—for my sometimes taciturn Pappou, for the children and grand-children whose needs and desires filled her hours and her home. She would wait.

I slept the sleep of exhaustion and hope. Like YiaYia, I was not superstitious, but a night of chanting in prayer and leaping over the bonfire under the moonlight had awakened my Greek roots. Several dreams filled the hours before dawn. Andreas did indeed make an entrance.

Where are you? I need you. My art is drying up without you.

The curious element of the dream was that rather than being a thousand miles away, I was in the same room. But instead of facing him as his model, I was turned away toward my own easel. The tree fungus I had first sketched when I began to create art again was on the canvas, coming alive under my hand. In the dream, Andreas reached out for me and I shook off his touch.

The other dreams were more fleeting, reaching back in memory to childhood and snatches of conversation not meant for a child's ear. My Viennese grandmother telling my mother I had returned from Skiathos a heathen, sun-browned and wild. I woke from that dream remembering the shame and anger I had felt at the age of ten. I sat up abruptly in bed, shaken and grateful it had only been a dream. The summer I was eleven, I stopped coming to Skiathos during my vacation. Miserable and lonely that initial summer, missing my cousins, I gradually adapted. I forgot the joy and freedom that had been mine on Skiathos.

I couldn't sleep after that, and left my bed. I wandered down to the kitchen in my dressing gown and fed some wood into the stove to make a pot of coffee. When it was ready, I took my cup outside to the terrace and watched the sunrise. Pappou found me there on his way to tend to his goats. He didn't stop to speak, but merely acknowledged me with a wave. I took a final gulp of the thick, dark liquid and went back inside to dress. YiaYia wasn't awake yet. No surprise, since she had stayed up so late to wait for me. I pulled on a simple dress and grabbed an apron from the kitchen before gathering my painting supplies and setting up my easel on the terrace.

I lost track of time until I heard Irini in the kitchen chattering with YiaYia. I stepped inside to join them.

"Maya, I brought your ring and chain from the Klidonas vessel. Did you dream? Did you see your love?" She held out the jewelry, and I put it in my pocket. If YiaYia noticed that I didn't replace the chain around my neck, she didn't say anything.

Chapter Twenty-Two

ELISE AND I CONTINUED to paint, and as a result, our friendship flourished. I was struck by the lack of rivalry between us. Although we had begun as mentor and beginner, through Elise's generosity of spirit, we became peers. In contrast, I had been aware of an undercurrent of tension among Andreas's circle of artist friends. They were constantly comparing each other's success—who got a show or what the critics said about it.

Perhaps Elise and I weren't rivals because we weren't competing. There were no galleries or art critics on Skiathos. We painted without the pressure of convincing a dealer to exhibit our work or a critic to review it.

We spent more time together as the summer progressed, not only painting, but also walking the beaches, picnicking, and devouring YiaYia's pastries over tea. Occasionally, Elise pried Oscar away from his writing desk to join us for tea or a walk. Oscar was unlike other men I'd known, perhaps because he embodied contradictions. He was both a merchant seaman and a scholar, well traveled and also well read.

One day at the beach, we all trudged along the sand in our bare feet, he with his trousers rolled up and Elise and I with our skirts hitched to avoid their getting soaked by the waves. Elise had wandered ahead, gathering sea-smoothed stones.

"I saw the Secession exhibition of Brenner's paintings."

I stopped, but said nothing. Why had he kept this to himself all these months? Had he told Elise? It was not something I had expected to follow me to Skiathos.

"I'd also seen some of Brenner's earlier work. It was not even comparable to what was on display at the Secession. It was as if it had been painted by a different artist. The difference was the model. The difference was you."

"What is the point of this revelation?" I asked as I turned to face him.

"I believe you had a profound effect on his work, not just as his model but as his muse. I'm fascinated by the idea of the Muse—the power wielded, of course, but also the sacrifice, the sublimation, of the Muse's own creativity in service to another. I haven't seen any of your paintings, but Elise tells me you have a profound gift. Is that why you left Brenner, to free yourself to make your own art?"

A part of me wished to turn away, retrieve my shoes and stockings, and leave. I felt more naked than I had been modeling for Andreas. But I stayed because I was both outraged and curious.

"Why have you waited until now to tell me you knew who I was? Why provoke me now? Or have you been like some

explorer observing a rare creature in the wild, waiting to
see what I would do?"

"I didn't recognize you at first. It was only a few days
ago, when you and Elise were deep in discussion, that I
realized the woman in the paintings was you. I couldn't
hear what you and Elise were saying, but the subject was
one that seemed to elicit intense feeling in you. It was
the expression on your face, a kind of unguarded passion,
that triggered my memory of the painting—the one that
embodied longing and touched a hidden part of my soul,
just as you intended."

"Yes, that was my intention. It is what I believe great art
must do—reach our innermost being."

"I've been fascinated by you since we met. You are such
an enigma, a barely restrained energy bound to this island
and your people. Here, yet not here; belonging, and yet a
stranger. Why have you hidden yourself here? To escape
Brenner?"

I barely knew Oscar—he had joined Elise and me only
a few times on our excursions—and yet his acute observations rang true, except for his assumption that I was hiding
from Andreas. I found myself drawn to Oscar in ways that
were different from the comfortable sisterhood I'd found
with Elise or the searing and dangerous passion I had with
Andreas. I trusted Oscar.

"I'm here because I was banished by my father. The
scandal caused by the exhibition horrified him and also
threatened the good name of my family, as well as his business. It was not my choice. Despite my despair at being

separated from Brenner and the world I knew, my exile here has brought some surprises. Meeting Elise reminded me of what I lost in devoting myself to Brenner. I would not have started painting if Elise hadn't asked me why I wasn't. And meeting you has challenged me even further with your questions."

"Will you go back to Vienna?"

"I must. I cannot stay here and continue to develop as an artist."

"What about Brenner? Will returning to him allow your art to flourish or will you be caught up in fulfilling his needs and not your own?"

I did not have an answer to his question. "I still love him," I responded. And then I asked a question of my own. "Have you ever loved someone?"

By this point in our conversation, Oscar and I had begun to walk again. What I had perceived as a provocation and confrontation—my feet firmly planted in the sand until I had extracted answers from him—had evolved into an intimacy I had not experienced before with a man, not even Andreas.

"Now who's being provocative?" He smiled and then answered, "Yes, I have loved before. I could tell you a tragic story in which she dies, driving me to seek consolation by writing a novel, but that would be a lie, and it appears we have moved to a level of truth telling with each other in a very short period of time. The truth is, she married someone else while I was at sea. I was more angry than devastated, but the loss did engender some soul searching and the decision to write."

"You're an unusual man, Oscar Goldberg."

"I'm going to assume that is a compliment," he said and smiled.

"You elicit honesty as well as display it. I've never revealed so much of my inner thoughts to anyone, much less a man, as I have today."

"Nor have I, Maya."

Once again, we stopped and faced each other. Something passed between us, an understanding and appreciation, an acknowledgment of a kindred sensibility. I had just told him I loved someone else, and I was filled with an overwhelming regret.

The unspoken connection between us was interrupted by Elise.

"Look what I found!" She held out her skirt, which she'd been using as a collection basket for the various detritus one finds at the shoreline. In the midst of the smooth stones and shell fragments was a perfectly formed conch shell, its interior a highly polished swirl of pink and orange. "I can't wait to paint this."

She was so pleased with her find that she seemed oblivious to what was simmering between Oscar and me. But the spell had been broken, and the three of us turned back to the dunes, where we'd left our shoes and the remnants of our picnic. As we climbed up from the beach, Oscar went ahead and then turned to offer Elise and me each a hand up the last steep section. When he took my hand, he lingered, a silent message in the pressure as he pulled me up to the top of the cliff. I felt safe.

A few days later, I went to paint with Elise. We had convinced Pappou to allow us to use an empty shepherd's hut on our family's pasture land in the hills. This enabled us to store our art supplies and easels, and offered a shelter from the weather if we needed it.

When I arrived, there was no sign of Elise. Under a tree with spreading branches I busied myself unfolding the easel a carpenter in Skiathos Town had built for me. I'd brought a sketch of YiaYia that I intended to use as the basis for a color portrait. When I looked up, I saw Oscar approaching, notebook in hand.

"Where's Elise?"

"She's feeling ill, and has begged off. I thought I'd keep you company. I'll write while you paint."

He found a comfortable spot on the ground, and we spent a few companionable, silent hours engaged in our respective work. When my hand needed a break, I retrieved a basket from the hut and offered him half of my egg sandwich and some wine.

"Would you be willing to read to me from your novel?"

He hugged the notebook protectively to his chest, seemingly in jest, but I detected a strong reluctance to let his words be heard. My desire to know more about him, to deepen this kinship we had formed, caused me to press the issue.

"Not only have you seen my naked body, but you've also encouraged me to bare my soul. I think it's time for some reciprocity."

I put my hand out for the notebook.

"My penmanship is poor. You may not be able to read my writing."

"Then read it aloud yourself."

And so he did.

I stretched out on the grass, closed my eyes, and listened. His writing, like his conversation, provoked and pierced. It delved into the fears of a protagonist modeled loosely on Oscar, a seafaring man seeking a father who had abandoned his family years before. The story was mesmerizing and compelling, a literary version of his sister's paintings.

When he stopped reading, I was breathless. I got up and knelt in front of him. The look on his face was one of both hope and fear. I took that expectant, anxious face in my hands and kissed him. He responded with gratitude that then melted into heat. I straddled his lap, wrapping my legs around him.

"I take it you liked the story," he murmured into my ear. The physical longing, the aching for human touch that I had quelled for so many months, burst out of me that afternoon.

I had enough sense to still the hand that started to slide under my skirt and up my thigh.

"Not here." I stood, took him by the hand, and led him to the hut. "The island has eyes," I told him as I unbuttoned his shirt. Making love to Oscar was an epiphany. To be touched in the flesh by someone who has touched your soul is to be devoured, consumed, and then, somehow miraculously, transformed—to become neither him nor I, but a new being that contained us both.

I wept.

"You knew I needed this. You came to me today to give me this gift. That's what it was, a gift. Thank you."

"I needed this as much as you did. So thank you."

We slept in each other's arms until the sun came through the window of the hut and sliced across my face. The brightness and the heat served as my clock, letting me know it was time to go.

I repinned my hair and brushed off the straw that had covered the dirt floor of the hut. When I opened the door, I was met by a blast of hot July air and the sound of bells hanging from the necks of Pappou's goats that grazed on the hillside. I motioned for Oscar to stay back while I gathered my easel and the partially finished canvas. Oscar's notebook was still on the ground, its pages fluttering in the wind. I grabbed it before one of the goats could get to it.

I returned to the hut and handed Oscar the notebook. Breaking the connection between us was excruciating, but if I stayed any longer we could risk discovery. I knew Pappou had only agreed to my using the hut with Elise because he made sure someone was watching the hillside periodically to assure our safety.

"You go first, down the northern path. Right now, there's no one here except the goats. I'll lock up and take the eastern route back."

"Can you come again tomorrow?"

I shook my head. "Not until next Thursday."

He kissed me, his lips skimming along my skin from the bottom of my ear to the middle of my collarbone. Then I pushed him out the door before I could succumb once more to his touch.

It was late afternoon when I returned to the house. YiaYia, whose perceptive eyes missed nothing, greeted me with a pointed observation.

"You stayed a long time painting today. You look flushed. Didn't you wear a hat?"

"I stayed under the tree. It was hot walking home. That's probably why my face is so red."

"Be more careful next time. If the redness doesn't subside, it's probably sunburn. I have some salve you can put on your face."

I kissed YiaYia and thanked her, but wondered how long I could continue to meet Oscar before she would suspect more than sunburn.

The memory of that afternoon was both sacred and carnal. Throughout the following week, I often become lost in a wave of sensation that pierced me with its clarity. I felt like a pilgrim who had crossed a spiritual barrier and found the utter peace of knowing and being known by another. I had feared that I might reveal myself to YiaYia with the agitation of waiting, but instead I felt an unusual calm, as if Oscar were physically at my side and not simply in my thoughts.

But that stillness was shattered after only a few days.

I received a note from Elise, asking if I could join her to paint in the afternoon, explaining that she had recovered and was eager to get back to her canvas. YiaYia had no need of me and waved me off.

"Your painting has settled you. Go, join your friend. She's been good for you."

I nearly ran up to the pasture, hoping the note had come not from Elise but from Oscar. But both were there. Elise's easel wasn't set up; Oscar was without his notebook. The look of torment on his face dispelled any hope I had of recreating the splendor and wonder of our previous meeting.

Elise reached out her hands to me. "Oh, thank goodness you could come! I couldn't bear it if we hadn't been able to see you."

"What has happened?" I looked from Elise to Oscar.

"We are leaving. We received a telegram this morning. Our Uncle Jakob is seriously ill and has begged us to come. He's our mother's brother and our only living relative," Elise explained. "He raised us after our parents died. We must go."

"You're returning to Austria? How soon?"

"Not Austria," Oscar answered. "Argentina, where he emigrated several years ago. We leave on the boat to Piraeus this evening. From there we'll travel first to Marseille and then on to South America. Our only hope is that we can arrive in time."

What passed between Oscar and me at his words was a shared anguish, a tearing apart of our hearts. What we had experienced in the hut had forged an essential bond, but that bond was fragile still. It needed nurturing. It needed time.

Elise broke into my stunned silence.

"I've already retrieved my easel and paints, but I will leave the unfinished canvas with you as a pledge we'll meet again and I'll complete it with you. Maya, I used to be content painting by myself, but your companionship these last few months has been an unexpected gift. You *must* continue to paint. Promise me that you will!"

"I promise."

"You and Oscar need to speak, so I will bid you *auf wiedersehen* here. We *will* see each other again. I am sure of it." Elise embraced me. "Take care. I know one day I'll see your work on display in Vienna."

She turned and walked down the hill.

"How much does she know about us?"

"Everything. She's my twin and I'm unable to conceal anything from her."

"At least she can be a comfort to you." I tried not to sound as utterly alone as I felt.

"Come with me to the hut." Oscar took me by the hand and I acquiesced, knowing that the moments we still had would be both brief and searing. I needed to touch him, and we could not in the open.

Inside the dimly lit shelter the mingled aromas of art and animal released an immersive memory of our lovemaking. I was overcome with a breathtaking need for him as he pulled me into his arms.

Unlike the first time, this physical encounter was desperate and grief-filled. I wanted to consume and be consumed, to be filled up with the memory of him as sustenance for the empty days ahead, for an unknown future. I was furious with the gods who had conspired against us to deny us the fulfillment of a love we had only just discovered, and transferred that fury into reckless desire.

I was trembling when we were finally spent, and he held me until I was still.

"I promise I will come back for you, wherever you are."

I wanted to believe him.

Chapter Twenty-Three

IN THE DAYS AFTER Elise and Oscar left, I slipped back into the melancholy and numbness that had marked my first months on Skiathos. I refused to go to the hut to paint. The memories were too raw.

YiaYia watched without saying anything, until we were in her workroom distilling summer herbs.

"Elise's departure has been a blow to you. It saddens me to see you withdraw back into isolation. I find it especially tragic that you have stopped painting."

"I've lost the will to paint. I was learning so much from Elise, and now, attempting to fill a canvas without her wise advice seems pointless and empty." It was the safest answer, deflecting with some truth to disguise the greater loss of Oscar.

"You've never struck me as someone who gives up, Maya. You have a gift, and denying both yourself and the world of that gift seems shameful. If you are reluctant to go back to the hut alone, take Irini with you. Teach her what you have learned from Elise."

Reluctantly, I agreed to YiaYia's counsel, which I knew was closer to an order than a suggestion. The following

Thursday, Irini and I climbed the hillside and I unlocked the hut for the first time since Oscar and I had said our final, desperate good-byes. I took a deep breath and entered the dusty, cobwebbed space. The light from the window fell on the straw-covered floor where we had lain. I thought that being here would rend me with pain, but instead of the memory of our last afternoon exacerbating my loss, it suffused me with wonder. Something extraordinary had happened here, and I knew I was supposed to embrace it.

"Are you OK?" Irini asked. "You look like you saw a ghost."

I smiled at her. "No ghost. I'm happy to be back here, remembering the joy that painting gives me. Thank you for coming with me."

"I'm excited to learn from you. YiaYia and Mama think what you teach me I may be able to translate into weaving. Shall I help you bring the paints and easel out?"

Irini's exuberance spilled over the hillside as we set up and began to paint. YiaYia, as usual, was right. In teaching Irini as Elise had guided me, I hadn't lost Elise.

One evening, Leo surprised me as I returned from Nota's shop and walked with me back to YiaYia's. It was unusual for him to do so, and I detected an urgency as he launched into an observation.

"You have lost the emptiness I remember from your early days here. Your art has helped. But despite whatever satisfaction your throwing paint at a canvas is bringing you, I believe you are still unhappy. The company of your family—of YiaYia and Pappou, of Irini and me—it's not enough."

"I have come to understand how loved I am by all of you and how deeply my Skiathan heritage has shaped me. But you're right, it's not enough. I've been torn from my life, my friends, my studies, my city. I don't belong here, Leo."

"Then what I have to tell you is important."

I looked at him, not sure what he was about to say.

"Your father is considering marrying you off to an islander as the only way to ensure that you never return to the life you had before."

I stopped in the middle of the path, horrified by his words. If I had I felt as though I had been thrust back centuries by my banishment to Skiathos, I'm sure that is exactly what my parents intended. Modern life as it was unfolding in twentieth-century Vienna was a threat, especially because of the way I had embodied the changes—with defiance, longing, and a plunging into the darkness of the human soul. I shivered at the reality Leo was presenting.

"How long has this been planned? How is it that you know?"

"I learned of it only this week, which is why I wanted to talk with you alone. YiaYia received a letter from your father and came to our house to talk with my mother, Theía Ekaterina, and Theía Anastasia. They didn't know I was there. I overheard the conversation. Your father asked YiaYia to find you a good match."

"Did YiaYia agree?" I couldn't believe she would be complicit in such a plan.

"It sounded like she was reluctant, but feared that the only other alternative your father would accept would be the convent."

I felt physically ill, overcome with a sense of despair deeper than any I had experienced since my arrival. I needed to be alone. I needed to think.

"Thank you, Leo. You are a true friend for letting me know."

"I agree with you, Maya. You don't belong here. If there is anything I can do to help you, please know that I will."

He hugged me and I left his arms to return to the house, where I retreated to my room. I couldn't sleep, my mind racing through a myriad of scenarios of how to thwart my father's plans. If Oscar were still here, I would have turned to him. But Oscar was beyond reach. And even if I could somehow get word to him, there wasn't time. By morning, the only alternative that had any hope of success was to reach out to Andreas and convince him to come for me.

At midday I brought Leo lunch down at the warehouse.

"Can you take a break and walk with me along the harbor?"

He agreed.

"Did you mean what you said last night, that you'll help me."

"In any way I can."

"If I give you a letter for Andreas, can you get it off the island without YiaYia and Pappou knowing?"

"Yes. I can be the conduit of letters from you to Vienna and any that come in return. I'm down at the warehouse very day. The mail boat leaves from the adjacent dock every week and I'm usually the one who picks up the post for the business and the family."

"Thank you, Leo!"

After Leo agreed to get a letter off the island and on its way to Andreas, I retrieved the stack of pages I'd written in the early days of my sojourn on Skiathos, untied the strip of fabric, and read through every one, from the earliest to the latest. None would do for the message I wanted to convey to Andreas. I took them all and threw them into the fire.

I was no longer the empty vessel who had arrived on Skiathos. With Oscar, I had discovered the possibility of a very different kind of relationship with a man. We had experienced passion as two equals, not as power to be wielded over the other. But in addition to the connection I had shared with Oscar, I had also absorbed the pull of family and the island's beauty and wonder. I could not deny that Skiathos was a part of me. I did not want to stay, but I knew I would take a part of the island with me when the time came to leave.

How much of what I had experienced did I want to share with Andreas? How much of my experience mattered to him? When I opened my writing desk, I sat motionless for a long time. While I was desperate to stop my father's plan to arrange a marriage with an islander, I was no longer willing only to be Andreas's muse. I knew Andreas was my one hope for escaping Skiathos. But how much would I have to sacrifice in order to do so?

My desperation led me to lie.

I appealed to Andreas as if I were still the Maya who had inspired his portraits. The Maya who had adored, encouraged, and awakened his genius. The Maya who was offering herself to him again, if only he would come and rescue her. There would be time enough, once we were together again, to reveal that I, too, was painting. I brushed aside an inner warning that the studio might not be big enough for two artists, not because of its physical size but because of the size of the artists' egos. I would deal with that when I was finally back in Vienna.

I sealed the letter, addressed it, and placed it in my prayer book for safekeeping until I could get it to Leo. The envelope lay alongside my drawing of Andreas, a memento of another time, another Maya.

The birthday of Leo's mother, Theía Maria, presented an opportunity for me to bring the letter to Leo. I tucked it into the pocket of my skirt and passed it to Leo in the orchard, where we had volunteered to harvest a basket of peaches. He slipped the envelope into his own pocket and promised to get it onto the mail boat.

"Have you heard anything more about my father's plans?"

"My mother and your father have been corresponding. She and YiaYia have been visiting with a few families with sons. 'Opening the conversation' is how it has been described to your father."

"How much time do you think I have?"

"It's not clear. From what I've heard from my mother, YiaYia is not satisfied with any of the prospects."

"I can't marry someone here, Leo."

"If I could, I would rescue you. I would marry you."

"You are rescuing me by taking the letter."

"I hope this man in Vienna loves you enough to move heaven and earth to come for you. If I were him, I would have been on the first boat."

"He doesn't know where I am, and my father threatened him if he came near me." Why was I making excuses for Andreas?

"And do you believe he'll defy your father now, after all this time?"

"I know he loves me and he needs me. He'll come." I said the words to convince not only Leo but also myself.

Weeks passed without any word from Andreas. Finally, as I returned from painting one afternoon I met Leo on the path. He tapped his chest pocket. My heart contracted in anticipation. A letter from Andreas.

"You have something for me?"

"YiaYia told me you had gone to paint, so I came to look for you. He withdrew the envelope from his pocket. "This came on the mail boat."

It was addressed to Leo, as I had advised Andreas to do. The envelope was covered in Austrian stamps.

"You didn't open it."

"It's clearly for you."

I ripped open the envelope with trembling fingers and scanned the familiar handwriting.

"He's coming."

"I thought you would be overjoyed."

"I am. I'm stunned, actually. I was afraid he'd forgotten me. Found someone else. I'm trying to fathom what will happen next."

"All hell will break loose is what will happen next. You knew that. When does he expect to arrive?"

I read the letter again.

"He planned to leave Vienna on the twentieth of August. It will take him two or three weeks. That's how long it took Papa and me to get here."

"That was winter. The boats make better time in the summer. He could be here next week. What's your plan?"

"My only alternative is to convince Andreas to marry me."

"How can I help?"

"Oh, Leo, thank you. My life is about to get very complicated, isn't it?"

"As if it wasn't complicated already? Listen, I'll come this evening to take you to Stefanis's place. It's Friday night. YiaYia and Pappou will think it's a good idea for you to get out with the young people. We can make plans there."

YiaYia fussed over me at supper when I barely ate.

"Are you sure you didn't get too much sun?" She felt my forehead.

"I'm fine, YiaYia, just not hungry."

As promised, Leo came after supper to pick me up. I changed into a summer dress as if we were joining friends for music and dancing in the square. We took a table in a corner of the courtyard and ordered some soda and pistachio nuts. I was still too much on edge to eat.

"Did you bring the letter?"

I pulled it out from my pocket and opened it flat on the table.

"Did your artist give any indication as to what he intends to do when he arrives in Skiathos Town?"

"I told him in my letter, if he should come, to find you."

"That make sense. He knows I'm the go-between. Once he's here and you meet with him, will you leave immediately?"

"If I don't, there's a risk that Pappou and YiaYia will try to stop me. I can't let them know. I hate this! The betrayal will kill them."

"Would your father reconsider his threat to marry you off here?"

I rolled my eyes. "You didn't see Papa the day he took me away from Andreas. He promised to break Andreas's hands if he tried to interfere."

"Andreas must love you deeply if he's willing to risk his livelihood to rescue you."

"I'm not sure it's love. Need, perhaps. I'm important to him, but only because of what I've been able to do for him."

"Do you love him?"

"I don't know anymore. I thought I did. I had a sense of destiny with him—that his destiny and mine were intertwined, and that I was the source of his explosive creativity."

"But you weren't painting when you were with him, and now you are. Will you have enough to nurture both your talents? What is the price you'll pay for marrying him, Maya? Do you believe marriage to your artist will stop your father?"

"Once I'm married, I'm no longer under my father's control."

"And so you exchange one man's power over you for another's?"

"What choice do I have, Leo? Marry Andreas, or marry the pharmacist's son or the doctor's son or the mayor's son and remain on Skiathos for the rest of my life? How much painting do you think I'll get done once the babies start coming?"

I tried to keep my voice low. In addition to there being eyes everywhere on the island, there were also ears.

"I'm sorry, Maya. You always chafed about the rules being different for boys and girls when you were a child."

"And as you can see, they are still different. No one is forcing you to marry."

I threw up my hands. I wasn't going to be able to change the rules, as I had so confidently imagined in Vienna. I could flaunt them, persisting until I obtained a place at university and then immersing myself in the avant-garde as model and muse and lover, but that was where it ended. Marriage was a different thing entirely, a convention I was not likely to escape. My quest for freedom had only entangled me in the net of my own illusions.

"I'd like to go home."

As we walked up the hill to my grandparents' house, I told Leo I would write a letter to Pappou and YiaYia for him to give to them after I left the island.

"I know that means they'll blame you for helping me. I'm sorry."

"I'm trying to think of a solution that doesn't require you to marry anyone."

"I once believed that was possible, but not anymore. By coming for me, Andreas has given me a choice. Marrying him is the better alternative."

We had reached the gate. I kissed Leo on both cheeks.

"Thank you for everything."

"I'll watch for Andreas and come for you when it's time."

The next day I went to the hut to retrieve Elise's landscape that she had left to complete when we met again. I removed the canvas from its stretcher and rolled it up, placing it in a cloth bag to hide it as I returned to the house. I did not take my portrait of YiaYia. I planned to ask Leo to collect it and give to her after I was gone.

I took one last look at the hut and all it represented—my art and my bliss—and locked the door.

Chapter Twenty-Four

ON SATURDAY MORNING, YIAYIA announced we would be having guests for dinner on Sunday, Dr. Bakarezos and his family.

"His son has returned from medical school and will join his father's practice. It's good for the island to have a young doctor. I want to establish a cooperative relationship with him."

YiaYia's reason for inviting the Bakarezos family to dinner was plausible, but warning bells were ringing in my head. Only a few nights earlier, while Leo and I sat in the square discussing next steps, I had flippantly listed off the sons of the prosperous men on the island as possible husband candidates. I hadn't known whether or not those men actually had marriageable sons, but I knew my father would only look at a professional man as a possible son-in-law.

I believed YiaYia wanted me to have a say in whom I would marry, and would not support forcing a union, but I also believed she thought the choice should be made among men approved by my father. I helped her prepare the meal and tidy the workroom on the chance that the younger Dr. Bakarezos might ask to see it. But I did not probe for any more information.

On Sunday, Pappou wore his good suit and polished his boots. YiaYia asked me to arrange her hair in a style she'd seen in a women's magazine Ekaterina had showed her.

"Wear one of your Viennese dresses, Maya. It's important that we appear sophisticated. Young Dr. Bakarezos has been away a long time. I want him to have a good impression. It's important that he doesn't think of me as a primitive, superstitious village healer, the way his father does."

The Bakarezos family arrived promptly at noon. Old Dr. Bakarezos's wife was dressed expensively in a dress that had definitely not been made on Skiathos. A diamond brooch glittered on her collar. Young Dr. Bakarezos was also fashionably attired in a well-cut suit that would have been appropriate in Vienna. He was self-assured and somewhat pompous. When he entered the house, I saw him sweep the room with his eyes, appraising everything from the rugs on the floor to the many books on the floor-to-ceiling shelves. I waited for the same appraisal of me, the potential bride. That I came from an educated, prosperous family was only one part of the bargain.

We were seated next to each other at the dinner table. Young Dr. Bakarezos was attractive and articulate, and this brought a look of relief to YiaYia's face. But my attempts to converse with him yielded only bored responses at best and dismissive opinions of most of the island at worst. His parents and my grandparents watched us intently—YiaYia with barely contained anxiety and Mrs. Bakarezos with pursed lips and a degree of suspicion that hinted she knew something unsavory about me. Eight months on the island had not been enough, apparently, to quiet the rumors. With relief, I expected that Mama Bakarezos would not approve this match for her perfect son.

After they left, YiaYia tried casually to gauge my reaction to young Dr. Bakarezos. At first, I was going to feign ignorance of the true purpose of the visit, but that seemed pointless. I had been making difficult decisions based on the belief that a marriage contract was underway between my father and a prominent island family. As angry as my father had been, I didn't believe he'd be cruel enough to force me to marry a farmer or a fisherman, so I confronted my grandmother.

"YiaYia, I know you aren't asking for my opinion about whether he might be a willing partner with you in keeping the island healthy. Please be honest with me. Is Papa planning to arrange a marriage for me here with a Skiathan son?"

YiaYia sighed and asked me to sit down. "Yes, he has asked me to suggest a possible match for you. I know the island, and now I know you. It was wrong of me to pretend that this dinner was for building a bridge for me. I shouldn't have underestimated you. I won't do it again. I will always involve you in any possible decision."

"Thank you, YiaYia, but please understand. I don't want to marry on Skiathos. As much as these months have enriched my life and brought me closer to you and Pappou, this is not the life I want. Can you understand?"

She took my hands in hers. "I understand you, Maya, but your parents, especially your father, fear for your future. If you defy him in this matter, he will no longer merely exile you to Skiathos. He will banish you from the family and send you to a convent. You'll be dead to him. An arranged marriage is his compromise. Please consider the consequences, my child."

I squeezed her hands and left the table. I needed to get out of the house. The moon was full, making the path to the cove easy to follow. When I reached the beach, I removed my shoes and stockings and walked along the water's edge. My father's plans, as my grandmother had described them, seemed unreasonably cruel and unwarranted. The condition he was setting—marry his choice or be cut off from the family entirely—was utterly soul crushing. I didn't know which would devastate me more. I wandered deeper into the water and lay back, floating with my arms outstretched and my hair drifting like seaweed on the tide. At some point, the salt of my tears mingled with the sea.

When I became cold, I turned and swam back to the beach. My dress clung to me, and I shivered in the night air. I found my shoes and stockings and started back toward the path.

In my room that night, I wrote my farewell letter to YiaYia and Pappou.

Late the next afternoon, Leo came to the house. Andreas had arrived and had taken a room near the harbor with the widow Asimina—the same guesthouse where Oscar and Elise had had lodgings. Andreas had booked passage for both of us on a boat leaving in the morning. I had already packed a bag and handed it off to Leo to deliver to Andreas. I could leave the house in the morning with no sign that I was traveling.

I did not sleep. Once again, I was fleeing with Andreas. This time, I felt none of the exhilaration that had marked my departure from Café Sacher on Christmas Day. Back then, I had felt free and on the cusp of a new life. This time, I felt only the weight of my choice.

Floating on the sea the previous night, I had tallied the cost of pursuing my art: the loss of my family, the loss of the soulmate I had found so briefly in Oscar. The burning need I felt to create, to bring to the canvas the vision that had begun to take shape this summer, outweighed everything else.

In the darkened house after my grandparents had gone to bed, I dressed in my traveling suit and crept downstairs.

I reached the harbor just before dawn and waited for Andreas. When I saw him approaching, I held still. He had, in fact, come.

He had lost weight, and his face was ravaged. In all the months of my exile, I had assumed that I was the one suffering. Although I had assumed my absence had annoyed and frustrated him, I had never imagined that my departure from his life had caused him pain. My fears that he had replaced me evaporated as he reached out for me and sobbed.

I hesitated, unprepared for his outburst, and put my arms around him, stroking his back. Around us I heard the sounds of the harbor coming to life—the squawk of seagulls, the thump of cargo being deposited on decks, the shouts of sailors as the ship was being readied to embark. I knew the street along the waterfront would soon be crowded with carts. Someone who knew me could appear at any moment.

"Andreas, we need to board the ship."

I released my hold on him and turned him toward the gangplank. "Do you have the tickets?"

"Is that all you have to say to me?"

"Until we are below deck and out of sight, yes."

There are eyes all over the island, I reminded myself, even on the ship. I kept my own eyes down and was glad I had a hat with a wide brim. I said a silent prayer that the purser checking our tickets was not a local man who would recognize me. Andreas seemed oblivious to the risk of discovery. I wondered how much Leo had explained to him. It was entirely possible Leo had been explicit and Andreas had dismissed the danger. But surely he remembered my father's threats! On Skiathos, no one would protect him from the wrath of Kostas Sircos.

I almost pushed him down the stairs to our cabin and then locked the door.

"We need to talk."

"Yes, we do. I heard nothing from you for more than seven months! I did not even know your father had taken you out of the country until I received your letter. I watched your house for weeks hoping to see you. Your absence paralyzed me. I've created nothing new since you left me."

"I didn't leave you, Andreas. I was taken from you, but we are together now. I am more grateful than I can express that you've come for me. I'm overwhelmed. Thank you."

Safe from the eyes of Skiathos Town, I grasped the enormity of what Andreas had done in making the journey and of what we were doing in escaping. Only then did I allow myself to collapse into his arms. It was my turn to weep.

He took me to the narrow berth and lay with me. I felt no passion, only a loosening of the tension that had sustained me since I had received his letter and learned that he was coming. It wasn't until the ship's bell rang and I felt the rise of the vessel as we left the dock that true relief flooded my body. I was exhausted and fell asleep in Andreas's arms. We would talk later.

I woke at midmorning. Sun poured through the porthole and lit Andreas's face where he sat. The brilliant light accentuated the sharp planes of his haggard cheeks and the smudged shadows under his eyes. Had my absence alone done this to him? If so, the burden did not sit comfortably on my shoulders. I had ached for him in the first months of my exile, but I hadn't starved myself. In the short time since our reunion on the dock, I confirmed my belief that Andreas had come not only for me but for himself.

I climbed out of the bunk, washed my face, and tidied my hair. The moment had come for the final element of my escape. I knelt before him and took his hands.

"Your coming for me has fulfilled a dream that I have wished for for months. Thank you, my love. But with every mile this ship is putting between Skiathos and us, it is also bringing us closer to my father. When we return to Vienna, we cannot hide, because he will find us."

"We can go elsewhere."

"And we'll always be looking behind us to see if he has caught up with us. Leaving Vienna is no solution, not if we wish to be together and not if your painting is to flourish."

"Without you, I've been unable to complete even one canvas that approaches the work I was able to do with you."

"I suspected that. I can see it in your face. You will paint again. You must paint again."

"And your father? How are we to avoid him if we don't go into hiding?"

"By marrying." There, I'd said it.

He let go of my hands and shifted back in his chair away from me.

"You know what I think of marriage. I thought you agreed. How can I explore the depths of human emotion in new ways if I'm shackled by the bourgeois strictures of marriage? Abiding by society's rules is the antithesis of breaking the rules. It's why the Secessionists defied the Academy."

His reaction was exactly what I expected. I got up off my knees.

"I'm going above. I need some air." I paced the deck, avoiding the other passengers. It occurred to me that I was still in danger. We weren't so far out at sea. A telegram to Skiathos could summon a cutter to take me back. I marched back to the cabin. Andreas was still in the chair drinking from a flask. I slammed the door.

"Until I am married, I am still Kostas Sircos's daughter and under his control. If I do not marry you, he will force me to marry a man of his choice. He already has a candidate, a doctor on Skiathos who dined with me and my family last Sunday. The marriage contract is probably already drafted, and the terms of the dowry already negotiated."

"This isn't the Middle Ages."

"It might as well be on Skiathos. If I do not marry you, I will be someone else's wife. I will never be able to set foot in your studio again. I will not be your lover. I will not be your muse."

Andreas looked at me in disbelief.

"I came for you. I rescued you."

"And for that, I am grateful. But it's not enough."

He took another swallow from his flask and got up.

"I need to piss," he said and left.

While he was gone, I unpacked. In addition to a few dresses and underthings, I had included my drawing materials. I thought it best to put them away. One hard conversation at a time. First marriage, then art.

When the bell for dinner sounded, Andreas had still not returned. Until I was Mrs. Andreas Brenner, I wanted to remain out of sight. I rang for the steward and claimed to be ill, asking for soup to be brought to the cabin.

I was sipping the broth when Andreas finally reappeared. The cabin was not spacious, but he paced the short distance between the porthole and the door back and forth.

"I can't live without you. You ignite my very soul, drive the hand that holds the brush. These months without you have been hell."

He ran his fingers through his hair, which looked as if it hadn't been cut since I'd left. He stopped pacing. "Very well, I'll marry you."

And then he grabbed my hand and pulled me up. "Let's do it now, before I lose courage."

I wiped my mouth, put on my hat, and climbed to the deck with him in search of the captain. That afternoon on a calm, sunlit sea, I became Maya Sircos Brenner. Our marriage was witnessed by the ten other passengers on board, and celebrated with a champagne toast provided by the captain.

We used the ring I had placed in the Klidonas bowl.

PART THREE
VIENNA

1907-1910

Chapter Twenty-Five

I KEPT OUR MARRIAGE certificate in my prayer book, knowing that the day would come when my father would demand to see it.

We had to spend a few days in Athens waiting for the ship to Trieste. As I had while on board the ship from Skiathos, I remained in hiding in our hotel room. I watched the street from the window, expecting to see Pappou at any moment. Andreas, his head firmly in the twentieth century, could not fathom my fear of being forced back to Skiathos.

"I've never been to Greece. As long as we have to be here, I'm going to take advantage and explore. I wish you'd come with me."

"It's fine for you to wander among the ruins. No one knows who you are, except for Leo, and he won't betray me. But I have to stay out of sight. We'll have time enough together on the next ship."

He sulked but didn't slam any doors when he left to climb the Acropolis. While he was gone, I retrieved my sketchbook and drew from memory the faces of my family.

Given YiaYia's warning that Papa would sever all ties with me, those images would be all that I had.

My anxiety didn't subside until we were once again aboard ship. Andreas had booked us a first-class cabin, an indulgence I was not expecting.

"You seem surprised, Maya. Did you think I couldn't afford to travel the way Kostas Sircos does?"

"I don't doubt you can afford it, Andreas. I'm grateful for your thoughtfulness. Delighted by it. Thank you."

His need to compare himself to my father was no surprise. His last and only encounter with Papa had been a hostile one fraught with the threat of devastating violence. I understood his need to prove to me and to himself that he was my father's equal, even if only financially.

The luxury of a comfortable bed and attentive servants gave us both an opportunity to forget for a few days what we were about to face in Vienna. Though the route was the same as the one I had taken with Papa over the winter, it was the antithesis of that harrowing journey. I soaked in a warm bath, was delighted to experience no seasickness, and was able to focus on rebuilding my relationship with Andreas. We were strangers to each other despite our intense, passionate history.

We had not made love on the passage from Skiathos to Athens. I was too agitated, and fearful of being snatched from the ship at any moment. He was mostly drunk. The cabin bunk had been narrow and damp. We had only held each other in sleep for the one night we were on board.

The bed in our cabin on the ship to Trieste, on the other hand, was large enough for both of us, and after my bath, I approached Andreas wearing only a loose dressing gown.

He was sitting in an armchair smoking, and watched me as I moved across the room. The expression on his face was unreadable. I deliberately flicked away the thought that he no longer found me desirable. It was difficult not to compare this new state of our relationship to the past—we were now a married couple rather than lovers—but I also found my memories calling up the look on Oscar's face in the shepherd's hut.

I willed my wandering mind to return to the present, breathed deeply, and took the cigarette out of Andreas's hand.

"Come to bed."

I grasped his now-empty hand and placed it on my breast, moaning softly when I felt his once-familiar calloused fingers stroke my nipple. My reaction pleased him, and the uncertainty I'd seen on his face and mirrored in my own ambivalence disappeared as he pulled me into his arms and onto the bed.

Our lovemaking was tentative, questioning. I don't know what he imagined my life had been like on Skiathos. How could any twentieth-century Viennese resident? But I could picture what his life had been like because I had lived it. I had often, over the months we were apart, feared that he had replaced me, both in his studio and in his bed. Although he was here with me now, that fear had not completely left me. My eyes were open, watching him, searching for some sign of the passion and obsession that had once shaped not only our lovemaking, but our daily existence. I tried to feel it within my own body, hoping to transmit to him that I wanted him physically. I responded to his touch, gasping with the surprise of a virgin when he first entered me and moving with him as his excitement accelerated. I did not lie passively beneath him, as some women do, enduring their wifely duty. I gave him every reason to believe that I was with him, gripping his back, pulling him into me, urging him on.

But emotionally, I was somewhere else.

Not with Oscar in the hut. My betrayal was not sexual in nature. Rather, my mind took me to waves lapping at my bare feet as I walked with Elise and Oscar on the beach; to afternoons in the orchard with my paintbrush in hand; to memories of dreams in which I was free.

I was not so far removed that I wasn't aware of Andreas's impending climax, and I met his ecstasy with a facsimile of my own. I knew I would not reach orgasm with all the thoughts crowding my head, and I did not wish to explain to him why I could not. And so I pretended.

When he collapsed in a contented tangle of exhaustive limbs, I smiled and kissed him.

He traced my lips with his finger.

"No one excites me as you do."

I refrained from asking him how many experiments he had conducted during my absence in order to reach that conclusion. I was not innocent and had no right to have expected him to remain celibate.

He was asleep within minutes, leaving me to ponder this new state. It occurred to me that the passion and intensity that I had directed toward Andreas and his art before I was taken to Skiathos had been displaced. Over the last several months, I had turned inward. How long could I dissemble my state of mind as I had my physical reaction in our lovemaking?

Chapter Twenty-Six

BY THE TIME WE docked in Trieste, we had settled into a rhythm that seemed to satisfy Andreas, most likely because he appeared oblivious to my state of mind. He had expressed no curiosity at all about my life on Skiathos.

In Trieste, we boarded the first available train to Vienna. When we crossed the border from Italy into Austria, I pressed my hand to the glass of the window. Meadows and forests sped by, and then the familiar crags of the Alps, like the fingers of a stone giant. In all the months I'd been away, I had not longed for the land. But the sight of the mountains caused a hitch in my breath.

I felt not a longing for my homeland, but a sense of seeing the majestic beauty of the mountains with new eyes, the eyes of an artist.

It was night when we arrived in the city. A misty rain scattered light from the street lamps into pinpoints on the windows of the cab Andreas had hailed to convey us home. The clatter of the horses' feet and the rhythm of the wheels, the smell of damp clothing and horse droppings, the plaintive notes of a violin wafting from an open window—all these smells and sounds surrounded me. I felt as if I was immersed in a kaleidoscope, and smiled like a child at the Prater.

"I have a surprise for you," Andreas murmured as the carriage came to a stop in an unfamiliar street. "I sold several paintings while you were gone, enough to afford new quarters with more space."

He led me into a four-story apartment building and up the lift to the top floor. With a flourish, he opened the door to the apartment and lit a lamp, revealing a long corridor with several rooms leading from it.

"Let me give you a tour."

The front of the apartment encompassed a kitchen, parlor, bedroom, and bath. To the rear, a spacious room with a wall of windows had clearly become Andreas's studio.

"It's impressive."

I wondered who his benefactor was to have enabled such an extraordinary change in Andreas's living accommodations. The single room that had been our quarters before would fit twice inside the studio alone. My eyes wandered around the space. A stack of medium-sized canvases leaned against one of the walls, their faces hidden. Two easels situated by the windows held canvases, but muslin covered them and I could not see what they contained. The only light came in from the street below, as Andreas hadn't turned on any lamps and seemed disinterested in remaining in the studio.

In fact, he took my elbow and turned me back to the living quarters.

"Let's have a drink. I think there's a tin of cake if you're hungry."

I wasn't. We'd eaten on the train. My curiosity postponed, I followed Andreas down the hall to the parlor. He had been so eager to show off the apartment that neither of us had removed our coat. I unpinned my hat and strolled around the room while Andreas poured us drinks.

"It's all quite elegant."

"You seem surprised."

"I didn't know you were unhappy in the old studio."

"It wasn't big enough for the size of work I'm doing now."

"I noticed one of the canvases on the easel was definitely bigger than what you had been using. When you're ready, I'd like to see it."

"Not tonight."

I smiled. "No, not tonight. We have better ways to spend our time. Let's take our drinks to the bedroom."

That calmed him. I knew from comments he'd made during the trip from Skiathos that he'd been frustrated in his work. There would be time enough in the coming days to see the painting and also to make space for myself.

When I woke in the morning, Andreas was still deep in sleep. On the table by his bedside, I saw the bottle of whiskey we had we had filled our cups with the night before, its contents much depleted from what I remembered. He must have awakened during the night and poured himself another glass—or two. It was no wonder he still slept.

I eased myself from the bed, wrapped myself in a dressing gown, and rummaged in the kitchen. Of course, because he'd been away for at least a month, I found precious little to eat, except for a tin of coffee. I made a pot and drank a cup in the parlor, standing at the window, observing our new neighborhood. The street was coming to life with the bustle of deliveries and men hurrying to the trolley at the end of the street. Directly across the road, beyond an iron fence, a park hosted a chorus of birds and early walkers with small dogs on leads.

Andreas had apparently done very well in order to afford an apartment of this size in a neighborhood such as this. I could imagine hosting a salon here, attracting the sort of clients who could afford an Andreas Brenner painting.

While Andreas continued to sleep, I left my post at the window and trod in my bare feet down the hall to the studio. I eased the door open, feeling like an interloper. Andreas had rushed me out the night before, which had only heightened my curiosity. What was he hiding? Another model? I was curiously indifferent to the idea, considering the fears that had plagued me on Skiathos. But I was here now. He had wanted and needed me enough to come for me. I had achieved what I had so desperately longed for. Not Andreas, I admitted, but freedom.

As I stepped into the studio, I acknowledged there was a price for that freedom, but I would consider it more fully another time. Right now, I was more interested in the unfinished painting.

I moved swiftly to the two canvases that had been draped in muslin to protect them from the sun and dust.

I whipped off the cloth on the first easel and studied the face staring back at me. It was not that of another model, but my own. He had attempted to paint me from memory. I say attempted because he had failed. Oh, the bone structure and shape of my eyes were a precise rendition of my own, but the coloring was off. He had painted the Maya of a Vienna winter, not the woman who'd been out-of-doors for months on a Greek island. But that was not the only difference between this painting and the series he had created for the Secession. The eyes, though accurate in their shape, lacked the spark of life. The portraits Andreas had made of me before had shimmered with vitality, as if the woman on the canvas was about to step into the room, pulled by a filament into the arms of the artist—or the viewer. This painting was flat, not only in the brushwork but in the impassivity and indifference of the subject. I felt no connection, even though the face in the image was mine.

I moved on to the second canvas and lifted the cloth with less energy, already expecting to be disappointed. Instead, I was shocked.

It was the portrait Andreas had painted of me when I was fifteen. Why was it here? And then I answered my own question: My father, in his rage, must have pulled it from its place of honor and sent it back to Andreas. I stood motionless before my image, remembering the profound impact the painting had had on my perception of myself.

But I also contemplated the meaning of its removal from my parents' home. Not only had they banished me in the flesh, but they had refused even to look at my portrait.

My decision to flee Skiathos was never in doubt, but still I had recognized that doing so would rend the fabric of my life with my family. That understanding now loomed before me as prescient.

I had cried only once during my banishment, when I walked into the sea the night before I left my grandparents' house for good. Then, I had contemplated the consequences of defying my father's wishes by marrying Andreas. Now, I was confronted with the reality of those consequences. I was clearly dead to my parents if they could not even bear to look at my face.

I sat on the floor, my back to the windows and my knees drawn up, and wept before the two very different portraits of me.

I didn't hear Andreas stirring in the other part of the apartment, and was startled by the sound of the door to the studio being flung open so forcefully that it slammed against the wall.

"What are you doing in here?"

I lifted my head from my knees and wiped my damp cheeks with the sleeve of my dressing gown. His vehemence stunned me. I had detected his reluctance to have me examine the studio closely the night before, but hadn't expected him to be outraged.

I rose from the floor and addressed him in a calm and confident voice that belied my own anger.

"I have missed your work as well as your touch, Andreas. I've been hungry for the sights and smells of your studio." I didn't say what I thought: *I have a right to be here. I have a role here.*

"You should have waited for me to explain."

"You're here now. Tell me."

"I have tried to recreate the magic you conjured up when you modeled for me—how you moved, how you looked at me, how you spoke to me—but it was impossible without you here. Look at this." He flung his hand at the first painting. "It's barely recognizable, not just your face but the immediacy of your being, how you offered yourself to me and ultimately to the viewer. I thought if I placed your adolescent portrait next to the new canvas as I worked, I could absorb some of its energy."

"Why do you even have this painting?"

"Do you remember when I told you I went to your parents' house after your father took you away, hoping to see you? I arrived early in the morning, and outside the gate, piled with the weekly trash, was your portrait. It had been cast away but thankfully hadn't been damaged. I took it."

What my father had done and my mother had agreed to was worse than I had imagined. I had assumed that my parents had sent the portrait back to Andreas, not that they had discarded it like a broken vase. All I could eke out in my shock was "Thank you for rescuing it."

"It wasn't enough to inspire me, but it was consoling to have it here, a fragment of you."

"But now you have all of me." I wasn't being completely truthful, but it wasn't the moment to reveal to him that I was no longer entirely his. Admittedly, however, given his fragility and its tendency to manifest itself in anger, I wasn't sure when the right moment would come.

"Let's get dressed and find some food. Is there a decent café in this neighborhood? I'm also going to make an assumption that you haven't hired a housekeeper yet, and we need to do the marketing."

"Are you missing your dear Gertraud already? How many servants did your grandparents have?"

"Only farmhands for the vineyards and orchards. Managing the household was my grandmother's domain, with my help. I'm perfectly capable of caring for our domestic needs. Getting some food in the house seems to me to be a priority. If you'd rather not accompany me after breakfast, you can point me in the right direction and provide me with some shillings."

His reference to the life I'd left to be with him still rankled. I retrieved the market basket from the kitchen and we left.

He at least knew where the green grocer, the butcher, and the baker could be found.

I smoothed my expression as I pushed open the door to the butcher's shop and made an attempt to be both knowledgeable and pleasant.

"You are new to the neighborhood," observed the young girl behind the counter, who, I soon learned, was the daughter of the butcher.

"I am indeed. What do you recommend today?"

After the usual exchange between customer and shop-keeper, she handed me the wrapped package of chops and sausages.

"Thank you for your business, Frau . . . ?"

I almost gave my name as Sircos before realizing that wasn't who I was anymore.

"Frau Brenner. Good day to you."

I had certainly been addressed as Frau Brenner aboard the ship, but that had been an experience out of time, outside of the lives both Andreas and I had been living. Now, in the midst of a butcher shop in Josefstadt, I came to realize what being Frau Brenner meant. I added the package of meat to my basket and moved down the street to the green grocer.

When I returned home, I could hear music coming from the studio. I unpacked the groceries, acquainting myself with the kitchen, and then made my way down the hall. Andreas was sprawled across the divan in the studio, eyes closed and a cigarette in hand. The music emanated from the brass horn of a gramophone, another new element that had been added in my absence.

I watched Andreas, not sure if he was sleeping and not wishing to disturb him if he was in a state of contempla-tion. Perhaps the music was an inspiration, a preparation before he took up his brush. I felt a sense of disorientation. Had I been away so long that nothing was familiar to me? Or had Andreas changed his methods as well as his environment?

When I saw the end of Andreas's cigarette approaching his fingers, I moved instinctively toward him. But the heat from the glowing tobacco reached him first and he bolted upright, quashing the cigarette into an empty saucer on the floor.

"You're finally home," he greeted me, with a combination of relief and irritation.

"I am, and ready to work if you are."

In the few moments I had observed him, I feared that Andreas had lost the drive and obsession that fueled his extraordinary talent. I remembered my own paralysis when I first arrived on Skiathos and wondered if he had faced the same lassitude and collapse of desire. My encounter with Elise had rescued me. I grasped with certainty that Andreas would not rescue himself.

"Do you want to resume the portrait of me that you found so unsatisfactory, or do you wish to begin anew?"

As I spoke, I moved toward the canvas, unbuttoning my blouse as I walked, and rummaging in my brain for the most effective means of restoring Andreas to his former brilliance. Rather than using words to encourage him to pick up his brush, I counted on my nakedness to ignite the spark.

It felt starkly unfamiliar to appear unclothed. The months of modesty on Skiathos had left their imprint on my psyche. Even in the shepherd's hut with Oscar, I hadn't stood naked before him. When we had lain together, it had been through the communion of touch rather than gaze. I wasn't feeling shame as I faced Andreas, but for the first time, I questioned what it required of me to provoke him to create.

He joined me at the canvas and rubbed his face, wiping away whatever he had seen in his mind while I was away and preparing himself to see what now appeared before him.

"You look different."

I am different, I thought, but didn't say it aloud.

"Shall I move around? Try a few poses before we settle on one?"

"Be my guest. I'm going to start fresh." He removed the old canvas and replaced it with a new one.

"Do you have anything in mind for a new series? A theme?"

I may have pushed too quickly, for I saw a flicker of hesitation cloud his face before turning to resentment. I surmised that he hadn't given any thought to what he wanted to achieve with this next iteration of his vision. Surely he hadn't planned to repeat an exploration of sexual awakening?

The music on the gramophone had stopped, and I took the opportunity to busy myself in restarting the recording to give both of us time to gather ourselves. We were not only in a new studio, we were each in a new state—emotionally, mentally, artistically. I felt resistance from him after months alone. Despite claiming to desperately need the inspiration he knew I would bring to him, Andreas was chafing at any attempt of mine to lead the way. I could sense he heard my questions as provocation, not encouragement.

For my own part, I was finding the task of managing his creative direction exhausting. My God, it was our first day of collaboration, and already things were going awry. The connection between us that had before seemed so effortless now felt onerous.

I stretched and shook out my arms and fingers, trying to loosen my mental constraints through a physical release. Then I returned to him and moved behind him, rather than posing in front of him.

I placed my hands on his shoulder blades and began to massage the tight muscles. His entire body was coiled, a panther about to pounce on his prey. *This is good*, I thought. He needed to attack the canvas, to approach it with conviction, not doubt.

"This is the Andreas I remember, the one I longed for, the one whose strength of purpose and brilliance awed me," I whispered into his ear as he bent his neck to my touch.

Only then did I move around him, positioning myself half in shadow and fixing a look of defiance on my face. I presented him with a warrior. As the idea started to take form, I reached for the cobalt blue pigment pooled on his palette and smeared two lines on my cheek. The antithesis of the blood on my thigh.

Chapter Twenty-Seven

WE WORKED THROUGH THE afternoon with only short pauses for me to break the pose while Andreas had a cigarette. When the natural light began to dim, he was willing to stop. I knew better than to approach the canvas and ask him what he thought. It was enough that he had painted all afternoon with vigor and purpose. I didn't want to disrupt the energy by studying the canvas. I was glad because I was afraid of what I might see and of my potential inability to disguise my reaction.

He seemed equally reluctant to ask for my opinion.

I gathered up my clothing and retreated while he cleaned his brushes. There was still dinner to be cooked.

Because he had not yet furnished our elegant rooms, we ate by candlelight, sitting on the floor in the parlor. The cooking skills I had honed in YiaYia's kitchen seemed to meet with his satisfaction. Although he said nothing, I knew he was surprised. Before I'd left Vienna, my repertoire had consisted of omelets and sausages in our makeshift kitchen, merely a corner of the studio. I had cooked then on the top of the tiled stove, kept our bread and eggs in a tin box to protect them from the mice, and stored cheese wrapped in cloth on the windowsill. Now I had at my disposal not only a cast-iron stove with an oven but also an icebox. The kitchen rivaled that in my parents' home, minus the attentive skills of Gertraud.

I gathered up our plates to carry them back to my well-equipped kitchen while Andreas stretched out on the rug. He flexed his fingers and studied them, still flecked with paint.

"Thank you for today. It was a good beginning."

I nodded. "I thought so, too."

By the time I finished washing up, he had abandoned his recumbent position and begun pacing in the hallway. He hesitated at the door to the studio and then abruptly turned away.

"Let's go out. I haven't been to the coffeehouse since I left for Greece. We can catch up on the news."

"Give me ten minutes and I'll change."

We took the stairs, and he nearly danced down the steps. My husband was a happy man as we ventured out to meet his friends. He'd had a productive day painting and a warm meal in his belly. Why shouldn't he be happy?

We were greeted at the coffeehouse by quite a ruckus, mostly for me.

"You're back! Thank God! We no longer have to listen to Andreas bemoan your absence."

I teased back. "What? You're not happy to see me because of my sparkling conversation?"

Andreas eased back into the circle of his comrades. He had lost the tension of the morning and laughed with a lightheartedness that had been missing since his arrival on Skiathos. Had one productive afternoon with me been enough to effect such a pronounced change of mood?

I sat opposite him at the long end of the table and marveled at his contentment as he regaled the group with tales of his travels.

Max leaned over to whisper in my ear. "You're quieter than I remember," he said, and then, "We've missed you, and not just because you manage to keep Andreas steady. Where have you been?"

"Visiting family in Greece."

"We thought you'd escaped to the anonymity of the country after all that commotion at the Secession last January. You certainly cast a spell on Andreas. He'd never produced anything as profound as that series before you. Would you consider modeling for me?"

I nearly spit out my drink. He meant more than modeling; of that, I was sure.

"I have no more magic to spare."

"Saving yourself for Andreas, are you? I can assure you, he did not do the same while you were away, although none of the substitutes he brought to his studio came close to giving him what you did."

So there *had* been others. Had he hidden the canvases he'd created with them?

If Max was hoping I would join him in his bed as recompense for news of Andreas's behavior, he was mistaken.

"And now I'm back. He won't need any more substitutes."

"Oh, loyal muse, I commend you—even though I wish you were mine."

He held up his glass, and I raised mine in response.

On our way home, Andreas questioned me.

"What were you talking to Max about?"

I saw no reason to dissemble.

"He asked me to model for him."

"And what did you tell him?"

"No, of course."

A look of relief swept across Andreas's face.

"Did you truly think I would have agreed? I am yours, Andreas, body and soul. No one else will paint me."

Unless I do myself, I thought

He made love to me that night with less desperation, confident that I was his on the canvas as well as in his bed.

Andreas painted the Warriors series over the next five months. I scoured literature, the Bible, Greek tragedies, and Shakespeare for stories of women warriors. Instead of nothing, these women wore the symbols of their fierceness. He painted Athena and Penthesilea from my own Greek mythology, Joan of Arc, and the Bible's Esther confronting King Xerxes. For each one, I gathered physical representations of their identities and read their stories aloud to him at night in bed.

He painted furiously, recapturing some of the passion that had emerged when he had worked on the Sexual Awakening series but transforming the women into the embodiment of female power. The deeper he immersed himself in the esthetic of Expressionism, the more vivid and complex the images of the women became. Their stories were perfectly suited to the raw, instinctual truth that Expressionism was seeking.

The paintings were another triumph for Andreas. I don't know how I managed to extract such brilliance from him, yet again, when I was so wary of the cost to me. And the cost was immense. Between finding subjects for the paintings, constructing the tableaus, posing for them, and narrating the stories to him, I had little time or artistic energy for my own art.

Later, I questioned why I had given the concept of the women warriors to him, but I suppose at the time, it was a form of appeasement. I thought if I could engage him in a satisfying project that stimulated and engrossed him, it would free me from his insatiable need for inspiration. I was so wrong.

Not only did the Warriors paintings consume me, but I was also managing our household and assuaging Andreas's constant crises of confidence. I collapsed into bed every night, barely able to respond to his sexual needs. I stopped going out in the evening to the coffeehouse, hoping that I could spend those hours in the studio. But I faced my sketchpad with dismay. The ideas had fled, and I felt as if the muscles of my hand were atrophying without any direction from my brain.

My only respite was mornings. Andreas slept late, the result of the hours he spent out at night. He insisted his best creative time was in the afternoon. In the early hours of the day, before I did the marketing and began the dinner preparations, I took myself out. At first, it was only to the park across the street, but then I began to venture farther afield.

One morning, Andreas had come in exceptionally late the night before, and I knew he wouldn't stir until nearly noon. My excursion took me as far as the Danube, where I contemplated the movement of the river as a surrogate for my own yearning. I berated myself for falling back into the same pattern of behavior with Andreas that I had escaped when painting on Skiathos. I knew I couldn't continue in this way, but extracting myself seemed beyond my reach. I turned from the river and made my way home.

As I approached the Kunsthistorisches Museum, I noticed a poster on the kiosk for the Vienna School of Applied Arts. Like the Academy of Fine Arts, it had been closed to women at the end of the nineteenth century, despite welcoming women when it was first founded. But the words "Women invited to apply" at the bottom of the poster reached me amidst the cacophony of advertisements for concerts and gallery exhibitions and theater presentations plastered on the kiosk. I rushed up and read it closely. I still carried a small sketchbook and charcoal with me, despite no longer taking part in the daily discipline I had once practiced. I quickly copied the address and promised myself I would make my way there.

At home, I penned a letter of inquiry and within a week received an invitation to schedule an interview. I had to wait several days before the opportunity of a free afternoon presented itself. Andreas's portrait business was still viable. Although my parents' social circle had eschewed any work by the scandalous Expressionist painter, there were still wealthy men who had never been to the Secession Building and had never seen one of Andreas's earlier portraits. So, when he received a much-needed commission, I encouraged him to schedule a meeting with the new client, explaining that we still needed to eat. Meanwhile, I wrote immediately to the school to secure my own appointment.

As soon as I saw him leave our apartment building, I put on my hat and coat and retrieved my art portfolio and the school's address. I splurged on a carriage to allow me as much time as possible to get there and back before Andreas returned. When I entered the building, I was led past several rooms humming with activity—painting classes, pottery demonstrations, drawing studios. I was then ushered into an office with the director of the school and a female painting teacher. I had dressed sensibly, and hoped I would not be recognized as the model for Andreas's breakout exhibition. But if any of the people I met with surmised who I was, they did not reveal their suspicions. I had used my maiden name when writing for admission, avoiding any connection with Andreas Brenner.

They examined my portfolio carefully, stopping to comment on my portraits.

"These are quite accomplished. They show not only a practiced technique but astonishing emotion. Where have you studied before?"

I explained my good fortune in finding Elise as a teacher, and the director was impressed.

"I think you will do well here. Welcome."

The art instructor gave me the schedule of classes with a recommendation of one for more advanced students. Somehow, I would find a way to attend.

Chapter Twenty-Eight

ONE MORNING AS I returned from the marketing, I noticed a woman standing at the gate to the park across the street. Her hat obscured her face, but the way she carried herself as she moved toward me was unmistakable. I put down my basket.

"Mama!"

She reached her arms out, and I walked into her embrace.

"Come have a cup of coffee with me." I motioned toward the building.

"Is he home?"

I nodded. "He was still asleep when I left."

"Not here. Is there a café in the neighborhood?"

I led her around the corner to Café Eiles, and we found a quiet table in the rear.

"How did you find me?"

"It wasn't difficult. Andreas Brenner has made quite a name for himself. I expressed interest at the Secession Building in purchasing one of his paintings, and they were quite happy to give me his address. He must be doing well to afford this neighborhood. I'm glad for you. At least you're not living in squalor."

I tried not to react to her cutting remark. I was truly happy to see her.

"I'm glad you found me. How are you? How is Papa?"

"We've managed. As you know from my letters, the scandal simmered for a few weeks, but without anything more being revealed about you, Vienna moved on to the next bright object. I survived Omama's criticism and the ostracism from those we might have once called friends."

"I'm sorry."

"I won't spend any more of my energy berating you. You've made many choices I would not have made, but in the decision to marry Brenner, I see it as the better alternative. A marriage on Skiathos would have killed you, and I mean that quite literally—either childbirth or the deep suspicion all islanders hold of outsiders would have driven you to your death."

"So, you know I married Andreas."

"Of course. Kaliope wrote when you ran away yet again. I cannot blame you, given the consequences for you of staying. But word of your marriage reached Vienna later. Vienna is its own island, Maya. Word passes from coffeehouse to church pew to opera stall. The sea captain who married you mentioned it to someone in Piraeus, and the message found its way home."

"How did Papa react to the news?"

"How do you think? With the fury of a man who has been defied. However, I've convinced him of the folly of forcing you into a life that neither of us meant for you. He still loves you despite his anger. With time . . ."

"Thank you for that. I've missed you both."

"But apparently not enough to let us know you have returned. We waited to hear from you after the letter from Kaliope and knew you'd left Skiathos."

"I didn't trust Papa."

A fleeting pain darkened her brow. She didn't defend him.

"Will I see you again?"

"Maya, of course! Papa doesn't know I've come, nor does he have your address. For now, it's best to remain in your own world. May I ask how you are finding life as a wife?"

"I'm adjusting. We both are. I'm not the same woman I was when I left Vienna. I started to paint on Skiathos, and I've just been accepted at the School of Applied Arts."

"Your face just lit up when you said that." She reached across the table and squeezed my hand. "Hold on to that joy. Keep painting."

She promised to come again, and did. We met every month, sometimes to visit a new exhibit at the Kunsthistorisches Museum or walk in Danneberg Park or, like the first time, to sip coffee at Café Eile.

Chapter Twenty-Nine

ANDREAS COMPLETED THE LAST of the Warriors paintings in late January. I say completed, but I knew he would be going back to each one to make modifications up until the moment they were packed into crates and on their way out the door. But my role as model had ended, and my afternoons were my own.

Over the months, I had carefully managed our household funds, setting aside a small amount each week for my art class and supplies. Andreas had an account at a supplier for canvas, pigments, and brushes, but I was reluctant to use it. I hadn't told him about the class yet, and I didn't want some clerk to mention my purchases if he happened to stop by. More and more, he'd relied on me not only to shop for him there but also to prepare the mammoth canvases and mix his paints. I didn't mind the work because it meant I'd received the training of an apprentice and learned how to build a frame and stretch and gesso the canvas. I knew someday I would put those skills to work in my own art.

The first afternoon I set out for class was blustery. Piles of dirty snow formed obstacles at street corners, and I had to navigate the mounds carefully. I felt like a child on her first day of school, but instead of a gaily decorated cone filled with sweets, I carried a simple leather satchel packed with a large sketchpad and a slim metal box of sketching crayons and charcoal.

I arrived early, found a place near the front, and set out my materials. By the time the class began, twenty women had filled the room. The director had assigned me to a life class, and as the model entered, the instructor made a few introductory comments and then set a metronome. We began with an exercise of one-minute poses, during which we sketched in broad strokes, capturing movement and emotion without taking recourse in details. After so many months of motionless posing for Andreas and little use of my own skill, I found both the pace and the object of the exercise challenging.

My charcoal stick broke in half when I pressed too hard in my haste to replicate the model's pose, and I missed an entire pose as I scrambled to retrieve the fragment. I voiced my frustration in what I thought was a whisper, but a few people nearby were clearly disturbed by the noise. All of them seemed to be moving their hands smoothly across the page. Perhaps the director had been wrong in placing me in this class.

My outburst drew the attention of the instructor, who moved to my side. She took the broken charcoal from my hand and demonstrated a technique that used a lighter touch.

"Try this way," she suggested and handed me back my implement. Red-faced, I began again. I felt much the same as I had my first day painting with Elise—rusty, stiff, unpracticed. I anticipated crumpling several sheets of paper by the end of the class and tossing them in the stove. As the class progressed, however, the pace of the poses lasted longer and my hand began to obey my eye. The longer time limit gave me an opportunity to study the model. It was a unique experience to be on the other side—to be the viewer, not the viewed. I was interested in her face, as well as the placement of her limbs. With the flat side of the charcoal, I began to use varying degrees of pressure to contour with shadows.

The next time the instructor came by, she smiled.

"You learn quickly. I understand your frustration at the swift tempo I set at the beginning, but its purpose is both to warm up our hands and to train the eye to recognize the key elements that are necessary to convey shape. Practice will strengthen your technique. But be of good cheer. You've done well for your first day."

My hands were black with coal dust, and probably my face as well. I found a washroom and tidied up before returning home.

Over the next few weeks, Andreas fussed with the Warriors for a few hours every day, but the rest of the time he spent either at the coffeehouse or pursuing the attention of galleries in order to secure an exhibition. My class met only twice a week, and it was not difficult to keep my activity from him. I had never revealed to him the extent of my painting on Skiathos. During the intense months of creating the Warriors, I hesitated to distract him. The state of his psyche, brilliant as he was, seemed too fragile to accept my own desire to create art.

I knew at some point I could no longer hide my developing mastery if I were to fulfill my own artistic future. I needed space and time to work. I needed the studio. At first, I convinced myself he'd be less apt to perceive me as a rival after he had obtained a gallery show. But it soon became clear to me that tying my development as an artist to his success was a mistake. So I presented myself with two tasks: stop hiding my desire to create and, at the same time, put my persuasive powers to work to find a gallery that would show Andreas's work.

I had had the sense, as time went on, that Andreas was spending most of his days and evenings at Café Museum and not seeking out the gallery owners who held his future in their hands.

At the school, I found a photographer who was willing to help me. It was another woman still learning her craft, and she was happy to come to the studio and photograph the Warriors. She developed card-sized prints that I placed in an album, along with the stories of each of the Warriors written by me in a concise but dramatic form.

When the album was complete, I donned my most memorable outfit—a deep magenta suit accented with a painted silk shawl I had purchased from another student and a hat with a veil that partially obscured my face.

Gustav Klimt had split with the Secession, disagreeing with its turn toward in a more conservative direction, but I thought it best to start there, given Andreas's success with the Awakening series. I visited every member of the Secession committee, including Carl Moll and Rudolf Bacher and presented myself as Andreas's agent. No one recognized me as the model from either the Awakening paintings or the Warriors series. I negotiated. I cajoled. I promised a robust turnout. I succeeded in getting them to come to the studio to see the paintings.

I delivered the news to Andreas over a special dinner I had prepared of Wiener schnitzel and asparagus.

"I have invited the members of the Secession committee to visit the studio. They're interested in mounting an exhibition."

"How did you manage that?"

"I showed them prints of the Warriors. I wanted to surprise you and also demonstrate to you I can be more than your model."

"So that's where you've gone on those afternoons when you weren't home."

Ah, he'd noticed. I decided it was better for him to think I spent all those afternoons doing his work instead of mine.

"You're amazing! I've been trying to get in front of the committee for the last month. I thought my previous success at the Secession would have been enough for them to notice me, but I didn't even get in the door."

I knew he hadn't even tried. Carl Moll had told me himself he hadn't had any contact from Andreas. For all his ambition and bravado, it appeared that my husband didn't know the first thing about promoting himself.

"I've made an appointment for Moll and other members of the association to come next week. After dinner, let's talk about how best to display the paintings in the studio."

The following week, I gave up my class to host the committee. Choosing not to disguise myself this time, I wore the draped costume I had created for the Penthesilea portrait. I had wine and cakes ready, and had printed each story on a separate card accompanying its painting.

Andreas paced the hallway waiting for their arrival, and I calmed him with my touch.

"What if these paintings don't measure up? They lack the visceral power of the Awakening series. The Secession chose those paintings for their ability to confront the viewer with hidden desires. These Warriors are too conventional. I'm no longer the *wunderkind*, the young genius turning the art world upside down. Too many of the committee saw the work I did while you were gone, and I could sense them shaking their heads in pity that I'd never be able to create another series that matched the Awakening one."

"When did they see them? You're usually so circumspect about showing your work in progress."

"I invited Engelhart and Bacher here one day last year. We'd been drinking the night before, and I wanted to get their opinion on the direction I'd taken. It was a stupid mistake."

It was no wonder he'd been flailing in trying to convince the Secession to give him another show. Those paintings he did without me were unremarkable compared to the Awakening nudes.

"Have a drink and stop pacing. They've agreed to come again despite what they saw last winter. I don't believe they'll be disappointed."

He took my suggestion and was less agitated by the time the committee arrived, but I was concerned to learn about the previous visit. It meant the committee would be more skeptical about what they expected to see. They knew from the prints that the subject matter of the work was different, but I hoped that in viewing the original paintings, they would understand Andreas had not lost his ability to capture the truth of human experience.

I opened the door to the studio for them with a flourish. Music emerged from the gramophone exactly as it had been playing when Andreas painted. I said nothing, letting them wander from easel to easel. I had cautioned Andreas not to interject his own comments.

"Let the paintings speak for themselves."

More than once, the men looked from the paintings to me. They could see I was the face of the Warriors. They needn't know I was also the driving force behind the series.

When they had finished their perambulation of the studio, I offered them glasses of wine and then stood back while they conferred, first with each other and then with Andreas. When I saw them smile and offer their hand to Andreas, my breathing eased and I released the stiff posture that had held me up.

After the men from the committee had left, I returned to the studio with Andreas, and together we collapsed on the divan. He poured us each another drink, double this time.

In the euphoria induced by the committee's decision to mount another exhibition of Andreas's work, I decided the time had come to reveal my own aspirations.

"Are you familiar with the Vienna School of Applied Arts?"

"Max studied there about ten years ago. I think he teaches there now."

I hadn't known that. The possibility of encountering anyone I knew in the halls had not occurred to me. Our artist friends were all serious professionals, well on their way to recognition and not in need of instruction. But of course they might teach. I now had even more reason to tell Andreas about my drawing class.

"Why do you ask?"

"I've been accepted to study there."

"Study what—interior or fashion design? That's wonderful. I've been thinking of contacting them for a referral for a designer for the apartment. Now you could do it."

"Not design. Painting." I held his gaze.

"I see."

What do you see, Andreas? A rival or a partner whose work you will support? I didn't express my thoughts out loud, but

I knew this was a crucial question that remained unanswered.

"I'm taking a drawing class two afternoons a week, but expect to add painting to my schedule soon. I'll need space here." I extended my arm to take in the studio.

"Fine."

"With the Warriors going to the Secession Building, it will open up some room for me."

He didn't ask to see any of my work or inquire where my interest in becoming a painter had originated. I didn't expect him to, and was grateful that he hadn't voiced any objections over losing space to me or losing my attention. For the moment, I had avoided those battles.

"What shall we do to celebrate your new exhibition?" I thought it best to shift the focus back to him. I'd carve out a corner of the studio another day.

He wanted to go to Café Museum, so that's what we did. He bought a round for everyone and took some teasing from our friends that his fortunes had, once again, turned with my presence.

With the revelation that I, too, was painting, our daily lives took on a different rhythm. I was relieved that the new exhibition kept Andreas sufficiently occupied such that he wasn't ready to begin a new painting. My modeling duties were in abeyance, and I embraced the freedom, immersing myself in my own work.

I was asked to contribute to a student show at the school and decided to concentrate on portraits of faces I'd seen on my morning wanderings—a fisherman, a mother reading on a park bench while her infant slept in a wicker cart beside her, a chestnut vendor on the Ringstrasse, a carnival operator at the Prater. In all, I created six character studies, the faces depicted on small canvases.

I invited Andreas to the opening, a modest affair with punch and cookies that was attended mainly by the families of the students. Because he had students exhibiting, Max was there. Until the show, I hadn't crossed paths with him at the school, although I'm sure Andreas had mentioned to him that I was studying there.

While Andreas strolled around the gallery, I stopped to chat with a classmate. Max soon approached and joined the conversation. After the other woman had drifted away, Max turned to me.

"You are a woman of many talents."

"Thank you."

"Those faces are quite good."

"You sound surprised."

"I didn't intend to imply that you weren't capable. Nevertheless, they show mastery that one might not expect from a beginner. You must have studied elsewhere before enrolling here."

"I did, in Greece. I developed a passion for portraits while working with Elise Goldberg. Do you know her work?"

"I'm not familiar with many women artists, though it's clear she taught you well."

I nodded in agreement. "Yes, she did."

I detected that it was a concession from him to acknowledge Elise's skill as a teacher. It also saddened me that he did not recognize her name.

Chapter Thirty

While my debut did not garner a mention in the newspaper, I was pleased that Andreas's Warriors show elicited almost as much attention as the Awakening exhibition. The critics were predictable in their praise or condemnation. Members of the Secession committee hinted that some institutions, not simply private buyers, were interested in purchasing his paintings. His name was also being suggested for permanent and monumental installments, including a mural for the university and a commission from a count who had become enamored of avant-garde art.

Andreas spent his day sketching ideas, many of which ended up torn from the pad and left scattered on the floor, stained with coffee and wine. I did not intervene. My corner of the studio took on its own identity. I was encouraged to experiment and had a mix of successes and failures. I was still working in small forms. Canvases were expensive, and I hadn't sold anything.

Unfortunately, the hints and suggestions that had been circulating at the Secession Building hadn't yet materialized for Andreas, and the exhilaration we had both experienced when the show opened was difficult to sustain. We needed Andreas to sell a new painting or take a commission for a society portrait to keep food in the larder, though the latter option did not appeal to him.

"I despise these portraits. I need to continue the new path I forged for my work. The tedium of Vienna's simpering belles is devouring my creativity. But you are becoming remarkably proficient at your character studies. A portrait commission would be perfect for you."

"Except that I'm unknown. Those with money to spend want the status of an Andreas Brenner portrait."

We needed to solve our financial situation soon or our elegant abode, and especially our magnificent studio, would slip from our paint-stained fingers. The worries about money weighed more heavily on me than on Andreas. He seemed to blithely ignore the pile of bills on the dining table as he left for the coffeehouse and esoteric discussions of the meaning of art in the modern world.

Despite my privileged upbringing, I was well aware of what was required to run a household. Both my mother in Vienna and my grandmother on Skiathos had, each in her own way, taught me the skills I needed. I prided myself on transforming the apartment into a home as well as a workplace for both of us.

I knew it would fall to me to find another source of income. On one of my morning walks, I made my way to Friedrichstrasse and rang the bell to Max's studio. Unlike Andreas, Max was awake and working.

"Maya! What brings you here?"

Before I could change my mind, I blurted out, "Are you still interested in having me model for you?"

A smile spread across his face as he ushered me into the studio.

"Don't misunderstand me, Max. I'm offering to be your model, not your muse and certainly not your lover. You know I can transform how a painter sees and subsequently reveals his subject. I am offering that skill to you, for a price."

"And what might that price be?"

We negotiated terms, and I left to convince Andreas of the necessity of my working with Max. It was not a tranquil conversation.

"You promised me that you wouldn't model for him."

"That was before I knew we would both need to bring in money to support ourselves. We've already been through this. My paintings are unknown, but my reputation as an experienced and skillful model is recognized. I can at least keep a roof over our heads while you find another lucrative commission."

"But why did you go to Max of all people?"

"Because we know him, he had already asked me, and he can pay."

"I don't like it."

I refrained from throwing the bills at him and instead said, "Then tell me how you intend to pay for these." I pushed the pile across the table. "Among many other things, our line of credit for art supplies has been shut down. We can't even get more canvas or pigments to create work we might be able to sell. What alternative do you propose?"

He flipped through the stack, glancing at the amounts without reacting to their magnitude. I couldn't understand how he could be so oblivious to the costs of daily living. Perhaps the steadiness of his income when he was only painting society portraits had lulled him into thinking he would always have a continuous stream of funds. His decision to move to the apartment had been based on the success of the Secession paintings, but the income from their sale was gone—through carelessness or ignorance or drunkenness. It didn't matter how. The money had been spent.

"Very well. If there's no alternative, go ahead. But I want my own time with you."

"When you are ready, of course."

With an excruciating attention to the needs of three artists—Andreas, Max, and me—I built a schedule both men could live with and from which I could extract a few hours each day for myself. The fact that Andreas did not have a major new project underway was the only blessing in an otherwise complicated and fraught arrangement. But over the next six months it paid the bills.

Chapter Thirty-One

I WIPED MY HANDS on a coarse rag after cleaning my brushes and pressed my palms against the small of my back, leaning back into a stretch. I was tired; I was stiff; I was cold.

I hadn't wanted to stop to stoke the fire, and now I was paying for it. I had been immersed in color and form, experimenting again with the layering I found so compelling, and had ignored my physical needs. Normally, I could paint for hours without exhaustion. Emotionally drained, yes. Euphoric sometimes on those days when what I have conceived in my head flows through muscle and sinew and blood and leaps from my hovering hand onto the canvas.

But this time, it was different. An ache gripped me, almost crippling me, as I attempted to move across the room to the stove. I grabbed the back of a chair and steadied myself, then slid around to sit down. I could feel my scalp prickle, sweat emerging from the roots of my hair under the scarf I had bound around my head, as though I was a washerwoman bent over a steaming cauldron or a peasant plowing the garden. A wave of nausea accompanied the sweat, and I imagined the color draining from my face, as if the canvas had absorbed it all.

I shivered. Was I becoming ill? I sat for a few minutes, forcing myself to take deep breaths. As I recovered from what I could only describe as a "spell," as if a curse had been placed on me, I reacted with anger. I had always had command of my body, whether I was modeling for Andreas or pouring my soul onto the canvas or arching into orgasm under Andreas's hand. Perhaps for the first time, I felt betrayed by my body.

I shook off the discomfort and stood forcibly, almost marching across the floor to the stove. I hooked the handle of the stove with a poker and pulled the door open. A pathetic glimmer of dying embers greeted me, and I stirred them up and blew, puffing them back to life. I threw in a few logs from the basket and held my hands up to the open door to warm them. Once the fire caught, I shut the door and went to the kitchen to make a cup of tea. After some effort, I found a cup that wasn't overflowing with ashes from Andreas's cigarettes or serving as a holder for brushes. By the time the water boiled, I was wrapped in a shawl. I moved back to the studio to study the canvas, but not too closely. I wanted an impression from a distance, as if I were a visitor in a gallery and not the artist who had wielded the brush. I walked slowly around the room, observing the canvas from several angles as I cradled my tea.

It was important to me to do this before Andreas returned. Unlike Andreas, who craved my attention when he was in the midst of a painting, I needed solitude. It was my own fault. I had alternately cajoled and challenged him from the first moments of entering his studio. I believed so fervently in his talent, his vision, that I could not hold myself back from expressing both what I saw on the canvas and what I saw with my mind's eye that he could still bring forth.

It was a power I wielded over him that both fulfilled and drained me.

But in that moment, standing before my own canvas, I needed to listen to the voice I had too often directed to Andreas and failed to offer myself. The canvas rewarded me for the attention I offered it. There was much to like in what I saw: the way the light caught a thickened layer of goldenrod I had slathered onto the forehead; the shape of the nose, accentuated by the shadow fading from indigo to lavender; the reflection in the green-gold iris created by a speck of zinc white. But when I shifted my position again, I saw a flatness of expression confronting me in the woman's image. *My* image. This was my fifth self-portrait, and still something continued to elude me.

A niggling voice asked if it was the execution or the subject that was the source of my disappointment. Was my own face so devoid of energy? Was it I who presented a blank visage, a mask that even the artist herself could not remove?

I lifted the canvas from the easel and placed it face to the wall alongside the other four. I draped an old shawl over the collection of wood and cloth and gesso, and turned to make Andreas his supper.

He was late arriving home, slightly drunk, but not so deep in his schnapps that he had slipped into melancholy. He ate his soup and bread with little conversation and retired to his armchair by the stove in the parlor with the newspaper. By the time I finished clearing the table and washing the dishes, I was too tired to join him. I went to bed. Sometime during the night, I stirred and found him snoring beside me.

In the morning, he was gone when I finally woke, still exhausted. It was just as well he wasn't there, because as soon as I rose, another wave of nausea overcame me and I barely reached the basin I'd left overturned in the sink the night before.

I wiped my mouth and cleaned the basin. I clearly was ill and abandoned my plans for the day. I knew I couldn't tolerate the aroma of coffee, but I managed to brew myself a cup of chamomile tea before retreating to bed.

I woke again around noon, famished and no longer queasy. I had a few eggs and some potatoes in the larder and made one of YiaYia's omelets, although I had no feta to truly replicate a meal as familiar and comforting to me as mother's milk.

Fortified, I dressed and went out to do the marketing. I returned with my market basket laden and deposited it on the kitchen table before seeking out Andreas, who was home early. I found him rummaging through a trunk.

"We've been invited this evening to Madame Zuckerkandl's salon. I saw Walter at the café, and he managed to secure us an invitation. Where's my white silk cravat?"

I crossed the room and opened the armoire. There on the floor in a shimmering puddle was his cravat. I shook it out.

"It will need ironing. I'll take care of it. What time does the salon begin?"

"Eight o'clock. Wear the red dress."

Of course. A signature. I pulled it from the same armoire and hung it by the window to air out. By the time I'd ironed the cravat, fixed my hair, and donned the dress, it was time to go. Thankfully, I hadn't had another episode of nausea.

We took the trolley to Madame Zuckerkandl's and made our way up the staircase to her apartment on Nußwaldgasse. The rooms were bustling with activity. Crystal goblets brimmed with Burgundy. Pearls, sapphires, and golden bangles flashed in the candlelight as the hands they adorned gestured in emphasis or greeting; an electric hum vibrated throughout, carried on the smoke of cigars, pipes, and a few cigarettes decorating the tips of ebony holders. I absorbed it all, watching as if it were a mural or, rather, a theater piece, which, of course, it was. Every guest there was a performer, singing for the attention of the money in the room, or a professor who could recommend a fledgling academic to a prestigious post, or a bored wife who would appreciate and reward an attentive new lover.

Andreas and I split apart five feet inside the apartment. We never moved through these events together. There was too much to glean and gather. It was better for us to be in two places, hearing different stories and comments. It was better for each of us, as well, to be performing alone. If I was by Andreas's side, it was too easy for people to recognize me from the Awakening paintings and dismiss me. But on my own, even in the red dress, I could exist as my own person.

Normally at these soirees, I would pluck a glass of wine from the wandering trays, but my spells warned me off imbibing that night. I did not want to make a mad dash for the lavatory in this company.

Instead, I roamed the rooms, catching fragments of conversation until I found a circle of unfamiliar faces paying rapt attention to a formally dressed middle-aged man. I slipped in between two young men. Neither exhibited the flamboyance or studied carelessness of our artist friends. They were eager, hungry almost, for whatever wisdom was being offered.

"It's Dr. Freud," the man on my left whispered to me in a tone of awe. He clearly expected me to be suitably impressed, and I nodded with a knowing smile. I did know who Freud was. I'd come across one of his monographs about the subconscious. I was curious.

Freud had alternately fascinated and outraged Vienna with his theories. Had my parents moved in more academic circles, they might have sent me to him instead of to Skiathos when my own eroticism and flagrant disregard for the rules of polite society had horrified them. What secret longing might Dr. Freud have excavated in what my parents perceived as my troubled soul?

As it was, I preferred to delve into these secrets myself, uncovering them on the canvas instead of on Freud's infamous couch. I suppose for those who did not have the outlet of creativity as a means of expressing themselves, Dr. Freud's explorations could be beneficial or curative—if one were seeking a cure, that is.

I was not.

But I listened and observed. The circle consisted only of men, earnest and attentive. Were they there to find answers for their own uneasy spirits? More likely, I suspected, it was to weigh Freud's usefulness for someone else—a sister, a lover, an unhappy wife—because these men did not appear to me to be the type who did much soul searching. As I listened to Freud pontificate, I began to realize that his understanding of women's longings and hidden desires was not only meager but ridiculous.

I quickly became bored and slipped away.

I was parched and also longed for a cigarette. Somewhere in the warren of rooms, I thought I might at least find a glass of bubbly mineral water. Madame Zuckerkandl was deep in conversation with Walter, and I could see Andreas standing in the doorway. His eagerness for her attention was practically oozing out of his pores, and I knew he was preparing to launch himself into their tête-à-tête. I turned to my back, happy to have been presented with a sideboard upon which a seltzer bottle and several glasses were laid. As I reached for the water, another wave of nausea attacked me, and I bent over with a small gasp. Grasping the edge of the sideboard, I gritted my teeth, willing it to pass, and then felt a cool hand slip around my waist and a voice close to my ear murmur, "My dear, come with me where you can recover yourself."

It was Madame Zuckerkandl, who had abandoned Walter and thwarted Andreas to come to my aid. I had no energy to be embarrassed by the attention and allowed myself to be led to a quieter corner of the apartment away from the alcohol- and ambition-charged din. We were in a bedroom, most likely Madame Zuckerkandl's. I eased back into a chaise longue and then felt the ministration of those cool hands again, this time pressing a wet cloth to my brow.

"I imagine you are still in the phase of not being able to keep down much food. When was the last time you ate?"

I thought back to the morning and shook my head. "Not since breakfast. I had a bit of tea and bread." Was my illness something familiar to her? Was it spreading through the city?

"When are you due?"

"Due?" I looked at her in confusion, and then saw an awareness spread across her countenance.

"My dear, I'm afraid I've made an assumption out of my own experience. Forgive me, but may I ask you a few personal questions in order to better help you through this episode?"

I nodded, still floundering.

"When was the last time you bled?"

I raised my eyebrows. This was not a question I'd ever been asked. At first, I was unwilling to even consider it. I'm not particularly modest. God and all Vienna know that, but it had stupidly never occurred to me. I had taken precautions, using a pessary. Andreas and I having a child at this moment in either of our lives was simply unthinkable.

But Madame Zuckerkandl was forcing me to think. I turned away from her and pounded the back of the couch with my fist.

"No! No!" My outburst was muffled in the cushions, but did not escape Madame Zuckerkandl.

"I felt the same way when I first realized I was with child. You may not remember me, but I know who you are. No, not as Brenner's infamous nude or even as Brenner's lover. I saw your work at that group exhibition at the Vienna School of Applied Arts a few months ago, but I haven't seen anything since. I'd be honored to stop by your studio for tea. Shall we say next Wednesday? You can show me what you've been working on, and I can share with you some wisdom about the unique challenges women face as both artists and mothers. What do you say? Now come wash your face and tidy your hair and return to the salon when you are ready. And eat something in the dining room. I assume Andreas does not know yet of your condition, and I shall not be the one to tell him."

I was not quite ready to rejoin the salon. My physical discomfort had subsided, but the terror of Madame Zuckerkandl's suspicion about my condition had hardened to a deep chill. I was paralyzed. My limbs refused to move, as if remaining hidden in Madame Zuckerkandl's bedroom would keep my condition in stasis. No growth, no change. I was a child who closes her eyes and believes she is invisible.

I could not think. I could not anticipate the next week when Madame Zuckerkandl planned to visit, nor the next months of heaviness and fatigue and the occupation of my body by another being. I could not even imagine the next few hours, when I would have to face Andreas as an entirely different woman, because that is how I felt. I was no longer Maya Sircos Brenner the nascent artist, the muse in the red dress, the outspoken flaunter of Vienna's repressive rules. I felt obliterated by the tiny being that had taken root in my womb.

Nevertheless, as kind as Madame Zuckerkandl had been, she would not countenance my hiding for much longer in her boudoir. She, at least, had seen a side of me that existed mostly in the shadows of Andreas's talent. She knew my work and had remembered it, even though my few pieces had been surrounded by others. I stiffened my spine, both literally as I rose from the couch and metaphorically as I prepared to reenter the fray of the salon.

I had gone that evening with nothing to prove, no one to impress. It was Andreas who needed the approbation and attention. Until the unexpected conversation with Madame Zuckerkandl, I had been merely an observer, amusing myself with the various scenes unfolding in the heady atmosphere of Viennese art and literature and science. But now the spotlight would turn toward me, at least in the form of Madame Zuckerkandl's astute gaze.

I was determined to be glittering, to sparkle like the jewels that had first attracted my attention. I would appear to have stepped out of one of Klimt's paintings. I would not slink away, tugging at Andreas's velvet sleeve to take me home.

I set my feet on the floor and swept out of the room. My red dress flowed, floating evocatively around my body. When I entered the parlor, I saw Madame Zuckerkandl nod and I returned the gesture.

It was well past midnight when Andreas and I arrived home. I could barely peel the dress off before collapsing on the bed. Ordinarily, after a night like that one, Andreas would have been hungry for my touch and for my affirmation that the evening had been a success for him. But that night, he was drunk and either as exhausted as I was or subdued by the reception he felt he had received from the august company at Madame Zuckerkandl's salon. He stretched out beside me, managing to remove only his shoes and his cravat, and promptly began to snore. I pulled the duvet over us and turned on my side, cradling my still-flat belly. Tomorrow, I would face this new awareness and decide what to do.

Chapter Thirty-Two

ANDREAS WAS STILL SLEEPING when I awoke to another bout of nausea. I knew I could use the excuse of too much wine if Andreas questioned my pallor and discomfort, but he did not stir when I left our bed for the lavatory. After a slice of dried bread and a cup of tea, I regained my equilibrium and decided to escape the confines of the apartment. Although the air was brisk, the sun was bright and the allure of an energetic stroll tugged at my spirit. Walking while thinking had often been a balm to me. Stillness wasn't one of my strengths, and I feared slipping into a morass of despair and defeat if I remained at home, brooding over my future and my relationship with Andreas.

I secured my hat, buttoned up my coat, and left the building for Danneberg Park. A cacophony of jackdaws greeted me as I strode the familiar paths. Winter's dull browns and bare branches seemed to match my mood, but the spare landscape revealed hidden feasts for the eyes. A black squirrel dug furiously in the barren flower beds, hunting for a long-buried acorn. Above him, a chattering bird warned of some unseen threat. A beetle crawled across my path, its iridescent carapace reflecting the late morning sun. I sealed the shapes and shadows of these images in my memory to retrieve at a later moment in front of the canvas. I didn't often paint landscapes, except when I was on Skiathos, but this morning's urban creatures intrigued me. My brain churned with unexpected possibilities, and I stopped my striding to sit on a bench. Rather than wait until I could return to the studio, I pulled from my pocket the small sketchpad I tried always to carry with me and, with a few quick strokes, captured the small scenes I had witnessed. I regretted only having a slim carbon pencil, as it was the colors that had most fascinated me—the varieties of brown in particular, from the deep, textured bark of a tree to the faded dun of an expanse of lawn. I promised myself I would come back soon with my small easel and my box of pigments. I prickled with urgency. How much time did I have until the physical burdens of pregnancy and then the demands of motherhood cut short my creative spirit?

I didn't want to leave the park and return to Andreas. I wasn't ready to tell him, and I doubted I could hide my anxiety. I had hoped that my walk would clear my head and open a path forward, but instead, it had only reminded me of how passionate I felt about transforming images from the world into art. I gasped at the thought of losing moments like this—small glimpses that become the seeds of something far greater. I was too new, my talents still forming, my vision not yet defined. I needed more time. I counted the days until Wednesday, when Madame Zuckerkandl had promised to visit. What did I have to show her? The five self-portraits were raw, unfinished, a pastiche of experiments, none of which had succeeded. I threw myself from the bench and hurried back to the apartment, hoping Andreas had finally slept off his stupor and gone out. I wanted solitude. Our rooms were dark and cold, the bed empty. I hurried to light the stove in the studio and throw open the curtains. I was famished. Is that what I would be confronted with in the coming months, a constant need for food? I slapped some cheese on a slice of bread and ate with one hand as I wrestled a small blank canvas to my easel. I smeared globs of burnt umber, burnt sienna, Cassel earth, yellow ochre, and cadmium yellow on my wooden palette and propped my notebook open.

I worked quickly, the shapes and colors that had captured my attention in the park emerging onto the blank canvas. But I quickly realized that I truly didn't want to paint birds and trees. What I wanted was to use the colors of that winter landscape as a language for what I truly wanted to paint—the human form. I took my brush and painted over what I had begun with swaths of yellow ochre. I opened the armoire door in the studio to expose the full-length mirror fastened on the reverse side. It was speckled, revealing its age, but I could see my entire body within the length and breadth of the oval. I moved the easel closer to the mirror and stripped to my petticoat, leaving my breasts bare, and began to create my outline on the canvas. Gradually, the image took shape, revealing through the slashes of color the tension emanating from my body. It was as if the woman in the painting was possessed by something outside herself. I was stunned by the unfamiliarity of my breasts as they emerged on the canvas. Had I not looked at myself recently? These were not the breasts Andreas had painted that heated night when we had made love for the first time. That body was one that had just been awakened to pleasure.

This body both contained secrets and revealed itself to hold a mysterious power. It was defiant and proud, but also still wrestling with whatever changes were taking place beneath the surface. I dipped my brush into a daub of cadmium red and added it to the brown I had used to define my nipples. That was what I had been trying to isolate, to identify as the difference between the nude of the young lover and the nude of the mother.

When I had begun the day, it had been with uncertainty and dismay, but when I stepped back from the canvas, I saw something entirely different—not quite acceptance, but a knowledge, at least, that I was strong enough to distill these profound physical changes into my art. I would make it work—my motherhood and my painting. I put my clothes on again and placed the new canvas face to the wall with the others. I felt a plan forming in my brain to chronicle the progression of my pregnancy. I smiled as I anticipated yet another scandal following in the wake of my actions.

My reverie was interrupted by the turn of the key in the lock. Andreas was home. The time of reckoning had arrived, but I was ready.

Or so I thought.

He was drunk. Alcohol never loosened Andreas up, relaxing him into the sort of comrade who could joke with his friends and buy another round for everyone because he was feeling the warmth of companions sharing good times. Alcohol made Andreas sullen.

He tossed his key and his hat on the table by the door; kicked off his boots, caked in mud; and crossed the room in his stockinged feet to the cabinet where we kept the whiskey. He held up the bottle to measure how much was left and poured himself half of what remained into a clouded glass.

It would have been futile to speak of anything important to him while he was in this state. In fact, it wasn't wise to speak to him at all. I waited to see which Andreas he would be this evening—the furious maestro, channeling whatever anger the drink had awakened into several hours in front of the canvas, or the despairing fraud collapsed in self-pity over squandered talent. He shuffled over to the chair by the stove, stretched out his feet, and nursed his drink with his eyes closed.

I shrugged. It would be a quiet evening. I retreated to the kitchen and beat together some eggs, flour, milk, and salt for *palatschinken*. I had a bit of plum compote, and thought the light pancakes and some fruit would be a gentle enough meal for my sensitive stomach.

I was preoccupied at the stove, pouring the batter into a pan, and didn't hear Andreas come into the kitchen until he had his arms around my waist and was nuzzling my neck. He reeked of cheap liquor and another cloying scent that was unfamiliar but undoubtedly feminine. I reached in my pocket for my handkerchief and pretended to sneeze to prevent the unpleasant odors from causing me to retch.

I slipped out of his embrace to flip the pancake and then slide it onto a plate.

"Hungry?"

He tore off a piece of palatschinke and popped it into his mouth.

"I'm meeting Tomas and Johannes for dinner later. Come to bed with me now. I have a different kind of hunger."

He pulled me toward the bedroom.

Reluctantly—did he even notice?—I turned off the gas, removed my apron, and followed him. He fumbled with his trousers and lifted my skirt. We might as well have been doing it against the wall and not in our own bed. He was seeking release and nothing more, this time with my body instead of the canvas. I rolled out from under him when he was done, and pulled down my skirt. I lay next to him as he recovered, and then he began to speak.

"And how was your day, Andreas? Oh, darling, thank you for asking. It was a disaster."

His voice was caustic.

So it was not going to be a quiet night.

"What has happened?" I steeled myself. Andreas labeling the day as a disaster could mean anything from running out of a pigment at a moment of inspiration to a bad review in the *Tagblatt*. He hadn't had a show since the

Warriors, and I thought perhaps that was what had caused his agitation.

"The library has rescinded its offer to have me paint the mural in the entry hall. I received word from Dr. Tandler, a pompous member of the board."

"Did he give you a reason?"

"Some nonsense about patrons concerned about the scandal attached to me from the Awakening exhibition."

"But that was nearly two years ago!"

"I believe someone who wants me to fail brought all the negative criticism to the attention of the board."

"Andreas, I know the art world is competitive, but who among your colleagues would do such a thing?"

"Max. First, he took you as his model, and now he wants to take my commissions."

"Max didn't take me. He paid me to sit for him when we needed the money. We would have lost this apartment, and our studio, if I hadn't taken the job. We talked about this. You agreed."

"Reluctantly, if you remember. Now I regret that I ever let you go to him."

"Andreas, you've seen the painting. There is nothing about it that identifies the subject as me, so no one's going to compare your interpretation with his. His style is completely different from yours and appeals to an entirely different client. I doubt very much that the library would even consider him for a mural."

"If it isn't a rival, then who is whispering in the ear of the board?"

I had my suspicions, but I wasn't about to share them with Andreas in his current state of turmoil. My father sipped brandy and smoked cigars with many of those men. I didn't doubt that he would sabotage my husband's career as a way of demonstrating I had made the wrong choice. Was he trying to drive me away from Andreas by impoverishing us? If so, he was underestimating his daughter.

But my concerns about my father's intentions would have to wait. Andreas needed reassurance.

"It's only one commission. There will be others. Remember, you have more than a model in me. I know how to advocate for you. We'll find other patrons who believe in the brilliance of your vision. Pull yourself together and go enjoy your dinner with Tomas and Johannes."

He left in a better mood. The sex and the solicitous words seemed to have given him new energy. I, on the other hand, slipped back into bed. My plans to continue painting were postponed as I acknowledged my exhaustion.

I don't know what time Andreas returned home. I woke early in the morning to find him asleep beside me. I eased myself out of bed and entered the studio carrying a basin as a precaution. The deeper I withdrew into the painting, the more energy I felt feeding me. The idea for the self-portraits excited me. For perhaps the first time, I saw a definite path ahead of me, instead of the constant experimentation that had marked my work since starting at the School of Applied Arts. I felt a confidence and a trust in myself as an artist with something to say.

Chapter Thirty-Three

Berta Zuckerkandl arrived promptly on the Wednesday afternoon after her salon. I hadn't told Andreas she was coming; I feared his desperate need for attention would overshadow my own work. As convinced as I was of Andreas's brilliance and potential for greatness, my belief in my own talent was still tentative. I wanted Berta Zuckerkandl's confirmation that I was a serious painter, and hoped she had a connection who might offer me a show.

For all my acumen and understanding of what constituted great art, I wasn't able to judge my own. I only knew that painting had unleashed a hunger in me to remove the veil obscuring my deepest fears and desires. The revelations presented in Andreas's Awakening series were mere surface images compared to what I intended to do with my own work. I would show not simply bared skin, but a bared soul.

She greeted me warmly and handed me a small package.

"It's ginger tea. I found it most helpful in my early months of pregnancy. How are you feeling?"

"Mainly exhausted. Mornings are difficult, but I've been able to work."

"Good! Now let's see what you've been doing since the school show."

I led her down the hall to the studio, and she stood in the doorway for a moment, her eyes sweeping the room, absorbing its totality, before she moved to the canvases.

"I find there's much to learn about an artist from her environment. What does she surround herself with? How does she organize her materials? Are there books or music? Some critics wish only to see the painting itself, but I want the backstory. I can tell even after this cursory glance which corner of the studio is yours and which is Brenner's."

With that statement, she marched across the room and began to study the canvases I had arranged along the wall. The differences between Andreas's work area and mine, between his art and mine, were indeed stark. Chaos and order. The artist observing versus the artist revealing. Portrait versus self-portrait. I was the source of the images in both his paintings and mine, but in the work I had created for Berta, I was gazing out, not being gazed at.

Berta moved deliberately from one painting to the next. I had placed them in a specific order, ending with the self-portrait I'd created since learning I was with child.

She finally turned to me. "I knew you had potential when I saw your portraits at the Applied Arts exhibit. You have not merely a well-honed technique but a remarkable grasp of the interior life of your subjects. The mother reading while her child slept was prescient. You didn't know you were pregnant when you painted it, correct? And yet you've captured what is most likely swirling through your mind as you adapt to this new stage of your life. What are your intentions with this last self-portrait?"

"I plan to chronicle my pregnancy with a new portrait each month."

"Astonishing! A remarkable idea that may hold some surprises for you. The changes are not merely physical as the body adapts to motherhood. Come. Let's sit and talk about the future."

I had tea and cakes ready and presided as I'd been trained by the nuns and my Viennese grandmother. But instead of chatting about fashion and balls, Berta and I mapped out a plan.

"I'd like to see you complete six more self-portraits of the emerging mother, enough to build a respectable show around. At the same time, can you create a few more of the small portraits? We can call it 'The Faces of Vienna.' I applaud you for what must be a regular practice of wandering for you to have found such iconic characters. Continue doing that. Meanwhile, I have an idea. Egon Schiele is proving to be quite a supporter of women artists. He's planning a show for women next spring at Salon Pisko, and I'm going to suggest he include your work."

"Hofratin Zuckerkandl, how can I thank you?"

"By producing more of what you've shown me today. And please, call me Berta."

I was overwhelmed by the gracious offer, and consequently threw myself into fulfilling Berta's expectations. I pushed myself to explore new neighborhoods on my walks, searching for subjects. I kept in mind Berta's characterization of the portraits as the faces of Vienna, and realized that I needed to include more than the workers who kept the city functioning. I took myself to Schönbrunn Palace and the Belvedere, even back to the university. As I sat sketching students who had been my former classmates, I thought I would feel regret. I had given up a place that I had fought for and that women like Liesl had practically begged me to maintain as a show of solidarity with the other women in my class. But as the faces took shape beneath my charcoal, I felt only exhilaration. I was doing what I was meant to do.

I knew I had paid dearly for the privilege of sitting on a bench and drawing in the middle of Vienna with the prospect of a gallery opening looming in the near future. The price had been marriage, not only the piece of paper that had been my passport out of Skiathos but also the time and energy expended in being a wife.

The greatest challenge to creating the work for the women artists show was, of course, Andreas. I wasn't sure which news was going to be more devastating for him to hear: that Berta Zuckerkandl had arranged an introduction to Egon Schiele for the purpose of including me in an exhibition, or that I was pregnant.

I couldn't delay too long in telling him either news—outside forces controlled the timetable. In the end,

I decided to inform him of both developments simultane-ously. One big disruption, rather than a prolonged draw-ing out of the inevitable.

We had just made love. He hadn't had too much to drink and wasn't about to slip into the profound sleep that usually followed our sexual encounters. I lit a cigarette for him and propped myself up on my elbow.

"I have some important news." That got his attention.

He looked expectantly at me, assuming I had wrought another one of my magical feats and obtained either a major commission for him or another exhibition, despite how little new work he'd produced since the Warriors.

"Berta Zuckerkandl apparently saw my portraits at the Applied Arts show and inquired about me. She thinks I have potential and has recommended me for an exhibition of women artists."

I wasn't going to reveal she'd also been to the studio and had taken on the role of mentor to me in matters of art as well as motherhood.

"That's interesting. Good for you."

I was relieved. He wasn't threatened. A women's show, in his eyes, wouldn't match the prestige of a Secession exhibit.

"Thanks. I have something else to tell you."

That made him uncomfortable. I suspect his mind went immediately to Max. Ever since I'd modeled for him, I had gotten the sense that Andreas was expecting me to confess to infidelity.

"I'm pregnant with our child. I expect we'll be parents by the end of May."

His silence confirmed for me that he was not pleased by the news. I reminded myself that I, too, was adjusting to my impending motherhood.

"It's overwhelming. I know."

"I thought you were taking precautions against this sort of thing." He made it sound like a disease that I had carelessly exposed us to. "What are you going to do about it?"

"Do? I'm going to have the baby. There is no other option at this point."

"I hadn't envisioned myself as a father. How can I paint if there's a child screaming in the background and the studio has been transformed into a drying room for nappies?"

"I hadn't envisioned myself as a mother either, but I'll adapt. I'm not the first woman to manage a child in addition to other responsibilities."

"But how can we be spontaneous, immersing ourselves in art and each other, if another human being is tilting our equilibrium?"

"Married couples have been resolving that dilemma for millennia, Andreas. I'm the one primarily responsible for our daily lives. If I have to, I'll strap the baby to my back the way tribal women do."

He was not reassured. I found it curious that he was more dismayed by the thought of the baby than he was by news about the Salon Pisko exhibition. The next day, he roamed through the apartment, fretting about where the baby would sleep.

"It's a big apartment, Andreas, and it will be at least a year before the baby will need its own room."

Perhaps he was looking for some aspect of this untenable situation that he could control. Because I was still coping with my own fears about what motherhood would mean for me, I could barely provide him the solace and reassurance he craved that his life and his art would not be disrupted by the presence of a child. At least he accepted without question that it was his child. I should have been grateful that he didn't accuse me of sleeping with Max, giving him an excuse to abandon me and the baby and pursue his art alone. But I knew he would not leave, because he could not imagine creating his art without me.

We achieved some rapprochement in the months leading up to the Salon Pisko show. My nausea abated as suddenly as it had begun, and I painted in the mornings while Andreas slept off whatever carousing or morose descent into frustration the alcohol caused him. In the afternoons, I posed for him. I had devised a new theme for him to pursue depicting the Merseburg charms, and it kept him focused.

Still, I was aware he was struggling. He painted for only a few hours every day, instead of being driven by the obsessive, energetic pace that had accompanied his earlier work. Instead of coaxing him to work longer, however, I let him be. With my newfound time, I walked around Vienna to find more subjects for my portraits.

Chapter Thirty-Four

I WAS EIGHT MONTHS pregnant when the Salon Pisko exhibition opened. Until I arrived to oversee the hanging of my paintings I didn't know who all the other artists were. Berta had mentioned a few but told me Schiele was approaching others as well.

Despite my cumbersome body, I was excited by the physical act of mounting my display in the area assigned to me. As Berta had recommended, I'd completed six more of the pregnancy chronicle, bringing the total for the exhibit to seven. An eighth was in progress at the studio. I also had a dozen small portraits, including one of my former classmate Liesl, who had agreed to sit for me. Her initial disappointment that I had given up my seat at university was tempered by her realization that I was forging a different path for women artists.

When I finished supervising the hanging of all the paintings, I wandered through the gallery to see who else was there. To my utter delight, I saw a painting I recognized immediately—a field of poppies.

"Elise!" I ran as quickly as my awkward and increasingly unfamiliar body allowed. She turned at the sound of her name and recognized me immediately, despite the radical change in my shape since we'd last seen each other. We embraced and exclaimed with joy over the prospect of finding ourselves in such remarkable circumstances.

"You must tell me everything that has happened since you left Skiathos."

"Likewise! I didn't expect to see you in Vienna, but I'm more than pleased you're here."

After her work was hung to her satisfaction, she came to see my paintings and then we retreated to a coffeehouse.

"We only arrived back from Argentina about a month ago, and I apologize for not seeking you out. It's been a whirlwind. Our uncle passed away after a lengthy illness, but at least we were able to be with him in his final months. We stayed on after his death to wrap up his affairs and because we found Buenos Aires a conducive environment for both of us to work. We came back because Oscar's novel was purchased by S. Fischer Verlag and is about to be published in Berlin. He's been furiously making corrections and proofreading, and I've been helping. As a respite from that intense work, we attended Berta Zuckerkandl's salon for an afternoon, and that is where I met Egon and why I'm a last-minute addition to the show."

"How is Oscar?" I tried to modulate my voice. Of course he'd be here with her in Vienna. When I had left Skiathos, I had never expected to see him again. My hands unconsciously went to my belly, now clearly visible under a loose dress I had discovered that was designed by Klimt's lover, Emilie Flöge. It wasn't specifically a dress for pregnancy, but it allowed a freedom of movement and level of comfort that made me feel stylishly adorned. What would Oscar think when he saw me? I wondered.

"Oscar is astonished, as I am, that he not only finished the novel but sold it to such a prestigious publisher. He was almost unbearable to live with in the last months of writing, burying himself in his work even more deeply than when we were on Skiathos. You should know that he experienced a burst of creative energy after we left that he attributed entirely to you. He called you his inspiration, an intensely burning filament of light. What you and he shared on Skiathos unleashed a torrent of words.

"But it appears you've undergone an artistic transcendence as well. The canvases you're exhibiting at Pisko are an incredible leap from your first tentative work when we began painting together. And you're experiencing yet another transformation in your personal life. May I offer my congratulations or . . . ?"

She glanced at my belly. My mind was still mulling over her remarks about Oscar and our apparent influence over each other, and I knew I would need to consider her words later, alone, so I pulled myself back. Did I trust Elise enough to reveal my complicated feelings about my pregnancy? If not Elise, who else could I speak with? Berta was an extraordinary mentor and voice of wisdom, but I hesitated to expose my vulnerability to her. Too much depended on her opinion. But Elise was my friend, and was apparently perceptive enough to sense that my pregnancy was a challenge.

"I certainly burrowed under the bedclothes for a few days when I realized why I was nauseated and exhausted, but I am coming to accept my situation. I have no idea how I will feel once this very active creature is out in the world and in my arms. So far, I haven't lost the ability to create, and I intend to fight fiercely to maintain my career."

"Your work on the maternal nudes speaks to everything you've just expressed in words—ambivalence, curiosity, and the stance of a warrior mother."

I smiled at her use of the warrior label to describe my defiant nudes. Is that how I defined myself, not only in the persona I created for Andreas but also in my self-portraits? How curious.

"I have missed you so much. Your provocative observations push me to consider aspects of my work and my life that have remained hidden."

"I have missed you as well. Dare I ask if you are married?"

"Oh, you may ask anything. Shortly after you and Oscar left for Argentina, my father decided marriage would put a stop to my scandalous behavior—particularly marriage to someone on Skiathos, far from the wagging tongues and scandal sheets of Vienna."

"You're married to a Skiathan!"

"No. I had enough warning to thwart my father's intentions. I knew marriage to a Skiathan would steal from me whatever remnants of my soul I'd been able to salvage. I came to the difficult realization that my only option for escaping marriage on Skiathos was to marry Andreas

Brenner. I reached out to him and he came, because it was in his interest to rescue me."

"And, how has it been...?"

"It has been an experiment, a series of lessons, a walk on a tightrope suspended above a river filled with monsters. But none of that was a surprise. I knew who Andreas was, and I took that step out onto the tightrope because behind me was a mountainous forest also filled with monsters."

"So no regrets?"

"My only regret was my naïve belief in my own power. I once thought of myself as an independent woman, but that has proved to be an illusion."

"Don't berate yourself for your choices, Maya. We make the best decisions we can with the information we have at hand."

I reached out my hand to her across the table. "You are the dearest friend."

We parted knowing we would see each other the next day at the opening. I hurried home as quickly as I could with my cumbersome body. Andreas would be waiting. As my pregnancy had progressed, I had become less desirable to him as a model. He'd been dismissive of my self-portraits, but I suspected that was only because he hadn't thought of the idea as a subject for his own paintings. I don't think he understood that the portraits were chronicling not only my physical changes, which were rampant, but also my emergence psychologically as a mother.

Instead of painting me, he was completing two paintings depicting the Merseburg charms, filled with horses and gods and forests, transforming the primitive spells into a twentieth-century exploration of humanity's descent. When he spent time at the canvas, he approached it with vehemence and a piercing vision. If only he would go there more often.

Chapter Thirty-Five

THE OPENING OF THE show hummed with a vibrancy and kaleidoscope of color and form. The champagne was pink, the artists were arrayed in gowns as flamboyant as their arresting paintings, and the critics could not disguise their enthusiasm. Credit was lavished on Egon Schiele for his foresight in collecting such an eclectic group of paintings. Schiele's association with the show had attracted an outsized audience for the salon. The rooms teemed with viewers surging and ebbing as they pressed from one group of paintings to the next.

I stood near my own work, an endless smile fastened to my face as if I had daubed it on with a brush. I ignored the backache and the fatigue as I acknowledged greeters, answered questions, and ignored the shocked responses of those who considered the fecund body of a pregnant woman an inappropriate subject.

I was longing for a chair when a flute of champagne was thrust into my hand.

"You look like you could use some refreshment."

It was Oscar's hand that had offered me the drink.

"My gallant savior!" I took the glass, but my hand was shaking. Even though I knew he would come, the nearness of him shattered my composure. "I could kiss you for this, among other things," I whispered.

But I didn't. He slid next to me as the crowd made its way around the room.

"I assume your husband is here somewhere in the room, and I shall therefore refrain from taking you in my arms."

I kept my eyes ahead and sipped my champagne, savoring every drop and every word.

"A wise choice, but I would reciprocate were we in another place and time."

"Tomorrow, then. We are staying at the Hotel Stefanie."

I nearly spit out my drink.

"I meant another lifetime."

"If no embrace is in our future, may I at least offer you a cup of coffee and a piece of cake at Café Central?"

"You may. Congratulations on your book's publication. I look forward to reading it in its entirety. I expect to hear the voice of a generation."

"Thank you. My congratulations, likewise. Elise told me I could expect to see you here, in order to prepare me. Otherwise, I suspect it would not have been a good scene—a grown man moved to tears at the sight of you."

Throughout our exchange, we did not look at each other but kept our eyes straight ahead. The conversation was broken periodically by my acknowledgment of a greeting or a comment as someone approached the paintings.

"I would never want to cause you to weep."

"It has already happened. I thought I was empty of my grief, but seeing you here tonight has rendered asunder my carefully rewoven heart."

"When I saw Elise yesterday and learned you were in Vienna, I also felt torn in two. I believed I could leave Skiathos and marry Andreas as long as I never saw you again. I've been swathed in cotton batting, my longing muffled for nearly two years, in order to survive. I'm no longer numb, feeling your warmth next to me, hearing your voice and your breathing. God help me."

"I can leave if you would prefer—the gallery tonight and Vienna tomorrow. My publisher would be happy to see me in Berlin."

"Please stay," I whispered. "I cannot bear for you to go away when I've only now allowed my heart to open again. It is excruciating to see and not touch you, but it is more agonizing to have no part of you at all."

"Then I shall stay and we shall nurse each other's wounds with words and not kisses. I enfold you in my thoughts. You have never left them. You are the source of the outpouring that became my novel."

I bowed my head in thanks. As I did so, my eye caught a movement by the door.

"My husband has arrived. It would be a kindness if you would drift into the crowd. I am too overwhelmed by your presence to dissemble in front of him that you are a stranger. I would rather not explain to him who you are tonight."

"I understand. Consider me a piece of flotsam floating away on the tide of these art lovers. Tomorrow, at Café Central at two o'clock?"

I nodded, and, as promised, he disappeared into the crowd. By the time Andreas arrived, I had recovered my composure and greeted him with a kiss.

"The place is bursting! Schiele has a magnetic pull. You ladies are fortunate to have his imprimatur."

I ignored his tone of belittlement. "We ladies" had earned our place on the walls tonight.

By the time we arrived home, my ankles were swollen. The baby had woken up and was pummeling me, and I was famished. The fancy canapés proffered on silver trays at the salon had hardly sufficed. Despite my exhaustion, I was still fizzing with exhilaration. My first professional show had exceeded my wildest dreams. Although I'd hoped Andreas might have been more excited for me or even simply supportive, I didn't allow his disinterest to dampen my joy.

I peeled off my shoes and stockings, hung my Emilie Flöge gown, and wrapped myself in a kimono.

"I'm going to scramble some eggs. Do you want some?"

"No, thanks. I'm heading out to the coffeehouse. If the early edition of the *Tagblatt* is out before I come home, shall I pick up a copy?"

"Yes, thanks. Do you really think the review could be out before the end of the night?"

"The night is still young for most of us, Maya."

I heard the door close slightly more forcefully than necessary as Andreas left. It was a relief that he had decided to go out. I didn't have the energy to assuage whatever resentment he was feeling. For most of my pregnancy, I'd not been able to keep the late hours that once had been a natural part of our artists' rhythm.

My mother had suggested it was nature's way of preparing mothers for the early months of an infant's life, when a baby has no concept of day and night. She had been remarkably supportive during my pregnancy and had suggested that when my time came, it would be wise to give birth at my parents' home.

"You'll need the support of women. Gertraud and I will be there with the midwife. Let me do this for you."

I thought back to YiaYia's story of the frightened young woman alone in her labor and agreed readily to my mother's offer.

I ate my eggs and curled up on the sofa, balancing the plate on my very large belly. In quiet and solitude, I allowed myself the luxury of contemplating Oscar's reappearance in my life. I had sealed away the longing, binding it tightly from the moment I left Skiathos. To dwell on the memory of the profound connection we had formed in those extraordinary months would have prevented me from salvaging what was possible in my marriage. I had made a commitment, a vow, despite the circumstances under which the marriage began, that I intended to keep. And although it had not been easy, I had put Oscar away in a secret place in my heart because he was no longer in my life.

It was both excruciating and overwhelmingly joyful to know he was near me once again. I had agreed to meet him, but I knew I had to be cautious with my heart and with my marriage. I could not allow myself to give in to what I so desperately wanted. But would I be able to resist? Could I see him, drink a cup of coffee with him, share with him the swirling contradictions and ambivalences of my impending motherhood and emerging recognition as an artist, and still keep from him the love I had buried and denied?

I thought it was a wonder that he did not hate me for the decision I made, even though it had been made out of necessity. But I knew I lacked the imagination and the daring to choose another life—a life with him.

I had been able to convince myself that I had no regrets. Despite Andreas's descent into a self-destructive melancholy I had not been able to rescue him from, I believed in Andreas's genius and in my capacity to nurture it. But the unanticipated demands of my pregnancy and the recognition of my own talent had left little energy or desire for saving Andreas.

Who was going to save me, nurture me? In my vulnerability, Oscar appearing at my side at the gallery, offering himself, had pierced the armor that was sustaining me. I knew I was at risk of letting him truly be the savior I had dubbed him to be when he had handed me the champagne.

My eyelids began to droop, and my hand nearly dropped the plate. My exhaustion was finally manifesting itself, and

I needed to go to bed. I would confront my dilemma in the morning.

Chapter Thirty-Six

THE BABY MIRACULOUSLY ALLOWED me to sleep late—no middle-of-the-night urgency to use the toilet or find a more comfortable position. Andreas's side of the bed was empty, and I detected immediately that he hadn't slept in it. This was a first. In the past, whatever he'd done during the night, whomever he'd been with, he had always come home.

What had precipitated the change? The exhibition? It wasn't yet clear if it had been a success for me. Had he seen me speaking with Oscar? It was possible, and would give him yet another reason to be angry.

With these questions swirling in my head, I rose, ate something nourishing, and riffled through the armoire for something suitable to wear for my meeting with Oscar. There was no possibility of recreating the carefree look of summer. I sighed and settled on a suit. It was my most conservative outfit, a relic of my university days that I had let out to allow for my changing body. I was trying to shield myself with the carapace of a disciplined, serious woman.

I pinned on my hat and left the apartment. My countenance was resolute, my stride as deliberate as possible in my condition. It was a practice I often engaged in when I was unsure of what I was about to face. I would act the role, even if I didn't believe it.

I hesitated at the door to Café Central. I understood myself well enough to know that stepping inside was a decision toward Oscar, toward revelation and risk, toward the possibility of joy and the destruction of the fragile walls of my marriage.

I pushed open the heavy glass and entered into a haze of smoke. The sound of clattering dishes and buzzing conversation filled the air. I scanned the room not only for Oscar but also for the faces of others who knew me, including Andreas's. It wasn't uncommon for him to stop here, and, in retrospect, I should have suggested another place. But it was too late now.

It appeared I was the first to arrive. Oscar wasn't among the murmuring guests. As I searched for a seat at a table where I could see the door, I felt eyes on me and saw heads tilted toward each other. I heard my name and references to Salon Pisko. Was word about the exhibit already out? I was glad of my hat and my modest outfit. Both protected me from what felt like an onslaught of attention. Was this a repeat of the public reaction to Andreas's Awakening series?

I found an empty table and took a seat. I didn't sink into it, but instead positioned myself with an erect posture and then looked out at the room. A number of people stared at me, and I stared back with defiance.

At that moment, Oscar arrived with three newspapers under his arm. He saw me across the room and strode quickly to join me, beaming. He placed the papers on the table.

"Have you seen the reviews?"

"No, but apparently half the people in this room have."

"You're a sensation. Berta Zuckerkandl has christened you, and the critics Arthur Roessler and Ludwig Hevesi were equally superfluous in their praise. You are a star."

I picked up the papers. Oscar had folded them with the reviews facing out. The only one I cared about was Berta's, and I devoured it. Warmth spread up my face, and I felt as if I was releasing a breath held too long underwater.

"I'm happy to see how highly she speaks of Elise's work. Without your sister, I wouldn't be sitting here today reading about myself. Please give her my congratulations and my thanks."

We ordered and waited until our coffees and pastries were on the table to begin the conversation I had been both dreading and longing for.

"Tell me truthfully how you are."

"Your sister asked me the same question. Did she not tell you?"

"She was quite circumspect, I think to protect me from hurt. Elise and I are close. As twins, we can often sense the other's feelings. She knows when we left Skiathos that I had lost more than a summer companion. I had lost my soulmate."

"How did you cope?"

"By pouring all of it into my novel—the wonder of discovery, the deepening of trust, the exhilaration of connection, and the devastation of loss. And you? What did you do?"

"Buried myself, as you did, in creating something that could only arise like a phoenix from the ashes of my grief and regret."

"So you do feel regret. I thought you told Elise you had no other choice but to marry Brenner."

"At the time, in my panic and fear, I could see no other way forward. I felt bound by constraints that I now understand were of my own weaving. Can you forgive me?"

"Only if you forgive yourself."

"I'm not at that point yet. My life has become enormously complicated by this child, but also by the child who still resides in my husband's troubled soul."

"Are you telling me once again that you're choosing him over me?"

I did not expect us to reach this point so quickly.

"Are you asking me to choose? Last night, you told me you'd abide by my wishes, that you would stay even though I could not offer you the flesh that hungers for you."

"It was easier to say that last evening, before a sleepless night spent wrestling with what sacrifice I'd be willing to make in order to stay."

All the turmoil that had disrupted my thoughts since Oscar had walked into the gallery now threatened to erupt. All the trappings of control and civility that I had structured around this meeting fell aside. I was aware of two shifts taking place simultaneously. I knew I wanted this man sitting across from me with all my soul, and I would find a way to convince him of my love.

At the same time, I gripped the edge of the table as a wave of pain convulsed me. It lasted less than a minute, but in the lull afterward, I sensed a sea change in my body. By the time the second wave rose through my body, I knew what was happening.

"Oscar, the baby. It's coming. It's too early."

"What can I do?"

"Get me a carriage."

He helped me up, threw some money on the table, and escorted me to the street. He was able to hail a cab before the next pain surged through me.

"Where to?"

"My mother. Elisabethstrasse, 23."

He held my hand and wiped my brow. If he was as frightened as I was, he did a magnificent job of disguising it. He murmured to me of halcyon days on the beach and the meadows of Skiathos. He even sang to me.

When the carriage arrived at my parents' house, he bounded up the steps to announce our arrival and then came back for me. It was Gertraud who answered the door and took me in her arms. My mother was close behind.

I sagged with relief, and my hand slipped out of Oscar's, but only after I felt a squeeze of reassurance. I was only half aware of the few words exchanged between him and my mother.

"Who are you?"

"The brother of her friend Elise."

"How long has she been like this?"

"About fifteen minutes. We were having coffee at Café Central to celebrate the exhibit."

"Thank you. You are most kind to bring her home."

And then the door was shut.

My labor lasted eight hours, one for every month of the pregnancy. I was attended by my mother, Gertraud, and the midwife who had delivered me two decades earlier.

My daughter, Sophie, was born at ten in the evening. Her lusty cries and her two-and-a-half kilo weight belied the fact that she was nearly a month early. As she nuzzled at my breast, I examined her perfect fingers and toes, stroked the downy black fuzz on her head, and felt the heft of her in my arms. I would have stared at her face for hours in awe of the sheer miracle of her existence, but my mother gently lifted her sleeping body from my arms and cradled her.

"She'll be hungry again before you know it. Get some rest. I'll be right here."

I dozed, ensconced in my old bedroom and cherished by the women who had cared for me as if I had never left home. When I woke to Sophie's cries an hour later, I asked my mother if Andreas had been told.

"I sent a message to your apartment, but he wasn't there. Your artist friend Elise stopped by around seven to ask about you. Her brother, the young man who brought you here, had told her. She was lovely, in the few minutes I could spare to talk with her."

"What about Papa?"

"He took himself to his club for the night when he realized what was going on. Men have no idea what it takes to sustain the human race."

Andreas arrived the next day. Elise had taken it upon herself to get word to him, tracking him down at Café Museum. His presence in the house was awkward but not disastrous. Anticipating that he might show up, my mother had convinced my father to stay the week at the club out of solicitous concern for his sleep.

Spared from a confrontation with my father, Andreas approached the bed and our daughter in my arms.

"She's tiny. I was surprised by the news when that friend of yours found me. You told me the baby wasn't due until next month."

"Most babies are small, but she's healthy. I may have miscalculated."

"You mean when you got pregnant?"

I could sense him counting back the months. Was he still obsessed with my modeling for Max? I waited. I knew it had been months after the session with Max before I became pregnant, but I was not going to defend myself.

"Would you like to hold your daughter?"

She was beginning to squirm, and I could see he was reluctant to take her. She answered for him with a hungry squall and latched onto my breast with a voracious slurp.

"Your breasts are different."

"They're full of milk."

"How long will you feed her?"

"Do you mean right now, or until what age?"

"What age."

"It depends on her. A year, perhaps."

She was only a day old, and already he was counting how much longer she'd have a hold on me, keeping me from him.

"How much longer will you stay here?"

"A few weeks, until I recover from the birth and have my energy back. I told you that was my plan."

"I want you home. I miss you."

I leaned my head back on the pillow as Sophie nestled against me in sated contentment.

"I can come home sooner if we get some help, someone to cook and clean."

His lips thinned in disapproval. "Still the debutante. You know we can't afford a servant."

"Then I imagine I'll be here for a while."

He left soon after, with no mention of when he'd be back. Flowers arrived from Berta, along with a note from Salon Pisko letting me know that seven of the Faces of Vienna series had sold and at least three buyers had expressed interest in the maternal paintings. While Sophie slept, I made notes in my journal. The proceeds from the sales would help keep us solvent.

Elise came to visit again, this time bearing gifts for both Sophie and me—a beautiful embroidered dress for her with a matching bonnet, a sketchpad and a painted silk scarf for me. During her visit, we danced around the topic of Oscar.

"He was quite overcome with awe and fear when he returned home after he brought you here."

"He was magnificent, Elise, keeping me calm with stories and songs. I don't know what I would have done if I hadn't met him at the café. I would have been alone in my apartment. We don't have a telephone. I'd have been down on the street attempting to hail a carriage while praying my water didn't break."

"Why did you agree to meet him?"

I sensed her guardedness, her wish to protect her brother from hurt. I'm sure she had borne the brunt of his pain after they had left Skiathos.

"I will admit to you that when I went to meet him, I was torn between my marriage vows and my love for Oscar. But I came to a decision once I was with him and was on the verge of telling him that this time, I had chosen him."

"But you didn't tell him."

"No. When I went into labor, every cogent thought flew out of my mind."

"He needs to know, Maya, and not from me."

"I know, but he can't come here. My mother knows he is your brother, but I do not need her disparaging yet another choice in my life. Can he wait until I return home?"

"And then what, Maya? Will you be any more free to talk with him? Where will Andreas be?"

I buried my head in my hands.

"Give me time, Elise. I'm exhausted, and I'm now a mother with a daughter to protect."

"I don't mean to push you beyond the limits of your capacity to balance all the elements of your complicated life, Maya. I understand that the tightrope you are walking now requires you to juggle knives as you traverse the wire. But Oscar is fast approaching his own limit, not knowing what you want. He's making plans to leave for Berlin."

"I cannot lose him, Elise! I will pull myself from this bed and go to him. There's a park around the corner. I'll meet him there tomorrow morning at eleven. Promise me you'll see that he gets there. Come for me, and I'll tell my mother you and I are walking."

"I promise."

The next morning, I bathed and dressed after feeding Sophie. She was too young to take outside, even swaddled in quilts and protected in the new pram my mother had bought. I told Mama I needed some fresh air and that Elise was coming to accompany me on a brief walk.

"You never could sit still for long. It will be good for you to have a break, but don't overextend yourself. Between us, Gertraud and I can manage Sophie."

Elise arrived promptly at quarter to eleven and led me to a secluded bench within the park. When Oscar arrived, she slipped away with a promise to return in fifteen minutes. I took Oscar's hand as we sat together.

"You were my savior once again."

"You're well? Elise tells me your daughter is beautiful."

"I can't thank you enough for the instrumental role you played in the birth of my daughter. But I haven't come here to talk about that. I've come to finish the conversation we began at Café Central before Sophie's arrival took us by surprise.

"I love you, Oscar. I did not have to struggle over the decision. How I become a part of your life, I still have to determine. But I am not looking merely for words from you. I want all of you. I want what we began in the shepherd's hut. Will you have me? I do not come unencumbered."

"I love you, Maya, and I already feel connected to your daughter, given my role in her birth. I want to spend the rest of my life with you, but I can wait."

He pulled me onto his lap, and I leaned against his chest. His arms around me and his heartbeat echoing mine gave me the strength I knew I would need in the coming days.

Chapter Thirty-Seven

SOPHIE AND I STAYED at my parents' house for two weeks. I wasn't ready to leave, but between the impatience of my father to sleep in his own bed and the urging of my husband for me to sleep in his, it became clear that the only way to restore equilibrium was for me to bundle up my daughter and go home.

Gertraud made soups and baked breads to stock my larder. My mother had bought out the children's shop on the Ringstrasse, and my grandmother had unearthed from her cedar chest the christening gown all of her children had been baptized in. I wrote an effusive thank-you note, recognizing that it had been a miracle Omama had even acknowledged Sophie, but I didn't mention it was unlikely we'd be bringing Sophie to church. My ostracism from Mama's family was loosening. I had actually produced a child within a marriage, however nonconforming the rest of my life had been, and for that, apparently, people were willing to forgive—to a point. Even Papa allowed himself to be mesmerized by his granddaughter.

He came home unexpectedly one evening for fresh clothes, and Mama and I were in the drawing room making a list of the gifts Sophie had received in her young life. Sophie slept contentedly in a basket at my feet. It was one of the few brief periods between feedings when I could actually do something with my hands. Papa stood in the doorway, watching us silently, before announcing himself.

I stood to greet him. It was the first time we'd had contact since the day he left Skiathos nearly two and a half years earlier. I was glad I wasn't holding Sophie. I'd already learned that my moods transmitted themselves directly to her when she was in my arms. The tension and suppressed anger engulfing me at the sight of my father likely would have caused her to scream inconsolably.

"Papa."

"Maya, you're up from your childbed. Good, good. Mama tells me that you and the babe are well, *Efcharisto stan Theo.*" Thanks be to God.

Sophie murmured in her basket, and I watched Papa struggle to remain stoic and unmoved by the scene before him. But he could not resist the pull of his grandchild, her tiny fist pummeling the air above the basket. He took one step into the room and then another. Surprising both my mother and me, and I think himself, he knelt down on the floor and gazed at Sophie, who opened her eyes at that moment.

"She has your mother's eyes."

He turned his head away from me as he stood up, avoiding my own eyes, but I saw the tears.

He left the room murmuring about his clothes, and Mama followed him up the stairs. I wasn't ready to sit down again to finish the list. Instead, I paced across the Persian carpet, keeping my steps light in order not to disturb Sophie.

I had understood somewhere in my milk-fogged brain that I might encounter my father, given that I was staying in his house, but I had been lulled by his absence. His unexpected appearance had caught me unprepared, but it seemed that he, too, was surprised to find me up and about. The shock of facing each other apparently muffled our reactions. While the air between us had rippled with tension, no words of anger had crossed our lips—but no words of forgiveness either. I had no expectation of his ever forgiving me, but I also knew I could not find it in my own heart to forgive him.

During my time on Skiathos, I had understood that my father's love was lost to me, but that night had given me hope that even if he no longer loved me, he would love my daughter.

I did not see him again before I left to return home to Andreas.

My departure took place in my father's largest carriage because of all the infant paraphernalia that needed to be transported. Sophie slept contentedly in my arms the entire ride. Andreas, who had come to retrieve us, sat opposite us and flicked his eyes from his sleeping daughter to his exhausted wife. Sleep interrupted every two hours by a hungry infant is no sleep at all. My mother, who had insisted on accompanying us, spent the entire ride observing Andreas; from her expression, it appeared she found him lacking.

When the carriage stopped in front of our building, its soporific effect on Sophie also ceased, and she woke with a howl. I managed to get her, screaming, into the lift, but not before the concierge stuck her head out the door of her apartment and fixed a look of intense disapproval on my struggles to calm Sophie. I left Mama and Andreas behind to deal with the luggage and the pram, and urged the lift up the four stories to our door. With the screaming Sophie in one arm and my keys in the other, I struggled to get inside. I put Sophie momentarily on the carpet while I peeled off my coat and my blouse, cooing gently to her. Sweat poured down my neck and dampened my chemise under my arms. She was hysterical by the time I put her to my breast, and it took her a few minutes to settle down. At such a young age, could she already detect the change in her environment?

I smelled traces of turpentine and linseed oil, the onions and sausage Andreas must have cooked the night before, and his Turkish cigarettes. When I had lived here before, I had barely noticed the odors, but now they assaulted me, just as they had affected Sophie and warned her she was in a strange place. By the time Mama and Andreas came through the door, Sophie had calmed down, although she was by no means her usual placid self. I didn't think I could place her in her basket and help with the unpacking, so I instead played the role of director, determining where the boxes and crates should go. Mama took over in the kitchen, unpacking the hamper of food Gertraud had prepared and muttering that she should have sent Gertraud ahead to scour the place.

It was true. Andreas, living on his own for two weeks, had left a trail of debris in the kitchen and beyond. As I walked through the apartment, determining where to store things, I found dirty plates on the floor by the bed, newspapers strewn on tables and chairs, empty bottles of wine and beer everywhere. I avoided the studio. I couldn't bear to see if he had done any work, and I didn't want to contemplate when or how I'd find time to paint myself. When Sophie finally fell asleep in my arms, I gingerly set her down in the pram and rocked it for a few minutes until I was sure she was asleep.

Only then did I put on an apron, open all the windows, and set about establishing some semblance of order in my home. Andreas's discomfort with my mother's presence and the piles of Sophie's belongings was so pronounced that I suggested he retreat to the studio. He did so with alacrity, relieved to be free from the unfamiliar faces and things around him.

Mama and I worked together in synchrony. Before Sophie's birth, I had rarely witnessed her doing any kind of serious domestic chores, but she rivaled YiaYia in terms of both her competence during my labor and later her ability to manage the household around the demands of a newborn. Now, she rolled up her sleeves and donned one of my aprons as she scrubbed and swept and made room in my armoire for Sophie's clothes and nappies. She found an enameled tub for soaking dirty nappies and placed it in the bathroom, along with an array of laundry powders to clean them and creams for Sophie's tender skin.

By the time the bells in the nearby church were tolling the noon hour, the apartment was orderly, the table was set in the parlor, and Gertraud's chicken and dumpling soup was simmering on the stove. Sophie still slept, which was something of a miracle. I knocked on the studio door to call Andreas to the midday meal. When he didn't respond, I opened the door to find him sprawled on the divan asleep. A half-empty bottle of whiskey was on the floor next to him. I closed the door and joined Mama for the last of our meals together.

"You'll let me know if you need anything? I'm happy to come back or send Gertraud once or twice a week to clean and put in some food."

"Thank you for the offer, Mama. I will think about it. For now, I'd like to get settled into a rhythm that I can sustain on my own."

"Don't overdo it. You are still in a weakened state and need to rest. If you don't want Gertraud, surely Andreas can afford to hire someone for a few hours a day. He's a successful artist."

"We'll see. Until I start selling more of my work, we'll need to be frugal."

My mother stayed to do the washing up and helped me bathe Sophie after she woke and fed again. After Mama left and I closed the door behind her, I pressed my forehead to the wood. I was relieved to be once again mistress of my home and my life, but I was also frightened to hold the life of my daughter in my uncertain hands.

Chapter Thirty-Eight

SOPHIE WAS ASLEEP WHEN Andreas emerged from the studio.

"If you are hungry, there's soup."

"I'll eat out."

I studied him. Despite his complaints while I stayed at my parents' that he wanted me home, now that I was here, it appeared he couldn't get away fast enough. I didn't have the energy to persuade him to stay. At some point, he would learn that Sophie's quiet moments would be the only opportunity he had for my attention. I didn't ask him when he'd be back.

After he left, I thought about napping, as I often had at Mama's, but the pull of the studio was stronger than the pull of my bed, and I opened the door. On my easel was the last of my pregnancy self-portraits. It had not been completed in time for the Salon Pisko show, and, of course, I'd gone into labor the next day. I stood in front of it, examining the face of a woman on the verge of motherhood but not quite sure what the future held. I was glad of the record, because already, after only two weeks, I had forgotten how worries about the unknown had hovered around my dreams. I was no longer the expectant mother. I was the mother.

I took the painting off the easel and placed it against the wall.

Then I wandered around the room, fingering tubes of pigment and running my hands through the brushes stored in a glass jar. I thought about putting a record on the gramophone, but I didn't want to wake Sophie. Curiosity finally pulled me to Andreas's corner of the studio.

A canvas was propped on his easel, and I walked around it to look, hoping I'd find that he'd started a new project. But what I saw confused me. The painting was vastly different from Andreas's work. It was vaguely reminiscent of paintings by the old masters that I'd studied in my art history class. It appeared to be an exercise in copying, a practice I'd often engaged in when I'd been a student sketching at the Kunsthistorisches Museum. The chiaroscuro was definitely an imitation of Caravaggio's style, but the subject wasn't one I recognized as a Caravaggio masterpiece. Perhaps Andreas was experimenting as a source of inspiration. I'd ask him about it when he got home.

I was interrupted in my musing. Sophie's cries let me know she had woken up.

Andreas came home after I'd gone to bed. He grunted and turned away from me when Sophie cried and I lifted her from her basket by my side of the bed. The exertion of the move back home had extracted more from me physically than I realized, and I dozed intermittently as Sophie nursed. I woke with a jolt when I realized she had fallen asleep on my chest. I eased her back into her basket and hoped she'd sleep for a few more hours. When she did wake again, it was nearly dawn, and I took her with me out of the bedroom in order not to wake Andreas. She was soaked through and needed a fresh nappy. I made a pot of coffee and sat at the table sipping it while Sophie cooed and pedaled her tiny legs. Was she going to be like I was as a girl, never willing to be still?

When she finally slept again, I managed to dress and brush my hair. Mama had wisely suggested that I wash my hair before I left my parents' house. Even less than twenty-four hours later, I understood how bound I was to Sophie's schedule, Sophie's needs. Everything else slipped from importance, including Andreas.

He slept past noon, apparently deaf to Sophie's wails. When he finally emerged, he spent a scant thirty minutes with me eating Gertraud's warmed-over soup, and then disappeared into the studio. I wanted to ask him about the painting on the easel, but Sophie's hunger interrupted us. As he had the evening before, he left for the coffeehouse and did not return until late.

Our days took on this pattern for about a week. As I began to understand Sophie's rhythms and she blessedly settled into longer periods of sleep, my energy began to return. I wasn't ready to face the studio, but I did have more stamina for expressing my own needs to Andreas.

Over a midday meal I'd been able to cook, I questioned him.

"You were so eager to have me return home, and yet I barely see you, except across the table at midday. That appears to be the only time you have available for me. I spend hours in the evening alone. If you were here, I'd want to hear about your day, your work."

"Are you truly interested? Then I'll tell you. I'm in conversations with an agent who may have some commissions for me."

"Is that what the painting in the studio is? It is so unlike your style, I thought perhaps it was simply an experiment copying the look of Caravaggio."

He became very still. "When did you see it?" He sounded deeply suspicious, as if I'd violated his artistic privacy.

"I went in the first day I was home. I missed the studio. I missed working. Your painting was there, not covered up. You haven't been reluctant to show me your work in the past—not since you painted my first portrait. Has something changed?"

He waved his hand as if to brush my concerns away. "It's not important. You were right. I was simply trying out my hand at understanding Caravaggio's technique of chiaroscuro. One can always learn from the masters, even as we break away from their traditional concepts of beauty and truth. That was clever of you to recognize the elements of Caravaggio."

He got up to return to the studio for the rest of the day. The conversation was the longest we'd had since my return. The next time I went into the studio, however, the painting was gone.

As Sophie grew, her presence pushed Andreas further from me. He claimed her crying disturbed his creativity. And when she was a month old, he decided to paint at a loft used by Helmut, one of his drinking companions. Alone with Sophie, I was both lonely and free of the conflict I felt in trying to care for both Andreas and my daughter.

My solitude was intensified by the absence of any direct contact with Oscar. I had been honest in professing my love to him that day I had met with him in the park, but I had no conception at the time of how difficult it would be to extricate myself from Andreas. The simple logistics of caring for Sophie on my own were overwhelming. Finding room for Oscar in my daily life, as well as in my heart, was proving to be impossible.

My isolation drove me to a deeper despair than the one I had experienced when I first arrived on Skiathos. But this time, I was responsible for keeping Sophie alive as well as myself. There were moments every day, sometimes when she was screaming inconsolably in my arms, that I howled along with her. At other times, in the blissfully quiet hours when she slept, my tears flowed soundlessly.

My mother came to visit unannounced one morning. I hadn't dressed or bathed in days, and had been walking the floor with Sophie for hours. Andreas was still coming home at night after painting at Helmut's loft, but he had moved to the divan in the studio to sleep because of Sophie's wakefulness. He hadn't yet emerged when my mother arrived.

"Maya, my darling." She put down the basket in her arms and reached out for both Sophie and me.

"Let me take Sophie. Have you eaten? You've lost weight since I was last here. As soon as Sophie quiets, I'll make you something to eat."

She rocked and burped Sophie while directing me to her basket. "There's a packet of chamomile tea in the basket. Brew some and set it out to cool. We're going to give some to Sophie to help settle her stomach. That's why she's crying like this. She has colic."

I went through the motions as instructed by Mama, who continued to amaze me with her skill. As promised, the chamomile tea eased Sophie's discomfort, and she fell asleep.

"Now off to the bath while I cook." Mama pushed me down the hall.

By the time I returned to the kitchen, freshly dressed, a pot of goulash simmered on the stove and bowls of spaetzle and cucumber salad stood ready to be set on the table in the parlor. The two of us ate in peace while both Sophie and Andreas slept.

"I will be blunt with you, Maya. You do not appear to be coping well. You've lost weight, the dark circles under your eyes reveal that you aren't sleeping, and the larder is nearly bare. You need help."

I knew she was right. I'd become undone by the tiny being who had entered my life. My usual confidence in my ability to meet any challenge was in tatters. My marriage was a sham. I hadn't set foot in the studio in days because every time I went in, I was reminded that my creative spirit had been sucked as dry as my breasts.

"I don't know what to do."

"Come home, then. Let us care for you and Sophie. From what I witnessed the last time I was here, your husband will barely notice."

I was tempted. Andreas's hostility toward me wasn't entirely unexpected. I had lost the passionate belief I had had in his talent as I witnessed his descent into drunkenness and carelessness. His dependence on me to nurture his gifts and to convince the art world of his genius had exhausted me even before Sophie's birth. Now it was simply impossible. His mounting resentment and jealousy, which had taken root when I began painting myself and then won a place at the Salon Pisko show, was now in full bloom. So leaving Andreas to return to my parents' home was not an obstacle in my decision. I had already left him emotionally, if not physically.

But I needed to weigh the price of stepping back into my life on Elizabethstrasse. First, as loving as Mama had been, both throughout my pregnancy and especially since Sophie's birth, my father was still the head of the family. My decisions would no longer be my own. The few moments of civility we had extended to each other after Sophie's birth had occurred because I was a guest. Once I moved back under his roof, I would once again be subject to his will.

"Thank you, Mama. Your offer is truly generous, but I'll find a way to manage on my own."

"I don't want to undermine you, Maya. But what I saw today when I arrived, I would hardly call managing."

"You're right. I've allowed myself to slip into paralysis, and you've helped me to see that. I'll take better care of myself and Sophie, I promise."

She sighed and rose to clear the table. "Very well, Maya. I'll try to visit more often. Will you allow me at least to order a regular delivery of food until you're able to get out to do the marketing?"

"Thank you, Mama."

She stayed another hour, spending most of it cooing at Sophie. After she left, I sat at the table with my notebook and reviewed the sums I was expecting from Salon Pisko for the sale of the Faces of Vienna portraits. Then I penned a note to the gallery inquiring about the interest in the maternal self-portraits. If I could sell even one, I'd have the resources to hire help.

I had just sealed the envelope when I heard the door to the apartment open and Andreas's footsteps in the hall. I slipped the envelope inside my notebook.

"Are you hungry? There's goulash and spaetzle."

"You cooked?"

"My mother did. I'm happy to warm some up for you."

He wandered into the kitchen, lifting pot lids and sniffing. "I'll have some. I suppose I should take advantage of Sophie sleeping while I can, before you have no time for me."

I got up from the table and lit the stove. As I stirred the goulash, something roiled within me after the numbness that had engulfed me since arriving home. My arm was ready to throw the wooden spoon coated in gravy at him. I only held back because I didn't want to clean up the mess it would make, both in the kitchen and between Andreas and me. I swallowed the retort to his sarcastic remark. Now was not the moment to have this conversation. I needed an answer from the gallery and the knowledge that I did not need Andreas before I gathered up Sophie and my art supplies and left him.

He ate alone because I withdrew to the bedroom to fold laundry while Sophie slept. By the time she woke, he was on his way to Helmut's to paint. I wrapped her in the painted silk scarf Elise had given me, tied it like a sling across my chest, and opened the door to the studio. I had no grand ambitions. I thought only to expand with color some of the faces from my neighborhood walks that I hadn't completed for the Pisko show. I forced myself to ignore the squalor that Andreas had left by the divan. The bedding stank of tobacco and sour wine. Instead of cleaning it up, I opened the windows and retreated to my easel. I found that I could gently rock Sophie while I worked with my oil pastels. It wasn't painting. It wasn't done with intense focus, losing everything around the periphery except the image in my head. But I was working. What at first was the distraction of Sophie's body curved against mine, her murmurs and bubbles of gas punctuating the silence, soon became a part of my process. I swiped the pastel across the page as I swayed.

The experience was similar to how I had felt in the closing days of my pregnancy, maneuvering myself in front of the canvas as I felt her moving inside me. Perhaps, as close as she was to my heartbeat, she was also experiencing that same sense of safety and contentment.

My back hurt after a while, but it was an ache that had produced something. I gave myself permission to stop. Sophie was beginning to fuss, and I did not want to push myself to exhaustion. I could not. I wiped my hands and closed the windows. I knew I'd come again to the easel.

Chapter Thirty-Nine

A FEW DAYS LATER, I heard the doorbell in the late afternoon. Other than Mama, I had had no visitors since I had returned to the apartment. For a moment, I thought perhaps it was the food delivery she had ordered, but I decided that was more likely to come in the morning. I walked down the hall with Sophie in my arms and opened the door.

"Elise, how wonderful to see you!" I hugged her awkwardly, encumbered as I was with Sophie. She returned the embrace and entered the apartment, her arms laden with a pale wooden pastry box from Café Sacher and a bouquet of purple calla lilies.

"Are you alone?" She looked past my shoulder cautiously.

"Yes. Andreas is painting elsewhere these days. I don't expect him home until late this evening, if at all."

"Good. Are you open to entertaining two Goldbergs? I brought a torte and will be happy to make the coffee if you point me to the kitchen."

"Two Goldbergs? Is Oscar here?" I put my hand up to my hair and felt the wisps escaping from my braid. I was sure I also had streaks of pastels on my cheeks.

"He's downstairs in the hall. We thought it best to wait and be assured of your willingness to see him. He didn't want to create difficulty for you."

"Please ask him to come up."

She went out, leaned over the balustrade, and whistled. Then I heard footsteps mounting the stairs. I tried to calm myself, but the anticipation of seeing Oscar, despite my disarray, sent a warmth through me. In the fog of the last month, I had been unable to fathom how I would find room for him in my life as I had promised, considering I had barely been able to dress myself.

I waited in the doorway as Elise made herself useful in the kitchen.

His smile as he reached the top floor, slightly breathless, was that of a man who had scaled a mountain and was about to plant a flag on the pinnacle. We stood wordlessly facing each other.

"You've come."

"I have. When I realized that you could not come to me, I enlisted Elise to be my scout and run reconnaissance. As much as I wanted to storm the building, she cautioned me that many obstacles might stand in my way, not the least of which was your husband. She also warned me that the demands of motherhood and the need for privacy might cause you to be reluctant to see me, even if Andreas were not here. I have come unannounced, but I hope not unwelcome. I had to see you, to know that you are well."

"You are welcome here, and thank you for understanding that my silence has not been intentional. I am so very glad to see you."

At that moment, Sophie stirred. I could feel her body begin to tense, and knew she was about to wail. I started to apologize, but Oscar simply put out his hand to stroke her head.

"So this is Sophie," he whispered. "I am very pleased to meet you."

She turned her head at his voice and his touch, and her body melted in contentment.

I could not prevent myself from reflecting on how different Andreas's engagement with our daughter had been. Had he spoken to her, touched her? I decided not to dwell on the questions, since it would only distract me from enjoying these very precious moments with Oscar.

I led him to the parlor while Elise continued to putter in the kitchen, retrieving the paraphernalia necessary for a proper afternoon of Kaffee und Kuchen.

Despite Oscar's calming touch, Sophie was clearly hungry.

"Will it disturb you if I nurse her here? I don't want to leave you for even a few minutes of your visit."

"Nothing you do can disturb me. Please feed your daughter."

As a nude model, I was accustomed to removing my clothes. But baring my breast to nurse Sophie in Oscar's presence stirred something in me. At first, I kept my gaze down on Sophie's rosebud lips, but then I turned to look at him. His face reflected an awe, a reverence, that I had not anticipated.

"You are a Michelangelo Madonna, and you are Gaia, Mother Earth. What a combination of nurturing and eroticism. You are a life force."

I forgot my bedraggled appearance and my exhaustion, basking in the words the act of nursing Sophie had elicited.

By the time Sophie was sated, Elise arrived with a tray laden with the Sacher torte and coffee.

"You seem to have found everything. Thank you for taking over my hostessing duties."

"It is the least I can do after barging in on you. After I pour, I'm going to insist on taking that beautiful child in my arms while you eat, drink, and soak up the adulation of my brother. I can see it on his face."

"I think his adulation is for my daughter."

"I told you what I saw—a goddess. If I were a painter, I would want to capture the ineffable image of peace and strength of a mother and child. I want to remember this scene and re-create it in my next book."

I handed Sophie to Elise and sipped my coffee. My arms felt bereft at first and then filled again when Oscar reached across the table and took my hand. Our fingers remained intertwined.

"Tell me about the world outside these walls."

Both Oscar and Elise regaled me with Vienna's news, gleaned mostly from attending Berta's salons on Sunday afternoons.

"I must tell you that your maternal self-portraits have created quite the stir," reported Elise.

Vestiges of the aftermath of the Secession exhibition of the Awakening series filled my thoughts.

"Have I caused another scandal?"

"To the contrary," Elise assured me. "The paintings have sparked a much-needed conversation about the demands of art and motherhood. Berta was one of the first to broach the topic. Did you know she has a child herself?"

"Yes, I did. It was Berta who encouraged me to pursue the series when I showed her the first one."

"You have a gift for capturing the depth of emotion in your subjects, not only in the faces but in the language of their bodies and their relationship to space." Oscar's assessment affirmed what I had attempted to do with the paintings.

"Have you begun to paint again? Or is it premature to ask?" Elise, as ever, got directly to what I suspected was the purpose of this visit.

"Don't worry, I won't burst into tears at your question. I've revisited some incomplete work on the Faces of Vienna series, and have devised a method of working with Sophie nestled in a sling across my chest. That alone was an achievement."

"You are remarkable."

"Thank you, but it's no more than my will overcoming my exhaustion. I haven't dared to try anything new yet. My brain hasn't caught up with my desire, my need to create."

"All in good time."

"I wonder if you could do me the favor of delivering a note to Salon Pisko. I'd like to receive payment for the paintings that have sold and pursue the interest in the maternal portraits. They sent word after the opening that a few people had inquired about purchasing one, but they didn't tell me who."

"Of course, Maya! I'm happy to do more than deliver the note and will speak with them directly. May I ask another delicate question? We've heard that Andreas hasn't sold anything recently and is no longer in contact with most of his coffeehouse comrades. Is everything between you well?"

I tried not to show my surprise. That Andreas had been lying to me about his whereabouts was puzzling.

"As well as can be expected in what has become a marriage in name only. I don't mean to sound bitter. You both know why I married him. I barely see him, now that he is no longer painting here. I haven't the energy or the will to coax him out of whatever pit of despondency he has allowed himself to fall into."

"We, of all people, don't expect you to. Our concern is for you and Sophie. You know you can turn to us, if you need us." It was Oscar who jumped into the conversation to reassure me.

I squeezed his hand. "I know. Forgive me if I have appeared stubbornly insistent on untangling the complications of my life on my own. I do not want to be dependent on anyone again."

If my words cut Oscar, he did not show it.

"I understand. Elise and I have always had each other, but in a way that drains neither of us. We would welcome you into our castle, pull up the drawbridge, and defend you against the siege of the world."

"Thank you, my dearest. If ever the world becomes too much, I know I will find refuge with you."

As the shadows of dusk settled over the city, Oscar and Elise said their goodbyes with a promise to return.

"Each time I come, it will be with a different pastry. I intend to try every bakery in the city, and we can all decide on the best. I'll be back with news—and payment—from Pisko soon."

Chapter Forty

THE NEXT DAY, ELISE returned after her visit to Salon Pisko.

"Maya, I am the bearer of bad news. The salon already made payment to Andreas for your paintings."

I grabbed the edge of the table in the hall and nearly collapsed onto the floor.

"How did this happen? I submitted those paintings as Maya Sircos, not Maya Brenner. Why would they pay him?"

"Apparently, he identified himself as your husband and indicated you were incapacitated after the birth of Sophie. Legally, the salon was obligated to give the funds to him. As a married woman, you have no control over your finances. Come sit. I'll make you some tea, and we'll try to sort this out."

My hands shook as I took the cup of tea from Elise.

"I am going to assume Andreas did not tell you."

I shook my head. "Did Pisko tell you how much it was?"

"Originally, they refused. It was only after I threatened to take my work off their walls that they relented. They've done well, selling my paintings."

She told me the sum, and I burst into tears. I had always been more likely to bury my emotional distress or to transfer it to my art than to cry, but since Sophie's birth, I'd been less able to manage my feelings. My whole body heaved with uncontrollable sobbing, and Elise took me into her arms.

"That money was supposed to be our future, Sophie's and mine. How stupid of me not to foresee that he would take it. I should have gone to Berta and asked her to hold the funds for me."

"All is not lost, Maya. All except one of the maternal portraits and a few of the Faces of Vienna are still unsold. It's only been a little more than a month since the opening. The interest is still high in the exhibition, and you'll sell the rest. I'll go to Berta and Egon immediately. They'll be able to put a stop to any more money going to Andreas. Will you confront him about it?"

"He's been so secretive about everything—his work, where he spends his evenings—it would be a waste of breath to ask him."

After Elise left, I took advantage of Sophie's lengthening naps and went to the studio. My outburst had cleansed me, and I picked up my sketchbook and a pencil. I was going to need more art to sell.

Berta came to see me with Elise and Oscar two days later. Together, the four of us devised a plan to assign Elise and Oscar as my agents so they would be able to receive funds for me. It was unorthodox and temporary. As long as I remained married to Andreas, he controlled any money I earned. There was a risk with the salon as intermediary of Andreas learning of additional sales.

"It might be best if the remaining works were sold privately," Berta suggested. "Pisko might balk at losing the potential commissions, but I'll have Egon speak to them."

"Without Pisko, how will I sell the paintings?"

"Leave that to me. There are women in Vienna of independent means—widows, heiresses—who would be very interested in seeing you succeed. In the meantime, I want to urge you to continue painting. Have you hired a nanny for Sophie?"

"Not yet." I wanted to express my outrage as to why. How could I when my income had been stolen by Andreas? But Elise placed her hand over mine and shook her head almost imperceptibly to warn me not to say more.

When Berta left, Elise was firm.

"We are hiring a nanny for you. After all," she said with a smile, "Oscar and I have an investment in you now."

The following week, we enlisted my mother to help in the search for someone to care for Sophie while I painted. Through Gertraud and her extended family, we found a young relative who had cared for several younger siblings. Matilda came to the apartment three days a week. At first, I found it difficult to relinquish Sophie into her arms. I still needed to have her close in order to nurse her, but as she grew and thrived, the hours I had to myself became a balm and a source of growth for me as well.

Two of the maternal self-portraits sold through Berta, a boost that fed my spirit and allowed me to consider once again securing the freedom that had thus far been elusive. It was not only the creative breathing room that Matilda provided that unleashed a new burst of artistic production for me. Andreas's frequent absences played a role, too. Although we were not legally separated from bed and board, in practicality we were. He had begun to spend fewer and fewer nights at home. It was a relief that lulled me into a false sense of contentment. I should have suspected that something was amiss, but it was too easy to attribute his absences to another woman. I assumed he had found someone else to serve as his adoring muse and inspiration.

Apparently he was selling his art, because he continued to pay the rent on the apartment. It was a dependence I reluctantly acquiesced to, if only because the prospect of uprooting Sophie and me, especially leaving the studio, was too overwhelming to ponder.

Andreas was not entirely absent, though. At least once or twice a week he would arrive to eat or bathe or sleep. His haggard appearance, sallow skin, and agitated behavior led me to suspect his excessive drinking was taking its toll. Even if he had shown any attention to Sophie, I would have been reluctant to allow him to hold her. But as he had in the early days of her life, he seemed indifferent. At three months, she was developing into a charmer, engaging even the dourest of neighbors when I was out with her in her pram. But those charms hadn't worked on her father.

The erratic nature of Andreas's appearances kept me to a certain extent on edge. Berta's lawyer had cautioned me not to entertain male guests. Any sign of impropriety, especially with our highly observant and judgmental concierge, could give Andreas grounds for accusing me of adultery and allow him to take not only the funds I was now earning but also Sophie. I couldn't imagine that he would want her, but as an act of revenge against me, it was certainly possible.

That meant my contact with Oscar was severely limited. We wrote to each other, with our letters passing through Elise, but except for a celebration of Elise's new work at Berta's salon, I did not see him. His patience astounded me, so I understood when he wrote that he was leaving for Berlin at the end of the summer. His book was about to launch, and Fischer, his publisher, had arranged for several readings and signings throughout Germany.

Berta had offered to host him at her salon when he returned, and I tried to hold on to that prospect of seeing him again when he was back. But it was not enough. I decided to meet him on one of my walks with Sophie, and begged Elise to arrange it.

"Are you sure?"

"I'm willing to risk it. We could meet at the Tiergarten Schönbrunn. Sophie is still a little young for the zoo, but if you come with him, we could meet accidentally at the aviary."

When we arrived at the zoo, I made my way along the path to the bird enclosure. I had brought Matilda along, and we watched as family groups, excited children, and doting grandparents enjoyed their summer outing.

When I saw Oscar and Elise ahead, I caught my breath and felt my face flush. Perhaps meeting in such a public place was not the wisest idea. I was more nervous than I expected. All the words that had passed between us over the last three months, including drawings I had sent him, had intensified the emotional intimacy between us. I longed for him, and I knew that seeing him now would only make his departure for Berlin all the more agonizing. I put a smile on my face and approached them. We feigned our surprise at meeting, and they cooed over Sophie before agreeing to walk together for a while. Elise joined Matilda, pushing the pram, and Oscar and I followed. We did not touch.

"I shall miss you in ways I cannot describe. I'll continue to write via Elise."

"I want to hear all about your adventures. I'm sure you'll be a sensation."

"I received my advance copies yesterday. Elise is placing one in Sophie's pram. I want to hear your frank opinion when you read it. I can't judge it anymore."

"Perhaps it will inspire a whole new series of paintings for me."

He laughed. "It is you who have been the inspiration. Thank you."

"I want to thank you for being so willing to accept my constraints."

"I've told you, I do so gladly. I am ever the optimist that one day you'll be in my arms again."

"I share your optimism. Your presence in my life has given me hope."

"I promise I'll return to you."

"I promise I'll be here waiting for you."

We caught up with Elise and Matilda, and the four of us enjoyed some ice cream. When we finally separated, I turned the pram away without looking back.

That evening, I began to read Oscar's book, the first pages of which had resonated with me so strongly on Skiathos. I read well into the early hours of the morning, stopping only to nurse Sophie. It was brilliant, searing, and captured the upheaval of the times, both in the individual lives depicted on the page and in its description of the Vienna that had shaped our generation. It would garner the same kind of praise and outrage that avant-garde artists had elicited. God help him.

The days took on a comfortable pattern. Matilda wove herself into Sophie's and my life seamlessly with her good-natured care of both of us. My art became more expansive as I allowed myself to work in a larger format. Oscar's letters passed from Elise's hand to mine, filled with humor and wonder as he continued his peregrinations through the literary landscape.

Once again, I felt lulled into complacency. I should have been more attentive to Andreas's erratic behavior. It was not only his unpredictable comings and goings but his fretful moods that were disconcerting. Any unusual sound in the building—footsteps on the stairs, the lift groaning late at night, or doors slamming—caused him to cast a fearful glance at our door and retreat to the studio. More than once, I heard him turn the lock as if he was in hiding.

Chapter Forty-One

THE NIGHT THEY CAME to arrest Andreas, Sophie had a fever and I was bathing her, sponging lukewarm water over her as she thrashed and screamed. I felt the pounding on the door as if the fists were battering my head. I had been walking the floor with Sophie for hours, frantic with worry that she had contracted scarlet fever. I had begged Andreas to go to the pharmacy earlier, but he was locked in his studio. When I called to him to answer the door, I was met with silence.

The pounding became more insistent and, afraid that whoever was on the other side of the door would break it down, I gathered Sophie in a towel and made my way down the hall. I struggled to contain Sophie, who was throwing her agonized body away from me as I fumbled with the latch.

"I'm coming. I'm coming."

I pulled open the door to two uniformed policemen, their faces twisted in anger at the delay. They pushed past me.

"Where is he?" one of them shouted, his spittle spraying my cheeks. I had no free hand to wipe away the drops, which reeked of tobacco and sausages. The men began pulling open doors, searching the parlor, the kitchen, even our bedroom. But, of course, they didn't find him. When they reached the studio, the last place he could be, they screamed his name and were confronted with the same silence I had endured all day.

The heavier man turned the door handle and it opened without resistance, no longer locked as I had thought. Both men rushed in. I waited in the hall, pacing with Sophie, expecting them to emerge with Andreas in shackles.

But he wasn't there. He must have slipped down the service stairs in the kitchen when they were searching the other rooms—perhaps when he heard the shouting—or left hours ago while I'd been struggling with Sophie.

The policemen emerged from the studio.

"Where has your husband gone?" they demanded.

I shrugged, still attempting to calm Sophie, who was now frightened as well as sick.

"He does not share with me his nightly escapades," I answered. I truly did not know where he might have fled, but at that moment, my only thought was *good riddance*.

The police left. In their wake, I felt violated and tried to calm myself enough to soothe Sophie. She finally fell asleep in my arms, her fever receding in the early hours of the morning. When Matilda arrived the next day, I decided not to stay in the apartment. I was badly shaken, afraid that Andreas might return and invite another police raid that could escalate into a more violent confrontation. We packed and took a carriage to Elise's. She took one look at us and drew us into the safety of her apartment.

It was days before I learned why the police had come for Andreas. He was arrested at Helmut's studio, where he'd fled. Word reached me when I went out to do the marketing and bought a newspaper on my way back. The headlines on the front page of the *Tagblatt*, normally a more sedate paper, shouted of an art forgery ring broken up by diligent detective work. Andreas was one of the five artists charged, along with Helmut.

Back at Elise's, I read the article twice, reeling from what it revealed and what Andreas had concealed from me. How could I not have known? I thought back to the copy of the Caravaggio that had suddenly disappeared from the studio. I trembled with rage. What had driven him to such a criminal act? I left Sophie with Matilda and Elise and went to the police station where Andreas was being held.

At first, I wasn't allowed to see him, but I refused to leave, waiting for hours until the sergeant in charge grudgingly let me in.

Andreas looked worse than usual, and I suspected that not having access to his whiskey was contributing to his agitation.

"Tell me everything."

He kept his silence for several minutes. When I offered him a cigarette from the packet I had brought for him, he took it with trembling fingers and began to talk, as if speaking would transfer the weight of his transgressions to me.

"I got into debt gambling. When I couldn't pay, I was approached with an alternative: create some paintings in the style of well-known artists. At first, it was only a few. The Caravaggio you saw was the first. But I was too good. The people controlling the ring put pressure on me to continue, and began paying well. I was making far more than I could selling my own paintings. It spiraled until I didn't want to stop."

"I can ask my father for help with a lawyer."

"He'd rather see me rot in prison. You know that."

He was right.

"But you could go to Berta Zuckerkandl. She has influence. Unless you don't want to taint yourself with my damaged reputation. Your career is on the ascendancy, I hear in the coffeehouses. You gained notice as the muse in the Awakening series and rode my coattails to your own notoriety. Without me, you'd be painting watercolors for sale at ladies' society church bazaars. Or, worse, you'd be some goat farmer's wife on Skiathos. You owe me, Maya."

If he thought he could coerce me into saving him by making me doubt my talent or showing gratitude for the charade of our marriage, he was gravely mistaken. The rage that I had contained for months since he had stolen the money I'd earned from the Salon Pisko exhibition had no more reason to be suppressed.

I scraped back my chair and rose from the table.

"I owe you nothing, Andreas."

And with a nod to the guard to let me out, I left.

I returned to Elise's apartment shaken but determined. I had decisions to make, the first of which was finding a new home for Sophie and me. Whatever the outcome of Andreas's trial, I did not want to remain in our apartment in Josefstadt, nor was it likely I could. The lease was in his name, and up until his arrest, he had been paying the rent.

I suspected my mother would swoop in again to offer us refuge in my parents' home, and I wanted to be prepared with an alternative. The day after I visited Andreas, Elise and I went house hunting while Matilda cared for Sophie. Many landlords were suspicious of a single woman seeking housing, so Elise and I devised a story that I was a widow and Elise's sister-in-law. We finally found rooms in an older building that would provide me with a well-lit space to paint and a bedroom large enough for Sophie and Matilda to share. Elise had convinced me that Matilda should be living with us. I would sleep on a divan in the sitting room.

Even Elise, with her independent wealth, needed her lawyer to sign the lease in Oscar's absence. I was anxious to move in as quickly as I could. Although unlikely, it was possible Andreas might be granted release on bail, and I wanted to be out of the apartment before he returned home. Elise, Matilda, Sophie, and I returned to the apartment to pack up our clothing, my art supplies, some kitchen utensils, and Sophie's bassinet.

When everything was in crates and baskets, I walked through the rooms that I had made into a home in the two years since I'd returned to Vienna. I stood in the studio, soothed by the northern light filtered through the bank of windows that had enraptured me the first time I'd entered the room. I brushed away the tears that had been my companion in the tempestuous months since Sophie's birth. Leaving this space was a bittersweet experience. It was the scene of my emergence as a painter in my own right, but ghosts still lingered in the shadows—a trunk filled with the robes and weapons used in the Warriors series; the hammered copper table on which I'd served wine and cakes to the Secession committee and Berta; a dusty album filled with the photos of the Warriors paintings that I'd created to entice the Secession to reconsider Andreas's work; a water-stained poster for the Salon Pisko exhibit. The room represented both my entanglement with Andreas and my liberation from the burdens and the power of a muse. I shut the door and left the keys with the concierge on our way out of the building,

In the following days, Elise and I wandered through open-air markets gathering necessities for my new home: a table and chairs, dressers, a bed for Matilda and a divan for me, carpets, curtains, and a few toys for Sophie, who, at six months, was sitting on her own and banging wooden spoons on turned-over pots and starting to pick up blocks.

We scrubbed and dusted, hung curtains, and made up beds. I had put off my mother's concerned inquiries after the newspaper article came out, assuring her we were well, but I wanted to be settled in our own home before she mounted her offensive to take us in. On the day we were to move from Elise's to the new apartment, Elise prepared coffee and cake for us as both a farewell celebration and an inauguration of our new life.

"I heard from Oscar today. He should be back in Vienna by Christmas. There was a letter for you as well."

She slipped it out of her pocket and handed it across the table. In the whirlwind of Andreas's arrest and our move, I hadn't had an opportunity to write to Oscar of the dramatic changes in our circumstances.

But Elise let me know he was already aware. "The news about Andreas made the Berlin papers."

I wondered what he would make of it all. The letter remained unopened until the evening, when Sophie and Matilda were asleep. The words were scrawled across the page in a far less measured way than he normally wrote, as if he was rushing to finish his thoughts and convey them to me. He wrote that he wished he could be at my side to support me through the ordeal of Andreas's trial, but also acknowledged that to do so would be a mistake. For my sake, he felt he shouldn't be seen publicly with me. I had to agree this made sense, but for a different reason: As I had expected, his book was a sensation and he'd become a well-known name, so the last thing he needed was to be dragged down by an association with me.

He also expressed hope that once the trial was over, my life might be more my own. It appeared that Oscar, like most of Vienna, believed Andreas was guilty. I shared that opinion. But even in prison, Andreas would still be my husband and still have power over me.

I put Oscar's letter aside. I'd hoped that the first night in my new home might offer me a glimpse of a new beginning, but little seemed to have changed.

Despite my unease about the future, our daily lives proceeded with little time for morbid reflection. Sophie flourished, my painting nourished me as I continued to explore and develop my style, and Matilda became an integral part of our little family.

Andreas's trial began in November. I dressed somberly and wore a veiled hat. Sitting back in the gallery, I hoped that enough years had passed since the Awakening series to keep the newspapers from recognizing me. A few of Andreas's more stalwart friends showed up, but I knew from the rumors within the avant-garde community that his reputation had been destroyed.

What I saw in the dock was a broken man. He looked seriously ill, far more than I would have expected his dependence on alcohol to cause. He hadn't been granted bail because he was considered a flight risk, and two months in a dank jail cell had taken its toll. I saw before my eyes what my absence from his life had precipitated—far more than the months I'd been on Skiathos, when his artistic efforts had been thwarted. This time without me, he'd not only been unable to sustain his physical well-being, but had also collapsed in spirit. I understood well the paralysis that can overwhelm the will to thrive. But perhaps because I had Sophie, I'd been able to rebuild my life and redefine Maya Sircos, Andreas Brenner's muse, as Maya Sircos, artist.

I listened to the list of my husband's transgressions, the portrayal of him as a venal, greedy man unable to make a success of his own art, and instead turning himself into a veritable factory of fake masterpieces. I felt no culpability for not being able to save him from himself.

I left the courtroom after the guilty verdict was announced and slipped down a side street to avoid the crowd that had gathered.

Chapter Forty-Two

OSCAR RETURNED TO VIENNA in December as promised. We celebrated Christmas Eve together at the home he shared with Elise. Matilda was with her family for the holiday. Sophie, at nine months, was the center of attention. She fell soundly asleep before the Christkind could shower her with gifts. Both Oscar and Elise encouraged me to spend the night. It had begun to snow, and they convinced me it would be impossible to get a carriage.

We sat companionably before the fire sipping a Riesling wine Oscar had brought back from his travels as far west as the Rheingau. He regaled us with tales of several cities, until Elise got up yawning and excused herself.

Oscar and I sat in silence, hands entwined.

"I want to show you something. I asked Elise not to share it with you until I returned."

He led me to his own rooms, a study and a bedroom. Elise had been true to her word. I'd never gone in them, all the times I'd been in the apartment. He opened the door and lit the lamp. On the wall opposite his desk was one of my maternal self-portraits.

"It has been a poignant reminder of how you looked that day at Café Central before you gave birth to Sophie. Your trust in me in those frantic hours has sustained me, reminded me why I wait for you."

I walked into his arms. "Tonight you do not have to wait."

We made love, the sense memories of that long-ago day in the shepherd's hut returning without effort. It was a tender exploration, a joyful discovery of the pleasures we had forgone for so long. We fell asleep in each other's arms and woke again to a need for something more, want unleashed after months of waiting. I had forgotten how it felt to be desired, to be cherished, and opened myself to all that meant—the vulnerability, the longing, the breathlessness of being submerged in each other.

It was one night out of time, snowbound with the city hushed around us.

We ate roasted goose and red cabbage on Christmas Day, and laughed as Sophie ripped apart the wrapping on the gifts left for her under the tree. Sophie and I spent a second night with Elise and Oscar before the roads were cleared and we could make our way to our own home.

We had been invited to my parents' home on the day after Christmas, a concession of my father's because of my mother's entreaties for him to let go of his fury about Andreas.

"The man is in prison. Isn't that enough?" she had asked him. Apparently he was willing, for the sake of his granddaughter, to put aside his disapproval for at least one day.

I wasn't prepared for the onslaught of relatives that greeted us when we arrived at Elisabethstrasse. Omama, in all her regal splendor, sat in the parlor holding court and waiting for the presentation of her great-granddaughter. I had dressed Sophie in a burgundy velvet confection my mother had sent, and she looked every inch the Viennese cherub. My aunts had also joined the throng, and it appeared that I was being welcomed back as the prodigal daughter. Perhaps the hope was that with my criminal husband behind bars, I might return to the fold. Since the newspapers had ignored me this time, I might be viewed as a tarnished Madonna.

I have no doubt that there would have been scant welcome for me if it hadn't been for Sophie. She was dandled on several knees and offered specially baked biscuits to teethe on by Gertraud. Overall, she succeeded in winning everyone's hearts. As she began to show signs of fatigue that I knew could erupt into a tantrum at any moment, I whisked her up to my old bedroom for a nap.

When she was settled, I got up to return to the family but was interrupted by a knock on the door. It was Papa. He had remained on the edges of the cooing and fussing over Sophie earlier, and I was surprised and somewhat cautious to encounter him now.

"Maya, a word."

I braced myself.

"I had occasion to meet Hofratin Zuckerkandl and her husband, the professor. They are customers of mine. When she recognized the name, she told me she knew you. She commented not only on your extraordinary talent but also your strength of character and sharp mind for business. She told me it was clear you were her father's daughter. The story in particular of how you convinced the Secession to exhibit Brenner's work, despite my abhorrence of that work, struck me as forward-thinking.

"I hope you'll use that skill to advance your own work now that he is out of your life. Not the nudes. No father wants to see his daughter's body on display. But the character studies are brilliant. I bought two for my office."

For a moment, I was speechless. My father hadn't spoken so many words to me since Skiathos. Mixed though they were, he appeared in his own way to be accepting who I was—and even taking pride in who I had become. Her father's daughter. That was a phrase I would hold on to.

"Thank you, Papa."

"Come and see us more often, not only at Christmas."

"I will."

I wasn't ready to kiss him, and he, too, seemed to stiffen at the idea. It had probably taken all of his reserves of generosity to speak to me. Instead, I reached out for his hand and squeezed it.

Chapter Forty-Three

AS SHE HAD PROMISED, Berta hosted a reading for Oscar on New Year's Day. It was his first appearance in Vienna, and a crush of literary society filled the apartment on Nußwaldgasse, eager to hear him. I hung back, happy to observe the effusive accolades and listen to the knots of conversation about the book as I moved through the rooms after he spoke. Every now and then, we caught each other's eye and he shrugged. Women, especially, seemed eager for his attention, placing their hands on his arm and leaning in to offer their whispered praise.

"My brother is the man of the moment," commented Elise as she approached me and handed me a glass of champagne.

"A well-deserved tribute," I replied, and smiled as we clinked glasses.

During the afternoon, I found Berta to thank her for speaking to my father.

"He was surprised I knew you, and I think at first he thought I was going to express disapproval. He mistook me for a staid Viennese society matron in the market for exotic decorative art items for my home, rather than someone knowledgeable and appreciative of modern art. As I recited your virtues, the look on his face moved from wariness and dismay that he was about to lose my business to the unabashed pride of a father who loves his daughter. I can see where you get the determination, resilience, and sharpness of mind. It cannot have been easy for him to build a successful life in a parochial city like Vienna."

Through Berta, both my father and I gained new insights into each other.

Over the next several months, life settled into yet another routine. I painted. Oscar and I deepened our connection, but with discretion. Once a fortnight, I delivered food and art supplies to Andreas in prison. I did not visit with him or write to him, as both activities would have demanded more from me than I was willing to give. But I also could not totally abandon him. Too much of my life had been shaped by my connection to him, but I did not realize how even those small acts of compassion continued to bind me.

It was in April, shortly before Sophie's first birthday, that I received a telegram informing me Andreas had died of tuberculosis. My first reaction was sadness. What a waste of a life that had once held such promise. He might have emerged after his prison sentence to reclaim his stature as an avant-garde master. Although, if I were being honest, I doubted he would have been capable on his own unless prison had transformed him.

The last act I performed for Andreas was to arrange his funeral. Although he had not been observant in his religion, I sought Berta's assistance in finding a rabbi willing to conduct the service, and secured a plot in the Jewish section of the Vienna Central Cemetery. He had never revealed his true identity to me or any of his colleagues. I only knew it because of my father's investigation of his past. On the gravestone, I asked the engraver to carve both his names: "Aaron Bochner, known as the artist Andreas Brenner." Only a handful of his artist friends attended the service at the grave site, which took place on a glorious spring day. I brought Sophie and gave her a white rose to lay on her father's grave. The press miraculously ignored us. They had already moved on to other scandals.

Those who attended the funeral joined me at Café Museum afterward. I had sent Sophie home with Matilda. The reminiscences were somber. No one had humorous stories to recount, and there were few words of fondness. It wasn't merely Andreas's fall from grace that had silenced the voices. I became aware of how few true connections Andreas had forged. No one knew him, not even I.

When I got home, I removed my widow's weeds and rocked Sophie.

The snipping of the final thread that had connected me to Andreas released me in unexpected ways. A few months had gone by when Berta planted a seed, as she often did.

"I'm leaving on an extended trip to Paris to visit my sister. You should consider coming at some point. What is happening there artistically is world-changing. You've reached a point where spending time there can deeply enrich your work. Think about it."

Think about it, I did. I was no longer an estranged wife. I was a widow. I was free to choose where and how I would live, and I could afford to do so with my own money.

Elise was particularly enthusiastic about the idea for herself as well when I approached her with the idea.

"I've begun to feel my art stagnating. Oscar and I don't usually stay in one place this long. We don't have roots here in Vienna, except for our connection with you and Sophie."

Her words offered me an opportunity to suggest a solution to the one obstacle I had felt impeding my decision to leave—my relationship with Oscar. I never intended to marry again. But I certainly intended to love.

"Why don't we all go?" I proposed. "We can find a house, live together, and support each other's endeavors."

"I love this idea! Our own artists' commune."

Oscar was equally enthusiastic, and in the summer of 1910, he went ahead to find us living quarters. Within a month he wrote he had discovered a former piano factory where artists were settling to live and work. We followed eagerly and moved into Le Bateau-Lavoir in September.

On our first morning in Paris, with Sophie in my arms, I looked out from Montmartre at the city below me. A lightness filled me, suffusing me with newfound hope.

I turned and walked back to the studio, ready to begin anew.

PART FOUR
BOSTON and PARIS

1977-1978

Chapter Forty-Four

VALERIE LANGDON REMOVED HER loupe, closed her jars of solvents, and cleaned her brushes and scalpels. She stepped back from the fourteenth-century Italian altarpiece she was restoring as a consultant for the Boston Museum of Fine Arts. The work was painstakingly slow, requiring her to deal with everything from wormholes to cracked panels before she had even begun to analyze and repair the colors. But that is what she loved—the slow process of discovery, as layer after layer of dirt and human contact began to be lifted, and then the spark of realization when she could see what the artist had originally intended.

Sometimes she felt as if the devout artisan were whispering in her ear, complaining of bones that ached from the damp cold held in by the thick walls of the cathedral and explaining any oddities that revealed themselves. *"I had to rush in this corner,"* he confessed. *"The priest was pushing me to finish the piece before the Feast of Corpus Christi and the arrival of the archbishop."*

Valerie's husband, Malcolm, an erudite art historian at Harvard with several books to his name, scoffed at the stories she invented for the artists of the late Medieval and Renaissance periods in which she worked. He did not understand that part of her process was to discern as much as she could about the artists—not only from their materials, the thickness and movement of their brushstrokes, and the length of time it had taken to complete a work, but also the milieu and the tenor of the times in which they painted. If she was to honor their work and bring it as close as possible to its original state, she needed deep in her psyche to know who they were and how they created. Before she had switched her undergraduate major to art history, she had been a theater major at Yale. Although she'd recognized early that a career on the stage was not what she wanted, she had nevertheless retained a sense of craft. Immersing herself in the life of the artist whose work she was restoring was akin to delving into a character as an actress.

She was satisfied with the restoration so far. Unlike its original artist, she didn't feel harried by the museum. The altarpiece would have a prominent place in the gallery, but not until it was ready.

She buttoned up her coat, wound her scarf around her neck to protect against the bluster of Boston in February, and turned off the lights in the lab. On her way home, she stopped at the Broadway Supermarket to pick up some things for dinner. When she climbed the steps to the front porch of her and Malcolm's apartment in a two-family house on Ware Street in Cambridge, Malcolm was already home. She could hear him in his study listening to the evening news. She popped her head in to let him know she was home and was about to offer him a drink when she saw he already had one.

"Your Aunt Wanona called earlier and wants you to call her. She left this number."

"Is everything all right?

"She didn't say. Only that it was important."

Wanona Dobbs was Valerie's mother's older sister. She had retired early from her work as a teacher and moved to the Catskills to care for her aging father, Valerie's grandfather. He had been living in Birch Cottage, the house in Twilight Park that had been in the family since Valerie's great-grandparents had built it in 1888. Grandpa had passed away the summer before, but Wanona had decided to stay.

Before she started making dinner, Valerie dialed the unfamiliar number, reaching the Ellenville Hospital. She waited anxiously as the switchboard connected her with Wanona's room.

"Hi, Aunt Nonie. What has happened? Why are you in the hospital?"

"Oh, Val, I'm afraid I slipped on the ice when I was out for my morning walk, and now my right leg is in a cast from my ankle to above my knee."

"Oh, no! Is there anything I can do?"

"Sweetie, I need a huge favor. The hospital is sending me to a nursing home for a few weeks, but in order for me to go home, I'll need someone to be with me. I hate to ask you, but you're all I've got. Do you think you could come up to Twilight Park?"

Valerie took a deep breath. "For how long?"

"I'm not sure. A month maybe."

Valerie did some mental calculations. She had at least three more weeks of work left on the altarpiece. If Wanona could stay in the nursing home until then, she could possibly manage it. She didn't have any new consulting assignments lined up and could afford at least a month without work. She understood that Wanona had no one else to ask. She hadn't married and had no children of her own. But she'd been a loving aunt and godmother to Valerie.

Wanona had sacrificed to care for her father when she, too, had been the only one in the family who could do it. Valerie's parents had passed away in an automobile accident when Valerie was at graduate school at New York University. Valerie and Wanona were the only ones left in the family.

"Of course I'll come!" After writing down the details of the nursing home where Wanona was going to be sent, Valerie poured herself a Scotch and made dinner.

She wanted Malcolm to have another drink and a good meal before she announced her plans. As she suspected, he wasn't thrilled.

"What about the edits for my new book? I was counting on you to tackle them as soon as you finished the altarpiece."

"I can take the manuscript with me and send you corrected pages every week in the mail. Birch Cottage has electricity. It's not completely primitive, so I can bring the electric typewriter."

Valerie had been helping Malcolm with his books since they'd met as students at the Institute of Fine Arts at NYU. He had been earning his PhD, and she typed papers for other students to earn extra money while she was studying for her Master of Science in art conservation. Eventually, after they'd begun dating, she had expanded her work to include editing for him and then researching. It was work she enjoyed, and after they had married five years earlier, their academic partnership had produced his two well-received books on twentieth-century artists.

Valerie wrapped up her restoration of the altarpiece at the end of February, bidding farewell to her imagined artist. She left for Twilight Park the next day with a trunk full of groceries, her typewriter, and Malcolm's manuscript. She stopped at Greene Meadows Nursing Home in Catskill, New York, to pick up Wanona, who was waiting in the lobby, her bag next to her on the floor.

Wanona gave Valerie a whoop and a big hug when she arrived. "I'm so happy to see you, sweetheart! You are a lifesaver. I was so ready to escape this place, I would have hitchhiked out on Route 23."

Valerie managed to fit a pair of crutches, a commode, and a collapsible wheelchair into the station wagon she and Malcolm had inherited from his parents. She followed the serpentine road that led up the mountain to Haines Falls and Twilight Park, grateful that it was a sunny day and not snowing or sleeting. She knew weather on the mountain at this time of year was unpredictable. As they reached the curve where the waterfall was visible, she could see that it was still partially frozen. It would be May before the torrent was totally released from its winter sleep and filled the rocky creek that wound through the valley.

Twilight Park was quiet when they passed through the gates. Only a few of the houses constructed along the three roads that clung to the hillside were winterized. Valerie's great- grandparents had been among the original homeowners in the community that had been established by a diverse group of New Yorkers to escape the heat of summer in the city. In the 1940s, Valerie's grandparents had winterized the Victorian cottage and added a wing with additional bedrooms and a second bath. Valerie's childhood summers and Christmas vacations had been spent on the mountain. More than any other place she had lived, Birch Cottage at Twilight Park was home.

When she pulled up to the house, she was surprised but grateful to see that a ramp had been erected from the side yard to the front porch.

"I had Bill Morris, the park caretaker, build that for me while I was in Greene Meadows," Wanona explained. Valerie wasn't surprised. Wanona had always been practical and organized. She helped Wanona into the wheelchair and pushed her up the ramp and into the house.

"Bill's wife, Rosemary, came this morning to turn up the heat and give the place a bit of spit and polish. I was in no condition after I fell to tidy the place up. I didn't want you to be faced with a mess in addition to being my nursemaid."

"You know I would have been happy to do it, Aunt Nonie, but I'm also glad we'll have more time to get settled. Do you want a cup of tea before I unload the car?"

"I'm fine. Just park me over by a lamp and give me that book in my bag."

After she hauled everything in from the car, Valerie lit the fireplace with the kindling and logs stacked by the hearth, probably another thoughtful instruction from Wanona to Bill and Rosemary.

"I made some chili for us last night. Sound good for dinner?"

By the time Valerie had finished washing up the dishes, it was after eight, and she could see that the strain of travel and resettling had worn Wanona out.

"Are you ready to go to bed?"

With a combination of awkwardness overcome by humor, Valerie managed to help Wanona access the commode, bathe, and get into bed.

"You're a dear to put up with this, my girl." Wanona hugged her good night and turned out the light.

Over the next few days, Valerie and Wanona worked out a system for meeting Wanona's needs, and Valerie was able to carve out time for Malcolm's manuscript. They settled into a comfortable rhythm in the house that both of them cherished.

One evening, the temperature dropped precipitously as storm clouds gathered over the mountain and it began to snow.

"I think we're going to need extra quilts tonight, Val. You'll find them in the cedar chest in the storage room off the second-floor landing."

The door to the storage room stuck, probably from disuse, but Valerie managed, with some pounding and jiggling, to get it open. A single incandescent bulb hung from the ceiling on a pull chain, and she turned it on to survey the crowded shelves, multiple stacked crates, garden tools, and ice skates that had been stuffed into the room over several decades.

She wove her way through the boxes to what appeared to be a cedar chest, and propped it open after dusting off the cobwebs that clung to it. Folded inside were the quilts Wanona had described, and Valerie lifted them out, remembering the chilly summer nights when her mother had tucked her in with the colorful covers.

"Granny Phyllis made these, sewn from fabric scraps from her calico and gingham dresses," she remembered her mother telling her.

As Valerie went to close the chest, she noticed what appeared to be a large framed canvas facing the wall behind the chest. She hadn't remembered it being there in her childhood. After she brought the quilts downstairs and helped Wanona to bed, she couldn't still her curiosity. She climbed back up the steep staircase and returned to the storage room.

It took some maneuvering to pull the canvas out from its tucked-away position. She dragged it out to the hall and turned it around. It was an unfinished painting of a pregnant nude, painted in the bold colors and dramatic brushstrokes of Expressionism. In the corner was the artist's signature—M Sircos—and the year 1909.

In all her art history studies, Valerie hadn't encountered an Expressionist painter named Sircos. She wondered if he were the husband of the pregnant model. She left the painting propped in the hall and went to bed.

Chapter Forty-Five

AFTER THE MORNING RITUALS were performed and breakfast was finished, Valerie broached the topic of the painting with Wanona.

"Aunt Nonie, I found a painting in the storage room when I got the quilts yesterday. Do you know anything about it?"

A wistful look passed over Wanona's face, and then she brightened.

"That's a painting of Maya Sircos when she was pregnant with her daughter."

"Who was she and who painted it? Why is it here? Did grandma and grandpa buy it?"

"Slow down, hon, and I'll answer each question. Maya painted it. It's a self-portrait. She was a well-known artist, first in Vienna and later in Paris, in the first part of the twentieth century. The painting wasn't your grandparents'. It's mine."

"Why haven't I heard of Maya Sircos? And how did you come to have the painting?"

"You haven't heard of her and countless other women artists because of two world wars and the Nazi destruction of what they considered decadent art. Maya did a series of self-portraits when she was pregnant. But as far as I know, the painting upstairs is the only one that survived."

"Why do you have it?"

"Because her daughter, Sophie, gave it to me when I was living in France. When I moved in to care for Grandad, I brought it with me from Springfield."

"I'm beginning to think that the Aunt Nonie I've known all my life has a hidden history. When did you live in France? Will you tell me about Sophie?"

Wanona considered Valerie's request.

"Let me think about it. I was there during the war. It's not an easy story to tell."

Had Wanona served in the military? Valerie's father had been in the navy in the South Pacific during the war, and except when he went to the VFW hall to play cards with his fellow vets, he had refused to talk about the experience.

"War is something to put behind us. No one wants to relive those days. It wasn't all Bob Hope putting on USO shows," he had told her.

Remembering his words now, Valerie understood she should not push Wanona.

Later in the afternoon, as the snow continued to fall, Wanona asked Valerie to bring the painting downstairs.

"I stored it when I first arrived because the house was Grandad's then, and it wasn't my place to hang the painting."

"This is your home now, Aunt Nonie. You can do what you want with the painting."

"It's your house, too, Val. Let's decide together where to put Maya."

Valerie wrangled the large frame down the stairs, careful of the birch limb that formed the handrail. She propped it against a wall in the living room, and Wanona wheeled over to study it.

"It's still in good condition, wouldn't you say, considering Maya painted it nearly seventy years ago?"

"Is that how old Sophie is now?"

"No. Sophie will always be thirty-three."

Wanona turned in her wheelchair and retreated to her bedroom.

Valerie watched her go, and understood even more fully Wanona's reluctance to talk about the painting. If Sophie died at thirty-three, it would have been early in the war after the fall of France. Why was Wanona in France then, if the Americans didn't land on French soil until D-Day in 1944?

Valerie made a pot of tea and sat on the floor in front of the painting. The only part that was incomplete was the background. But Maya, cradling her belly, gazed out at the viewer fully formed. Valerie was completely consumed by the image. Her conservator's eye saw patches that could use some cleaning. But given its age and the fact that it had survived the Nazi purge of Expressionist art, probably hidden somewhere in the French countryside, it was in remarkable condition, as Wanona had noted.

It was an exceptionally private, vulnerable painting; Sophie must have cherished it as the baby held unseen by her mother. Valerie was particularly drawn to Maya's face and the expression of both unbridled expectation—any day that child would be born—and apprehension. It was unclear whether Maya had been concerned about the birthing process or the unknowns of motherhood—or both.

Valerie placed her hands on her own belly, mimicking Maya's pose, and became engulfed in the memory of the baby she had lost a year before, a miscarriage in her first trimester. Her obstetrician had assured her that miscarrying in the first twelve weeks was not unusual, and that she'd most likely be able to conceive again and carry a baby to term. But those words had provided little comfort. The loss had altered something in her relationship with Malcolm. He had seemed to recover and move on to his next book, while Valerie had floundered. Obtaining the commission to restore the altarpiece had helped to keep her from dwelling on her grief, but seeing Maya's portrait had opened up the wound.

"It has a powerful effect, doesn't it?" Wanona sat in the doorway to her bedroom. Valerie didn't know how long her aunt had been watching her.

"Why don't you make me a cup of tea, and I'll tell you as much as I can about how that painting became mine."

They settled themselves across from the painting, Valerie on the couch and Wanona in her wheelchair.

"I was in Europe teaching in an exchange program at the University of Lyon when Hitler invaded Poland and the war began. Gran and Grandad wanted me to come home at

once, but I resisted. It was easier in those days to claim letters had been lost. Phone calls were expensive and difficult
to schedule, so I blithely ignored my parents' entreaties.
I wasn't a child. I was twenty-seven, and I understood
deep in my being that I needed to do something to make
a difference. The world was falling apart, descending into
chaos and uncertainty, and I knew I had the perseverance
and the ability to face the turmoil and perhaps ease some
suffering."

"What did you do?"

"I found my way to the Brits and offered my services.
At first, I was stuck in an office translating French and
German messages."

"I didn't know you spoke those languages."

"I imagine there are many things you don't know about
me. Eventually, my facility with languages and my knowledge of Lyon, where I'd been living for over a year, came
to the attention of the consulate leadership.

"When Hitler invaded France in May of 1940, Lyon became the heart of the French Resistance. I was recruited
then, and didn't have to think twice about accepting. Sophie had evacuated Paris with Maya, and they, too, made
their way to Lyon. They had removed as many of Maya's
paintings as they could from their stretcher bars and rolled
the canvases into their suitcases, buried under their clothing. Sophie had already been a liaison for the Resistance in
Paris. She was a few years older than I, and a savvy, fearless
operator. She was put in charge of a small team that I
was assigned to, all women. She had an uncanny ability

to disguise herself as anyone from a nun to a prostitute to a farmer's wife selling cheese in the market square while passing on covert messages.

"In quiet moments, we gathered at the apartment Sophie shared with Maya, and Maya would cook for us and regale us with stories of Gustav Klimt in Vienna and Picasso in Paris."

"She knew them?"

"She had been an active part of the avant-garde scene in both cities. She'd lived and worked in Le Bateau-Lavoir, the abandoned piano factory where Picasso lived and painted.

"Before that, in Vienna, she'd been a sensation with her pregnant nude series. She painted one every month while she was with child. Maya was a treasure, full of life, despite the circumstances of the war.

"After the Germans occupied Lyon in 1942, we stopped going to her place in order to protect her. Sophie and I and the rest of the women had to move around a lot, never staying in any one place more than a few days. As the activities of the Resistance intensified, we became more than couriers. Sophie, in particular, pushed our superiors to let us do more. We blew up train tracks, received and distributed airlifted supplies—weapons and explosives—and operated clandestine radios that had to be dismantled and rebuilt with every use.

"We thought we were invincible, operating right under the Nazis' noses. Even as we saw them make brutal examples of Resistance fighters, sometimes even executing them, the danger of our situation reinforced our commitment to the cause.

"One night, before a particularly risky mission, Sophie and I were in hiding in a shepherd's hut near a bridge we'd been assigned to blow up. We'd already lost several men in the Resistance, and the likelihood of being killed or captured escalated with each day. Maya had left Lyon to hide in the countryside. The paintings she'd salvaged from Paris had been placed for safekeeping with different people. That night, Sophie told me of the whereabouts of Maya's last pregnant nude, the one she had painted just before Sophie's birth. Of all the paintings, it was the one most precious to her. Sophie made me promise that, after the war was over, if she did not survive, I would retrieve the painting and hold it in her mother's memory."

Valerie was transfixed by Wanona's story. "Sophie didn't survive that night?"

"No, she didn't die then. It was months later. As it became clearer that the Germans were losing, they unleashed a vicious spree of killing, and Sophie was caught up in it when delivering a message to a drop-off point."

Wanona's gaze moved away from the painting and out the window at the world covered in the silence of the mountain snow.

Valerie took her hand.

"She was your friend."

"She was the bravest, smartest person I've ever known. Every day, I've tried to emulate her conviction and her belief in fighting for the freedom of others. I've tried to impart her nobility to my students."

"I know you've transmitted those values to me," Valerie said.

Wanona squeezed Valerie's hand. "Thank you, love. This story has exhausted me. Can you help me to bed?"

Valerie pushed Wanona to the bedroom and supported her as she shifted onto the bed.

"I think I'll skip dinner. All these memories have robbed me of my appetite."

Valerie spent the rest of the evening in front of the painting. Her mind wandered to Maya, the mother who had lost the child she had carried in her womb to the brutality of war. How had she survived that devastation, and what had happened to her after the war?

Chapter Forty-Six

IN THE MORNING, AFTER Valerie assisted Wanona with dressing and built a fire in the fireplace, she took a walk along the ridge. The snow had stopped during the night, and the walkway and ramp to the cottage had already been cleared and the road plowed.

The sun glistened across the mountain, and Valerie took a bracing gulp of air. After months of enduring a gray Boston winter, replete with mounds of dirty snow on every street corner that she had to climb over to make her way to the T, the wonderland before her was absolutely magical.

Wanona had encouraged Valerie to get outside.

"I have the phone and can give a shout out to Bill to find you if I really need you. So go. You need some color in your cheeks after listening to me blather last night."

"You weren't blathering. I know how reluctant Dad was to talk about his experience of the war, so I'm honored that you were willing to tell me such a difficult story. Thank you."

Valerie walked for nearly an hour. When she returned to the house, she shook off the snow from her boots onto the porch and immediately went to Wanona, who was reading by the fireplace. Valerie set about adding logs, while exclaiming to Wanona that it was like Narnia outside.

"C.S. Lewis must have known a landscape like this to be able to create such a mystical place beyond the wardrobe."

"One of these days, I'll get back out there. But for now, how about some hot chocolate?"

Over cups of cocoa with marshmallows, Valerie carefully reopened the conversation about the painting.

"What happened to Maya after the war?"

"I don't know. In the final days of the war, the Germans set about destroying as much as they could. Her association with Sophie, which Sophie tried desperately to hide, could have made her a target. But I didn't hear anything to indicate she had become a victim. Waves of people returned to Paris, and it's possible she made it home. She was young enough, only fifty-seven, when Paris was liberated in 1944. With nothing to keep her in Lyon, she might have made the journey. Why do you ask?"

"I'm intrigued by her. The painting resonates with me so powerfully, and I'm astounded that I've never come across any of her art or even her name."

"As I told you, so many women artists of her time simply disappeared from public view."

"I want to know more about her—particularly whether she was able to return to Paris with any of her work."

"I've often thought of her over the years. It would be a gift to Sophie's memory if you could find out more about Maya and her art."

Valerie was limited in how much she could research while at Twilight, but she wrote to a classmate from NYU who now worked at the Clark Art Institute in Williamstown, Massachusetts. The Clark had an extraordinary art library that Valerie had used frequently when conducting research for Malcolm. Her friend, Catherine, was fascinated by Valerie's description of a lost artist, and was willing to delve into the Clark's resources.

A week after Valerie had contacted Catherine, she received a manila envelope stuffed with photocopies of newspaper reviews about exhibitions that featured Maya Sircos as an artist, along with images of her as a model in several paintings by Andreas Brenner. Valerie recognized one of the Andreas Brenner paintings, that of the warrior Penthesilea.

"That's Maya's face!" Valerie exclaimed. "I knew there was something haunting about her self-portrait. But the difference in how she is portrayed in each painting is striking. I wonder how she transformed herself from model to artist at a time when she would have been dismissed as out of her element."

The more Valerie discovered about Maya, the more she wanted to know.

"Did you ever see any of the other paintings Maya and Sophie had rescued from Paris?"

"I did, in the early years before the Germans occupied Lyon and the canvases were hidden. What I remember of them was their vibrancy. The colors were so bold, and the faces told a story. They were like Maya herself—full of energy and generosity."

A few days after Valerie received the manila envelope in the mail, the phone rang. It was Catherine.

"Valerie, she's alive! Maya Sircos lives in Paris."

"How did you find her?"

"I have a colleague at the Louvre. I asked her to search the archives for the artists who lived at Le Bateau-Lavoir, since your aunt said Maya had shared studio space in the same building as Picasso. On a hunch, my colleague also checked the phone book. It turns out Maya lives on the Left Bank. Here's her address."

Valerie was stunned. She wanted to learn as much as she could about Maya's art but never imagined the artist might still be alive. When she shared the news with her aunt, Wanona burst into tears.

"Aunt Nonie, what would you like to do with this information?"

"I'd like to get on a plane for Paris. But showing up at Maya's door unannounced may not be the best idea. I don't even know if she will want to see me."

"Because you'll remind her of the daughter she lost? Do you think she's resented you all these years because you survived?"

"I don't know. It was so chaotic at the end. After Sophie was killed, what was left of our team scattered, as she had trained us to do. After the Allied Forces arrived in Lyon, I went to retrieve the painting Sophie had told me about, the one she had hidden in a cave in the hills. The cave overlooked the road to Paris, pockmarked with craters from artillery but swarming with people heading north. Maya must have been among them, because when I went to the farm where she had been hiding, she was gone. I didn't have a chance to offer her my help or even say goodbye."

"You could have that chance now if you reach out to her."

Wanona agreed to Valerie's suggestion that she write to Maya. "My French is a little weak from disuse. See if you can find my *Editions Larousse* dictionary over there on the bookcase."

Wanona labored over the letter, tossing several versions in the wastebasket before she was satisfied.

"I told her about you and how you are researching her work. I also told her I wanted to come to Paris to see her."

Valerie took the letter to the post office when she went into town to do the grocery shopping. She also stopped at the library to pick up a few books for Wanona.

Harriet, the librarian at the Haines Falls Free Library, remembered Valerie from her visits there as a child.

"What brings you to Twilight Park in winter?"

"I'm helping my Aunt Wanona. She recently fell and broke her leg. This is a list of books she'd like to borrow."

"Oh, no! Wanona has been a regular here. I was wondering why she hadn't been by. If you give me the list, I'll find the books for you."

While Harriet gathered the titles Wanona had requested, Valerie went to the card catalog and searched for resources related to Maya's story. When Harriet saw her jotting down some call numbers, she offered assistance.

"Are you looking for a specific title or topic?"

"Yes, artists in early twentieth-century Paris."

"We may not have much here, but I can order books for you through our consortium. Several of the college libraries may be able to help."

Weighed down by Wanona's requests, plus a few titles for herself that Harriet had been able to round up, Valerie made her way back to Twilight Park.

"Malcolm called while you were out doing errands. He asked about the status of his manuscript. Are you writing another book for him?"

As Valerie unpacked the groceries, she assured Wanona she was editing Malcolm's book, not writing it.

"Your editing is essentially a rewrite of that man's murky prose. I've seen the magic you've worked in turning his ideas into a readable text. You have a knack for fixing things, whether it's a painting or your husband's books. Have you ever thought about creating something that is yours alone? Being a fixer is a fine thing—look, you're even fixing me up—but I've always felt that you've held yourself back. Forgive me for sticking my nose where I shouldn't, but over the last few days, I've observed you throw yourself wholeheartedly into the mystery of Maya Sircos's art. In fact, those books you brought back for yourself from the library don't appear to have anything to do with Malcolm's work."

Valerie stopped stacking cans in the cupboard. Stunned by Wanona's comments, her mouth dropped open, but she was speechless.

"Have I overstepped?"

"You know I've always respected your opinion, Aunt Nonie, even when it's hard to hear. You're right. I've become immersed in Maya's story, and I've been ignoring Malcolm's work since discovering the painting. His work has always taken precedence over my own interests. Coming here has helped me to see that more clearly." Valerie hugged Wanona. "You've always been the one out ahead, hacking through the underbrush to get to the heart of what I truly need."

"So no hard feelings?"

"None. I still have to edit Malcolm's manuscript, but I won't let it get in the way of my curiosity about Maya. I can whip through it while we wait to hear from her."

Two weeks later, two items arrived for Wanona: a postcard of Montmartre and a letter typed on onion skin and signed with the same scrawling flourish as the name on the painting. The postcard was an exuberant acknowledgment of Wanona.

"You're alive! You found me! More to come."

The letter contained a brief description of Maya's odyssey back to Paris. She had found lodging in Montparnasse and was slowly able to reconnect with others who had survived the war and then rebuild her life.

She closed with the words, "I have a lovely apartment now on the Left Bank. You must come visit me."

"She wants to see me." Wanona reveled in the invitation.

"Then let's make sure you're fit to travel soon."

Valerie stayed another month with Wanona, until she was able to navigate the house with crutches. Rosemary was able to help with cleaning and shopping and ferrying Wanona to physical therapy after Valerie left.

"Keep me up to date on your progress. With perseverance, you could be in Paris by June. Meanwhile, get a passport!"

"It's a powerful motivation. Thank you for making this possible—both my recovery and my potential reunion with Maya."

Valerie hugged Wanona goodbye with a promise to call every week.

Chapter Forty-Seven

IN THE MIDDLE OF June, four months after her fall, Wanona announced to Valerie she'd been cleared by her doctor to travel.

"Let's book the tickets."

Valerie was circumspect with Malcolm about her reasons for the trip to Paris. She said Wanona wanted to attend a small reunion of people she'd known during the war and needed a traveling companion. Malcolm was set to give a series of lectures at the Chautauqua Institution during the weeks Valerie and Wanona were planning to go to Paris, and he reluctantly agreed it was a good time for Valerie to help her aunt.

Valerie said nothing to Malcolm about Maya. She had finished editing his book, and there was a lull while his agent negotiated with Houghton Mifflin, the publisher of his two earlier books. She hadn't picked up another restoration commission yet, although she'd been contacted by the Isabella Stewart Gardner Museum to give her opinion on a Michelangelo drawing of La Pietà created for the poet Vittoria Colonna it had recently acquired.

Once Valerie had returned to Boston, she explored every resource on early twentieth-century women artists available at the Museum of Fine Arts, the Fogg Museum at Harvard, and the Gardner. A poster from the 1909 Salon Pisko show had proved to be a treasure trove, revealing the names of the seven other women artists who had been part of the exhibition with Maya. With some assistance from Catherine at the Clark and the twentieth-century European art curator at the MFA, Valerie had been able to track down some of the paintings by the Pisko exhibitors in museum collections, but, as Wanona had warned her, most of their artwork had disappeared.

The two women flew from Logan to Orly on July 8. As they approached the city to land, Valerie saw Wanona turn toward the window and take in the landscape with a sigh.

"You haven't been back since the war, have you?"

Wanona shook her head and reached in her pocket for her handkerchief. She dabbed at the tears spilling from her eyes.

"I didn't expect to be so affected, and it's only the Eiffel Tower. I can't imagine how much I'll blubber when I finally see Maya. I need to get a grip on my emotions."

"I don't think Maya will be any less emotional, if her letters are any indication."

Wanona and Maya had corresponded throughout Wanona's convalescence, the letters increasing in length and revelations as the weeks went by. Wanona had let Maya know Valerie would be accompanying her on the trip, and Maya said she was looking forward to seeing both of them.

They took a cab to the Hotel Pont Royal. Valerie had chosen it not only because of its proximity to Maya's apartment, but also because Jean-Paul Sartre and Simone de Beauvoir used to frequent the hotel's bar in the 1940s. Valerie thought Wanona might have had an occasion to drink there as well.

When the cab deposited them at the hotel, Wanona had another sharp intake of breath.

"Have I made a mistake in booking us here?"

"Not at all. I need to expect that everywhere we turn, I'm going to be confronted with memories."

They had decided to give themselves a day to settle in before visiting Maya, mainly to give Wanona an opportunity to rest.

"You don't need to be my nursemaid on this trip," Wanona said sternly, as Valerie fussed over her. "I don't need a nap. I need a croissant and a cup of very strong coffee."

Together, they struck out to find a patisserie. Wanona had a cane and sensible shoes, and strode with her usual determination through the streets of the Saint Germain-des-Prés neighborhood.

After the two women were revived by coffee and sweets, Wanona asked Valerie what she wanted to do.

"It's your first time in Paris. Shall we spend the day seeing the sights, taking a boat ride on the Seine, or going shopping? I know you've set up appointments at the Louvre and the Musée d'Orsay for later in the week, so let's be tourists today."

"I don't want to wear you out. Let's do the boat ride. And then if you're up to it, we can shop at Le Printemps and Le Bon Marché. From what I've heard, they'd fit the budget of an intermittently employed conservator."

"That sounds like fun, and I'm a big girl. If I'm fading, I'll be good and rest. I want to be at my best tomorrow with Maya."

They spent the rest of the day floating down the Seine, followed by a bistro meal at La Coupole and a stroll through the book stalls before venturing to the iconic department stores. They returned to the hotel laden with shopping bags filled with scarves for themselves, linens for Birch Cottage, and a stylish pair of pale denim bell bottoms with gorgeous floral embroidery on the hem and on the matching vest. Valerie even found some bowties and matching pocket handkerchiefs for Malcolm.

"Very professorial," commented Wanona, "without being stodgy. I think you should wear the bell bottoms when we visit Maya tomorrow," she added, with a twinkle in her eye.

They collapsed onto their beds with some ham baguettes they'd picked up during the day. Both were asleep by eight o'clock and didn't wake until nearly ten the next morning.

They had invited Maya for lunch and planned to pick her up at her apartment at one. On the way, they stopped for flowers, fruit, and chocolates. Maya's building had an inner courtyard that could be reached through large green wooden doors. A chestnut tree grew in the middle, its branches reaching up to the balconies of the floors above.

Valerie was relieved, for Wanona's sake, that there was an elevator. It was an ancient cage that creaked and groaned, but it got them successfully to the third floor, where Maya was waiting at the door of her apartment. Valerie knew Maya was ninety, but what she saw standing before her was a woman she recognized immediately as the twenty-two-year-old who had painted the self-portrait she'd discovered at Birch Cottage. Her hair was jet black, pulled away from her face in a very French chignon. From her ears hung long, beaded earrings. She was dressed in yellow slacks with a white blazer over a paler yellow camisole. On her feet were Birkenstock sandals. Her startling blue eyes crinkled with pleasure, her face a striking example of her Greek heritage. She was slender and not stooped.

She reached out her arms to Wanona, who walked directly into her embrace. Maya kissed her on both cheeks and then stepped back to take all of her in.

"My Nonie, here you are at last. I would have known you anywhere."

"Likewise, Maya!" Then she turned to Valerie, whose arms were filled with the gifts. "My niece, Valerie. If not for her, we wouldn't have found you."

Maya extended the same kisses to Valerie and then welcomed the visitors into her apartment. The sitting room had a small kitchenette on one wall and a door to a balcony overlooking the courtyard. Beyond the sitting room, an open door revealed a bedroom. Maya busied herself placing the flowers in a vase while Valerie and Wanona turned slowly around the room in amazement.

A deep burgundy Persian carpet covered the floor. A divan upholstered in moss green velvet was piled with pillows of every fabric in shades and patterns of green and burgundy. Two upholstered armchairs flanked a low, hammered copper table. But what most drew their attention were the walls, which were covered in very recognizable art—a Chagall drawing, a Picasso portrait of Maya, an Egon Schiele painting of a young girl. The center wall opposite the divan was dominated by a portrait of Maya; it was *Woman in a Red Dress*, which Valerie had seen a photo of in the materials sent by Catherine from the Clark archives. It was extraordinary to see it in person—the fluidity of movement, the presence and passion of Maya that Andreas Brenner had captured.

Maya carried the flowers across the room and set them on the copper table. "That painting stops everyone when they see it for the first time. It was the second one he did of me, when we met years after he had painted me at fifteen, a portrait commissioned by my father."

"I thought I read it was in a private collection, purchased at Andreas Brenner's first Secession show. I didn't realize it was in your possession."

"Only recently. Someone very dear to me saw when it came up for auction at Sotheby's and purchased it for me. It defined who I was at one time in my life. Andreas's early death caused the value of his work to skyrocket, and fortunately, most of it survived the Nazis despite his Jewish heritage."

"And what about your own work? Aunt Nonie has told me how you were able to hide the canvases during the German occupation."

Maya waved the question away. "We can talk of that over dinner. Nonie has promised me a meal at a three-star Michelin restaurant, so I suggest we not be late."

Valerie detected some reluctance on Maya's part to speak of her art but also understood it would not do to arrive late for the reservation at La Tour d'Argent, so she dropped the subject. The meal was beyond anything Valerie had imagined, but it was the conversation that remained with her. Maya was sparkling, deeply expressive of her joy at being reunited with Wanona. Although they had shared in their letters much of their separate histories since they had last seen each other, they still had much they could only speak of in person. They held hands as they recounted the chaos of the last days in Lyon. Maya spoke of the losses endured when she returned to Paris: Jewish friends who had managed to escape to America and stayed there; others who had been rounded up in the first days of the German occupation and never returned from the death camps; soldiers who had perished in the fighting.

"We were mostly women who had survived the war. Some of us lived together in Montparnasse. We fed ourselves and the children by selling paintings to the American soldiers. The galleries sniffed at us, considering us only a short step above street artists. Most of my contemporary women artists slipped into obscurity."

"Have you continued to paint?"

Maya held up her arthritic hands. "I can play with small ideas, which I do almost every day, until the pain is too much. The art sustains me in the midst of so much loss. So many who filled my life are now gone. This is why, my dearest Nonie, your presence is such a gift."

"Will you forgive me for not seeking you out sooner? I was so frayed by the time I returned to the States after the war that I could not absorb any more loss."

"All is forgiven. I didn't try to find you either. Part of my reasoning was selfish. I didn't want to know if you had lived when Sophie had not. But having you here now has brought a piece of her back to me."

After the meal, the trio strolled slowly through the Jardin des Plantes, Maya and Wanona leaning on their canes and Valerie snapping photos of them. A few hours later, Valerie and Wanona escorted Maya home, and then returned to their hotel and collapsed on their beds, sated with both food and stories.

Chapter Forty-Eight

THE NEXT DAY, WHILE Maya and Wanona spent some quiet time together, Valerie met with curators at the Louvre and the Musée d'Orsay, thanks to introductions from both Catherine and the Gardner Museum. Her hope was to track down works by the other seven artists from the Salon Pisko exhibition, but she was frustrated by the lack of interest as well as the lack of information. It was suggested her search might be more fruitful in Vienna, despite the fact several of the women had spent time working in Paris.

After a long day, Valerie looked forward to joining Wanona and Maya at Maya's apartment for a light supper. She had been given a list of cheeses, paté, and bread to pick up on the way. Over wine and victuals, Valerie expressed her disappointment.

"Why is this so important to you?" Maya asked.

"It was your self-portrait. It spoke to me in powerful ways, far more so than the portrait Brenner painted of you. I believe you capture women's experience in a visceral way, and yet so many art lovers don't even know you exist. Art scholars for generations have focused only on male artists. But at the museum where I consult in Boston, we're beginning to see a trickle of newly rediscovered art by women from eras like the Renaissance, for example. There's been a movement stirring, at least in America, to acknowledge the hidden contributions of women in all fields. If I can bring this small group of artists into the light, I'll feel I've contributed as well."

"Let me know how I can help you."

"Thank you, Maya. Letters of introduction would help. If others from the Pisko exhibition are still alive, can you help me find them?"

"I can introduce you to one tomorrow—Elise Goldberg, my closest friend. She and her brother miraculously hid out in the Pyrenees during the war and survived. She's frail, but her mind is sharp. She's what you Americans call a force of nature."

The three women visited Elise the next day. Her lodgings were larger and more elegant than Maya's bohemian flat, but the warmth with which she greeted them matched Maya's.

"Please forgive me for not greeting you on the landing, as I know Maya does, because she's always so excited to welcome people to her home. I'm equally delighted. But I have a few years on Maya, and these fragile bones scold me if I make them do too much. Now tell me, Valerie, about this burning desire you have to tell the world that women have been creating art for centuries."

Over tea and pastries, Elise and Maya tossed names, places, and paintings back and forth as Valerie furiously took notes. The conversation built in layers as one memory inevitably triggered another.

"It sounds like I should go to Vienna to hunt down some of these galleries and question them on where the art might have ended up."

"Absolutely. Let's make a list for you."

Wanona elected to stay in Paris. Maya had insisted she give up the hotel and move in with her for the rest of her stay. Valerie took the train to Vienna, armed with names and addresses and introductions to galleries and museums. She had bought a notebook at Le Bon Marché and was beginning to see her ideas taking form. She just needed to fill in some missing pieces: Where was the art? What was known about the women who had died?

Valerie's week in Vienna was exhausting and almost as unfulfilling as her time in Paris had been, until she achieved a breakthrough with a representative at Salon Pisko, which still had a record of addresses that had been kept up to date. She was able to meet with relatives of two of the original artists, and through them obtained the locations of several paintings. One family had a written biography, the other several catalogs from exhibitions. She took photos and penned notes. By the time she left Vienna, her notebook was nearly full.

When she arrived back in Paris, she had formulated a proposal that she thought she could present to the three Massachusetts museums that had been kind enough to of-fer her at least a start in her search. She was bubbling with excitement by the time she reached Maya's apartment. The women were eager to hear of her progress, and Valerie sensed a softening of Maya's initial resistance to talk about the canvases she'd hidden during the Nazi occupation.

"I want to take you to my studio. It's not far."

Together, they walked a few short blocks to an industrial building near the Sorbonne. Maya unlocked the outer door and led Valerie down a long corridor. The building seemed to hum with activity—muffled voices behind brightly painted doors; the whir of a potter's wheel punctuated by the slap of clay; the sound of a flute somewhere above them. Maya stopped at a door and led Valerie inside to a high-ceilinged space with a wall of northern-facing windows. A number of easels set up around the room held works in various stages of completion that had clearly been created by different hands.

"I teach here a few days a week. Those are my students' projects. My own work is over here."

She directed Valerie to a corner of the room where a single easel with a small canvas contained a nearly completed portrait of Wanona.

"Oh, it's wonderful! I read in the Pisko catalog that you had exhibited a series of portraits called Faces of Vienna. Unfortunately, I could not find any of them, not even photos, but seeing Nonie's face, I'm reminded again how compelling your portraits are."

Maya stood aside and pointed to the wall behind her.

"These are the paintings I hid during the war. I eventually re-stretched and framed them, but never sold any of them. Tastes had changed, and galleries weren't interested in handling them."

Valerie walked along the wall. There were two more of the maternal nudes, some portraits, and a few seascapes that were so complex and colorful she could almost hear the sea.

"Where is this?"

"The island of Skiathos in Greece. I spent my childhood summers there, and also a year in exile after the scandal broke of Andreas's Sexual Awakening exhibition at the Secession Building. The island is where I began to paint after meeting Elise."

"May I photograph them? I want to show the museums in Boston what they have been ignoring."

"Of course. I did the same to promote Andreas's work when he was being sidestepped for exhibitions. We think alike, you and I."

There was also a striking portrait of an intense, dark-haired man who resembled Elise.

"Who is this?"

Maya hesitated for a moment.

"Oscar Goldberg, Elise's twin brother."

"He bears a remarkable resemblance to Elise, but the portrait is also incredibly compelling, even without the comparison. His eyes burn, not only with intelligence but with witness to the world's pain. Is he also a painter?"

"No, a novelist. As a young man, he was a major voice of our generation."

"Did he write later in life?"

"Up until the war; then, after he returned from hiding in the Pyrenees, he penned one more book, a searing indictment of greed and venality. He was still the voice of a generation that had lived through not one but two wars."

"Is he one of the ones you lost?" Valerie's voice had dropped to a whisper. Something about the way Maya spoke of Oscar suggested he was more to her than she was letting on.

Maya put her hand up and stroked the face of Oscar Goldberg.

"He was my soulmate and the only father Sophie ever knew, because Andreas was dead before she was two. When Oscar reappeared in Paris, he mourned with me, held me together when I didn't think I had the strength to endure Sophie's death."

"When did he die?"

"The twenty-fifth of October, 1973. A brain tumor. I lay with him in his bed and held him in my arms until his last breath. From the moment I met him, when I was only twenty, he brought me happiness and peace."

"I am so sorry." Valerie put her arm around Maya's shoulders.

"I was lucky to have had him in my life for so long." She patted Valerie's hand. "Come, it's time to get back to Wanona. I hope you have what you came for."

"Far more than I had hoped."

The next night, they were invited to dinner at Elise's. Elise had managed to gather two more artists from the Pisko exhibit, as well as descendants of the final two. Over aperitifs and hors d'oeuvres in the drawing room, Elise announced Valerie's project and encouraged all the guests to share what they could of their own or their mother's history. Although a few were skeptical at first, by the fish course they were murmuring their approval.

"It seems like a monumental undertaking, fraught with the risk that no one will care about us or our art," said Freya Nadler, one of the reluctant artists. "But Valerie, you have impressed me with your diligence, your experience in art research, and your ability to mine connections. If you think you can resurrect our reputations and our art, you have my support."

Maya raised her glass in a toast, which was seconded by Elise. One of the women joked that Valerie would have to work quickly if something substantive—a book or an exhibit—were to materialize before they were all gone.

"On the contrary," interjected Maya, "this has given me the will to live until I see Valerie's project through to fruition."

In their checked baggage the next day was the portrait Maya had painted of Wanona. After they landed, Valerie drove Wanona back to Birch Cottage and helped her to hang the portrait.

When she returned to Boston, Valerie was on fire with the project. She had a couple of days to herself before Malcolm returned from the Chautauqua Institution, and she used them to spread out her work on the floor of her studio in the apartment, just as she did when she conducted research for Malcolm or approached a restoration. She had a pile for each artist, a pile of photos of the artwork she had found, a list of who owned the art that still existed, and the start of an inventory list. She was so absorbed in the work that she barely stopped to cook, grabbing takeout from the Chinese restaurant in Harvard Square and eating on the floor while she made more notes. The second night, she was too tired to undress and go to the bedroom, so she pulled one of her grandmother's quilts over her and slept on the couch in the studio.

As she sorted and organized, she was absorbing the lives of these women, much as she did when restoring a piece of artwork. She had the advantage of having met and spoken with Maya and Elise, as well as Freya and Anna, the other two women who had attended Elise's dinner and who had been gracious enough to promise to write with answers to the questions she had. As also was her practice, she wanted to place the art in context, and had drawn up a bibliography to educate herself on what Vienna was like at the time these artists were flourishing. Soon, she had an outline to begin writing the proposal. Her intention was to convince one or more of the museums to mount an exhibition and produce a major book on the women. She was at the dining table with her Smith Corona humming as she pounded out the introduction to what she was calling "Lost Vienna."

When Malcolm arrived home, dropping his bags in the hall, he kissed her and then took in the stacks of paper and the open notebook next to the typewriter.

"What's this? Did Maude get back already about the changes Houghton Mifflin wants on the book?"

"I haven't heard a word from Maude. I only got back on Tuesday, and there was nothing in the mail I picked up at the post office."

"What is this, then?"

"It's from my trip with Wanona. We met with some remarkable women artists who exhibited together at the turn of the century. Unfortunately, two world wars and the destruction of most of their art by the Nazis led to their work—and them—being largely forgotten. I'm putting together a proposal for the major museums to do a retrospective on their art."

Malcolm flipped through the notebook.

"Do you really think this is worth your time? We should be hearing any day from Maude, and you know how much work that can entail."

"I'll worry about that when Maude calls. Until then, I'm pursuing this."

He shrugged. "What's for dinner?"

"Curry from the Indian place. I'll order it if you'll pick it up."

Several days passed, and Maude did not call. Valerie was relieved, but Malcolm was anxious; eventually, he called Maude.

"Malcolm, every publisher is heading either to Nantucket or the Hamptons for August. I don't expect to hear from Houghton Mifflin until after Labor Day. So cool your engines. Go to the beach yourself."

The breathing room was what Valerie needed. The finished proposal included photos and was neatly bound with a clear cover. Fortunately, not every curator followed in the footsteps of editors at major publishing houses in taking the month of August off, so she was able to get appointments through the kindness of the same people who had opened doors for her at the Paris museums. However, neither the Clark nor the MFA was interested. They had booked programs for the next eighteen months. But even if they had had room, they told her, the idea wasn't relevant to their mission.

"There's a reason these women artists have disappeared, Mrs. Langdon. Their work no longer has meaning in the modern world."

Discouraged and disgusted, but not surprised, Valerie crossed those museums off her list. She wondered if their answers would have been different if the curators were women or if she had presented a cohort of male artists. Valerie knew, from her contacts in the art world, that women scholars were beginning the arduous work of identifying women who had been forgotten or deliberately written out of history. Women's studies courses were starting to show up in college curricula, but only after persistent efforts to overcome the dismissive attitudes of academic leadership. Apparently, museums were just as resistant to entertaining the idea of accomplished women.

Undaunted, Valerie skirted the Back Bay Fens as she crossed from the MFA to her meeting at the Gardner. Despite her lack of success so far, she remained hopeful about her chances at the Gardner because it had been founded by a woman whose eclectic collection had provided the basis for the museum's renown. It was small, and its collection was unique. Perhaps she could appeal to its reputation for mounting what other, larger museums considered too minor in terms of their importance. Valerie believed fervently that these artists had produced work that was neither small nor unimportant.

She took a deep breath, held her portfolio close to her heart, and opened the door to the museum.

Rather than meeting with the director, a man, she instead was introduced to his assistant, a knowledgeable woman in her fifties. At first, Valerie was dismayed that the appointment wasn't deemed serious enough to warrant the ultimate decision maker's attention. But as the meeting progressed, it was clear that presenting to Marjorie Whittaker was a stroke of good fortune. Unlike the director at the MFA, who had considered Valerie merely a conservator out of her depth, Marjorie knew of and respected Valerie. In fact, it was Marjorie who had read Valerie's assessment of the Michelangelo La Pietà drawing. She probed Valerie's interest in the Viennese artists and listened attentively to the story of how Valerie had discovered Maya's self-portrait and how it had spoken to her as a woman.

Marjorie studied the photo of the painting Valerie had provided in her proposal.

"Even in this photo, I see what you mean. I can only imagine what effect the actual painting can have on the viewer. As I'm sure you know, the majority of our visitors and patrons are women. I could see an exhibition of this kind appealing to them. I'd like to take this to our committee. If they agree, we might have a slot open next fall. I know something we had previously planned has slipped through our fingers. I'll be in touch either way in a few weeks."

Chapter Forty-Nine

WHILE VALERIE WAITED FOR the Gardner to make a decision about the exhibition and Malcolm paced in his office, anxious to hear from Maude about his book, the summer wound down. To distract themselves from the agony of waiting, they took a short trip to the Berkshires to attend a couple of concerts at Tanglewood, followed by a few days of hiking. While they were out in the western part of the state, Valerie treated Catherine to lunch in Williamstown to thank her for her help, and then visited the Clark's library herself to explore in person.

The library had bound copies of the Secession art magazine *Ver Sacrum*, and Valerie was excited to find lithographs and block prints by one of the Salon Pisko artists. Every time she came across another fragment of information about them, she experienced a shiver of excitement, reinforcing her belief that she was on the verge of producing something important and truly her own, as Wanona had urged her to do.

When Valerie and Malcolm returned to Cambridge, it was Maude's call that came first. She let Malcolm know that Paul Thompson, the Houghton Mifflin art history editor, would be sending a memo with developmental editing changes. This was typical in book publishing, but Valerie had hoped for a reprieve from Malcolm's work. If she got the go-ahead from the Gardner, she'd be faced with navigating a precarious balancing act that would also limit her ability to take on any restoration work that could pay the bills.

She tried to shift her focus away from the details of "Lost Vienna" and concentrated on getting Malcolm's revisions done as quickly as possible. In the past, she had been keenly interested in and proud of the work she did on Malcolm's books. She loved art history and the window it opened to the hearts and minds of artists from the past. But recalling her conversation with Wanona from a few months earlier, she now found herself resentful of the energy she was expending as Malcolm's fixer.

Nevertheless, as the weeks wore on without word from Marjorie Whittaker, Valerie had time to devote to Malcolm's book and no other responsibilities. It also became clear she needed to seek out another conservation project, and sent out inquiries.

Returning home after a day at the Fogg Museum gathering background for one of the holes that needed plugging in Malcolm's book, Valerie picked up the mail that had landed on the floor inside the front door after being delivered through the slot. She quickly flipped through the bills and flyers, looking, as she did every day, for the Gardner's return address on an envelope. Today, finally, the envelope was in her hand. Inside was a single sheet of paper. The Gardner was willing to mount "Lost Vienna." Marjorie Whittaker asked Valerie to contact her soon to set up a planning meeting. Handwritten at the bottom was a message: "Congratulations! Looking forward to working with you."

Valerie did a little dance in the hall before calling Marjorie.

The initial planning meeting went well. The exhibition was scheduled for September of the following year, and Valerie was hired as a consulting manager to coordinate all aspects of the show. The list of tasks required to implement an exhibition of such complexity—eight artists whose works were almost all in Europe—was extensive and daunting enough. And then Marjorie told her, "We see the advantage of creating a major book to accompany the show. We'd like to commission you to pull it together. You've already done the major detective work, and are probably, at this moment, the most knowledgeable researcher on the art produced by these women."

Valerie was both thrilled to have been offered the chance to compile the book and overwhelmed at the prospect of tackling such an enormous project. She called Wanona to share both the news and her trepidation.

"This is exactly what you set out to do, Valerie. Don't be dismissive of your talents or your experience. Remember what I told you in the spring. It's time to be more than someone else's helpmate. Put on your big-girl pants and write a book with your name on the cover. Meanwhile, I'll let Maya know. Perhaps we can persuade her and Elise to come for the opening."

Fortified, Valerie plunged into the work of organizing the show and creating the catalog. For a while, she continued to gather the background information Malcolm needed for his revisions, but soon realized she couldn't do the rewrites and the typing for him and still keep to her timeline for "Lost Vienna."

The conversation with Malcolm was challenging.

"How can you drop this in my lap when you've been my partner on my books since grad school? I have a deadline. How am I going to find someone who knows the material as well as you do?"

"I have a deadline, too, Malcolm—a museum opening that can't be postponed the way a book's publication date can slip. And if you think of me as your partner on the books, why have I never been listed as co-author?"

"I don't know who you are anymore. You haven't been yourself ever since you found that painting at your aunt's house, went off to Paris with her, and came back with all these grandiose ideas about raising the visibility of women in art. Frankly, I'm surprised the Gardner agreed to exhibit this show at all, but perhaps they have some wealthy Austrian donor who needs coddling."

"I won't stoop to your level to rebut your ridiculous allegations, but I'll find someone who can do your typing for you."

Malcolm sulked, flipping through the copious notes Valerie had provided for him and slamming pens on his desk.

She found a flyer for a typist on the bulletin board at Harvard's Extension School, interviewed her, and introduced her to Malcolm. She was a grad student at Boston University and familiar enough with the period Malcolm was writing about.

Valerie wished them both a productive day and left for the museum, which had provided her with a desk and a phone and a state-of-the-art IBM Selectric typewriter. With a smile on her face, she forged ahead.

The following year was intense, and involved a substantial amount of minutiae that was Valerie's responsibility to manage. Over fifty works of art from several owners in different countries had to be insured, their packing overseen, and shipped. She made two trips to Europe to supervise the preparation and crating of the paintings herself. Artwork that existed only in photographic records had to be arranged in suitable displays. The text identifying each work and its provenance had to be painstakingly created and reviewed. The exhibit space had to be designed. And all of that was just for the exhibit.

The catalog was even more complex, as Valerie hunted down scholars who might have studied the artists or who could be persuaded to delve into their work and write essays. She wrote the biographies herself, based on the interviews she had conducted and the letters she had received from the living artists and the relatives of those who had passed away. The introduction of women's studies departments at universities around the country was a help, but most of the programs were in the early stages of development. She was finally able to identify two art historians willing to participate.

In the midst of the complex administrative work she was handling for the exhibition, Valerie took on another conservation project for a private client referred to her by Catherine. Although she had negotiated a fair consultancy fee for managing "Lost Vienna," she and Malcolm still needed her income as a conservator. Although it meant more time devoted to work, she found conservation an effective counterpoint to the stress confronting her in her curatorial role. As much as she loved the work of creating the exhibition, she was in new territory, constantly learning and sometimes making mistakes. The conservation project, on the other hand, was restorative to her spirit as well as to the painting.

The painting arrived in February, a Sybil that was believed to be the work of Ginevra Cantofoli, a seventeenth-century Bolognese painter. When Catherine had told her of the assignment, Valerie was pleased to learn it had been created by a woman. Valerie's work on "Lost Vienna" had converted her into a missionary, passionate about bringing the work of women artists into public view. Restoring the Sybil was another way of shedding light, literally, on paintings lost to obscurity.

She inspected it first in natural light before examining it closely with her loupe and then under a microscope. Under UV light she searched for signs of repainting and burnish, shiny or polished areas that indicated mishandling. She was relieved to find no burnish, which would have been time-consuming and delicate to repair, if at all. The main issue with the Sybil was the discolored varnish that had darkened the painting. With an array of solvents at her disposal, she began to test small areas for one that would dissolve the varnish without harming the paint. After she found a suitable solvent, she removed the varnish and replaced it with a new coating. One of the key elements of conservation that Valerie adhered to was the concept of reversibility. Anything she did to the painting could be undone. Nothing would permanently change the original work.

She became absorbed in the task, letting go not only of the many balls she was juggling for the exhibition but also of the mounting tension between her and Malcolm. Finding him a substitute typist and researcher had helped, but his resentment and perception that she had "abandoned" him had led to a palpable emotional distance between them. The hours she spent in her studio focused on work that required both concentration and control were a respite.

As the date for the opening of the exhibition neared, Valerie arrived home every night both exhausted and exhilarated as everything began to take shape, filling in the framework she had created. The museum was doing an effective job disseminating information and building excitement about "Lost Vienna." But the mounting interest added another layer of conflict between her and Malcolm when he announced that *ARTnews* had called the house to interview him about the show.

"Why you?"

"They had heard that the curator's name was Langdon and naturally assumed it was me."

"And you corrected them, right?"

"Well, I told them I'd be happy to schedule a conversation to provide an overview of the exhibition."

"Malcolm, ten months ago you told me this show wasn't worth my time, that no one cared about these women except some wealthy Austrian dowager, and now you want to be a part of it because it's caught the attention of a prestigious art journal? You can't be serious. You know nothing about these artists because you chose not to."

"But think of the added weight it would give the exhibition if my name, as an expert in twentieth-century art, was associated with it."

"There is only one member of this family who is an expert on *these* twentieth-century artists, and that's me. Give me the name and number of the editor who called. I'll do the interview."

She barely contained her fury as she snatched the slip of paper from his reluctant hand. As if she didn't have enough on her plate, she would now have to be vigilant in preventing Malcolm from inserting himself into what he had finally recognized as a significant event.

At the museum the next day, she spoke to the publicity department about identifying clearly who the press should be contacting. She didn't want to reveal that she couldn't control her husband and his interference, but at least she could try to minimize his involvement.

She really didn't need this, with so much at stake. After the exhibit opened, she realized, she would have to give some serious thought to the state of her marriage. The tension her new role had caused between her and Malcolm was something she should have anticipated. She was changing, growing in ways she hadn't imagined possible. She still loved the quiet, intense work of restoration and the way she could lose herself in a painting. But she was discovering talents that probably had been within her grasp all along; they simply had not been exercised except as Malcolm's amanuensis.

It frightened her to realize that Malcolm might not be able to accept this new version of his wife. He already had shown signs of it when she stopped rewriting his book, but this latest stunt—assuming he could speak more authoritatively than she to *ARTnews* and take credit for the development of the exhibition—was one she couldn't ignore.

For the first time, propelled by Malcolm's arrogance, Valerie considered a future without him. She sat with the idea as she pursued the rest of her responsibilities for the show. The thought was overwhelming at first, but eventually she felt lighter as she imagined casting off the burden of needing to please Malcolm.

It had only been since discovering Maya's painting and meeting the artist herself that Valerie saw the possibility of another life—a life still marked by losses and challenges, but one she believed she had the resources and resilience to embrace. The realization brought with it a sense of freedom that influenced her relationship with Malcolm as the opening drew closer. Her firmness over the issue of the magazine had surprised him, and she noticed a dawning realization on his part that she was no longer as pliant as she had been earlier in their marriage.

Although she had hoped they could postpone a confrontation until after the exhibit opened, it was not to be. A major issue arose one night over whose needs took precedence when Malcolm's editor sent the manuscript back for more edits, commenting that it lacked the coherence and originality he was used to seeing in Malcolm's work.

"You need to help me salvage this. It was your absence in the last year that has caused the book to suffer."

Something snapped in Valerie.

"I won't do this anymore, Malcolm. You know as well as I do that I've essentially written your books for you. Find yourself another ghost writer. I have my own book to write."

Malcolm left that night, claiming that he had already found someone willing to be a more supportive partner—his new typist, of course.

After he left, Valerie sat in the quiet house. She had galleys to proof for the catalog and a logistics meeting in the morning to prepare for. She would get to both. But for a few minutes, she needed to acknowledge that she wasn't falling apart. Life would undoubtedly be messy in the coming months as she and Malcolm unraveled their marriage, but she knew she could weather it.

Chapter Fifty

BY THE MIDDLE OF August, Malcolm had moved out of the apartment and taken half the furniture. He and Valerie had spent a strained evening slapping colored stickers on bookcases and lamps—orange circles for Valerie, green for Malcolm—to divide up the possessions they'd accumulated in five years of marriage and two years of living together during grad school. After the last box was carried out the door and loaded onto the rental truck, Valerie took a broom and swept up the bits of debris that had lain under Malcolm's desk and dresser: notes in her handwriting, gum wrappers, a crumpled cigarette pack. She hadn't known that he smoked, but she supposed there were many things she didn't know about him.

The next day, Catherine drove to Cambridge from Williamstown and she and Valerie went shopping to replace the household items that had left with green stickers on them. Valerie found that purchasing a new set of dishes and glasses that matched her taste was invigorating, an outward sign that she was starting over at the age of thirty. In a housewares shop at Porter Square, she even found a set of flatware that would have been at home on Maya's table in Paris.

With Malcolm gone, Valerie realized she could host Maya and Elise when they arrived for the exhibition and looked forward to welcoming them to her home. The museum had offered to cover their travel when it invited them to attend the opening. A flurry of letters and a couple of phone calls from Wanona and herself encouraging them to consider the invitation finally succeeded in convincing them to make the trip.

Wanona joined Valerie in greeting Maya and Elise each with a bouquet of flowers when they arrived at the airport three days before the opening. Valerie had had the foresight to arrange for wheelchairs to pick them up at the gate. Despite the long flight, both women looked animated—even a bit giddy—as they emerged from customs.

After their luggage had been collected, they were bundled into a cab and whisked off to Cambridge.

Although it was early evening, Maya and Elise were still on Paris time, and after a short visit and a light snack, the two women went to bed. Valerie had transformed Malcolm's study into a guest room. Despite the crush of last-minute details for the exhibition that needed attending to, she'd taken the time to make the space both beautiful and functional for two artists in their nineties.

They were both more fragile physically than Valerie remembered, and she hoped she'd made the right decision in urging them to come. She was grateful that Wanona was available to shepherd them around and manage the pace of the next few days. Not only would they be the center of attention at the opening, but a writer from *Art in America* had secured an exclusive interview with them, scheduled for the day before the launch. It would be a whirlwind, one that Valerie thought Maya would relish, but she was anxious about Elise's stamina. As Elise herself had noted the first time she'd met Valerie, her age and her more subdued personality set limits on how much she could do, despite her desire to be fully present.

The next morning, Valerie was off early to work. Wanona brought Maya and Elise to the museum later in the day to preview the final hanging of the paintings and drawings. Maya with her cane and Elise with her walker stood at the entrance to the gallery. Maya reached out her hand to Elise and squeezed it.

"Did you ever imagine we'd see our art once again on the walls of a gallery?"

Together, they wandered slowly around the room, oblivious to the awe of the museum staff who had stopped what they were doing to look at the artists. The buzz of voices and the hammering of tools came to a standstill as the two women stopped at one painting, the field of poppies Elise had been painting the first day she had met Maya on Skiathos.

"It was a lifetime ago, but I remember and cherish that day with exquisite detail—the moment that redefined who I was. Thank you, my friend."

"I merely offered you a different way of seeing your life, my dear. You are the one who transformed that life."

"We should let these young people finish their work. What a relief that we don't have to be the ones measuring the walls and aligning the edges of the frames. They have a tendency to tilt if you merely look at them, don't they?"

The press interview the following day was a runaway success, with the two women playing off each other's strengths. They were articulate, knowledgeable, and full of stories of the vibrant art scenes in Vienna and Paris that had shaped both their art and their lives. They were vessels of history, bringing to life a forgotten moment.

The afternoon of opening night, Valerie's apartment became part beauty salon, part fashion boutique. Rather than exhaust Maya and Elise with a trip to her local hairdresser, Valerie had arranged for the shop to come to them. It was no surprise that both women had firm ideas about how they wanted their hair done. As expected, Elise, with her silver hair and dark eyes, kept to her subdued, elegant style. She had her hair fashioned into a French twist and donned a Dior gown of black chiffon with a white linen collar and cuffs. Maya, with her raven hair piled on top of head, Aegean blue eyes, and statuesque height, wrapped herself in a vibrantly colored floral silk caftan from Givenchy.

The museum had arranged for a limousine to pick them up, which garnered the attention of Valerie's neighbors as the women emerged from the building in their finery. They arrived at the Gardner to a flurry of cameras as they walked a red carpet, both of them radiant and regal.

Valerie watched as they entered the gallery. The look of wonder on their faces as they gazed at the retrospective of the Salon Pisko artists was a precious gift more rewarding than the international accolades the Gardner would receive in the coming days or the excitement the exhibit would ignite among women art historians.

In a quiet moment, stolen after scores of guests chatted eagerly with the stars of the night in the receiving line, Valerie gathered Elise, Maya, Wanona, and four glasses of champagne. Together, the four women raised their glasses and toasted to the women artists of Vienna, who were no longer lost.

A MESSAGE FROM LINDA CARDILLO

Thank you for reading *Paint the Wind*! I hope you enjoyed it. As an author, I am always gratified to hear from readers and am deeply appreciative when you share your experience of the book—through a review on Amazon or Goodreads or simply by spreading the word to your friends.

If you'd like to learn more about my books, read excerpts from new work, and wander through my musings on the writing life, please visit my website and sign up for my newsletter at www.lindacardillo.com

If you have any questions or comments, or would like to invite me to your book club discussion, please write to me at linda@lindacardillo.com

ACKNOWLEDGMENTS

Every book is a journey, and I've been fortunate over the years to have a few fellow-travelers who accompany me. To my beta readers, Andrea Taupier, Brian Murphy, and Daisy Miller, thank you once again for your willingness to read my words and offer me your clear-eyed opinions of what resonates with you and what needs to change.

When the world became too much and I needed a quiet place to write, three wonderful friends opened their homes to me: Jean Barish at Twilight Park, Barbara Pearce on the Connecticut shore, and Andrea Taupier in Western Massachusetts. Thank you for rooms that offered both peace and inspiration.

I am especially grateful to Maria Kamoulakou, who led me through the history, culture, geography, and food of the Greek island Skiathos. I could not have written Part Two without your insight and generosity. *Efcharistó, file mou!*

Many thanks as well to Lydia Vagts, who took me into her conservation lab at the Boston Museum of Fine Arts and shared with me her history, her training, and her process when working as an art conservator. Any errors in the depiction of Valerie's work as an art conservator are entirely my own.

Thank you also to Wolfgang Platzer, who directed me to the indispensable works of Austrian writers of the time period, giving me a keen sense of Vienna and Maya's generation. Vielen Dank!

In addition to the historical figures in the story, one fictional character is named for a real person. Wanona Dobbs won the privilege of being named as Valerie's aunt and a member of the French Resistance in an auction supporting the Richard Salters Storrs Library.

My design, editing, and production team are incredible professionals. Thank you to Dar Albert, of Wicked Smart Designs, for her striking cover; to Erin Binney, whose sharp eyes and questioning mind found the flaws as she edited; and to Christine Richardson, who created an elegant interior of the book worthy of the Vienna art world.

And finally, to my husband, Stephan, my deepest gratitude for supporting me as I buried myself in this book. You are always there for me, my love and my champion.

ABOUT THE AUTHOR

LINDA CARDILLO IS AN award-winning author of historical fiction and historical romance. She writes about the old country and the new, the tangle and embrace of family, and finding courage in the midst of loss.

She is also co-founder of Bellastoria Press, an independent publisher, and a teacher of creative writing.

In an earlier life Linda worked as an editor of college textbooks before earning an MBA at Harvard Business School at a time when women represented only 15% of the class. Armed with her Harvard degree, she managed the circulation of *Inc.* magazine during its successful start-up, founded a catering business and then built a career as the author of several works of nonfiction, from articles in *The New York Times* to books on marketing and corporate policy. Throughout her professional life and while raising her family, she nurtured her intention to write fiction. Her debut novel, *Dancing on Sunday Afternoons*, which launched Harlequin's Everlasting Love series, was published in 2007.

Paint the Wind is her fifteenth book.

GLOSSARY

German Words and Expressions

Abendbrot – light evening meal

Abitur – graduation from high school

Acht Kunstlerinnen – a group of eight women artists who formed an association to promote and exhibit together

Brötchen – crusty roll, usually eaten at breakfast

Ferien – vacation, holidays

Frauenkunstverein – a women's art association

Frohe Weihnachten –Merry Christmas

Gott sei Dank – Thank God

Hofratin – title given to councilors, diplomats (female form)

Kaffee und Kuchen – coffee and cake

Kaiserschmarrn – sweet pancake torn into pieces

Kamillentee – Chamomile Tea

Kneipe – local bar

Mahlzeit – time to eat

Neue Wiener Tagblatt or *Tagblatt*–major Viennese newspaper

Palatschinken – pancakes
Schatz, Schatzi – my treasure, my dearest
Spaetzle – egg noodles
Sylvester – New Year's Eve
Weisswurst – veal sausage
Wiener Allgemeine Zeitung – major Viennese newspaper
Wiener Schnitzel – breaded cutlet
Wunderkind – child prodigy, genius

Greek Words and Expressions
Baklava – pastry of filo dough, walnuts, and honey
Efcharisto – Thank you
Efcharisto stan Theo – Thanks be to God
Engoni – Grandchild
Fasolada – bean soup
Hamalia – cookies made from almonds and orange
blossom water
Kalimera – Good morning
Kamara – traditional dance of Skiathos
Klidonas – Feast of St. John the Baptist; Summer Solstice
Metaxa – Greek spirit like brandy
Mitera – Mother
Omilito neró – "silent water" that is part of the Klidonas
ritual
Paparouna – poppy
Pappou – Grandfather
Pateras – Father
Retsina – wine flavored with pine
Theía – Aunt

Theíos – Uncle
Tiropita – casserole of cheese and eggs
YiaYia – Grandmother